# Death at the Paper Palace

*A Tales & Tails Mystery*

## KRISTIN BRELLEN & BEN ALEXANDER

Tales & Tails Publishing, LLC

First published by Tales & Tails Publishing, LLC 2025

Cover Art: Balexander
Chapter Illustrations: Balexander
Author Photos: Rachel Kepshire

First edition

ISBN: 979-8-9994960-3-4

# Contents

*It is the glory of God to conceal a matter;*
*to search out a matter is the glory of kings.*

Proverbs 25:2

# Prologue

Forks of lightning raked electric fingers across the sky over the Paper Palace. As heavy rain pelted the unkempt grounds, lightning lit up the old mansion. The curtains of the bedroom windows were drawn closed... all, except for one.

*Flash*. Light spilled into the master bedroom, revealing shapes in varying shades of gray.

*Flash*. The shadows of a large armoire, a secretary desk, and a canopy bed appeared on the walls and then melted into darkness.

*Flash*. A motionless figure lay on the bed, bony hands folded across her abdomen. Her toes, still in low-heeled shoes, pointed outward.

*Flash*. The figure, an elderly woman, wore a dress with an embroidered bodice and a smooth chiffon skirt.

*Flash*. Gleaming and glittering, a queenly tiara sat dramatically askew upon her short white curls.

*Flash*. The woman wore a scowl, and the paper-thin skin of her complexion was pallid and gray. Her eyes were closed. She did not breathe.

*Flash*. The bedroom filled with a great pulse of light.

Then darkness fell on the body of Phyllis Grant.

# Chapter 1

---

# Tales & Tails

# Bookshop

Breaking through the steely November clouds, a finger of sunlight touched upon a singular oak leaf. Although its brothers and sisters had long since fluttered to the ground, this fiery leaf had clung stubbornly to its branch where it played and swayed in the autumn wind. Finally, with a breeze like a gentle sigh, the leaf shivered and let go. An icy gust picked it up and carried it away from the grounds of the crumbling riverfront manor. At the end of the winding cobblestone driveway, the wind dropped the leaf onto a weatherworn pillar engraved with the name of the estate, *Paper Palace*. After several long moments, a mighty draft vaulted the leaf high in the air where it soared toward the park entrance and floated above a fountain that had been drained for the season. Dancing and swirling like a wayward spark, it glided toward Parchment Lane and Crystal Run's sleepy downtown. It pirouetted past the William Grant Memorial Library. It skipped by Sloane Apothecary. It brushed across Gerhartz Gallery & Studio. For a moment, the leaf seemed to settle on the sidewalk until a frigid blast sent it whirling in loops, the leaf's side grazing the ground. With a whoosh, the wind lifted the leaf and carried it under a cornice scripted with the words "Tales & Tails Bookshop." A warm light emanated from the windows, and, clinging to a pane of glass set in a glossy teal door, the leaf finally rested.

Just inside the door, a black cat sat nestled on a woven rug, its long tail wrapped around its body. Conceding that it would be a while before it would be able to greet customers, the cat rose, stretched, and headed in the direction of muffled voices in the back of the shop. Occupying a double storefront, the bookshop was spacious, and the cat had a distance to cover. Beyond the entrance was the story time area where a rocking chair with a basket at its base was situated between two stained-glass windows. Brightly colored children's books filled shelves and displays near the story time area, and a labyrinth of shelves, which were heavy with books organized by age group and genre, wound throughout the space. Comfortable chairs with downy pillows and side tables, like cozy little islands, could be found throughout the store. At the back of the shop stood a glass display case ready to be filled with the morning's fresh batches of muffins, scones, and cookies, and a hand-lettered chalkboard announced the featured coffee flavors. On the exterior wall to the side of the bakery counter, a grand stone fireplace stretched to the ceiling of the bookshop. Large, framed maps of Narnia, Avonlea, and Neverland rested against the mantel. Customers could sip their coffee or tap away on their laptops at the tables surrounding the fire, or they could doze in one of the squashy plump chairs. Having finally reached its destination, the inky-colored cat plopped down on the rug in front of the fire and turned its whiskers toward the warmth.

As the fire crackled merrily, three pairs of young eyes looked intently toward the head of a long, wooden table where a woman was seated. She was tall and thin with a runner's build. Her porcelain skin and attractive features glowed in the firelight and were framed by her vanilla-blonde hair. Her green eyes sparkling, Becca Gables returned her children's warm gaze. She smiled pleasantly. "I'm going to erase *all* of the words now," she announced. "Do you think you can recite the verse?"

"Easy." With his forefinger, thirteen-year-old Oliver poked a marshmallow, which bobbed in his hot chocolate. He was tall and gangly, his long limbs spilling over the glossy, rustic wood chair in which he slouched. He had chestnut hair that had been ruffled by his pillow and his mother's green eyes.

With a soft gray cloth, Becca wiped the remaining words from the dry-erase board she was holding. "Then you go first," she said encouragingly. She laid the board on the table and absentmindedly stroked the ears of the sand-colored golden retriever resting at her feet.

Oliver began in his husky voice, "We have this hope as an anchor for the soul, firm and secure. It enters the inner sanctuary behind the"—he paused and raked his fingers through his hair—"veil," he decided. "Hebrews 6:19."

"Wrong!" Violet appraised with a grin. At sixteen, she was all cream and chocolate. Violet had long, cocoa-colored hair, which was pulled back into her signature messy bun, and warm nut-brown eyes flecked with gold. Her cheeks bloomed on her clear complexion. Primly, she pulled up her thin frame and locked eyes with her mother. "We have this hope as an anchor for the soul, firm and secure. It enters the inner sanctuary behind the *curtain*. Hebrews 6:19." She flicked her eyes in the direction of her younger brother.

Oliver slapped a hand on the table. "It means the same thing!"

At the sound of Oliver's whack, the golden retriever startled. Becca leaned down and rubbed the spot between the dog's eyes with her thumb. "It's all right, Butterscotch," she soothed. She straightened and turned toward Hazel. "Would you like to give it a try?"

Ten-year-old Hazel leapt from her seat. "Oh, yes! But I would like to recite it *dramatically.*" Her voice had a sweet-sounding lilt, and she smiled charmingly at her mother and siblings. Long straight vanilla-blonde hair hung down her back, and her aquamarine eyes sparkled.

Oliver rolled his eyes and crossed his arms over his chest.

"*Really*, Hazel," Violet moaned.

"If that's what works for you," Becca said, stifling a smile.

The firelight was her spotlight. The girl cleared her throat and said in a loud, clear voice, "We have this *hope*"—she gestured toward the ceiling—"as an anchor for the *soul*"—she crossed her hands over her heart—"firm and secure." She pounded a fist into her other hand. "It enters the inner sanctuary behind the..." She paused, skipped over to the window, which flanked the massive fireplace, and grabbed a handful of white linen. "*Curtain*," she finished, throwing an impish glance at Oliver. "Hebrews 6:19."

Becca clapped. "Brava!"

Hazel released the curtain from her hand and curtsied. She noticed Toffee, their golden-brown cat with only a stump for a tail, perched on the windowsill in the weak morning sun. She scooped him up. As Hazel slid back into her seat, arranging the purring feline on her lap, Becca stretched across the table to distribute a glossy eight-by-ten print to each child.

"Keep them face-down for the moment," she instructed. A strand of blonde hair had escaped from her hairclip, and she tucked it behind her ear. "Hebrews 6:19 is one of my favorite verses. An anchor keeps us secure against life's storms, and we must always remember Who our anchor is." Her fingers moved unconsciously to the tiny cross necklace that sparkled at the base of her slender neck. Becca resumed her seat and rested her fingers on her own eight-by-ten print. "And in keeping with that theme, let's look at today's picture study. Flip."

As if on cue, the twinkle lights entwined around the bookstore lit up, and light instrumental music filled the space.

"Aunt Audrey's in!" Hazel declared.

"Good morning!" came the musical voice from behind the confectionery counter. All four of the Gables looked up to see a plump woman in her mid-thirties balancing a large bakery box against her hip. In the other hand, a set of keys jingled. Audrey had a cheerful heart-shaped face, and the shop's twinkle lights reflected in her eyeglasses, which topped very round cheeks. A tiny diamond sparkled on the side of her nose, and an auburn French braid hung down her back like a rope.

"Hi, Audrey!" Becca greeted.

"Are those glazers?" Oliver called.

Becca pointed to his mug of hot chocolate. "Don't you think you've had enough sugar for the morning?"

Oliver grinned.

"Hey, Bec, do you have a minute?" Audrey had set the bakery box on the counter and was hanging her keys on the wall hook. "I have the numbers for October's cash flow."

Becca grimaced and turned to Violet. "Do you think you could get started for me?"

Violet nodded dutifully.

"Begin by studying the painting—" Becca said.

"I know, I know," Violet replied, waving her mother away. "I've got it."

As Becca rose from her seat, the golden retriever lifted her head. Becca stooped down and stroked her velvety ears. "I'll be back soon, Butterscotch," she said. As she stepped away to join Audrey behind the confectionery counter, the children turned over their prints to reveal Rembrandt's *The Storm on the Sea of Galilee*.

She found Audrey pouring coffee into two teal stoneware mugs stamped with the bookstore's logo: Tales & Tails. A book with the word "Tales" stamped on its spine leaned against an ampersand bookend. To the right of the bookend stood a cat with "Tails" written across its body. Audrey handed one of the mugs to Becca, who immediately headed toward the refrigerator. Plucking a carton of cream from the door, she added two splashes and watched it swirl as it rose to the surface.

"Ready?" Audrey asked, settling in at a small round tiled table with her own mug. On the table's surface laid her laptop, which was plastered with brightly colored stickers depicting frogs, flowers, and the titles of Broadway musicals.

Becca felt a wave of dread wash over her as she slid into the other chair and surveyed the laptop. "I don't think I'm ever ready for these meetings," she admitted.

Audrey smiled sympathetically at her sister-in-law as she opened the laptop and revealed a digit-filled spreadsheet. She turned the screen toward Becca and scrolled to the bottom. "Here are our accounts receivable for October—the money coming in."

Becca squinted at the numbers. "Okay," she said hesitantly. "That's pretty good, right?"

Audrey glanced up and half-smiled in response. She clicked on a second spreadsheet. "And *here* are our accounts payable for October—the money going out." She scrolled to the bottom of the sheet.

Becca gasped. "Where does it all *go*?"

Audrey scrolled up a bit. "The lease on the bookshop and your apartment, the utilities, the stock of books, coffee, and bakery..."

"Okay, okay, I get it," Becca said. Her stomach twisted, and she glanced in the direction of her children, who were still seated at the table. She could see their heads bent over the art prints.

"You're turning green," Audrey observed. "Listen, I've got good news." She clicked on a third spreadsheet. "We're still technically in the black... but just barely. And Christmas is coming up, which is always a profitable time for us. Customers are purchasing Christmas gifts..."

Becca brightened at the word "Christmas" and leaned forward in her chair. "I will put together some book lists to help the customers with their shopping. We'll do special Christmas-themed story times. And the kids and I will do our gift-wrapping community service."

"That one tends to be more of a wash," Audrey commented without glancing up from the spreadsheet through which she was scrolling.

Becca frowned. "I wasn't thinking about profitability for any of those."

Audrey looked up from the screen and smiled warmly at her sister-in-law. "No, you were thinking about sharing stories and serving your customers like you always do." She drummed her fingers on the table. "You also have that catering job at the Paper Palace for Phyllis Grant's cocktail party. That should bring in a nice little profit."

Becca propped her elbow on the table and rested her chin on her hand. "You'd *think*," she said. "But Mrs. Grant isn't paying that much."

"Really?" Audrey's eyes widened. "You're providing the food, and both you and Violet are serving, right?"

"Yes," Becca said. "I mean, it's still worth *doing*." She tipped her head toward the laptop in acknowledgement of the ominous spreadsheets. "But Mrs. Grant isn't paying as much as one would expect from the founding family of Crystal Run."

"Founding family!" Audrey parroted in her most pretentious voice. She folded her arms on the table and leaned in toward Becca. "You know," Audrey continued in a whisper, "this actually makes sense. Rumor is that she spent her way through the family fortune, and just look at the Paper Palace! It has been looking *pretty* dilapidated lately."

Becca shrugged. "Maybe she's just frugal," she said, her voice lacking conviction.

Audrey raised an eyebrow. "In any case, here's what we need to do for the month of November and through year-end. Save money any way that you can. Every little bit will end up making a difference."

"Got it," Becca said, nodding.

Oliver's throaty voice suddenly cut through the air. "One of the disciples is throwing up over the side of the boat."

Becca's and Audrey's eyes met, and they giggled. "Are we done?" Becca asked.

"That's enough for now. Carry on schooling those nieces and nephew of mine," Audrey commanded. Closing her laptop with a smile, she glanced in amazement over at the children. "You know, it's just incredible to me how those children are able to work so independently."

"Yes," Becca said, beginning to rise. "Self-management is one of the goals of our homeschool, especially as the children grow older." She gazed wistfully in their direction and sighed. "It actually makes me sad sometimes because I *love* being around them. But it's about learning responsibility, and they can't do that if I'm always looking over their shoulders."

Audrey shook her head. "Well, I still think it's incredible."

"Thanks, Audrey," Becca said, stepping in the direction of her children. She stopped suddenly and pivoted back. "The field trip!" she gasped.

"To Chicago? What about it?" Audrey asked.

Becca's eyes were wide. "Can we still afford to go?"

Audrey smiled. "I already budgeted for it. Just make sure the kids stay out of the gift shop."

"Phew!" Becca exhaled. She lifted Audrey's heavy copper braid, playing with it between her hands. "What would I do without you? You have been such a blessing since we lost Matt."

"Hey!" Audrey laughed, holding up her right hand. "I was a blessing even when Matt was still here!"

Becca gave the braid a tug and strode back toward her children. She scanned the table, noticing that the prints of *The Storm on the Sea of Galilee* were still in front of them. Stepping over Butterscotch, she resumed her seat and turned toward Violet. "Thanks for leading, hun. Where are we at?"

Violet sat up a little straighter. "We observed the painting and then flipped it over and described it. We noticed how all the disciples are struggling to regain control over the fishing boat—"

"One of them is looking right at us!" Hazel declared.

Becca nodded. "Yes! That is actually a self-portrait of Rembrandt." She glanced down at her notes. "Oliver, what did you notice about the contrast between light and darkness in the painting?"

Oliver swirled the last dregs of hot chocolate in his mug and considered the scene. "There's light coming from this corner"—he pointed to the upper-left of the print—"and you can see a patch of blue sky. On the other side, the boat and the disciples are in shadow... including the one who is being sick over the side," he finished with a grin.

Hazel rolled her eyes. "Boys!" she scoffed.

Becca straightened her notes, tapped them on the table, and looked at Oliver. "That's a good observation about the contrast between light and darkness. Rembrandt used a treatment called *chiaroscuro* in this painting."

"Kee-ar-o-what-o?" Hazel said.

"*Chiaroscuro*," Becca repeated slowly. "It's Italian. The word literally means bright-dark, and it's a combination of two Latin derivatives." Her eyes twinkled. "Ten minutes of extra screen time to anyone who can figure out what the two words are."

Oliver's eyes widened, but it was Violet who answered unhesitatingly. "*Obscurus*, which means dark."

"Yes," Becca encouraged. "That's one of them."

Violet gazed toward the blaze snapping in the fireplace. Suddenly, her face lit up, and she turned toward her mother. "*Clarus*, which means clear or bright. And I don't want an extra ten minutes of screen time."

"I'll take it!" Oliver volunteered.

"Very good, Violet," Becca praised. She turned toward Oliver. "And no."

Oliver cracked a smile, crossed his arms over his chest, and tilted back in his chair. The muffled chime of a timer sounded, and Violet pulled her phone from her sweatshirt pocket. "Mom, it's time to open for the day," she said.

Becca glanced down at her watch. "Goodness! So it is." She rose from her seat. "For tomorrow, I want you all to think about *why* Rembrandt might have used *chiaroscuro* in this painting."

"Hey, Bec!" Audrey called. She was just replacing the glass dome over a cake stand she had loaded with raspberry muffins. Bustling over to a coat rack, she snatched a teal apron from a hook and flung it at her sister-in-law.

Becca caught the apron in one hand. "Oh, right!" she said. She shook it out and popped it over her head. Reaching behind her to tie the belt, she glanced at her children and asked, "Does everyone know what their school tasks are for today? Do you have everything you need from me?"

They nodded.

Hazel glanced down at *The Storm on the Sea of Galilee* in front of her. "Can I display it?" she asked.

"Oh! That reminds me!" Becca said, her cheeks flushing pink. "I have a special announcement. On Tuesday, we will be going on a field trip to the Art Institute of Chicago where we will be able to observe authentic works of art by Rembrandt, van Gogh, Monet—"

"And Degas' ballerinas?" Hazel pitched forward in excitement, and the toffee-colored cat jumped from her lap.

"And Degas' ballerinas," Becca confirmed with a smile. "And yes, you may hang up our art print."

Violet glanced at the time on her phone and pointed to the teal door across the bookshop. "Mom, you really need to open."

"Right, right," Becca replied, smoothing her apron. "Off we go!" She beamed at her children and pivoted in the direction of the bookshop entrance.

Grabbing her art print, Hazel headed to the fireplace and clipped it to a strand of twinkle lights that curled around the mantel. Oliver and Violet collected the remaining materials and tucked them into a basket. Oliver hoisted his boulder-like backpack, stopped by the bakery counter to grab a raspberry muffin from Audrey, and headed to the other side of the shop toward his favorite place to do schoolwork: a life-sized replica of a hollow tree. Violet hefted the basket behind the bakery counter where she tucked it away for the day.

Audrey wrapped an arm around Violet. "Good morning, kiddo!" she greeted. "Are you and Hazel going upstairs to work on your school?"

Violet squirmed beneath her aunt's embrace and smiled awkwardly at the floor.

Laughing, Audrey removed her arm. "I'll remember one of these days! You're more of a firm handshake kind of girl."

Violet nodded, her nut-brown eyes regarding her aunt warmly. "It's okay. You're going to need me for the story time rush, right?"

Audrey nodded. "Almost certainly, but you should have some time to get a head start on your lessons. We'll shoot you a text when we need you."

Violet glanced over at Hazel, who was sitting cross-legged in front of the fire. Toffee, the golden-brown Manx, wiggled his stub of a tail as the girl scratched under the cat's chin. The black cat, Licorice, rubbed and bumped against her other arm, anxious for his turn.

"Let's go!" Violet called.

Hazel dropped a kiss on top of each of the cats' heads and popped up to join her sister. As the girls trooped in the direction of the stairs that led to the Gables' apartment, Violet cast a final glance toward her mother.

Becca flipped the storefront sign to *Open*.

Through a pane of glass set in the door, Becca could see Phyllis Grant and her granddaughter, Lexi, standing in the chill. Before her fingers were even off the deadbolt, she felt the sturdy teal door tug outward as Lexi held it open for her grandmother. Accompanied by a frigid blast, the two women breezed into the bookshop. A fiery oak leaf caught the gust and slipped inside. Becca's eyes widened as she watched Phyllis Grant crush it beneath her heel.

# Chapter 2

# The Grants

Phyllis Grant, the great-great-great-granddaughter of a papermill magnate, was thin and frail, yet she carried herself with the regal posture of her predecessors. Her head was crowned with white permed curls. Despite the two deep vertical grooves etched between her penciled brows from her permanent scowl, she had deep-blue eyes and fine features that suggested she had once been a beauty. She wore a rust-colored wool overcoat. Pinned to her lapel was a gold "G" studded with diamonds.

"Good morning!" Becca greeted.

Phyllis peered down at her wristwatch then up at Becca. "10:02," she said curtly.

Becca smoothed the front of her apron. "I apologize, Mrs. Grant. I know it's cool and breezy out there today. A cup of tea by the fire will be just the thing."

Phyllis heaved a sigh, untied the belt of her overcoat, and then paused, waiting expectantly. "Alexandra," she prompted in a soft voice, "my coat, please."

"Oh!" Lexi set down the camel-colored briefcase she was clutching and hurried to help extricate her grandmother from her coat. The young woman, who was in her late twenties, was tall and very thin. With her shoulders rounded slightly forward, Lexi did not carry herself in the stately manner of the Grants; however, she shared her grandmother's ocean-blue eyes and straight nose. Her ebony hair was pulled back into a ponytail, and she wore a thick olive-green puffer coat that looked almost comical on her birdlike frame.

Phyllis watched as Lexi draped her grandmother's overcoat onto the coat rack by the door. "Thank you, dear," the elderly woman said, smiling her approval as Lexi then bent to take up the briefcase again. "Come now," she continued. "I must have my tea in hand and be prepared for the meeting before Donna—er—the ladies arrive." She turned on her heel and strode toward the back of the shop with Lexi, still bundled in her coat, hustling after her.

With a small smile and a slight shake of her head, Becca slid her hands into her apron pockets and watched the pair make their way through the bookshop. Then she stepped over to the story time area to make sure her picture books were in place for the 10:30 story time. This week's theme was "Squirrels and Acorns." Beside the stack of picture books was a pretty melamine bowl filled with acorns that Hazel had gathered to give the children as mementos. When she was sure that everything was in order, she headed toward the back of the shop where the smell of coffee and warm pillowy donuts filled the air.

She found Phyllis seated in the place that Becca had recently occupied, the head of the long table near the fire. The briefcase was open on the table, and Phyllis, donning a pair of reading glasses, was removing and arranging papers in front of her. Butterscotch, who had abandoned her spot upon the elderly woman's arrival and taken up a new one by the fire, lifted her head and let it fall back on her paws with a soft snort. While Audrey bustled about in the back, Lexi stood near the bakery counter, wringing her fingers. Becca slipped behind the counter to join her sister-in-law.

"May I help you with anything?" she asked.

Concentrating on her task of pouring boiling water from a kettle into a personal-sized teapot, Audrey replied, "Would you grab a scone for Mrs. Grant?"

Carefully selecting a triangular-shaped pastry from behind the glass, Becca set it on a plate and warmed it in the microwave. She then scooped jam and clotted cream onto the plate and headed toward Lexi. At the same time, Audrey joined her with the teapot as well as the saucer laden with a dainty teacup and a slice of lemon.

"That should be everything," Audrey said.

Lexi glanced back and forth between the teapot and pastry.

"Here, let me help you," Becca urged. Stepping around to the other side of the counter, she clutched the handle of the teapot with one hand and picked up the cup and saucer with the other. Lexi grabbed the pastry, and the two women headed toward Phyllis's table.

"You may put them there," Phyllis directed, indicating an empty place among the papers that the woman had reserved for her refreshments.

Becca scanned the table and glanced up at Lexi. "Did you order anything for yourself? Hazel created a brand-new crème brûlée latte that is absolutely delicious. It's smooth and creamy with a hint of vanilla and caramelized sugar sprinkled on top."

Lexi's eyes sparkled, and she opened her mouth to answer.

"Those types of drinks are terribly contrived, don't you think, Alexandra?" Phyllis interjected. "Give us a good time-honored black tea any day. That is what we Grant women have always enjoyed."

The young woman's face fell for a moment, but she tipped her chin in resolve and looked at her grandmother. "You're right," she said.

Phyllis nodded her approval and then turned to Becca. "Besides, those commercialized drinks are terribly overpriced."

At the words, Becca felt a warmth rise into her cheeks. She took a breath, smiled pleasantly, and turned to Lexi. "May I get you anything?"

"I'll have black tea, please," she muttered.

"With lemon," Phyllis added.

Becca met Lexi's eyes, and the young woman nodded. Phyllis turned her attention back to the papers in front of her.

Becca took a deep breath. "Will there be anything else, Mrs. Grant?"

"You are dismissed for now," she replied without looking up from her papers.

Becca did not waste any time in hurrying away from the table to prepare Lexi's black tea... with lemon. She selected a second teapot from the shelf, filled it with water from the kettle, and perched a wedge of lemon beside a teacup on a saucer. She placed all of the items on a tray and was about to deliver them, but her gaze fell upon Phyllis, who was breaking apart her scone and dunking it into the clotted cream. Setting her mouth in a hard line, Becca set down the tray and turned toward her sister-in-law. "Audrey, could you make a crème brûlée latte, please?"

Audrey raised an eyebrow. "Did anyone order it?"

"Take it out of my tips," Becca said.

Audrey rolled her eyes, but her lips curved into a half smile, and she turned to grab a large glass pedestal coffee mug from the shelf. While Becca greeted another customer and tapped his order into a tablet, Audrey made quick work of preparing the drink and finished with generous swirls of whipped cream and a heavy sprinkle of caramelized sugar. Taking the tea tray in one hand and the latte in the other, Becca scanned the room. Not seeing Lexi, Becca paused for a moment, puzzled, and then smiled in realization.

"I'll be right back," she whispered to Audrey as her sister-in-law poured black coffee into a paper to-go cup.

Licorice at her heels, Becca made her way through the maze of bookshelves toward the fine arts section. She glimpsed down at the black cat.

"Don't trip me," she warned playfully.

She found Lexi in her usual spot: an oversized worn leather chair beside a side table topped with a small stack of books. Her legs were curled beneath her, and she was slowly paging through a book titled *Caravaggio: His Life and Work*. On the book's cover was an image of an amazed Saint Thomas, his finger embedded in Jesus's side, with two other disciples looking on.

"That's a striking cover," Becca said, gesturing toward the book as she set the tea tray on the table. "Well... it *is* accurate, though."

Lexi glanced up from her page.

"I have something for you... on the house!" She beamed as she held out the sugar-topped latte.

The woman accepted the mug from Becca, took a sip, and licked the cream from her lips. "Do you have any more books like this?" she asked.

It took a moment for Becca to process the lack of acknowledgement. Then she pointed to a nearby shelf and said pleasantly, "All of our art books are over there. But if you're looking for something in particular, I'd be happy to order it for you."

Lexi nodded and returned to her page.

"You've been very interested in art for a while," Becca observed. "Pretty soon, you'll have read every book on that subject in our shop."

The young woman dragged her eyes away from her page to look at Becca. "My boyfriend, Harvey, majored in art," she said. "I like being able to talk about it with him. Plus, it gives me something to do when I drive Grandmother here for her meetings." She tilted her head in Phyllis's direction.

Becca nodded in understanding. "We were just studying Rembrandt ourselves this morning. How nice that Harvey is an artist!"

Lexi sighed. "I wish Grandmother would see it that way. She loves art, but she doesn't love that I'm dating an artist."

Glancing in the direction of the café, Becca's eyes rested on the elderly woman for a few moments. With a slight shake of her head, she turned back toward Lexi and smiled. "Well, you enjoy, and let us know if you need anything else." She watched as, with a graceful leap, Licorice jumped up onto the arm of the chair occupied by the young woman and massaged the soft, worn leather with his paws. Before he could settle in, Lexi pushed him off, and he landed on all fours with a soft thump.

Becca's eyes widened, and she stood frozen for a moment. "Come on, Licorice," she consoled, patting the side of her thigh and moving in the direction of the hollow tree. "Let's go see how Oliver is doing." Quickly recovering from the insult, Licorice hurried after his mistress as she wound her way through shelves of books.

With its faux leaves and scaly bark, the hollow tree was surprisingly realistic. When Becca arrived, she chuckled at the sight of Oliver's dirty socks protruding from the window. Not able to resist, she grabbed some of the toes and gave them a gentle shake. Both feet immediately withdrew inside the tree. "How's it going in there?" she called up.

"Good," came the flat reply.

Becca chided herself for asking a teenager such a closed-ended question. "What are you working on?" she asked.

"I'm working on math, Mom," Oliver said. His unenthusiastic tone was one which Becca knew well enough to mean that he was, indeed, calculating probability or solving an algebra problem.

She noticed Licorice at her feet and looked up at the window. "Do you want some company?" she called.

"Sure!" came the muffled reply.

Two hands, which were a little more manly than Becca would care to admit, emerged from the window. As she lifted the willing cat into them, her breath caught for a moment. Oliver's hands looked remarkably like his father's, even down to the freckle at the base of his thumb. Smiling at the realization, Becca passed off the cat, brushed her own hands on the front of her apron, and headed toward the café area.

As she approached, she found that the story time crowd had begun to arrive, and a line of customers had formed in front of the counter. Audrey was tapping an order into the shop's tablet, and she glanced up at Becca. "Help!" she mouthed.

Quickly texting Violet with a request to come down, Becca hurried to greet the next customer in line. She glanced over at Phyllis's table, which was now occupied by three additional women. The four ladies comprised the Crystal Run Improvement Society, CRIS for short. Becca's eyes sparkled as she recalled Audrey's name for the group: Crystal Run's Insufferable Snobs. The name was apt since the group's purpose was to assess the town's art, music, theater, and general appearance and offer unsolicited advice for improvement. Naturally, Phyllis was the president of the society.

To Phyllis's right sat Donna Sloane, vice-president of the group and wife of the well-respected town pharmacist. She was in her early sixties, tall in stature, and slim. Her silver hair was smoothed into a stylish pixie cut, and she was dressed in a tweed blazer. Across from Donna sat the group's secretary, Marjorie Marston, who, with her short round body, red hair, and ruddy cheeks, resembled an apple. The treasurer, Evelyn Hansen, was the final member of the group and sat to Donna's right. She was a small mousy woman with a pinched face and thick-framed eyeglasses. Historically, the Crystal Run Improvement Society had conducted its monthly meetings at Crystal Links Country Club. As Becca gazed at the group, who appeared to be voting on something, she wondered why they had decided to start gathering at her "little shop" as she had heard Phyllis call it a few months ago.

Violet appeared within minutes, and the three women were a display of efficiency and speed as they rang up book purchases, whipped up sugary drink orders, and fulfilled pastry requests. The whirlwind of activity was highlighted by a boy with golden curls who could not decide what he wanted more—a donut or a donut hole—only to burst into tears when his mother said that he couldn't have *either* because he had already had a cookie.

Becca, who felt like time had hardly passed, was shocked when she heard Violet's voice call, "Mom, it's time! You need to head over for story time now."

"Already?" Becca glanced down at her watch. "Ugh, late again!" She turned toward Audrey, who made a shooing motion at her. Becca smoothed the front of her apron and headed to the other side of the counter. As she passed the table of CRIS ladies, the sharp call of "Rebecca!" froze her in her tracks.

Becca turned toward the source of the voice and took a deep breath. With a deliberately pleasant tone, she replied, "May I help you, Mrs. Grant?"

Phyllis held up a finger to the women at her table. "One moment, ladies." She turned toward Becca. "Before Alexandra and I leave, you and I need to discuss the details for my—*ahem*." She coughed daintily and flicked her eyes in Donna's direction. "For my *event* next week."

"I would be happy to," Becca said. "I am running story time right now, but I should be available to chat after that."

The elderly woman scowled and paused, but then she finally responded, "Very well, we'll *chat* then." She said the word as though it left a bitter taste in her mouth. Phyllis returned her attention to the society members. "Now, the flowerbeds in front of the theater simply *must* be addressed."

Becca quickly stepped away in the direction of the story time area. As she made her way, she felt two little hands grip her arm. She glanced down to find Hazel, who had taken a break from her studies to join her mother.

"May I ring the chime?" the girl asked excitedly.

"Of course," Becca said. "I'm counting on you to do it."

As the mother and daughter approached, they found that parents and children had already begun to gather. Becca took her place in the rocking chair while Hazel plucked a mallet from the story time basket. With great importance, she struck each bar of a wall-mounted chime, and a melodious tune sang throughout the bookshop. Within a minute, the straggling children and their parents had gathered in the story time area. Butterscotch, who had also been summoned by the chime, ambled over toward the center of the rug. After making three leisurely turns, she lay down facing Becca as if she, too, wanted to hear the stories.

"Hello, boys and girls!" Becca greeted cheerfully. "Let's begin with our good morning song."

About twenty minutes later, Becca laid the final book, *Because of an Acorn*, on the stack by her feet. She clapped her hands together and smiled warmly at the children. "Our time together is over for today! If you enjoyed the books we read, I will be placing them over there"—she pointed to a nearby table covered with a golden-brown floral tablecloth—"so you can look at them more. As we sing our goodbye song, Hazel is going to pass out a little gift that she collected. Hazel, would you like to show the boys and girls?"

Hazel, who had been sitting cross-legged at her mother's feet, popped up like a cork. She stooped down to pick up the pumpkin-colored bowl filled with acorns, plucked one from the top, and held it up between her pointer finger and thumb.

"Ready?" Becca asked. To the tune of "Clementine," she and the children began to sing, "See you later, alligator. After a while, crocodile!"

The pink gauze butterfly on Hazel's apron fluttered as she darted among the children and placed acorns into their chubby hands.

Smiling and saying goodbye to the members of the dispersing group, Becca suddenly heard a voice that made her stomach tense as it said, "My grandmother is ready for you." Becca caught a hint of impatience in the voice and looked up to see Lexi.

"Oh, yes!" Becca said. "To discuss the cocktail party. I'll be right there."

Lexi turned on her heel, her blue-black ponytail whipping behind her. As Becca hurried to arrange the books on the display table, she could feel Phyllis's glare burning on her from across the room. She thought better of continuing and strode in the direction of the café area and found Phyllis where she had left her, at the head of the long table. The woman's fingernails made a clacking sound as she drummed them on the tabletop. The other CRIS ladies had departed, and Lexi was seated to her grandmother's right. Becca slid into the chair on her left.

"As you know," Phyllis said, "I am donating the Grant family portrait to the William Grant Memorial Library." She sat up a little straighter. "The Grants founded Crystal Run. The painting will serve as a permanent reminder to whom gratitude is owed."

Audrey, who had appeared by Becca's side to supply her with her catering notes, looked at Becca. Already stifling a giggle at the comically haughty words of the elderly woman beside her, Becca refused to make eye contact with her sister-in-law.

Becca took a breath to keep her voice steady. "Permanent? It's not a loan?"

"The library *is* the William *Grant* Memorial Library, named after my great-great-great-grandfather. Why shouldn't it be permanent?"

Becca glanced at Lexi, who stared glaze-eyed into her empty teacup.

"This is a monumental event," Phyllis continued. "It is exactly *why* I am hosting this party. To celebrate the history of the Grant family, to educate the most important citizens of Crystal Run about the portrait's history, and to celebrate its relocation to a more visible place."

Smiling and picking up the stack of papers Audrey had left, Becca tapped them on the table. "Shall we go over the action items for your party?"

Phyllis glanced down at her own stack of papers. "Alexandra mailed the invitations two weeks in advance." She picked up a pen and ticked a box on a list.

Lexi plunged a thin hand into her handbag and pulled out a cream-colored envelope. "What about Mrs. Sloane's invitation? May I mail—"

The stately woman shot her granddaughter a meaningful look. "Not. Yet," she said in a staccato and grinned cruelly to herself.

Becca raised an eyebrow and tried to catch Lexi's eye, but the young woman kept her gaze down as she tucked the neglected invitation back into her bag. With a slight shake of her head, Becca said, "I have the guests arriving at 7:00, so Violet and I will come well in advance before that. I am thinking 5:00?"

"That will be satisfactory," Phyllis acknowledged. The woman surveyed Becca's teal apron, and the creases between her brows deepened. "You and your daughter will have formal uniforms, of course."

Becca nodded. "Yes, Violet and I will both be properly attired."

Pursing her lips, Phyllis drummed her fingernails on the table and then looked up at Becca. "This is an elegant event, and I will not have children running around. I trust that you will be making arrangements for your other children."

"Oliver will be helping provide the music. He is playing his violin, and Charles Rochester will be on the piano. As for Hazel..." Becca glanced toward the story time area. "Well, you see, um... I'm having a hard time finding anyone to watch her." She looked at Phyllis.

The elderly woman stared at her, the furrow between her eyes deepening.

Becca took a deep breath. "I am wondering if it would be all right if I bring Hazel with me. You have such a big house—I could find a quiet room for her to be in. She won't be a bother."

Phyllis scowled. "You've exhausted *all* other options?"

"I have," Becca said.

The elderly woman picked up her pen and tapped it on the stack of papers in front of her. Finally, she said, "There is a spare bedroom your daughter may stay in during the party. I am not unreasonable after all. I do know your husband is dead."

Becca blinked, and an icy chill ran up her spine. Although it had been three years since the car accident, the curt delivery of the words hit her like a slap in the face. "Thank you," Becca said quietly, putting her fingers to her cheek. After a moment, she cleared her throat and added, "I *promise* that Hazel won't be any trouble, Mrs. Grant."

"See to it that she isn't, or you will be held personally responsible," Phyllis said, a threatening edge to her voice. Satisfied, the woman glanced at the checklist in front of her and continued. "Now, the drinks are the most important part of a cocktail party. Rebecca, you will need to find a bartender for the event."

"Oh!" Becca said, her heart fluttering. "I thought you had already secured a bartender, Mrs. Grant. It might be difficult to find someone on such short notice."

Lexi leaned forward. "Grandmother, I already asked Harvey to be the bartender. He's happy to do it."

Her eyes widening in surprise, Phyllis turned to her granddaughter. "You are still associating with that boy?"

Lexi shifted uncomfortably in her chair. "He's really nice," she squeaked out.

"Alexandra," the elderly woman said with measured patience, "in a few short years, you are going to be a lawyer. Appearances matter. While I'm sure he's perfectly pleasant, there are plenty of suitors more befitting for association with our family. That is why we agreed on your cutting ties."

The young woman lifted her dark-blue eyes to meet her grandmother's. "I understand," she said. "But could you give him a chance? For me?" Her eyebrows raised hopefully. "I think you will really like Harvey. Besides, he is the only bartender you're going to find on such short notice."

Phyllis studied her granddaughter's face and let out a relenting sigh.

"I do think it would be for the best, Mrs. Grant," Becca said. "The party is only nine days away."

Phyllis picked an imaginary piece of lint from her sleeve. "Very well," she said slowly, continuing to look at her granddaughter. "Your *friend* may tend bar at the party, and he will need to supply all the beverages." She returned her gaze to Becca, and her voice took on a businesslike tone. "However"—she raised a single crooked finger in the air—"there is something that I would like *you* to handle."

Becca picked up the pen and poised it over her notepad. "What is that, Mrs. Grant?"

"During the evening, I will be raising a champagne toast to the Grants, the founding family of Crystal Run." The elderly woman held up an imaginary champagne flute, and a hint of a smile crossed her lips. She dropped her hand and resumed, "I cannot drink alcohol, so I will require a non-alcoholic sparkling drink for myself. I am assigning you the task of procuring one for me."

"Non-alcoholic champagne," Becca said as her pen flowed across the paper in front of her. "Got it. And you have the drinkware you need, Mrs. Grant?"

Phyllis's eyes flicked sideways, and she reached for her teacup. "Alexandra and her friend will be taking care of that," she said. Suddenly, her deep-blue eyes widened, and she turned toward her granddaughter. "The guests' champagne flutes may be standard, but mine must be in one of the special Grant family heirloom goblets. You know the ones."

Lexi nodded. "Yes," she said. "I will see to it."

Phyllis returned her gaze to Becca. "In the coming week, I will expect a finalized menu."

Becca made a note on the pad in front of her. "You will have it by the end of the week."

The woman nodded. "Prepare for ten guests, the most distinguished citizens of Crystal Run."

Becca's green eyes sparkled. "Of course," she said, struggling to keep her lips from showing her amusement at the idea of there being distinguished citizens in this tiny town.

"And you will also be handling the clean-up afterward," Phyllis stated.

"Yes," Becca agreed.

"Then we are concluded here." At that, the elderly woman reached her clawlike hand into her purse and pulled out a check. She stole a final glance at the amount, and that cruel smile played on her lips again. "Here is the down payment that you agreed to," she said, handing the check to Becca.

Looking at the meager sum, Becca felt her stomach twist. With effort, she managed to form the words, "Thank you, Mrs. Grant." As she added the check to her stack of papers, she glanced up to see that Oliver had emerged from the hollow tree and was making his way over to her. She returned her gaze to the pair of women. "Please don't hesitate to contact me if you think of any questions or need anything else."

"We'll be in touch. Good day," Phyllis said dismissively and snapped the latches shut on her briefcase. Lexi shrugged her thin frame into the olive-green puffer coat. As Becca headed toward her son, she heard the elderly woman say, "Alexandra, will you please take the briefcase?"

Oliver raked his fingers through his unruly hair. "Is it lunchtime?"

Becca smiled, knowing that the prospect of food was one of the few things to lure her son from his secluded study space. "Let me just check in with Aunt Audrey, and I will meet you upstairs for sandwiches."

The gangly young man nodded and headed toward the stairs that led to their apartment.

Now that the story time rush had diminished, Becca found Audrey tidying up behind the bakery counter. She gave a final swipe and hung up the washcloth.

"I have something for you!" Becca said, holding out Phyllis's down payment.

Audrey wiped her hands on her apron, took the check, and frowned as she observed the amount. "I can't *believe* we are doing this for so little profit," she scoffed.

Becca nodded soberly. "I told Mrs. Grant the going rate for a catering event and that what she was asking for was way below. But she said it was *that* or no deal. And we need the income."

Audrey noticed the look of disappointment and worry etched on her sister-in-law's face, and she softened. "That we do. Besides, a high-profile gig like this will likely bring in more business." She smiled and glanced at her watch. "Isn't it time you join the kids for lunch?"

Becca hung up her apron, noticing that Violet's and Hazel's were already on the hooks. She turned toward the auburn-haired woman. "I'll see you in an hour."

"You mean that I'll text you when you forget to come down?" Audrey teased.

Becca pushed open the door to their apartment and headed to the kitchen. Despite its modest size, the room was bright and airy with its powder-blue-and-white tiled backsplash, creamy quartz countertops, stainless appliances, and light-oak lower cabinets. She slid into a seat at the table and found a tidy-looking turkey sandwich and scoop of fruit salad, which Violet had lovingly prepared for her. Between bites, Becca edited Violet's report on *The Screwtape Letters*, graded Oliver's algebra, and glanced over

Hazel's diagrammed sentence. Becca couldn't believe how the time had passed as her phone lit up with a text from Audrey:

*Lunch is over, and you've got a visitor.*

Quickly finishing the inspection of her children's work, she loaded her plate into the dishwasher. "Does anyone need anything before I head down?" The children shook their heads, and Becca skipped lightly down the stairs.

She stepped into the twinkle-lit bookshop where the soft piano melody of "Lo, How a Rose E'er Blooming" filled the space. With quick steps, Becca made her way to the café area. At first, she saw only Audrey, who was leaning over the glass bakery counter. Becca tilted her head. "I thought you said I had a visitor."

"You do," Audrey said, pointing toward the fireplace.

There she saw the broad back of a middle-aged man as he tossed a log onto the fire. He was tall, solidly built, and muscular. The man reached for a poker and began to adjust the log.

Becca grinned. "Well, hi, Uncle John!"

At her greeting, Captain John Olson withdrew the poker, turned around, and smiled. "Your fire was getting low," he said in his warm bass. He had thick white hair and a bushy white mustache.

Becca hurried to throw her arms around his neck.

"Careful now," he chuckled as he held the poker away from them.

Stepping back, Becca gazed into the kind blue eyes that reminded her so much of her father's. She glanced at the police uniform blazer, which was hung neatly over the back of a chair. A silver captain badge glinted in the firelight. "They're able to spare you at the station for a bit?" she asked.

"For a bit," the chief returned, hanging the poker back in its place. He glanced at his watch. "I have a three o'clock meeting, but I have time for a raspberry-filled donut... and a black coffee."

Becca stepped in the direction of the bakery counter, but Audrey waved her away. "I'm on it!" she said. "Go chat with your uncle."

As John eased himself into a chair at one of the wooden tables, Butterscotch, who had been snoozing by the fire, ambled over and placed her head on his knee. Becca seated herself beside him. Her eyes sparkled, and her lips spread into a smile.

"Oh no, here it comes," John chuckled.

"What's going on at the police station?" Becca asked. "Are there any interesting cases?"

"Always," the chief said, smiling.

"What about all the fence vandalisms? Do you have any suspects?"

"That's actually the subject of my three o'clock meeting," John said. He glanced up as Audrey placed a mug and a plate loaded with a sugar-crusted donut in front of him. "Thank you, Audrey." He leaned back in his chair, pulled out his wallet, and removed a fifty-dollar bill. Handing it to Becca, he said, "To the owner of this fine establishment. No change necessary."

Becca's eyes widened as she took in the denomination. "U-uncle John!" she sputtered. "We can't accept this!" She thrust the bill back in his direction.

Suddenly, Audrey's hand darted out and snatched the bill from Becca's fingers. "Oh, yes, we *can* take that! Thank you!" The auburn-haired woman gave the chief an appreciative smile and marched away happily with her prize.

Becca smiled and shook her head. "You're too generous, Uncle John."

"Not at all," the captain said, biting into his donut. "This treat is worth every penny." He broke off a bit and held it under the table for Butterscotch, who made quick work of it.

Becca shook her head again. Then her face lit up as she recalled their previous topic of conversation. "So, the fence vandalism case... Do you think it's someone trying to trespass? Or maybe kids who need something better to do with their time?"

John, who had been taking a sip of his coffee, set down his mug and laughed softly. "Becca and her questions," he said. "You never could help yourself. I remember when you were just a kid in pigtails, sitting next to your dad at his desk, unwrapping mint candies, and peppering him with questions about the cases. And even when you were working your way through school—sitting at the front desk at the station, answering phones, and filing papers." He smiled, the skin around his eyes settling into familiar creases. "You had to know everything about all the cases. Your father had that same insatiable curiosity. That's what made him such a great police chief. That's your father in you, you know."

Becca felt a surge of warmth rush into her cheeks. "Thanks, Uncle John," she said, a slight huskiness in her voice. "That's the nicest compliment." As she blinked away the tears, her eye caught her uncle's silver badge. Reaching over, she adjusted it slightly and smiled affectionately up at him.

# Chapter 3

# Lost and Found

"It's massive!" Hazel exclaimed. As the Michigan Avenue traffic hummed behind them, Becca and the children tipped their heads back and surveyed the colossal two-story limestone building in front of them. The family had paused by one of the two huge blue-green copper lions that stood guard on either side of the wide staircase leading up to the museum's entrance.

Oliver reached up and patted one of the lion's enormous paws. "Hey, Toffee, you've grown a bit."

Squinting toward the second story, Violet said, "You can certainly see the influence of Ancient Greece and Rome." She pointed a long delicate finger upward. "Look at the Corinthian columns."

Becca's eyes followed the line of her daughter's finger. Above the arches and columns, the words THE ART INSTITUTE OF CHICAGO were carved into the limestone. An icy gust blew, and she pulled her wool coat a little tighter around her. "Shall we go inside?" she suggested.

After paying admission, Becca waved the children away from the crowd and over to the side as she unfolded the visitor guide. She furrowed her brow as she took in the multiple floor plans shaded in a variety of colors. "I want to start with a Rembrandt, so that means we go to the Arts of Europe, but where is that? There are a lot of levels..." A strand of blonde hair fell into her eyes, and she blew it away with a puff from the side of her mouth.

"Would you like some help?" Violet offered. "Dad taught me how to read those."

Becca smiled gratefully and handed over the visitor guide. "Yes, please. I think we are here," she said, pointing to a spot on the map.

Violet scanned the large glossy paper. "You're close. We are *here*." She guided her mother's finger to the other entrance on the map. "We don't have very far to go. We just need to go up the grand staircase, and it will be close to the top."

Becca laughed. "Lead the way!" She adjusted the strap of her tote bag on her shoulder and grabbed Hazel's hand.

"Can we skip the modern art?" Oliver asked as they moved through the crowd.

"Most certainly," Becca said. "There may be a piece or two that we observe, but we won't be spending much time there."

"Mom, look!" Hazel tugged Becca's hand as they approached the elegant polished-marble staircase. Above the wide set of stairs, which eventually split into opposite directions, were lofty arches supported by more Corinthian columns. A white marble statue stood at the top of the staircase.

Oliver leaped up the steps, two at a time, and made his way to the statue. He had just finished reading the plaque by the time the others joined him in the sunlit space. "Samson wrestling the lion," he said proudly.

After a quick debate about whether *they* would ever eat honey out of a dead lion like Samson did (the consensus was "no" unless Oliver had skipped breakfast that morning), the Gables made their way to Rembrandt's *Self-Portrait* of 1636-38.

Becca stepped to the side of the painting so as not to block others' view. "We discussed etiquette on the way here, so we're all clear on that, right?"

"We all know that Oliver is not going to be able to help himself," Violet said, a note of amusement in her voice. "He is going to touch a painting and end up in art museum jail."

Cracking a smile, Oliver lightly elbowed his sister in the ribs.

Becca shook her head and tried not to show her amusement. "No one is going to end up in art museum jail." She took a breath, clasped her hands in front of her, and smiled brightly at the children. "Today is a very special day," she said. "We are going to be looking for goodness, truth, and beauty as we observe the artwork. This is a large museum, so there's no way that we're going to see everything today, and that's okay."

"It's especially okay if we skip the modern art," Oliver said.

Becca's mouth set in a straight line, and she tapped her foot. "First," she continued, deliberately not responding to Oliver's repeated comment, "we are going to tour the exhibits as a family. As we do that, I want you to keep your eyes open for a painting that really speaks to you in some way or is especially meaningful to you. Before we leave, you will each be sketching that painting. I have a sketch pad and charcoal pencil for each of you." She reached into her bag, pulled out the items, and held them up for her children to see. "When we get home, you will each be writing a research paper on the artist who created that painting. Do you have any questions?"

Hazel patted the beaded purse that hung across her chest. "Will we have time to go to the gift shop?"

Becca laughed. "No, I don't think so, Hazel. Do any of you have questions about the *assignment*?" The children shook their heads. "Then let's begin!"

After comparing *Self-Portrait* with *Storm on the Sea of Galilee,* the Gables made their way to the Arts of Europe: Medieval and Renaissance exhibit. It had a somber feel with its dark-gray walls and many religious-themed artifacts that likely had their origins in European churches and cathedrals. Head down, Oliver quickly walked past a pair of paintings, one portraying Adam and the other Eve with some well-placed branches.

Hazel gazed up at Eve. "That hairstyle does *nothing* for her."

Violet rolled her eyes.

Oliver's discomfort was quickly replaced by delight when the Gables entered the next section: Arms and Armor. The young man darted about the vast room, his nose a hairsbreadth from the glass as he eagerly took in the displays of daggers and swords, many of which were fanned out in impressive arrangements. Oliver's eyes widened as he stared at a sword that was taller than most grown men. He turned toward Violet. "The knight must have been a *beast* to be able to wield that."

"Mm-hmm," Violet said, glancing at her watch. She turned toward her mother. "Are we almost ready to move on?"

Becca smiled. "Soon."

Giggling, Hazel pointed to a pair of knights threatening each other with wooden lances. The knights' helmets were adorned with voluminous sky-high plumes, and they wore velvet pants and bows on their shoes. "They're going to have a tea party when they're done jousting!" Hazel exclaimed.

Oliver scoffed. "Whoa, look at those maces!" he said, hurrying over to another display.

Violet and Hazel exchanged glances. "I don't understand why boys are so obsessed with weapons," Violet said.

Becca shrugged and smiled. "I think God made men to conquer the world and women to make it beautiful." She glanced at Oliver, who was hurrying to another display case. "Five more minutes!" she called.

When they were finally able to succeed in dragging Oliver away from Arms and Armor, the Gables moved on to the Arts of Europe: Painting and Sculpture 1400-1900. The gray-green walls were filled with colossal canvases, some as big as walls themselves, in gilded frames by greats including El Greco, Caravaggio, and Rembrandt. Becca and the children moved slowly among the paintings, the subjects of which were primarily Jesus, Mary, and various saints or scenes from Greek or Roman mythology. As they were about to move on to the next room, Becca noticed that Violet was lagging. "Stay here," she instructed Oliver and Hazel. She found Violet with her arms crossed against her chest. Her head was tipped slightly to the side as she stared at the painting. Becca read the plaque next to it: *Pompeo Girolamo Batoni (Italian, 1708–1787). Allegory of Peace and War. 1776.* The painting depicted the armored god Mars gazing into the eyes of a woman personifying peace. She held an olive branch.

"Is this the piece that speaks to you?" Becca asked.

"Maybe," Violet said thoughtfully. "I was just thinking about how this painting demonstrates what you were talking about... about men and women."

Becca laughed. "So it does! Conquering and beauty."

When the family finished in the Art of Europe section, Becca asked Violet to lead them to the Impressionist wing. As they made their way down the hall, Hazel glanced up at a painting and gasped in delight. "Degas' ballerinas!" Although the ballerinas in the painting were still as they waited in the wing of the Paris Opéra, Hazel rose onto her toes and began to turn in a pirouette. Unfortunately, she spun right into the sizeable belly of a middle-aged man who coughed and sputtered. "Oops!" Hazel looked up at the man, and her cheeks flushed. "Sorry!" With a final grunt, the man tramped away, shaking his head. Becca glanced down at Hazel and raised an eyebrow. "Oops," Hazel repeated meekly. Becca smiled, and the group continued in the direction of the Impressionist wing.

As her eyes fell upon the blues, greens, and purples of Renoir's *Seascape*, Becca's breath caught. "Violet, Oliver, Hazel," she said dreamily, "I hope you're letting this soak in. You're seeing the *original* paintings of Rembrandt, van Gogh, Monet... You can *see* the texture of the paint created by the *actual* brushes they held in their hands."

Just then, she heard her phone chime. She pulled the phone from her purse and glanced at the screen. "It's a text from Aunt Audrey," she told the children. "This may be important." As Violet, Oliver, and Hazel stood admiring *Seascape,* Becca located a vacant bench in the room and lowered herself onto it to read the text:

> *You won't believe what just happened at the bookshop!! Epic granny showdown—Crystal Run's Insufferable Snobs. Two of the CRIS snobs went at it! Something about Donna not getting an invitation to Phyllis's cocktail party? Phyllis called Donna "the wife of a drug dealer"!!! I was sure Donna was going to claw her eyes out, but she stormed out with Lexi before Donna could get the chance. Don't worry, they were the only ones in the shop. Better than a soap opera, for sure.*

Becca sighed and shook her head. Glancing up, she saw Violet and Oliver still in front of *Seascape*. A museum docent was slowly walking away from them, and Oliver's cheeks were flushed. Becca rose and made her way to the children. "Is everything okay?" she asked.

"Oh!" Violet said, grinning. "Oliver just got threatened to be put in art museum jail."

"I didn't touch it!" the young man protested. "I just wanted to see the brushstrokes up close to see how he made the waves look so frothy." He flicked his eyes in the direction of the docent and lowered his voice. "Apparently, I got too close."

Violet tilted her head. "I wonder if they'll make you wear stripes."

Becca's eyes swept over the room. "Where's Hazel?" she asked.

Immediately, Violet's smile dissolved. She and Oliver turned and cast their gaze around the room and then exchanged worried glances.

Becca's fingers flew to the cross at her throat, and she took a deep breath. "Okay," she said. "Let's not panic." She closed her eyes and moved her lips in a short and urgent prayer.

"Hazel probably got bored and went on ahead," Violet suggested.

Becca nodded. "Let's see if she's in the next room."

With a final glance around the space, she led the two older children into the adjoining room. As the trio searched among the crowd, they swept past works by Seurat and Monet without a glance as though they were cheap prints displayed at a dentist's office. Unsuccessful, the group paused near van Gogh's 1887 *Self-Portrait*. Becca's heart pounded, and a thought flashed across her mind that the man who was peering out of his thick gold frame seemed far too unconcerned about her lost girl.

"She must be going through this *really* fast," Oliver commented.

Violet wrung her hands. "Maybe she was looking for the water lilies?"

Becca peered into the entranceway to the next room. "Do you think she could have gotten that far?" She tapped her foot and considered. "We'll try one more room."

They worked their way through the crowd and entered the next room, which was even more packed than the others had been. Standing out from the charcoal-gray walls like colorful jewels were two of Monet's water lily paintings. If Hazel were in this room, *surely* this is where she would be. Desperately searching the mass for her golden-haired daughter, Becca scanned the crowd. "She's not here," she choked out. Oliver reached forward and squeezed his mother's shoulder. The color drained from Violet's face. Becca took a deep breath. "Let's go back. I don't think she would have gotten this far."

More quickly this time, Becca wound her way back through the Impressionist wing. "It's still not time to panic," she said assuredly with a quick backward glance. "You all know the plan for if we get separated. Hazel will find a docent." Becca instinctively moved toward the last place she had seen Hazel, Renoir's *Seascape.* Her brows knit in concentration as she gazed upon the melancholy waves and all their movement. *Movement!*

Becca gasped. "I know where Hazel is!" Her eyes were wide as she grabbed Violet's hand and pulled her out of the Impressionist gallery and into the hallway in the direction of the Degas ballerinas.

Sure enough, there was Hazel, facing *Yellow Dancers (In the Wings).* Her eyes were fixed on a spot on the painting, and her expression was stoic with concentration as she moved through the various ballet positions: first position—heels together, toes out to the side; second position—feet hip-distance apart; third position—one heel lined up with the middle of her other foot.

To Violet's great relief, Becca released her vise grip on her oldest daughter's hand. "Thank you, God!" she exhaled. She rushed over to Hazel and flung her arms around her. The floral scent of her daughter's hair filled Becca's nostrils as she kissed the top of her head.

"Mom! Now I have to start o—" Hazel complained, but she stopped abruptly upon seeing the tears in her mother's eyes.

"Hazel Ruth Gables!" Becca admonished. "You know better than to go off on your own."

Hazel dropped her gaze to the floor. "I'm sorry, Mom. It's just that all of you were right over *there*," she said, pointing to the entrance to the Impressionist wing. "And I told Violet and Oliver that I was going back by the ballerinas. They must not have heard me."

Violet folded her arms across her chest. "Oh, sure, blame it on Oliver and me."

Becca smiled and wiped an eye with the back of her hand. She glanced around and suddenly gasped. "Oliver! Oh no, where's Oliver?"

Hazel spun, and Violet's head swiveled as she searched for her brother. "Ugh, not again!" the older sister groaned.

Becca was just drawing in a breath and considering what to do next when Oliver, a blur of gangly arms and legs, came sprinting up toward them.

"Walk, please!" sounded the sharp voice of a nearby docent.

Oliver skidded to a stop.

"Art museum jail..." Violet said in a sing-song voice.

"Mom! Mom!" he said, ignoring his sister's taunt. "You have to come see the exhibit I found!"

Becca let out an exasperated sigh and addressed all three children. "Okay, listen, unless you are given direct permission *by me*, we all need to stay *together.*"

Observing the mixture of frustration and relief on his mother's face, Oliver's excitement momentarily melted. "I'm sorry, Mom," he said sheepishly, tracing a circle on the floor with the toe of his sneaker. He looked up, and his green eyes sparkled. "But you all *have* to come see this. It's so cool!"

Becca nodded. "All right, let's all go... *together.*"

With quick steps, Oliver led his mother and sisters down the hallway.

As they strode through the hall, Violet narrowed her eyes slightly at her brother. "You must have been *really* concerned about Hazel to have stumbled across this exhibit."

Oliver shrugged and cracked a smile as he directed his family to take a right. "She could have been over there."

After a few twists and turns, they entered a room with a large sign on an easel titled *Special Exhibit: Stolen! Masterpieces Taken in Daring Heists.* "And some of them are still missing!" Oliver said, unable to keep the excitement from his voice.

Violet and Hazel exchanged glances, and Becca smiled, amused by her son's enthusiasm. She gestured toward another posterboard on an easel, which featured paintings by artists including Leonardo da Vinci, Michelangelo Merisi da Caravaggio, and Johannes Vermeer. "It looks like this is where we start," she said.

The Gables moved through the exhibit with Oliver leading the way. At the descriptions of the most daring robberies, Oliver hopped from one foot to the other, and Becca had to cover her mouth with her fingers to hide her smile.

"Look at *this*!" the teenage boy said. He was several feet ahead of his mother and sisters and motioned for them to catch up.

Violet was the first to join him. "Oh *no!*" she gasped.

At the sound, Becca and Hazel hurried over to the easel. Hazel's mouth dropped in horror as she took in the image: Rembrandt's *The Storm on the Sea of Galilee.* Becca nodded solemnly. "It's true," she said. "I didn't mention it because that wasn't the point of our picture study, but this painting was stolen and is still missing."

Oliver frowned and shook his head incredulously at his mother. "But that's the most interesting part!" he said.

When they finally reached the end of the exhibit, the teen searched the faces of his mother and sisters. "Wasn't that the *coolest?*"

Hazel adjusted the strap of her beaded purse. "I didn't realize how many stolen paintings there were... are," she said.

"It was... interesting," Violet admitted slowly. "Also, kind of sad."

Becca pressed her lips into a straight line. "Do you remember when we talk about how God said that this world has fallen into sin? These are the things that happen when selfishness and greed in a person's heart come out in their actions."

Oliver let out an exasperated sigh, and Becca turned to him and smiled. "This *is* a fascinating exhibit, Oliver. I'm so glad you found it and showed it to us." She ruffled his chestnut hair, and he jerked his head away with a lopsided grin.

Becca glanced at her watch. "Now," she said, "it's time for you to choose your paintings and do your sketches. Do all of you know what you'll be drawing?"

Violet nodded. "*Allegory of Peace and War.*"

"Good," Becca said approvingly. "Oliver?"

Oliver tipped his head to the side. "I'm going to sketch the firebrand one."

Hazel laughed. "Oh, yes, because there's fire involved."

Becca said, "*A Boy Blowing on a Firebrand?* That's a fine choice. I love the illumination of the firelight on the boy's face in that one." She looked down at Hazel and, with her forefinger and thumb, tipped her chin up to meet her gaze. "And I bet I know which one you will be sketching."

"*Yellow Dancers (In the Wings),*" Hazel confirmed.

"Wonderful," Becca said. She distributed the sketchpads and charcoal pencils and glanced at her watch again. "You will have an hour to do your sketches. I'll stay with Hazel. Violet and Oliver, do you feel comfortable going by yourselves to do your drawings?"

"Yes," Violet said, and Oliver nodded.

"We'll meet back by the Samson statue in one hour," Becca said, "and then we'll head home. Do you have any questions?"

The children shook their heads.

"Then let's go!"

Becca had hardly finished speaking before Violet was out the door. She gazed down into Hazel's aquamarine eyes. "Are you ready?" In response, the girl popped up on one leg and performed a graceful arabesque. Becca smiled and reached for her hand. As the two headed toward the exhibit's exit, she cast a glance back at Oliver, who was standing in front of an easel, rereading the description of the theft of the *Mona Lisa.* "Oliver," she said. He didn't move. "Oliver!" His head snapped up, and his mother pointed to the exit. "*Now*, please." With quick steps, Oliver made his way to the door. Chuckling softly to herself, Becca squeezed Hazel's hand and followed.

When the sketches were completed, the Gables took in as much art as they could until the museum's close. Their tour included, to Hazel's delight, the Thorne Miniature Rooms, which were the most historically accurate and detailed dollhouses the family had ever seen. It also included, to Oliver's chagrin, a brief visit to the Modern Wing to see the iconic *American Gothic* (the farmer and his daughter). When Becca and the children exited the museum and descended the steps toward Michigan Avenue, the sky was already dusky. Violet located their light-blue minivan in the parking garage, and the family climbed inside and headed home.

A light drizzle spattered the windshield. After making it through the frenzied big-city traffic and back into Wisconsin, Becca exhaled and allowed her body to relax a bit. "I think we're through the worst of it," she said to Violet, who was in the passenger seat.

Violet raised her hands to tighten her messy bun and gazed out the window pensively. She turned toward her mother. "What was *your* favorite painting at the museum, Mom?"

Becca tilted her head as she considered the question. "I don't know if I could choose a favorite, but I really love *Rainy Day*." She paused and then continued, "Although, don't you think Benson could have built up a big cozy fire for his daughter?"

"Like the one at the bookshop!" Hazel said wistfully. "How long until we're home?"

"It will be a while," Becca said, glancing in the rearview mirror at her younger daughter, who had cushioned the window with a squashy stuffed strawberry and was resting her head on it like a pillow.

"Never mind favorite *painting*," Oliver chimed in. "What was your favorite *art theft?*"

Violet rolled her eyes. "Oh no, not again." She swung around in her seat. "Can't you talk about anything else?"

"I don't know if 'favorite' is the word I would use," Becca directed toward Oliver.

The young man leaned forward and gripped the edge of his seat. "Could you believe how those guys dressed up as police officers to steal *The Storm on the Sea of Galilee?*"

Violet picked up her purse from the floor of the minivan and pulled her earbuds from the front pocket.

"And *The White Duck!*" Oliver continued. "That burglar used a smoke canister and a fan to create a smokescreen."

As Violet fitted the earbuds into her ears, Hazel sat up and started looking around for a second stuffed animal.

"*The Potato Eaters* was stolen *twice*," Oliver informed the group. "The second time, the getaway car got a flat tire, and the painting was recovered in thirty-five minutes." He flopped back in his seat and chuckled.

"I *know*. I saw the exhibit," Hazel said, cramming stuffed animals over her ears like earmuffs.

Becca caught Oliver's eye in the rearview mirror. Even in the dim evening night, she could see her son's eyes shining. "I love your enthusiasm," she said.

"Do you think I could write my research paper on stolen paintings instead of the firebrand artist?" he asked.

"Van Honthorst?" Becca tapped her fingers on the steering wheel as she considered. Finally, she said, "Yes, you may. I want you to be interested in your subject."

Oliver grinned and gazed out the window for a moment. Then he pitched forward again. "I wonder if Uncle John has ever solved any cases of stolen paintings!"

His mother smiled. "Not that I know of, but you'll have to ask him. He's been on the force for many years."

"When will we see him next?" the young man asked eagerly.

Traffic had begun to slow again, and Becca squinted as she searched for the cause of the delay. After a few moments, her gaze caught a "detour" sign. She tapped Violet on the arm, and Violet pulled the nearest earbud from her ear and looked at her mother.

Keeping her eyes on the road, Becca pointed to her phone, which was resting between them. "Can you get us home?"

Her daughter smiled, picked up the phone, and zoomed in on the map. "You'll want to take the next exit."

Nodding, Becca switched on the turn signal and glanced in the rearview mirror. She eased into the right lane and exited the highway.

"Now, take a left," Violet instructed.

As Becca followed her daughter's directions, the Gables soon found themselves on a nearly unoccupied stretch of road. Becca glanced back at Oliver, who was shuffling through the snack bag, and Hazel, whose eyelids were slowly opening and closing. With a small smile, Becca allowed her body to relax. Suddenly, she sat bolt upright, her fingers tightening their grip on the wheel.

Violet turned toward her mother. "Are you okay? I know how to get us home."

"Oh!" Becca said. "Sorry. I was just thinking about how much we have to do before Mrs. Grant's cocktail party. It's only three days away!"

Smiling, Violet leaned back against her seat. "Mom, you couldn't be more prepared. You've been planning this for weeks. Your checklists have checklists."

Becca chuckled and glanced at her daughter. "You're right. I've put in the work, and God will bless our efforts." With a sigh, she leaned back against the seat again.

With Violet navigating, it felt like no time at all before they were back at their cozy apartment above the bookshop in tiny Crystal Run.

# Chapter 4

# Final Viewing

"But, Mom, can't I stay with you?" the girl whimpered. "It's *spooky* in here!"

"Oh, it's not that bad, Hazel," Becca said, trying to sound convincing as she nonchalantly swiped at a cobweb. Dressed in her catering uniform of a white button-down shirt topped with a black linen apron, she crossed the large square bedroom. Determinedly, she passed a bed in the middle of the room, which was supported by mahogany pillars and hung with deep-red damask curtains. She stood in front of a window framed in matching fabric and opened the dust-covered blinds. The November sun had already set, and the twilight did nothing to brighten the bedroom's atmosphere. Against the window, the wind gusted, creating a howling sound that even

Becca found unsettling. Closing the blinds again, she moved back across the red carpet and examined a throne-like white cushioned easy chair near the head of the bed. She ran her fingertips across the moth-eaten upholstery, turned, and found her daughter seated on a low ottoman by the fireplace, an abridged copy of *Jane Eyre* in her lap and a backpack resting at her feet.

The girl was staring up at a grubby portrait of an unsmiling man. "Mom, Oliver said that Mrs. Grant's husband died in *this* room. May I *please* stay with you? I don't like it here. It—it feels haunted."

"Hazel Ruth," Becca said, pointedly looking back at her daughter, "you know full well that ghosts do not exist." She paused at the inopportune howl from the window and then continued, "That is just the wind outside. This room is perfectly cozy. You have your book and plenty to do while we serve at Mrs. Grant's party. You know that God is always watching over you, and you are perfectly safe. You need to wait here. Do you understand?"

Hazel smiled weakly. "Yes, Mom."

"That's my brave girl," Becca said with a final glance as she headed out the door.

As she hurried down the steps, she met Lexi, who was wearing a vintage-looking black crepe sheath dress and mumbling something about perfume. Becca headed to the living room where Violet was setting up for the party. The room was large and stately with fawn-colored walls, gleaming tiled floors, and dark boarded ceilings. Between an arched alcove with a window seat and a double door leading out to the gardens stood a massive carved-stone fireplace. Becca's eyes were immediately drawn to the enormous portrait of the Grant family that hung imposingly over the fireplace. A dignified man, his expression serious though not unpleasant, sat in a shining tufted mahogany chair. His wife stood on the man's right with one hand resting on his shoulder. To the left of the man, perched on the leather chair's arm, was a teenage girl wearing a baby-blue long-sleeved mini-dress. She had a small smile on her face, almost a smirk, and she cradled a Yorkshire terrier in her arms. Becca squinted up at the portrait and noticed that the entire surface was laced with a series of hairline cracks. *It's too bad that it didn't hold up better over the years,* she thought.

"How does it look?" Violet asked.

At the sound of her daughter's voice, Becca tore her gaze away from the portrait and surveyed the room. Tucked discreetly against a wall was a long rectangular table covered in white where the food would be placed. Round pedestal tables, which were draped in white linen and tied at the base with wine-colored bows, were arranged in a semi-circle in front of the Grant family portrait. Atop each table was a lantern filled with a pillar candle surrounded by rose petals. Additional floral arrangements and candelabras completed the décor.

"It looks positively elegant," Becca said.

With a smile, Violet, who was wearing a catering uniform that matched her mother's, nodded and adjusted the angle of a lantern.

Becca turned her gaze to the corner of the room where a grand piano stood gleaming beside a music stand and musician's chair. As she crossed the room toward her son, she watched as he carefully laid his father's violin into its worn black case.

"Did I *have* to wear a suit?" Oliver asked, tugging at his collar. "What time is Mr. Rochester getting here? And *how* much is Mrs. Grant paying me?"

Becca exhaled and tapped her foot. "Yes, you had to wear a suit. Mr. Rochester said he's arriving at 6:15 so the two of you can tune and warm up. And we already discussed payment. It's not polite to do that here."

Oliver frowned and looked around the room. "Can I at least light the candles?"

Amused by her son's love of fire, Becca smiled. "When it's time, yes." She glimpsed at her watch. "I need to check on the food." After taking a few steps, she glanced back at her son. "Did you *have* to tell Hazel that Mr. Grant died in that red room?"

"It's true!" he responded. However, seeing his mother's look of disapproval, Oliver smiled sheepishly and said, "Sorry."

Trying to muffle the click-clacking of her black heels as she hurried across the living room, she headed in the direction of the kitchen. As Becca passed the bottom of the grand staircase, the doorbell sounded. She paused, waiting to see if someone would answer the door. She heard the door creak and heave open.

"Mrs. Sloane..." Lexi's hesitant voice echoed through the hall. "You're here early."

Remembering Audrey's description of the "epic granny showdown" at the bookshop between Phyllis and Donna, Becca cringed and clenched her fists. Deciding that she could not be bothered with the drama, she continued to the kitchen.

The sweet smell of butternut squash mixed with apple and onion filled the kitchen as she stirred the mixture in the slow cooker. Becca lifted the lid of the food warmer to inspect the rosemary chicken skewers and added a splash of chicken stock. As she peered into the refrigerator to make sure that the lemony whipped ricotta and endive cups were in order, as well as the portions of avocado chocolate mousse, a lid clanged onto a counter. She jumped and slammed the refrigerator doors shut. Horrified, Becca watched as Donna Sloane, dressed in a navy-blue cocktail dress topped with a matching lace three-quarter-length-sleeved jacket, licked a bit of the squash mixture from the tip of her finger.

"Ex-excuse me?" Becca sputtered. "May I help you, Mrs. Sloane?"

Donna replaced the lid on the slow cooker. "This is delicious," she said. Taking in Becca's horrified stare, she pointed to a teaspoon resting on the counter. "Don't worry, I tasted it from the spoon."

Becca's hand flew to her heart, and she heaved a sigh of relief.

"Please," the woman said, "call me Donna." She smoothed her silver bangs across her forehead. "I'm here to help set up for the party. *And...*" she continued, lowering her voice conspiratorially, "I don't want to miss the fireworks when Patricia Koller arrives."

"The president of the library board?" Becca asked as she placed Donna's used teaspoon in the dishwasher.

"The very one," Donna said. "She oversaw the arrangements for displaying the Grant family portrait, and there wasn't a thing about them that Phyllis liked. She tried to get the poor woman *fired.*"

"Oh, that's too bad," Becca said, busying herself by counting out a stack of cocktail plates. "I hope they've worked things out."

Donna beamed. "Well, I don't. Patricia's arrival could be the most entertaining event of the evening!"

Becca continued counting.

Frowning and placing a hand on her hip, Donna finally said, "Don't mind me. I am just on my way to the butler's pantry to fetch Phyllis's goblet. I heard Lexi say that it would be needed for the toast." She took a few steps and paused, shaking her head. "Phyllis needs all the help she can get. She hasn't been sleeping well."

"Oh, she hasn't?" Becca asked, glancing up from the stack of napkins. "I'm sorry to hear that."

Donna gave a slight shrug. "It's one of the challenges when you are as old as she is, darling. She regularly sends her granddaughter into my husband's shop to pick up her sleeping pills. Without them, she just wanders the house at night." She shook her head again, and the tiniest smile played on her lips. "The poor thing," Donna added and then passed through the kitchen and made her way to the small adjoining room.

Becca's eyebrows furrowed as she watched the woman rise onto her tiptoes to peer into the glass-fronted cabinets. Donna's already towering stature was amplified by her sky-high pointed pumps, which were red-soled and embellished with tiny gemstones. Becca could only imagine how much they cost.

"Aha!" she said triumphantly, opening a cabinet and extracting a wine glass. She returned to the kitchen and held it up to show Becca. The kitchen light refracted brilliantly through the hand-cut lead crystal glass, which was ruby red in color except for the stem, which was clear as a diamond.

"It's beautiful," Becca breathed.

"It's a Grant family heirloom," Donna said knowingly. "There's a complete set."

"Oh!" Becca said. "That reminds me! She returned to the refrigerator and pulled a sapphire-blue bottle with a white label from the door. I have Mrs. Grant's non-alcoholic sparkling wine." She glanced at her watch. "Did you happen to see if Harvey arrived to set up the bar?"

Donna raised an eyebrow. "Isn't it *your* job to monitor the help?"

Becca's eyes widened slightly, but she pressed her lips into a smile. "I'll just go see," she said. "Would you like me to take that?" she asked, indicating the regal-looking goblet.

"No," Donna said. "I will deliver it myself."

With a nod, Becca hurried out of the kitchen, the bottle heavy and chill against her arm.

As she approached the living room, she was greeted by the sound of a piano and violin playing "Stand by Me," and she smiled at the sound. Sure enough, upon entering, she saw Oliver's music instructor, Charles

Rochester, seated at the piano, his long chestnut curls bouncing as his hands moved vigorously over the keys. Abruptly, the man stopped playing, leaned toward Oliver, and said something indistinguishable. The two resumed the upbeat melody.

Shifting the bottle to her other arm, Becca made her way to the dark cherrywood bar, which was located on the wall opposite the fireplace. With its half-moon shape and heavily carved columns and feet, the bar gleamed in the low evening light. Lexi, her chin propped on a fist, leaned on the shining Italian marble. She stared glaze-eyed across the room as Harvey finished slicing oranges on a cutting board. The young man was in his late twenties, and he was thin and average in height. He wore a white button-down shirt, which was rolled up at the sleeves, and a black buttoned vest. He had sandy-colored hair and a sprinkle of freckles across his nose. As Becca approached, Lexi straightened, cleared her throat, and peered over the bar. She watched her boyfriend's face contort and turn red as he unsuccessfully attempted to open a jar of maraschino cherries.

"Good grief!" Lexi snapped. "All you need to do is strike the top of the jar with a knife to dent it, and then it will open." As Harvey reached for a knife, she rolled her eyes.

At the outburst, Becca's eyes widened. Tentatively, she placed a hand on Lexi's back. "I know this party is important to your grandmother... and to you. Don't worry. Everything is going to go off just as planned tonight."

"What?" Lexi said, confusion tempering her annoyance. "Huh? Oh, yes, I'm sure it will."

Becca held out the bottle to Harvey. "Here is the non-alcoholic sparkling wine that Mrs. Grant requested. It's for her glass... for the toast."

"Thank you," Harvey said, shimmying the bottle into a stainless-steel container of ice, which was tucked into one of the drawers behind the bar.

Lexi straightened. "Oh, that reminds me. Grandmother wants her special glass for the toast."

"I've already got it!" Donna announced, her lips stretching into a mauve lipstick-framed grin. She pretended to toast with the ruby goblet and then carefully handed it to Harvey.

Lexi frowned, but her expression brightened when she saw her grandmother appear under the arched entrance to the room.

With quick steps, Becca crossed the space toward Phyllis, who stood primly, waiting to be greeted. Her short white curls were topped with a sparkling silver tiara. She wore a dress with a lace embroidered bodice, three-quarter-length sleeves, and a smooth chiffon skirt. For a moment, Becca's eyes flicked toward the impressive Grant family portrait, and she observed that the baby-blue color of Phyllis's dress exactly matched that of the teenage girl peering out of the gilded frame.

Noticing Becca's glance, Phyllis said, "It's so the guests know that *I* am the young woman in that painting." She chuckled to herself. "Of course, they'll know that when I give the history of the portrait, but it's all about the details." She exhaled, and the furrows between her brows deepened. "I will inspect the room now." She stepped toward a floral bouquet and examined a creamy white rose between her fingers. "This is a bit wilted," she croaked.

"It looks fine to me," a voice contradicted.

Phyllis turned sharply toward the sound of the voice and found Donna standing beside her. She straightened her frail frame and tipped up her chin. "You're here early."

Donna ran her fingers through her stylish silver pixie cut and shrugged. "Early arrivals, late invitations..." She laughed. "Time is relative, don't you think?"

Becca held her breath and busied herself moving the white rose, which looked perfectly lovely to her, to the back of the arrangement.

"I'm here to help set up for the party, darling," Donna said in a syrupy voice.

Phyllis narrowed her eyes. "You really didn't have to do that, *darling*."

Becca sucked in a breath and noticed that Violet had finished transferring the food from the kitchen to the long white rectangular table. "Mrs. Grant, may I get your opinion on the rosemary chicken skewers? I want to make sure you like how they're seasoned."

The regal-looking woman turned toward Donna. "I'm needed elsewhere. *Do* make yourself comfortable."

As they approached the long table laden with hors d'oeuvres, Becca admired her daughter's tasteful arrangement of the food, particularly the methodical checkerboard-style arrangement of the cups of chocolate mousse. "Violet," she said, "would you please make up a sample plate for Mrs. Grant? I'm going to have Oliver light the candles now."

Violet busied herself under Phyllis's critical eye while Becca reached under the table to retrieve a lighter. She moved across the room toward her son, and the music stopped sharply as she addressed the young man and handed him the lighter. Reproachfully, Mr. Rochester shook his head as Oliver, a huge grin spread across his face, leapt away in the direction of a candelabra.

Becca returned to Phyllis, who was now standing at the bar beside her granddaughter, nibbling a chicken skewer. She made her way toward her employer.

The elderly woman smacked her lips. "These could use a bit more salt," she told Becca, returning the skewer on her plate.

"Yes, ma'am," Becca said. "I'll add a touch more."

Phyllis turned toward Lexi and ran her gaze over her granddaughter. Her fingers fumbled for the clasp of Lexi's necklace, which had moved to the front, and she slid it to the back. She surveyed her granddaughter again. "Very nice," she appraised. "You look like a Grant."

Lexi gave a small smile and began pulling on her fingers.

Glancing at the watch that dangled from her bony wrist, Phyllis looked at Becca and snapped, "Are you watching the time? My guests will be arriving soon." Before Becca could answer, she continued, "Have your daughter let me know when everyone has arrived, no earlier than 7:10."

"I will give Violet the directions," Becca said.

Phyllis's gaze moved to her granddaughter's hands. "You can stop that, dear. Everything will be fine tonight." Her reassuring smile shifted into her usual scowl, and the elderly woman retreated to her chamber upstairs.

Becca smoothed her apron and scanned the room. Sipping an old-fashioned, Donna stood at the double doors and gazed out into the gardens. Harvey waited attentively at the bar. Oliver's bow worked back and forth across the strings as he and Mr. Rochester played "Let It Be." Twinkling invitingly, the lanterns on the pedestal tables beckoned guests to come and admire the grand portrait. The sweet smell of roses, tinged slightly by the woody fragrance of rosemary, permeated the air.

Becca looked at Violet, who stood by her side at the table laden with food, and smiled. "This is going to be a night to remember," she said to her daughter.

She had barely finished speaking when Dr. Stephen Davis entered the room. Having tended to the various members of the Grant family for decades, he was familiar with the house and had no need of an escort. He met Becca's eyes, nodded, and headed in the direction of the bar. As he made his way there, Becca thought that, with his snow-white hair and cropped beard, he resembled a svelte Santa Claus.

Donna made her way to the bar to greet him, and in a short time, the pair was joined by Andrew Curtis, Phyllis's lawyer, who was short and heavyset. "It's far too blustery out there!" the man said, sweeping the few strands of hair that remained over his balding head. "I delayed my vacation so I could be here for Phyllis tonight. Come this time tomorrow, I'll be stretched out on a beach in Maui." He smiled and closed his eyes and then polished his lenses on his untucked shirt.

The Crystal Run Improvement Society ladies arrived next—the apple-shaped Marjorie and the mousy Evelyn, along with her husband, Scott. Marjorie and Evelyn made a beeline for Donna, and the three women proceeded to attempt to outdo each other with insincere compliments about their dresses, including exclamations of "That lavender color is striking!" and "Is that lace imported from France?" The men chuckled, shook their heads, and moved away from the trio.

"When do we serve the food?" Violet asked quietly.

"We'll let them get their drinks first," Becca said. "And wait until Mrs. Grant arrives."

Violet nodded. She looked sideways at the table and then narrowed her eyes. "That's odd," she said.

"What?" Becca asked.

"One of the cups of chocolate mousse is missing. I know because I had it arranged so carefully."

Becca glanced over at the checkerboard of chocolate and frowned. "You're right," she whispered. "There's one missing in the corner." She glanced across the room at Oliver and tilted her head. Then she turned back to Violet. "It's all right. I have a few extras in the refrigerator. Why don't you grab one after you let Mrs. Grant know that the guests have all arrived?"

As her daughter nodded, Lexi appeared at the room's entrance with Patricia Koller, president of the library board, at her side. Patricia was average in height and build, but Becca couldn't decide which was more distinctive, the woman's cloud of frizzy red hair or her black-rimmed cat-eye eyeglasses.

At Patricia's entrance, Donna's head snapped in the woman's direction. Eyebrows raised hopefully, she searched the room for Phyllis and smiled mischievously as she clinked the ice in her old-fashioned glass.

Lexi smiled at Patricia and gestured toward the bar. The woman headed in that direction, glancing up at the Grant family portrait as she made her way there. With Patricia settled, Lexi approached Becca and scanned the room. "Is that everyone?"

Becca, who had been keeping a mental list, shook her head. "We're still waiting on Mr. Sloane."

"Mrs. Sloane and her husband rode separately?" Lexi asked, wrinkling her nose.

Becca shrugged. "Apparently. He must not have wanted to help set up for the party."

Lexi made a face, and turning on her heel, she returned to her station at the front door. Within a few minutes, she reentered the living room with David Sloane by her side. Tall and tanned with slick-backed hair that was gray at the temples, he looked the part of the well-respected town pharmacist. The other men in the room glanced up upon his arrival, and he responded by raising his hand in a half-wave. Giving his wife a peck on the cheek as he passed, David walked briskly toward the other men.

Violet glanced at her mother and raised her eyebrows.

"Yes, now," Becca said.

Discreetly, Violet slipped out of the room, and Lexi headed in the direction of the bar. She laid her black clutch on the marble countertop and accepted a glass of red wine from Harvey.

As Becca waited, she watched Patricia Koller, who had her own beverage in hand. Patricia took a step in the direction of the CRIS ladies, but she stopped abruptly at the sound of one of the women's piercing laughs. Glancing at the group of men, she gave a slight shake of her head. She finally settled on examining the Grant family portrait, which would soon be hanging in her library, the William J. Grant Memorial Library. Suddenly, Patricia's eyes snapped toward the entrance of the living room, and Becca followed her gaze. The music halted abruptly.

Phyllis Grant stood under the magnificent stone arch. With her regal posture, it was difficult to believe that her frame was actually frail and thin. Her tiara sparkled in the candlelight, and her deep-blue eyes looked down at her guests as though she was examining them from a tower. A slight smirk played on her lips, and Becca sucked in her breath as she realized that it was the *exact* expression of the girl in the portrait. A thick tension permeated the atmosphere as Phyllis stood there, her hands primly clasped in front of her.

The silence was broken by the sound of a guest's exuberant clapping. Becca cast her glance across the room to find its source, Evelyn Hansen. As the enthusiastic clapping continued, Donna rolled her eyes, but the other guests, thankful for a means to break the tension, caught on and joined her in a general applause.

Phyllis's smirk stretched into a smile as she gazed out upon the room. Lexi hopped down from the barstool and hurried to her grandmother's side. Linking her arm with her grandmother's, she accompanied her toward the guests.

Across the room, Becca locked eyes with Mr. Rochester, and she nodded. The pianist gave the cue to Oliver, and the young man raised his eyebrows as his bow skimmed the strings. In the candlelight, he looked too grown-up for Becca's liking, and her eyes pricked with tears as the room filled with the moody notes of his violin. Her hand reached down toward her apron pocket, and she felt the rectangular outline of her phone. Wistfully, she prayed for an opportunity to capture a few moments of Oliver's evening performance on video.

Lexi led her grandmother to the center of the room where she moved regally about her guests, greeting them and thanking them for coming. Becca couldn't help but chuckle at Violet's whispered observation that Mrs. Grant's air seemed to indicate that she had done her guests a favor by *allowing* them to come to this momentous event. Like a cat basking in the sunshine, the elderly woman lavished in her guests' praise and gratitude, finally dismissing them to enjoy some hors d'oeuvres.

After the guests had been served, Becca glanced down at her watch and turned toward Violet. "Mrs. Grant wants to start her speech at eight o'clock," she said. "I'd better let Harvey know that he can begin to prepare the champagne. You're okay on your own?"

Violet nodded, and Becca crossed the room to the bar where Lexi was perched upon a stool, and Phyllis was talking to Harvey. As she approached, Becca found that the elderly woman was already giving orders regarding the champagne toast.

"I shall have my special drink in the Grant family goblet," she said, a crooked finger raised in the air. "And you will need to fill nine additional champagne flutes for the guests."

*Nine.* Becca looked over her shoulder and scanned the room. An uneasy feeling twisted in her stomach.

"Mrs. Grant—" she said.

Phyllis dropped her hand to the marble countertop and drummed her fingers. "What is it?" The question came out like a statement.

Becca glanced around the room one more time. "I know it's important that all the guests are here for the speech and toast. Some of them are missing."

Lexi looked up from the red wine she had been swirling around the bottom of her glass, and the double lines between Phyllis's brows deepened. Her eyes grew stormy as she turned to examine the room. "Who's missing?"

Becca smoothed her apron. "David Sloane," she said, "Scott Hansen, Dr. Davis—"

"Dr. Davis!" Phyllis hissed. She narrowed her deep blue eyes. "I know *exactly* where they are." She turned toward Harvey. "Pour the drinks," she commanded. "I shall be back momentarily." The elderly woman puffed out her chest and moved determinedly across the room toward the door that led to the library.

Becca and Lexi exchanged glances.

"Should I follow her?" Becca asked.

The two women watched as Phyllis opened the library door with a force that was surprising for a woman of her age and closed it behind her.

Lexi shook her head. "It seems she has the situation handled."

As Becca nodded in agreement, Patricia Koller approached the bar. Pushing her black cat-eye glasses up the bridge of her nose, she looked at Becca and asked, "Do you know if the presentation will be starting shortly?"

With a quick glance at the library door, Becca said, "Mrs. Grant plans to begin her speech in just a few minutes."

Patricia turned her attention to the crystal champagne flutes that Harvey was filling. She picked up the empty red goblet and examined it by the candlelight. "I've never seen anything like it," she breathed as she turned it over in the light. Carefully setting down the ruby wine glass, she smiled and strode away in the direction of the hors d'oeuvres.

Becca turned toward Harvey. "I'm going to check on Violet."

As she left, she noticed Lexi reaching into her clutch, pulling out a compact mirror, and then tucking it away again. *That poor girl must feel so much pressure to appear "Grant-worthy,"* Becca thought sympathetically.

After asking Violet to restock the hors d'oeuvres, Becca stood and surveyed the room. The melody of "Piano Man" drifted through the air, and she gasped in delight at the realization that she had been granted the opportunity to record some of her son's performance. Becca pulled her phone from her pocket and, not daring to be too obvious, began to record Oliver from a distance. For a couple of minutes, she lost herself in the glow of the candlelight and the lovely melancholy notes.

Becca was shaken from her reverie by the sound of the library door swinging open. Quickly switching off her phone, she returned it to her pocket. Emerging from the library was Andrew Curtis, who, looking relieved, tucked some bills into his wallet, which he then placed in his back pocket. David Sloane followed close behind, punching Andrew in the shoulder and grinning. A much less jovial-looking Dr. Davis came next, and he made purposeful strides toward the bar. Finally, a pinch-faced Phyllis stood framed in the door, which she closed behind her. She paused for a moment and then marched after Dr. Davis, her mouth pressed into a firm line and her fists clenched at her sides.

"Oh, dear," Becca breathed as the hostess stormed past her.

Dr. Davis ran his hand over his short white beard as he observed Harvey distributing the champagne under Lexi's supervision. "When you have a moment," he said to the young bartender, "I'll take a whiskey on the rocks." The doctor turned to see Phyllis angrily striding toward him. "Better make that a double."

Phyllis joined the group in a huff and jammed both fists on her hips. "How *dare* you pull my guests away to play cards on a night like this," she accused in a low voice. "*You* of all people know how much this night—this portrait—means to my family."

The doctor glanced toward Harvey, who was still busy serving the champagne. Stepping behind the bar himself, he grabbed a whiskey glass. "Oh, calm down, Phyllis," Dr. Davis said, scooping some ice. "Your dad loved a good card game." He picked up the bottle of whiskey and poised it over the glass. "You know, you should really be apologizing to *me*. I was about to win when you came storming in." The doctor glanced at the red crystal goblet, which was filled and waiting behind the bar. "Is this yours? You're staying away from alcohol, correct?"

Becca approached softly as Phyllis leaned over the bar, her clawlike fingers turning white as they gripped the edge. The elderly woman's eyes narrowed dangerously. "I know full well what I can and cannot consume, and I most certainly do not need a degenerate like you reminding me," she whispered harshly. "*You* are the one who plied my husband into cards. You just *loved* enticing him into it. You have always been a degenerate and always will be. You're pathetic."

A bright-red color washed over Dr. Davis's face, and he slammed down his glass, whiskey sloshing over the side. He opened his mouth to retort, but Becca cut in first.

"Dr. Davis!" she said brightly, flashing her most charming smile. "Won't you come with me to sit down? I found a spot for you with an excellent view."

Dragging his eyes away from Phyllis, he took a deep breath and let it out. He turned toward Becca. "I think that would be a good idea," he finally said.

Becca smiled and nodded toward the glass of whiskey. "You can bring that with you if you want," she said. "Champagne is waiting at the tables, but we're saving that for the toast at the end."

The doctor considered the glass for a moment and picked it up. His face still flushed, he followed Becca toward the semicircle of tables.

As Phyllis watched him retreat, her sapphire eyes sparkled, and the corner of her lips rose into a smirk. She blew out a satisfied breath and turned toward Harvey. "I shall give my toast toward the end of my speech," she said. "When I motion to you, bring me my wine glass."

"Yes, ma'am," Harvey said, a slight quaver in his voice.

The elderly woman looked her granddaughter up and down and smiled. "Alexandra, it's time to take your place."

Grabbing her black clutch, Lexi hopped down from the barstool and took the seat nearest to where her grandmother would be standing.

When Dr. Davis had been safely settled into a seat and all the other guests were finding their own, Becca discreetly made her way over to Oliver and Mr. Rochester. She caught Mr. Rochester's eye and nodded. The pianist murmured something to Oliver, and the two of them gently faded out the music.

Oliver laid his violin and bow across his lap. "Food?" he mouthed.

"In the kitchen," his mother replied softly. Her gaze went back and forth between her son and his music instructor. "The music was excellent." She squeezed Oliver's shoulder. "Your father would have been proud."

Mr. Rochester smiled in agreement. As he and Oliver slipped out of the living room, presumably in the direction of the kitchen, Becca scanned the semicircle of tables to make sure everything was in order. Then she headed toward Violet, who had lined up a pair of chairs near the hors d'oeuvres. Becca slipped into the empty chair, sat up straight, and turned her eyes toward Phyllis at the bar.

The hostess took a deep breath, pulled herself into her regal posture, and strode forward to take her place under the colossal Grant family portrait. She paused for a few moments, sweeping her eyes over her guests, and then flashed a wide smile.

# Chapter 5

# Grant Legacy

"Good evening," Phyllis Grant said. "Welcome to the Paper Palace on this very special night. Thank you for being here." She glanced toward the double doors that led out to the gardens and noted tapered black branches clawing the air as the wind surged outside. "I know it's not the mildest evening, but you will find that your efforts to be here tonight will be greatly rewarded. You are among the few who will be the last to see the Grant family portrait in its original location before it is donated to the William J. Grant Memorial Library. You are witnessing history."

At these words, Patricia Koller, the president of the library board, glanced sideways at Phyllis and patted the red cloud of her hair. Evelyn's hands flew together as if to clap, but she stopped herself just in time.

Phyllis caught the movement and nodded appreciatively. "As you all know, in 1853, my great-great-great-grandfather, William J. Grant, built the first papermill in this area. Four years later, Crystal Run was incorporated as a city. Not only did William Grant found this town, but he also single-handedly started the company that brought prosperity to it. As the line of Grants continued to grow Grant Paper Company, we provided jobs to the families of Crystal Run so that you may have homes to live in and food on your tables. This is the legacy of the Grants." She paused, allowing the gravity of her words to settle upon the guests.

David Sloane coughed and straightened his tie.

As Phyllis turned and looked up toward the enormous portrait above her, her tiara twinkled in the candlelight. She raised a thin bony hand in indication of the painting. "What you see here is the portrait of *my* family, which was commissioned by my mother as a Christmas gift for my father. Seated in the middle is my dear father, William Grant III, who, as you all know, was the cornerstone of this community. Standing next to him is my lovely mother, Betsy, and—oh!" She placed an age-spotted hand over her heart and gave a forced laugh. "And *me*!" Failing to notice the stoic faces of her guests, she chuckled at her own joke and wiped a nonexistent tear from her eye. "Here I am at age seventeen. And of *course*, I must mention my beloved dog, Mopsie." She looked up at the Yorkshire terrier in the young woman's arms, smiled, and shook her head. "You can imagine how he *squirmed* while we were posing for this portrait."

Gesturing toward Lexi, she continued, "My granddaughter, Alexandra, has conducted extensive research on this pivotal work so that I may share its significance with you tonight."

Lexi's jaw twitched, and she started playing with the clasp of her clutch.

"Don't be shy about it, dear," Phyllis said, smiling reassuringly at the young woman. "You should be proud of all your hard work." Turning back to her guests, she continued, "Her study brings these wonderful facts to light. The portrait was painted in 1970 by Francesco Alberti, a renowned Italian painter, who had recently immigrated to America. I'm sure you've noticed the remarkable size of the portrait. Because of the prominence of the family and the size of the estate, Alberti insisted on this very large canvas, which came from Italy. Of course, my father demanded that everything must be the best, so Alberti used only the finest brushes and the highest quality paint. He even used a special coating technique that was specifically designed for important works of art."

Becca, who had been glancing at her watch, looked up at the portrait and recalled the network of hairline cracks she had seen across the surface. *I think Mrs. Grant may have been lied to,* she thought. *If he used the best paint and all of that, it didn't hold up very well.* The clunk of a glass lid behind her caused Becca to jump. Swiveling around, she watched Harvey remove a piece of rosemary chicken from a skewer with his teeth. She raised her eyebrows at him.

Harvey smiled as he chewed. When he had swallowed, he pointed to the platter of endive cups and whispered, "These are really good too."

With a small smile, Becca returned her attention to the speech.

Phyllis leaned in toward her guests and lowered her voice. "Now, over the numerous sittings we had to do for this portrait, this swarthy Italian became *quite* taken with me." She glanced up and smiled at the seventeen-year-old representation of herself in her baby-blue mini-dress and ebony hair spilling over her shoulders. "He was so smitten with me that even months after the painting was finished, he tried to get back into the house several times to see me." A simpering laugh escaped from her lips. "The impertinence!"

Donna Sloane rolled her eyes and raised her glass to her lips. Realizing it was empty, she frowned, rose from her chair, and strode to the unmanned bar.

Phyllis eyed Donna for a moment. "Impertinence!" she repeated. Then she turned back to her remaining audience and smiled. "There was the time he got caught picking the lock of the doors that lead out to the gardens," Phyllis said, counting off on her fingers, "and the time he tried climbing in the window. Oh! And the final time he tried entering through the servants' quarters disguised as a gardener!" She laughed. "He was *so* besotted with me." She gazed off across the room, lost in her memories for a moment.

Noticing that Donna had successfully managed a brief escape to refill her own glass, a few other guests found themselves with empty glasses (or drained them quickly) and followed her lead to visit the bar.

Clenching her jaw and shaking herself from her recollections, Phyllis turned pointedly to the guests who remained seated, raised a crooked finger in the air, and said firmly, "But I would have none of it! Artists, after all, while talented, are passionate and unruly. They're governed by their desires and are not people with whom *I* or any of the Grants would associate." She cast a sideways glance at Lexi, who looked across the room at Harvey and shifted uncomfortably in her seat.

"I told my father that I wanted nothing to do with him and asked him to take care of it once and for all. Daddy had that artist shipped promptly back to Italy, never to be allowed in America again." Phyllis's eyes sparkled as her lips curled into a cruel smirk.

Becca and Violet exchanged glances, and Becca raised her eyebrows.

Phyllis paused and once again gestured toward the colossal portrait in its gilded frame. "So, what you see before you is the *only* painting by master artist Francesco Alberti ever to be completed on American soil." The elderly woman clasped her hands in front of her and searched her guests' faces as she allowed the importance of her words to settle upon them.

Dr. Davis pulled out his phone and started scrolling.

Phyllis glanced at the unattended bar, searched the room, and then narrowed her eyes at the young bartender, still hovering by the hors d'oeuvres.

"Harvey!" Becca whispered urgently.

Eyes wide, he abandoned his plate and scurried across the room to retrieve the ruby goblet while Phyllis blew out an impatient breath and collected herself.

Once Harvey was in place, the regal hostess raised her hand vertically and gave a slight twist at the wrist. At her signal, Harvey carefully crossed the space and delivered the wine glass.

With her free hand, Phyllis gestured toward the painting and said, "This portrait has been in our family for fifty years and symbolizes the foundation and heart of our beloved city. Tomorrow, with the mayor doing the honors, this portrait will be officially donated to the William J. Grant Memorial Library. There, on display for the whole community, it will serve as a reminder of just how much the Grant family has done for the city of Crystal Run."

Phyllis raised her red goblet, and the candlelight bounced brilliantly from it. "Now, as we send off the portrait to its new home, I invite you to raise your glass with me." She paused, casting her eyes over the guests to make sure that their glasses were raised. Dr. Davis was still glued to his phone, and Marjorie elbowed him.

"Oh!" Davis laid down his phone and picked up his champagne flute.

Phyllis ignored him and raised her glass a little higher. "To the Grants! Long live the legacy."

"To the Grants!" came the reply with a mixture of enthusiasm and ennui.

Phyllis raised the glass to her lips and drank deeply.

Unable to control herself any longer, Evelyn Hansen jumped to her feet and exploded into applause. The remaining guests rose and joined her, albeit with less enthusiasm.

Her sapphire eyes sparkling, Phyllis stood like a queen beneath the grand portrait, soaking in the perceived laud and honor.

As the applause gradually faded, the piano and violin notes resumed and brightened. Evelyn was the first to approach the elderly woman and express her surprise and amusement at the anecdote of the "brazen" Italian painter. "Didn't you find it a *little* romantic at the time?" the CRIS treasurer asked.

Phyllis furrowed her penciled brows. "Not at all. I found it incorrigible."

Patricia Koller joined the women and cleared her throat. "On behalf of the William J. Grant Memorial Library, thank you for your generous donation." After a pause, she added cooly, "I'm so glad that we could finally agree upon a display that meets your approval." Patricia's eyes flicked toward the ruby glass in Phyllis's hand. "And I love your family heirloom goblet, by the way."

Phyllis gave no response except to narrow her eyes at the woman. In that moment, Lexi stepped toward her grandmother and, smiling apologetically at Evelyn and Patricia, offered her arm. Phyllis accepted, and Lexi led her to an empty seat at one of the tables surrounding the portrait. The elderly woman sank into the chair, her baby-blue dress puddling around her, and Becca appeared with a plate of hors d'oeuvres. Phyllis waved Lexi away in dismissal to make room for other guests and daintily dipped her spoon into the chocolate mousse. A few at a time, guests trickled over to converse with the hostess, who slowly began to wilt in her chair. Her eyelids drooped, and she didn't even have a reply for Donna's comment, "If I had known we were getting a history lesson tonight, I would have brought my notebook!" As the Hansens asked polite questions about the particulars of the portrait sittings, Phyllis's mouth gaped open in a yawn, which she quickly covered with her bony fingers. When she had spoken with all the guests, Phyllis looked toward the bar and motioned at Lexi. She then turned in the direction of Becca, who was stationed at the dessert table, and crooked a finger at her. The two ladies quickly made their way to the elegant woman.

"I am retiring for the evening," she said, stifling another yawn. "The excitement of this evening has taken a lot out of me."

"Of course, Mrs. Grant," Becca said. "I'll see that the party ends smoothly and clean up afterward."

Phyllis nodded and allowed Lexi to assist her from the chair. As the hostess freed herself from her granddaughter's support, a cry of, "Whoa, whoa, whoooa!" rang out, and all three women stared in horror as a bleary-eyed Dr. Davis dove to catch a large vase of white roses that he had knocked off a pedestal. Phyllis watched as Lexi and Becca hurried over to address the puddle of water and flowers on the floor.

Rolling her eyes to the ceiling, the woman sighed, turned back toward the table, and carefully picked up the ruby goblet. She pulled herself into her typical regal posture and headed toward the exit. Framed under the stone arch, Phyllis paused and turned to survey the scene. Her gaze moved to the Grant family portrait, and a proud little smile played on her lips that matched the one of the young woman in the painting. She admired the painting until a final yawn reminded her of her destination. Raising her hand to her tiara, she disappeared through the grand stone arch.

With their hostess gone, the guests remained for a while, chatting and nibbling, and they gradually drifted out to their cars. An angry gust of wind forced its way inside as Lexi pushed the heavy front door shut behind the Sloanes, the final guests to leave. She leaned against the door, heaved a sigh, and headed toward the living room to watch as Harvey packed up the bar.

Becca and Violet made quick work of tidying the living room. As the ladies packed up the remaining food, Oliver snuffed the candles and then joined Mr. Rochester in tucking the lanterns and decor into boxes. Becca pulled the white linen tablecloth from the hors d'oeuvres table and gasped in surprise as she found Hazel sitting cross-legged underneath and looking up at her.

"Hazel!" she exclaimed. "What are you doing down there? How long have you been under that table?"

"I don't know... For pretty much the entire party?" the girl replied. "That red room was creepy!"

Becca placed her hands on her hips.

"I'm sorry," Hazel added with an effort to make her voice sound remorseful.

Trying to hide her smile, her mother glanced down at her wristwatch. "It's late. As long as you're here, you can help us tidy up."

Hazel slid out from underneath the table, and an empty chocolate mousse cup skidded beside her.

"Aha!" Violet exclaimed. "*You're* the culprit."

Thanking Mr. Rochester for his help and insisting that they had the situation under control, Becca instructed Violet, Oliver, and Hazel to carry equipment and boxes out to the Gables' minivan. She made a final check of the kitchen and returned to the living room. Only the tables, chairs, and candelabras remained, all of which would be picked up by the rental company the following day. The flowers, of course, would stay as well.

Becca glanced at her clipboard, frowned, and made her way toward Lexi and Harvey at the bar. "Do you have your grandmother's red goblet?" she asked. "I was going to wash it and return it to the cabinet, but I can't find it."

Lexi shrugged. "It will have to turn up. It's part of a complete set."

Becca nodded. "And the payment for tonight—"

"I don't have it," Lexi said flatly. "I don't know where Grandmother put it, and I'm not going to disturb her. You'll have to come back another time to get it."

Becca opened her mouth to reply and then closed it again. She smoothed her apron and looked around the room. "In that case, I believe we are all done here, so we're going to head out. Have a good evening."

Lexi threw a cursory glance around the room. "Good night," she said, turning back toward Harvey.

As Becca headed out of the room, she smiled when she noticed her children waiting for her under the stone arch. Hazel hurried over to meet her, her white backpack slung across her shoulder.

"Mom! I left my copy of *Jane Eyre* in that room!" she said.

Becca stifled a yawn. "That's okay, at least you remembered before we left. Just run up and get it."

Hazel froze in her tracks and stared up at her mother with huge eyes. "By *myself*?"

Oliver chuckled. "Ooh, someone is scared of being in the red room where there was a *dead body*!" He glanced up at his mother's expression and clapped a hand over his mouth.

"Too late!" Becca said. "Oliver, you get to escort Hazel as she collects her book."

At these words, Oliver froze. "What! Uh..." His eyes slowly trailed up the grand set of stairs that led toward the second floor. "Can—can you come too, Mom?"

# Chapter 6

# Unexpected News

With the scent of coffee permeating the air and Butterscotch resting at her feet, Becca watched as rivulets of rainwater dripped down the bookshop window.

"Is there something fascinating out there?" a warm bass asked.

At the sound of his voice, the golden retriever rose and nuzzled the hand of Chief John, who was dressed in his police uniform. Taking in the welcome sight, Becca smiled and hugged him, resting her head on his shoulder. "I'm so *tired,* Uncle John!" she half-laughed, her voice slightly muffled against his blazer.

"That's right, you were partying at the Paper Palace last night." He chuckled at the idea of Becca partying. "You know I got an invitation to that, right?"

Becca lifted her face from his shoulder and looked at him squarely. "I did not! Why didn't you go? That would have improved the evening considerably."

His bushy white mustache raised a bit as he grinned. "Would *you* have gone if you weren't getting paid?"

At the word "paid," Becca glanced quickly at Audrey, who was running calculations behind the confectionery counter, and then she dropped her gaze to the floor.

The smile faded from John's countenance. "Don't tell me you didn't get paid." His tone was serious.

Becca looked up at him and sighed. "Mrs. Grant was exhausted and left the party before giving me the payment. I asked Lexi about it, but she didn't know where it was and told me to come back another time."

"We're going over there right now," John said determinedly, pulling his frame into its full impressive height.

"We? Now?" Becca asked.

"Oh, yes," John said. "I'm not letting that woman pull one over on you. I know how she is."

Becca glanced at her wristwatch. "Well, it is time for my lunch break. I'll just check with Audrey. She slipped behind the counter and stood beside the tiled table where Audrey was crunching numbers. "Is it all right if I run to the Paper Palace to pick up payment for last night?"

Audrey released her gaze from the figures before her and tilted her heart-shaped face toward Becca. "Actually, I would *love* it if you did. I'll watch the kids."

Becca smiled and squeezed Audrey's shoulder. "I shall not fail!"

Shaking her head, Audrey laughed. "If the chief is going with you, I have no concerns."

Becca returned to John's side and found him pulling his keys from his pocket.

"I'll drive," he said.

The windshield wipers thudded rhythmically as the chief maneuvered his black Ford Explorer between the stone pillars fixed at the end of the long cobblestone driveway. Although her view was slightly obscured by the rain on her window, Becca made out the familiar words *Paper Palace* engraved on one of the pillars.

"Well, what do we have here?" John said.

Becca looked up and saw that parked in the circular driveway were an ambulance, another black Explorer—this one marked distinctly as a police vehicle—and a white SUV labeled "Medical Examiner." Her eyes widened, and she looked at John. "Whatever it is, it isn't good."

John parked behind the other vehicles and grabbed a black umbrella from the compartment in his door. He popped it open and held it over Becca as the two made their way to the mansion's impressive front entrance. Becca glanced sideways at John as she reached out a finger and rang the bell. They waited. Gently maneuvering the umbrella's handle so that John would be more shielded, Becca smiled and shook her head when he shifted the umbrella back over her and tilted his face up to the sky. Becca rang the bell a second time.

After a long moment, the door swung open. There stood Lexi, her eyes red and swollen and her ebony hair matted and disheveled. She swiped at a wayward strand that clung to her forehead and looked back and forth between Chief John and Becca.

John cleared his throat. "May we come in?"

"Oh, yes, of course," Lexi said in a hoarse voice. She opened the door wider.

Becca stepped inside. After shaking the water from his umbrella and closing it, John followed.

"Miss Grant," John said, his voice warm and kind. "Are you all right?"

Becca's eyes were wide. "Lexi, what happened?"

Again, Lexi's gaze bounced back and forth between the chief and Becca. Finally fixing her eyes on Becca's concerned countenance, her lip quivered, and she choked out, "She's dead!" The young woman buried her face in her hands and sobbed.

Becca's eyes widened, and her hand flew to her heart. "Dead?" she repeated. She stood frozen for a few moments before stepping forward and wrapping her arms around Lexi.

"My—my grandmother!" Lexi stammered between wails. "She was all I had left!"

"I'm so sorry," Becca said softly.

Lexi extricated herself from Becca's embrace and collapsed into a striped upholstered chair by the entrance.

John deposited the umbrella in the stand by the door and turned toward Becca. "I'm going to talk to the officer on duty." He had only taken a few steps into the hall when the officer appeared, summoned by the renewal of Lexi's sobbing.

"Captain Olson!" the officer said, stopping short. The young man was tall and trim with his dark hair styled in a tidy crew-cut.

"Officer Spencer," John acknowledged. "I'd like to have a word with the medical examiner."

"Yes, sir," the officer said. "He is in the process of his assessment."

John nodded. "Lead the way, and you can fill me in."

Becca pressed her lips together and glanced at Lexi, who was staring out the window into the rainy landscape. "Has Harvey been here? Will he be coming?" Becca asked.

As a bolt of lightning illuminated the graphite sky, Lexi turned toward Becca. She pulled her cell phone from her pocket and, with tears in her eyes, held it up and waved it. "He's not answering," she said, her voice a mixture of frustration and grief.

"I'm sure he'll be here soon," Becca said, smiling sympathetically. A roll of thunder boomed, and she felt a vibration under her feet. With a final glance at Lexi, Becca hurried after the two men.

"The granddaughter called emergency response at 9:07 this morning," the officer said, mounting the grand staircase that led to the bedrooms. "She says that she had brought Mrs. Grant her usual breakfast tray and found her lying on top of the bed, fully dressed from the night before, and unresponsive."

"I see," John said. "Was anyone else in the house at the time the body was discovered?"

The officer shook his head. "No, sir. After the phone call, the paramedics arrived and performed their assessment. I came onto the scene and interviewed Miss Grant."

By this time, the trio had arrived just outside Phyllis's bedroom door. Officer Spencer gestured inside. "The medical examiner," he said.

John glanced inside the room and turned toward Becca. "You stay right here while I talk to Dr. Brennan."

As John disappeared, Officer Spencer nodded at Becca and headed back downstairs.

Frowning and leaning against the doorframe, Becca pulled her phone from her purse and started to scroll through her inbox. She couldn't help but hear John's recognizable bass.

"Will you be able to ascertain the time of death?" he asked.

Becca's finger froze on the screen as she listened intently for the answer. The second masculine voice, which had to be Dr. Brennan's, was too muffled to be discernible. She continued to scroll. After what felt like ages, the voices became audible again.

"She likely died of a stroke," the doctor said. "But the autopsy will be able to tell us for certain."

"Do you have an idea of when the autopsy results might come back?" John asked.

Becca strained her ears.

"Lately, the lab has been turning them around in about two weeks," Dr. Brennan said.

Outside, Becca waited several more minutes as the men continued their muted conversation. Finally, they emerged from the room.

"I'm accompanying Dr. Brennan as he signs the Certificate of Death," John explained to Becca as he passed. The police chief and doctor continued down the hallway toward the stairs, their voices low in conversation.

Becca sighed and returned her phone to her purse. She started to follow, but as their voices drifted away, she felt an irresistible pull toward Mrs. Grant's bedroom. *Just a peek*, she told herself. Gripping the doorframe with one hand, she leaned into the doorway and peered inside the room, which was richly decorated in mauve and gold. There, on the canopy bed, lay Mrs. Grant. Now that she wasn't pulling herself into her regal posture, the woman's body looked tiny and frail underneath the voluminous fabric of her baby-blue cocktail dress. Becca took a few hesitant steps into the room and noticed that the woman's hands were folded across her stomach, her bony fingers intertwined. Becca stood on her tiptoes, trying to get a view of the woman's face. Finding the effort futile, she lightly padded toward the bed. Mrs. Grant's countenance was pale, and she wore a deep scowl even in death. The woman looked like her queenly self in every respect except for the crystal tiara that sat conspicuously askew atop her short white curls.

After tearing her gaze away from the crooked tiara, Becca examined the nightstand next to Phyllis's bed. Nestled among a collection of vitamins and supplements, she noticed a daily pill organizer. Her brows knitted as her gaze lingered there for a moment, and then she crouched down to examine an orange prescription pill bottle from Sloane's Apothecary. Straightening, she wandered across the gaudy mauve-and-gold room and stopped at Phyllis's desk, which was littered with various binders and papers. She hesitated over one binder in particular, but her attention was quickly diverted when she noticed a check sitting on top of a pile of papers. There, written out in a spidery scrawl, was the catering payment. Becca drew in a breath and clasped her hands.

"Rebecca Gables!" a warm bass reprimanded.

Becca let out a squeak, and her hand flew to her heart.

"I should have known that this is exactly what would happen if I left you alone here," John continued. His voice was stern, but his blue eyes sparkled.

"I'm sorry, Uncle John," Becca said. "I don't know what came over me—"

John chuckled and shook his head. "I do. It's that insatiable curiosity. Now, hustle out of here. This is completely against policy."

"Yes, sir." Obediently, Becca took a step toward the door. She stopped suddenly, though, tucked a strand of blonde hair behind her ear, and grimaced at the police chief.

"Oh no, what?" he said.

Becca pointed at the check on Phyllis's desk. "Look what I found."

John eyed the check. "Grab it! That's what we came here for."

Becca glanced at Mrs. Grant's body laid out on the bed and then back at the check. "Oh no, I could hardly," she said.

John drew himself up protectively, and a warm fatherly smile spread across his face as he stepped forward.


Their business complete, John steered the Explorer down the long winding driveway. Becca glanced down at the payment in her hands and then lovingly back at Uncle John. Her gaze returned to the check, and she stared at the signature, Phyllis E. Grant. Becca leaned against the headrest. *It's amazing,* she thought as she watched the rain spatter her window, *how drastically circumstances can change in just a moment.*

# Chapter 7

# Processing over Pizza

Flipping the hood of her rain jacket over her head, Becca heard the roar of Uncle John's Explorer as he headed back to the police station. With quick steps, she made her way down the alley, pulled her keys from her bag, and let herself into the back entrance. As she hung up her purse and jacket, she could hear the buzz of the afternoon crowd within Tales & Tails, and she hurried toward the café. Catching a glimpse of Audrey taking orders behind the confectionery counter, Becca slid to a stop, pivoted, and dashed back to her bag to retrieve the catering payment.

Check in hand, Becca glanced around the crowded bookshop. Customers, relieved to find a cozy shelter from the storm, meandered through the bookshelves under the warm glow of the twinkle lights. Noting that

Violet was stationed by the register near the door, Becca headed straight toward Audrey, who was waiting with measured patience as a juvenile customer counted out coins to pay for her chocolate chip cookie. The man who was next in line folded his arms and glanced down at his watch.

"Can I help you count them?" Audrey asked the girl.

"I can do it myself!" she insisted, pushing her bangs out of her eyes. "And now I have to start over. One... Two... Three..."

The man behind her let out a long sigh.

Audrey smiled apologetically at him and turned toward Becca. "Oliver and Hazel are upstairs," she said. "Were you successful?"

Solemnly, Becca held out the check, which Audrey eagerly snatched and tucked into her teal apron pocket.

"What," Audrey laughed, "no self-congratulations or confetti?"

Becca shook her head.

Noting her sister-in-law's sober expression, Audrey's face drained of merriment. "Is everything okay?" she asked.

Becca glanced at the long line of customers and whispered, "Phyllis Grant is *dead*."

"No!" Audrey's jaw gaped open.

Becca nodded and muttered, "I'll explain more later." She moved toward the coat rack to grab her apron.

Gazing over her shoulder at her sister-in-law, Audrey shook her head incredulously.

"Done!" the girl announced, proudly pushing a jumble of coins forward with both hands. "One dollar and ninety-one cents! Now, I'll count out a tip for you." She glanced down at the pennies in front of her.

The man next in line shifted his weight, his eyes closed and his lips moving as if he were repeatedly counting to ten.

"Oh, honey, that's okay!" Audrey said reassuringly. "Just the payment for the cookie is fine for today!"

As the autumnal sky darkened throughout the afternoon and early evening, the glow of the bookshop's twinkle lights grew warmer. Soggy customers, in gradually decreasing numbers, dried themselves by the big fire, which crackled cheerfully in the fireplace. A few minutes before closing time, Becca and Audrey found themselves nearly alone except for a middle-aged man in a squashy leather chair. The man's hands rested on the arms of the chair, and the mug of tea by his side was cold. He let out a snore. Audrey giggled and looked at Becca, who gravely headed to the kitchen to retrieve a small stack of paper napkins.

Audrey frowned. "So, tell me about Phyllis Grant," she said as she laid out four paper plates on the long wooden table.

With a quick glance, Becca counted the plates. "You're not staying for pizza?"

"No," Audrey said. "I've got leftover soup at home that I really need to use up."

Becca nodded and eyed the customer who let out another snore. "When Uncle John and I arrived at the Paper Palace," she said, "there were several vehicles in the driveway, including an ambulance and a police vehicle. Lexi let us in, and she was beside herself. She told us that her grandmother had died, and then Uncle John went up to talk to the medical examiner. He thinks that Mrs. Grant died of a stroke."

Audrey nodded. "Phyllis Grant won't be missed by anyone. The only person she was ever decent to was Lexi, and that was probably just 'cause she carries the Grant name." She paused for a few moments, lost in thought. "In fact, rumor has it that the old crone was trying to get some high-up at the library fired."

"I actually heard that too," Becca said. "I don't know if there's any truth behind it, but apparently, Mrs. Grant was unhappy with the plan for how her family portrait was going to be displayed, so she tried to get the president of the library board fired."

"I'm sure there's truth behind it," Audrey said with a wry smile. "But I do feel bad for Lexi. As far as I know, her grandmother was her last living relative, and it's not exactly a secret that there's nothing left of the Grant family fortune."

Becca sighed sadly. "I don't know what Lexi will do." She paused and crouched down to pet Toffee, who had ambled over to her, and began rubbing against her ankles. "But the idea of Mrs. Grant dying of a stroke strikes me as odd."

"One sec," Audrey said, looking up at the clock on the mantel. "Seven o'clock." She stepped toward the man sleeping in the leather chair and gently placed a plump freckled hand on his arm. "Excuse me, sir," she said. "It's closing time."

While Becca warmed up his tea in the microwave and transferred it to a thick paper cup, the man roused and marveled at how quickly the afternoon had passed. Becca escorted him out of the shop, turned the deadbolt, and flipped the sign in the window to *Closed*. She headed back toward the fireplace where her sister-in-law waited.

Audrey placed her hands on her hips. "Why does the idea of Phyllis dying of a stroke seem strange to you? Old people have strokes," she said matter-of-factly.

"Well," Becca said slowly, gazing into the fire, "I spoke to Mrs. Grant just before she left the party. She didn't have problems speaking or understanding. She didn't seem to have any numbness or paralysis. And from what I could tell, she didn't have any vision problems."

Audrey shrugged. "Maybe the stroke didn't start until after she got to her room. I don't know, I'm not a doctor."

"Yes, maybe," Becca said, her eyes still fixed on the dancing flames. "It's also odd that Harvey wasn't there with Lexi today when she lost her only remaining family member."

Audrey nodded, placing her hands on her hips. "Yeah, that is strange."

"Pizza's here!" Oliver's husky voice called from across the room.

Becca turned to see her son approaching, hefting a stack of pizza boxes. He was followed by Violet, who was carrying a tub of precut vegetables, and Hazel, who ducked behind the confectionery counter to see if there were any baked goods left at the end of the day.

"Thanks for ordering the pizza, Vi," Becca said as she helped Oliver arrange the boxes in the middle of the table. The young man opened the lids, revealing three steaming pizzas, and the smell of melting cheese and tangy tomatoes and herbs infused the air. Butterscotch strolled over from her place by the fire and gazed up toward the table with hope.

Triumphantly, Hazel held up a white paper box as she joined them at the table. "Four oatmeal chocolate chip cookies!"

"I'm heading out," Audrey said. "I'll see you all tomorrow." She ruffled Oliver's hair, dropped a kiss onto Hazel's blonde head, and shook Violet's hand. After a moment's hesitation, Audrey leaned across the table and grabbed a piece of pizza. Biting off the end, she said, "For the road," and gave a final wave to Becca.

Becca slid into her spot at the head of the table. "Shall we say grace? I believe it's your turn to lead, Violet."

Oliver, who was just about to take a bite of pizza, glanced at his mother and set down his slice.

As Violet concluded the prayer, Becca kept her hands folded and head bowed for several long moments. She looked up to find her children staring at her quizzically. She pressed her lips into a small smile and reached for a slice of herb chicken Mediterranean.

"I have some sad news to share with you," she said.

Hazel stopped picking the sausages off her slice and looked at her mother with wide eyes.

Becca drew in a breath. "When Uncle John and I drove over to the Paper Palace this afternoon, we found out that Mrs. Grant had passed away during the night."

Violet's eyebrows raised a little as she transferred sticks of carrots and celery to her plate. "Oh, that's too bad," she said.

Oliver took a large bite of a meat-loaded slice, and Hazel resumed her task of sausage removal.

After a few moments, Hazel spoke. "I'm not sad," she said in her sweet lilt. "Mrs. Grant was a mean old lady."

Becca frowned. "Hazel Ruth, that is not a kind thing to say."

"You know, Mom," Oliver said, his voice muffled by his full mouth, "Hazel's right. She wasn't very nice."

As Violet nodded in agreement, Becca placed a finger in front of her lips to remind Oliver of his manners. She then picked up her slice of pizza.

"Besides," Hazel said, "they were saying that she wasn't going to be around very much longer anyway."

Becca dropped the slice back onto her plate. "Who was saying that? When?"

"Mrs. Sloane said that to her husband—at the party," Hazel said.

"You were under the table," Violet said, her tone accusatory. "How would you know that it was Mrs. Sloane?"

"Her shoes!" Hazel said defensively. "There were only two pairs of shoes around when I heard it. One was a man's, and the other was Mrs. Sloane's super-high sparkly shoes."

"With red soles?" Becca asked.

"Yes, the bottoms were red," the girl said.

Becca stared at her daughter. "Okay," she finally said. "Tell me everything that you heard around that conversation. What came before? And after?"

Hazel shrugged. "I wasn't paying that much attention at first because I was working on a friendship bracelet." Gracefully, she held up a thin wrist that was encircled by a bracelet in varying shades of pink. "But I *know* I heard Mrs. Sloane say that Mrs. Grant wasn't going to be around much longer. And then she laughed and walked away."

Feeling her stomach twist, Becca pushed the paper plate away from her. Oliver's chair scraped across the floor as he rose and headed toward the café's kitchen.

Violet, who had been sitting quietly in thought, spoke up. "Do we know what Mrs. Grant died from?"

"We don't know for certain," Becca said, "but the medical examiner thinks that she died of a stroke."

"A stroke..." Violet repeated. Thoughtfully, she twirled a carrot stick between her fingers. "I wonder if Dr. Davis saw any symptoms of it coming on."

Becca shook her head. "I don't know."

Violet's nut-brown eyes narrowed. She leaned toward her mother and said in a low voice, "Would he even have helped her? He was *so* angry."

Becca recalled the maroon color of Dr. Davis's face as she had led him away from Mrs. Grant and nodded. "He was furious," she agreed.

She raised her eyes to find Oliver returning from the kitchen, clutching a can of root beer in one hand. He stopped and yawned loudly. With eyes barely open, the young man swayed dramatically as he walked and pretended to nearly collide with one of the gleaming wooden tables.

"Oliver, *what* are you doing?" Becca said.

He covered his mouth as it gaped open in another fake yawn. "I'm Mrs. Grant," he said. He held up the can of root beer. "Here's my fancy red glass, and I just"—he paused, raising his hands above his head in a theatrical stretch—"am so *tired*. I must leave the party."

Becca pressed her lips into a line and placed both hands flat on the table. "*That* is not kind either," she scolded.

Violet took a bite of pizza to stop herself from giggling.

Fixing her eyes on each child in turn, Becca said, "We use our words and actions to build up and bless others. We are called to be kind to even those who are hard to love."

Oliver slid back into his seat, and the three children looked down at their plates.

Becca tapped her fingers on the table. "Oliver..." she said. "Why were you yawning so much?"

"That's what she was doing," the young man said innocently. "Before she left, she was constantly yawning."

With wide eyes, Becca gazed at him for a moment. She shook her head slightly. "Make sure you have some vegetables," she said to him, indicating the tub.

When dinner was over, Oliver set to work extinguishing the fire in the fireplace, and Becca and the girls cleaned up.

As Violet wiped the table, she paused near her mother's uneaten piece of pizza. "What should I do with that?" she asked.

Becca glanced at the plate. "You can leave it for now. Thank you," she said thoughtfully.

After returning the washcloth to the kitchen, Violet looked around the space with satisfaction. "Everything is cleaned up," she reported.

Becca smiled at her children. "Thank you all for your help. You head upstairs, and I'll be up in a few minutes to read to you."

Violet and Oliver headed in the direction of the Gables' apartment, and after locating Toffee and Licorice and saying good night to them, Hazel followed.

Tearing the crust from her slice of pizza, she held it down to Butterscotch, who gratefully started munching. Becca tossed the rest in the trash and headed toward the kitchen to retrieve her laptop. The computer illuminated her face as she typed, *What are the symptoms of a stroke?* Her eyes clouded as they moved down the list of symptoms—none of which she had noticed Mrs. Grant experience. She closed her laptop with a soft thud, feeling that twist in her stomach again.

# Chapter 8

# Ghosts in the Graveyard

Becca frowned at the tombstones—or rather, the large pieces of Styrofoam that she was *supposed* to turn into tombstones—and placed her hands on her hips.

"Lights up!" Violet's voice rang from across the other side of the sanctuary. Immediately, the single sound of a bell tolled.

Glancing over her shoulder, Becca saw Hazel appear from the right side of the stage. With her gleaming white robe and frosted evergreen circlet, she shone like an icicle in moonlight. Hazel spread her arms wide as she moved toward centerstage. She stopped in front of a teenage boy wearing a nightshirt, nightcap, and a gray beard. With wide eyes, the young man gaped at her and asked in a warbled voice, "Are you the spirit whose coming was foretold to me?"

"I am," Hazel said, her words loud and clear.

Out of the corner of her eye, Becca spotted Uncle John and Oliver slipping through the side entrance of the former sanctuary. She smiled as she considered the blessing of this old church. After two years of furious fundraising, Crystal Run Homeschoolers, also known as CRH, had purchased the building to repurpose for their music and theater programs. As funds allowed, they slowly updated the former church, now called Steeple Hall. Much of the financing came from the fine arts programs themselves, but there was also an anonymous donor who gave regular contributions. Although Uncle John would admit to nothing, Becca noticed a sparkle in his eyes whenever she mentioned the donations, and the police chief seemed unusually interested in the roof repair.

As the scene unfolded onstage, John and Oliver quietly made their way down the side aisle. John had exchanged his police blazer for a royal-blue CRH Hawks t-shirt, and Oliver's lumpy winter coat was unzipped over his blue-and-white basketball uniform. John said something to the young man and ruffled his hair. Oliver nodded and drew his lips into a half-hearted smile. Pulling his earbuds from his pocket, he collapsed into a back pew and closed his eyes.

Becca caught Uncle John's eye and motioned him over. On his way, he turned and waved to Violet. Seated in a director's chair, she had a binder labeled "Stage Manager" in her lap. John chuckled as Violet remained frozen, her gaze fixed on the scene in front of her. With a glance at Hazel, who was now scrutinizing Child Scrooge, the police chief made his way across the room and joined Becca on the tarp that had been laid out on the floor.

Smiling, Becca pecked him on the cheek. "We haven't seen you in a couple of weeks! Has it been that busy at the station?"

"Yes, lots going on." He grinned. "But I couldn't miss spending the evening with my favorite people. We're still on for ice cream when we're done here, right?"

Becca nodded. "Oh, yes, I've got my heart set on caramel cashew." She paused and added, "Thanks for taking Oliver to his game."

John raised his eyebrows slightly. "Did you hear how it turned out?"

Becca pulled her phone from her back pocket and held it up. "The basketball mom group text kept me informed of all the gory details." She returned the phone to her pocket, and her face grew serious. "How is he doing?"

A soft laugh escaped from John's lips. "He's doing all right. He got a basket, and his team displayed good sportsmanship. You would have been proud of him."

Becca smiled. "God is teaching him humility." She glanced down at the tombstone-shaped slabs of Styrofoam, cans of paint, and cardboard box of supplies at her feet. "And speaking of humility, how in the world did I get assigned to set design? I know nothing about painting a set."

Uncle John laughed. "Come now, you're very creative. What have you got?"

Becca pointed to the two cans of paint. "I thought that if I sponged on those two shades of gray, that might make the tombstones look aged." She paused and blushed. "But I don't even know how to open a can of paint."

John grinned. "Today's the day you learn!" Crouching down, he shuffled through the contents of the box. The man pulled out a couple of paint trays, spouts, and sponges. He then shook the cans vigorously and, grabbing a paint key, showed Becca how to pry it under the lid. John lifted a section of the lid himself and then motioned for her to come over and do the rest.

Becca slowly made her way around the lid's circumference. "Is there anything interesting going on at the station?" she asked. After a few prying motions, she peered up at him out of the corner of her eye and attempted a casual voice. "Did you get the results of Mrs. Grant's autopsy?"

John tipped his head slightly, and a small smile played on his lips. "Why are you asking?"

"Oh!" Becca said. "I'm just curious." Triumphantly, she lifted the lid from the can and held it up for John to admire. He pointed to the tarp, and she carefully laid it down and crouched by the second can of paint.

Folding his arms across his chest, John said, "As a matter of fact, the report did come in a couple of days ago. It turns out that Phyllis Grant didn't die of a stroke. The cause of death was a combination of alcohol and sleeping pills."

Becca inhaled sharply, and her gaze snapped to her uncle. "What! Alcohol? That's not possible!" Her hand, still clutching the paint key, was frozen mid-pry. "I *know* I brought her non-alcoholic champagne just like she requested."

"I'm sure you did," John said. "But there's no question she had alcohol and a sleeping drug in her system."

"Eszopiclone?" Becca asked.

John's jaw dropped. "How did you know that?"

"I saw a prescription for it on her nightstand when I was in her bedroom the day after the cocktail party." Becca looked up and smiled sweetly.

Shaking his head and chuckling, John said, "You've always had a good eye." He paused as he watched Becca peel the lid from the second can of paint and then added, "It appears to be an unfortunate accident."

Carefully laying the second lid by the first, Becca stood and wiped her hands on her worn jeans. "Do you think that's all there is to it?"

"We don't see any evidence of foul play," John said, stooping to pick up the pour spouts. "Are you watching?" he asked as he attached the first one to a can of gray paint.

Becca nodded.

He continued, "Sometimes elderly people get confused and combine alcohol with their medications."

Becca shifted her weight from one foot to the other. "Yes, but Mrs. Grant seemed pretty well aware of the fact that she couldn't have alcohol."

John glanced up at her and handed her the other pour spout. "Your turn," he said, straightening. "It's possible that she picked up the wrong glass at the party at some point. Or she might even have had a nip of something to ward off some pre-party jitters."

When she had attached the second spout, Becca stood and tucked a wayward strand of blonde hair behind her ear. She frowned. "I have this feeling that I just can't shake."

"I'm sorry, Bec," John said. "Unless there is evidence to the contrary, we have to treat this as an accident. At this moment in time, this seems to be nothing more than an elderly citizen making a mistake. It's sad, but it happens."

Becca nodded thoughtfully. "I understand," she said, hooking her thumbs into the pockets of her jeans.

"How are we doing over here?" a woman's deep voice bellowed from behind.

Becca let out a squeak, and her hand flew to her heart. "Meryl!"

"Well!" The director's eyes widened, and she looked at John. "I didn't think my presence was *that* alarming."

John chuckled. "Oh, that's something she's done all her life. She got that from her mother."

Meryl Rivera was tall and willowy, and her straight white hair was cut into a blunt bob. Large violet eyes peered out of a pair of thick-rimmed glasses. A lavender pashmina shawl was wrapped dramatically across the woman's shoulders. She nodded at John. "It looks like you have a helper here."

"Ms. Rivera," John acknowledged.

Meryl loosened her shawl so she could toss it artfully over her shoulder again. "We're working through a costume malfunction right now, so I thought that I would check on the progress of our graveyard."

Becca and John turned toward the stage, which was set for Bob Cratchit's house. Violet was attempting to run lines with the Cratchit family, which was seated around a large table. Noticeably absent was the head of the family, Bob Cratchit. As the girls' frilly capped heads bobbed in laughter and the boys snickered openly, Violet folded her arms across her chest. To the side of the stage, a costume mom frantically stitched a pair of black trousers.

Meryl placed a hand to the side of her mouth and said in a loud whisper, "Bob Cratchit split his pants. It's never dull!" She smiled and shook her head. "How is the progress over here?"

Becca gestured toward the paint. "We got the paint cans open!" she said proudly.

Meryl peered down her nose at the two cans of gray paint and sighed. "Well..." the woman said, "that's a necessary step." She paused and then smiled brightly. "Perhaps for our next show, what do you think about coordinating ushers?"

Becca frowned and opened her mouth to respond, but she stopped as she noticed the young man playing Bob Cratchit, now wearing a pair of jeans, hurrying onstage.

"Oh!" Meryl said. "I'm needed. Carry on!" With a final toss of her shawl, she flounced toward the stage.

John caught Becca's eye, and the two burst into laughter.

Taking a deep breath to steady herself and glancing at the open paint cans, Becca said, "Maybe I am more cut out for coordinating ushers."

"Never mind her," John said. "You're doing great. Now we pour the paint into the trays."

As Becca and John each picked up a can of paint and began to pour, Becca's countenance grew pensive. "How is Lexi handling the news?" she asked softly.

John straightened. "The granddaughter? I called her with the autopsy results when they came in." He smoothed his bushy mustache with his thumb and forefinger and continued, "I probably should have delivered the news in person. She was very distraught."

"Oh, no," Becca said.

John nodded solemnly. "The poor young woman blames herself. She normally handled her grandmother's medication, but she was distracted that night because of the party. She figures that Phyllis must have taken her pills herself and overdosed." John heaved a sigh. "She was overcome with grief, just wailing into the phone."

In thoughtful silence, Becca dipped a sponge into the darker shade of gray paint and then dabbed off the excess. Pulling a piece of Styrofoam toward her, she began to swab the paint onto the foam. Finally, she said, "Well, that explains the strange email I received from her yesterday."

John leaned against the back of a pew. "Strange in what way?"

"She sent me an email saying that the red crystal goblet that Mrs. Grant used for her toast is missing. Since I was the caterer, she says that it was my responsibility to keep track of it, and she is charging me an exorbitant amount of money for it."

Letting out a low whistle, John said, "Well, sometimes when people lose those close to them, they reach out for anything that reminds them of their loved one. She's probably really hurt that she doesn't have that anymore."

Becca nodded. "I figured that it was coming from a place of pain. This is something that shouldn't be handled over email or text." She leaned back on her heels, admired her work, and began dabbing gray paint onto the next piece of Styrofoam. "I gave Lexi a call as soon as I received the email, but it went to her voicemail. It makes sense. I believe her grandmother's funeral was yesterday. But if I don't hear from her by tomorrow, I'm going to stop by to see her in person."

"That will do her some good," John said. "But you're not paying for that goblet." He drew his frame into its protective stance.

"No, I am not," Becca confirmed, smiling.

With a sharp nod, the chief allowed his gaze to settle on the tombstone. "And yes, Phyllis's funeral was yesterday."

"I thought so," Becca said as she dipped her sponge into the paint tray to reload. "I overheard some of the CRIS women talking about it." She swabbed off the excess paint. "They asked me if I would be interested in joining their society."

John raised his bushy eyebrows. "And what did you say?"

"I didn't really give a response," Becca said, rocking back on her heels and looking up into her uncle's face. "I was just shocked that they would be trying to fill Mrs. Grant's place before she was even buried. It seemed so inappropriate." With a sigh, she returned to her work.

"That *is* cold," John agreed. He folded his arms across his chest.

Carefully, Becca dabbed the sponge around the outline of the tombstone. "Evelyn was the only one of them to show any compassion for her passing." For a few moments, she worked in silence.

"If there is any person in the town," Scrooge's agonized voice rang out from across the room, "who feels emotion caused by this man's death, show that person to me, Spirit. I beseech you!"

Incredulously, Becca and John looked toward the stage. Turning back toward each other, they locked eyes and shook their heads.

By the time Meryl Rivera had gathered the cast and crew for notes, Becca had finished painting five tombstones. She recruited Oliver to help clean up, and she, Oliver, and John headed toward the cast and crew, most of whom were seated cross-legged on the stage. Hazel, who was now wearing jeans and a pink sweater, flashed them a quick smile. Becca stifled a laugh as she noticed that Hazel still had ghostly blue-black makeup smudges under both eyes. With her pencil scratching fervently against a legal pad, Violet took careful notes of Meryl's comments on the evening's performance. Finally, the Gables and Uncle John filed out of Steeple Hall along with the crowd of burgeoning actors. Immediately, they were hit with a cold blast of wind.

"Ah, that feels good!" Oliver said, his open jacket flapping in the gust. He tilted his face up to the inky sky, closed his eyes, and smiled. "Oof!" he exclaimed suddenly as a playful punch was delivered to his shoulder. Oliver turned to see one of his friends. He grinned and returned the slug accordingly.

Becca shook her head and pulled the collar of her coat tighter around her neck. "Are we sure it's not too cold for ice cream?" she asked.

Uncle John wrapped an arm around her shoulders. "We've got to do something to celebrate the fact that you now know how to open a can of paint." He gave her a little squeeze. "Besides, I thought you said that you have your heart set on caramel cashew."

"Using my own words against me!" Becca laughed. She looked up at him and raised an eyebrow. "Now, for the serious question. What flavor are *you* going to get?"

# Chapter 9

# What Oliver Found

Oliver's fingertips inched beneath the pink-and-white striped lid of the bakery box.

"Oh, no, you don't!" Hazel scolded as she reached across the minivan to swat his hand away. "Those are for Miss Grant."

Becca's gaze snapped to the rearview mirror. "What's going on back there?"

"Oliver is trying to sneak a cookie!" Hazel tattled. She passed the striped box up to Violet, who laid it safely in her lap.

Folding his arms across his chest, the young man thumped back against the seat. "Sorry," he said, "I'm still hungry."

Becca shook her head in bewilderment. "How is that possible? We *just* had dinner."

Oliver shrugged and looked out the window.

"He's *always* hungry," Violet said quietly, and Becca stifled a smile.

"I don't understand why Miss Grant gets cookies," Oliver complained, light pulsing across his face as they passed a row of huge evergreens strung with Christmas lights. "She's accusing you of stealing a dumb glass and making us go to all this trouble. She probably just didn't look hard enough."

With a sigh, Becca eased her foot onto the brake and turned into the cobblestone driveway of the Paper Palace. She parked in the circular driveway and switched off the ignition. Unbuckling, she turned around and faced her son. "Miss Grant is in a lot of pain right now," she said. "She just lost her last remaining relative, and she's blaming herself. So, no, she shouldn't be charging me for the missing goblet. But she never got back to me after I called her, and I need to make this right. Do you understand?"

Oliver nodded solemnly. "Yes, ma'am."

Taking the box from Violet's lap, she held it up and smiled. "Besides, everything is better with baked goods."

Oliver looked at her for a few moments and then raised his mouth in a half-smile.

"But in all seriousness," Becca said, "before we go in, let's pray for Miss Grant and ask God to help us navigate this situation." She placed the box back in Violet's lap, and the children followed their mother's lead in bowing their heads and folding their hands. "Heavenly Father," she prayed, "we know you can do all things. We ask that you bring Miss Grant comfort and peace during this time of loss. Please use this experience to draw her close to your Son. And, Father, we ask that you help find a resolution to the missing wine glass. All this we ask in Jesus's name, Amen."

The snow crunched under their feet as the Gables approached the impressive front entrance of the mansion. Becca reached out a finger and rang the bell. Several long moments passed. "I think she's home," Becca mused, stepping back and observing light pouring out of some of the windows. She rang the bell a second time.

Hazel huffed hot breaths into the icy air, creating puffs of vapor. Violet shivered, and the cookies rattled in their box.

Gazing up at the windows again and tapping her foot, Becca stretched out a finger toward the bell a third time. Before she made contact, however, she heard the scraping turn of a deadbolt.

Slowly, the door opened a crack, and Lexi peered out at them. "Oh, it's you," she said.

Becca smiled warmly. "Hi, Lexi. I'm not sure if you received my voicemail, but I want to talk to you about the missing goblet."

Lexi opened the door a little wider. "Do you have the payment for it?"

"I am sure we can figure it out," Becca said. "May we come in?"

The young woman raked her fingers through her blue-black hair, and her eyes dropped to the snow-crusted ground. "I'm sorry, Becca, this isn't a great time. Harvey and I were down in Chicago all day, and he just dropped me off."

Becca smiled apologetically. "I understand," she said, "but I am sure this won't take long."

Hazel scooted around her mother and looked up at Lexi with large aqua eyes. "We brought cookies!"

Lexi's gaze shifted to the pink-and-white striped box in Violet's hands, and her mouth curved into a small smile. After hesitating for several moments, she finally said, "Oh, all right." The young woman opened the door wide and stepped back.

The Gables trooped inside and stamped their shoes on the mat. Violet handed Lexi the box of cookies.

"Thanks," Lexi said flatly, placing the box on a side table.

"I'm sorry to show up unexpectedly," Becca said, pulling off her gloves. "I did try to call, but I know you have a lot going on right now."

Oliver tugged on the wool sleeve of his mother's raspberry-colored coat. "Mom, is it okay if Hazel and I play chess in the library?"

Becca looked at Lexi. "Is that all right?"

"That's fine," Lexi said with a disinterested wave.

Violet glanced at her mother and raised her eyebrows.

"You may stay here if you like," Becca said.

As Oliver and Hazel disappeared into the hallway, Becca tucked her gloves into her pockets. She scanned Lexi. The young woman was pale, and dark circles ringed her ocean-blue eyes. Her ebony hair hung lankly around her face, and she wore an oversized sweatshirt over a pair of jeans.

"How are you doing, Lexi?" Becca asked.

Lexi stared blankly at Becca. Finally, she said, "I'm fine." She paused. "I mean, how am I supposed to be? I don't have any family left, it's my fault, and it looks like I'm going to have to sell the estate."

"I'm so sorry," Becca said quietly, stretching an arm forward to offer Lexi an embrace.

Reluctantly, Lexi accepted the hug, her thin frame stiff.

"Please let me know if there's anything I can do to help," Becca said, drawing back and looking into the young woman's wan face.

Lexi nodded. "Well, I'd really like the missing wine glass back... or payment for it. That set has been in our family for generations. It is an heirloom." She looked out the window for a moment.

Violet frowned and glanced sideways at her mother. Becca gave the tiniest shake of her head.

Turning back to Lexi, Becca saw that the young woman's eyes were wet with tears.

Lexi closed her eyes. "And— And I can just picture my grandmother raising that goblet as she toasted our *family*..."

"Oh, yes," Becca affirmed, gently touching Lexi's elbow. "I know that the wine glass is very special to you. May I help you look for it? It might be something as simple as having been put back in the wrong cupboard."

Lexi jerked her arm away from Becca and narrowed her eyes. "Listen, I have turned this house upside-down—"

"Mom! Mom!"

The two women and Violet turned to see Hazel racing toward them, her golden hair streaming behind her. She skidded to a stop and placed her hands on her knees.

Becca's eyes widened. "What is it, Hazel?"

"Come on!" the girl said, her voice shrill with excitement. "You have to see what Oliver found!"

Becca and Lexi exchanged looks.

"Come *on*," Hazel urged and waved them toward her. The trio followed as the girl led them up the grand staircase, across the landing, and into the hallway. As they approached the bedrooms, Hazel suddenly stopped and grinned. "Look!" she said, pointing.

Just outside Phyllis's bedroom stood Oliver, triumphantly holding up a ruby-colored crystal wine glass. Even in the artificial light of the hallway, it sparkled brilliantly.

"You *found* it!" Lexi beamed. "Where was it?"

A wide smile spread across the young man's face. "It was in Mrs. Grant's bedroom... behind the nightstand. It was mostly hidden by a curtain." Oliver lowered the glass to examine it. His smile faded, and he tilted his head. "There's something weird in it, though."

Lexi moved to take the glass from Oliver, and Becca drew in a sharp breath. "Wait!" she cried.

Lexi froze, and she and the children stared at Becca in surprise.

"Just a moment," she said and smiled reassuringly. Reaching into the pockets of her wool coat, Becca removed her gloves and slipped them on. She stepped toward Oliver and carefully took the glass from him. Upon a brief inspection of the goblet, Becca's eyebrows furrowed. "I see what you're saying, Oliver," she said thoughtfully. "The inside of the glass is coated with some kind of white sediment."

"But the glass itself is okay?" Lexi asked. "I'm sure that's just the dried residue from Grandmother's drink. It's not a big deal. I can wash it."

Becca held the glass in the light and squinted. "You're probably right," she said. "But we really should have this checked out, considering the cause of your grandmother's death." She moved the glass to her left hand and pulled her phone from her pocket. Pressing the button on the side, she spoke into it, "Call Uncle John."

Lexi blew out her breath and crossed her arms over her chest. She tapped her foot as Becca put in the phone call.

Pressing her lips into a straight line and returning the phone to her pocket, Becca said, "The police do want to examine it. The chief is sending an officer over to pick it up. He says that someone is already in the area, so that's a blessing."

"Really? Why?" Lexi said, her eyes widening. "The chief told me just the other day that Grandmother died from a combination of her sleeping pills and alcohol. It was an accident."

"That's probably the case," Becca said, "but I think it's wise to have this checked out." She glanced again at the sediment in the glass. "As far as I know, you never get this kind of residue from sparkling non-alcoholic wine." She tipped the glass toward Lexi. "It's white."

"I want to see too!" Hazel interjected.

Becca held up a single finger toward Hazel. "Violet, would you please take Hazel downstairs? Maybe the two of you could look at the books in the library."

Placing her hand on Hazel's shoulder, Violet nodded and obediently guided her sister toward the landing. Oliver began to follow his sisters.

"Oliver, you stay here," Becca said. "I think you'll be needed." She looked at Lexi and tilted the goblet toward her a second time.

Lexi's eyes narrowed as she peered into it. Suddenly, she gasped, stepped backward, and stared wide-eyed at Becca. "You— You don't think that somebody could have *intentionally* done something to hurt my grand-mother, do you?"

Seeing the startled expression on Lexi's face, Becca smiled softly. "Oh, Lexi, it's only a theory. I'm sure that when the police check out this glass, they will confirm that what happened to your grandmother was just an accident. They just want to make sure that everything is okay."

Lexi exhaled, and her shoulders relaxed. At that moment, the doorbell sounded, and the young woman looked at Becca.

"That's probably the police officer. He will want to come up here," Becca said.

Nodding, Lexi turned and headed toward the landing. Oliver followed and leaned over the railing to watch as Lexi led the police officer upstairs. It was Officer Spencer, the same man who had been present the day of Phyllis's death.

The officer's eyes widened in recognition of Becca. As he pulled on a pair of white gloves, Officer Spencer explained that the chief had already filled him in on the circumstances of the wine goblet. Carefully taking the glass from Becca, he said, "I'm just going to take some pictures, and I will collect the glass for the lab to examine."

After asking Oliver a series of questions, the officer led the group into the garish mauve-and-gold bedroom. Standing beside Phyllis's canopy bed, Oliver pointed behind the nightstand where he had found the goblet, and following the young man's directions, Officer Spencer replaced the wine glass exactly as Oliver remembered finding it.

On her tiptoes, Becca could see that not only had the goblet been located behind the nightstand, but it had also been almost completely concealed by the mauve window curtain. Only the tiniest bit of the base had shown.

When Oliver was satisfied with the placement of the goblet, Officer Spencer snapped several pictures. Sadly, Lexi watched as he carefully placed the ruby wine glass in a plastic bag.

"Don't worry, ma'am," the officer said reassuringly. "We will take good care of your property. It shouldn't be long before you get it back."

The investigation complete, Lexi escorted the police officer to the door, and Becca and Oliver followed. As the door closed behind Officer Spencer, Becca looked at Oliver. "Would you please find your sisters? I think it's time that we head out."

"Yes, ma'am," Oliver said and turned to head in the direction of the library.

Distraught, Lexi watched as the officer climbed into his marked SUV and pulled on her fingers. Noticing Becca's gaze, she forced the corner of her lip into a small smile and said, "Well, at least the glass has been found."

"Yes, the set will be complete again in no time," Becca said, smiling warmly at her. Her expression grew serious. "Truly, Lexi, I am so sorry for your loss. If there's anything I can do—"

Lexi waved away the words and lowered her tear-filled eyes to the floor. "Thank you," she finally choked out.

The sound of loud whispers and footsteps announced the children's arrival. Becca shifted her gaze from Lexi to the sight of Oliver leading his sisters toward them. She smiled at them. "Are you ready to head out?"

Violet zipped up her coat, and Oliver nodded.

Hazel skipped over to the side table where the pink-and-white striped box still laid. She looked up at Lexi, who swiped her eyes with the back of her hand. "Don't forget about the cookies!" the girl said. "Everything is better with baked goods." She shuffled her feet and added shyly, "That's what Mom says."

Placing her hand on top of Hazel's golden head, Becca felt her lips curve into a faint smile.

As the Gables stepped out into the chill toward their light-blue minivan, Becca heaved a sigh of relief. "Phew! Well, that turned out differently than I expected, but God took care of us. The goblet has been found." She turned toward Oliver and raised an eyebrow. "I am really glad you found the wine glass, but I thought you said you were going to play chess with Hazel."

Oliver gave a lopsided grin. "I *figured* that Miss Grant wasn't looking hard enough. And do you know what my reward should be?"

"What?" Becca said, stifling a smile.

The young man looked at her with conviction. "Cookies!"

# Chapter 10

# Combinations

As the organ notes faded from the final preservice hymn, John Olson slipped into the empty space Becca had left for him in their usual pew—left side, second row from the front. The chief was dressed in a full navy-blue suit, and he was slightly out of breath.

Becca turned to him, smiled, and held up a finger in faux admonishment. "You were almost late," she teased in a low whisper. "You're *never* late for church."

John raised his bushy white eyebrows and said in a low voice, "I'll explain later."

Becca eyed him quizzically, but John leaned forward and looked past her, winking at Hazel and then nodding to Violet and Oliver in turn. John then fixed his eyes on the Glory Cross, which, backlit by stained glass, shone radiantly between two towering Christmas trees. The organist finished the opening bars of "Hark the Glad Sound," and John's robust bass sang out, "Hark the glad sound! The Savior comes, the Savior promised long." Becca gave him one more sideways glance and then joined him in singing the hymn.

When worship was over, the Gables filed out of the pew and slowly made their way down the shining tiled aisle, standing in line to shake the pastor's hand. Pastor James was tall with an athletic build, which was currently hidden by his white robe and purple vestments. His light-brown hair was short, and he wore glasses.

Becca smoothed her wool navy-blue-and-green tartan skirt and smiled at the children. "Remember, eye contact and a firm handshake." She suddenly felt Uncle John's light touch on the small of her back, and she stepped forward to shake Pastor James's hand. "Good morning!" Becca said brightly.

The pastor smiled warmly. "And a good morning to you."

"Excellent message, Pastor," John said, gripping the man's hand.

Pastor James clapped his other hand over John's and shook the chief's enthusiastically. "Thanks, John," he said. "Always good to see you in the second row."

After the children had also greeted the pastor, the group headed to the atrium, which was buzzing with activity. Oliver immediately darted toward the kitchenette where donuts and cookies were being served on the counter.

Becca cringed as he nearly bowled over an elderly man with a cane. "Walk, please!" she called.

Oliver apologized to the man and obediently slowed his steps. Winding their way through the visiting congregants, Violet and Hazel followed at a more casual pace. As Becca stood in the beverage line to procure cups of coffee for Uncle John and herself, she shook her head as she watched Oliver stuff the remainder of a white-frosted Long John into his mouth. He wiped his hands on the front of his pants and looked up to see his friend Ethan, a sandy-haired teen several years his senior. Dropping into a slight crouch, Oliver mimed dribbling a ball and taking a shot, which Ethan promptly pretended to block. The two chuckled, and then Oliver headed toward a cluster of boys his age to wait for Bible study to begin.

A cup of steaming coffee in each hand, Becca carefully picked her way through the chattering crowd and found John waiting for her at one of the standing-height tiled tables. She handed John his cup, hung her tote bag on the back of a stool, and headed back to the kitchenette to grab two little tubs of cream. As Becca made her way back to John, she spotted a wisp of a woman in the throng and waved at her. "Maggie!"

Turning at the sound of her name, the young woman flashed a smile when she discovered its source. Maggie Sharpe, the librarian and preschool aid at Grace Lutheran School, stood on her tiptoes and returned Becca's wave.

"I have books for you!" Becca called. She gestured toward the tote bag slung across the back of the high stool near Uncle John, and both women headed in that direction.

Becca reached into her tote and smiled at the young woman whose wavy black hair was cut into a long bob. "I'm glad I found you!" Becca said, pulling out a stack of Christmas-themed picture books and handing them over. "These are for the library at Grace School."

"Oh, thank you!" Maggie said. "It's so kind how you support the grade school even when you homeschool your own children."

Becca grinned. "Of course! The school is wonderful. We homeschool because we wanted a more active role in our children's education. But I love the school, and I'm all for supporting it."

"Well, we are always grateful," Maggie said, raising the stack of picture books a few inches. "And I'm going to make it to your bookshop one of these days."

"You know," Becca said thoughtfully. "Our annual gift-wrapping event at Tales & Tails is on December 14th. We do it as community service, but all tips go to the church. You could swing by the shop and get some presents wrapped while you are at it." She tilted her head and raised her eyebrows.

Before the young librarian could reply, Becca saw a whirl of movement from the corner of her eye, and her attention shifted to Hazel, who was wearing a chiffon cranberry-colored dress with long sleeves, a ruffled collar, and a satin bow tied around her waist. She was the center of a cluster of elderly women who were oohing and ahhing as the girl twirled to demonstrate the "float" of her skirt. Violet, who, in contrast, was dressed in a white button-down shirt tucked into a charcoal-gray skirt, watched and rolled her eyes.

Becca smiled at Maggie. "Sorry, I'd better make sure Hazel gets down to Sunday School." She stepped toward her daughters and called over her shoulder, "I'll see you in Bible class!"

Placing her hand on Violet's arm, she said, "Would you please take Hazel down to Sunday School?"

"Glad to," Violet replied. She squeezed between two of the elderly ladies, glancing at them apologetically, and pulled her sister from the ring of admirers. "Hazel's got to go to Sunday School now," she said in explanation.

When the two girls were out of earshot of the elderly women, Violet glanced down at her sister and said reproachfully, "You know, there's more to life than pretty clothes."

Becca watched the girls descend the staircase toward the classrooms, and she turned toward Uncle John, who was still standing beside the tiled table, pensively sipping his coffee. Seeing her gaze, he pointed to her coffee cup, and Becca remembered the two little tubs of cream in her hand. As she busied herself with the cream, an elderly man sidled up to Uncle John.

"Lyle!" John said in greeting.

Lyle Gregory, a fixture at Grace Lutheran Church for as long as anyone could remember, maintained the building, kept the grounds, and greeted congregants every Sunday morning. He was a frail-looking man with fluffy white hair and remarkably large pale-blue eyes that looked even larger behind his thick glasses.

The man grinned at John. "I have a gift for you."

"Oh?" John said, raising his eyebrows.

Reaching into the pocket of his suit coat, Lyle fished out a sealed envelope and held it out to the chief. "The combination code to get into to the church office," he explained in his shaky, fragile voice. "Approval just came through."

John took the envelope from his hand. "Excellent! Thank you, Lyle."

"Use it well, young man," Lyle said, smiling.

At the words "young man," a giggle escaped from Becca, and she covered her mouth with her fingers. John looked at her and raised a bushy white brow, and then Becca truly burst into laughter. "I'm sorry!" she said, settling herself. "It's just so funny to me, Mr. Gregory, how you always call him 'young man.' How long have you known my uncle John?"

Lyle's eyes shone with merriment. "Oh, I've known this little troublemaker since I had him in Confirmation class." He smiled and sighed wistfully. "I taught that for over fifty years, you know. Your father was in my class too." Shaking himself from his thoughts, he held up a reproving finger at John, winked at Becca, and said, "Blessings on your day!" His tuft of white hair bobbing, he shuffled toward the display cabinet that housed the church's special antique communion set and began to polish the already immaculate glass front.

John glanced at his watch and then at Becca. "We have five minutes until Bible study. I'd like to have a word with you. Would you join me in the conference room?" He held up the newly given envelope containing the door code and grinned. "Let's put this baby to use!"

"Of course!" Becca said. She grabbed her coffee and tote bag and followed Uncle John.

Ripping the envelope open as he walked, John glanced at the series of numbers inside. He punched in the combination on the keypad mounted outside the offices and was rewarded by a click of the door. He and Becca slipped inside, and John led her to the conference room. "Have a seat," he said, gesturing toward one of the chairs pushed in around the long table. As Becca settled into the chair, John seated himself at the head of the table.

Again, he glanced at his watch. "Now, don't get overly excited, but you're going to hear about this soon enough anyway, so you might as well hear it from me."

Becca's eyes widened, and she sat up straight.

John stifled a smile and continued. "The reason I was almost late this morning is because an interesting report just came in. You know that goblet that Oliver found at Phyllis Grant's home?"

"Yes?" Becca was perched on the edge of her seat.

"The lab found traces of alcohol in the glass as well as an alarming amount of eszopiclone. We are now opening a homicide investigation."

"Murder," Becca murmured. "I just *knew* something was off." Pressing her lips into a straight line, she nodded and gazed out the window at a naked tree branch bobbing in the wind.

John leaned back in his chair, crossed an ankle over his knee, and looked expectantly at his niece.

Suddenly, she brightened and snapped her attention toward Uncle John. "Who are you putting in charge of the investigation? Did you get a warrant to search the Paper Palace? When will we need to go in for statements? Who are the suspects so far? Do you need me to make a list of everyone who was at the party? Where—"

"Whoa, now," John said, holding up a hand. "I was on the fence about sharing this with you because I knew you were going to be like this... all your questions." He laughed softly, and the wrinkles around his eyes crinkled in amusement. "Honestly, it's like being attacked by a hummingbird."

Becca blinked. "A hummingbird?" She laughed and then felt her cheeks warm as they flushed a rosy hue.

Still chuckling, the chief smiled at her affectionately. "Detective Post is in charge of the investigation," he said.

Becca raised an eyebrow. "Post? I'm not familiar with that name."

"He was recently promoted to detective. He will be contacting you soon to schedule a time to come to the station for statements and fingerprints." John glanced down at his watch. "But enough of this for now. It's time for us to get to Bible study."

Becca's eyes flicked to the wall clock. "It is," she agreed with a sigh. Rising from her chair, she slung the strap of her tote over her shoulder. John held the door open for her and gestured to Becca to go first.

The pair made their way down the hall and into the classroom for Bible class. Light streamed in from the many windows and spilled onto the tables, which were arranged in a U-shape. In the center of the U was a podium topped with an open Bible and a high stool with a brown leather jacket slung across the back. Half-sitting and half-standing on the seat's edge was the Bible teacher, Alex Gerhartz. He was in his early forties and tall with an average build. Alex had brown hair and eyes and a close-cropped beard. Never one to shy away from a good-natured debate, either theological or trivial, he was currently in the middle of a lively dispute with Lyle about the merits of snow. While Alex was a firm believer in the more snow, the better, Lyle, on the other hand, would prefer that his snow shovel not be needed all winter long. Glancing over his shoulder, he smiled and greeted them with a half-wave. "Good morning!"

"Morning, Alex," John returned in his warm rumble.

Becca smiled broadly, wished the Bible teacher a good morning, and then gave a general wave to the people already seated at the tables. Her eyes locked on the two open chairs next to Violet and Oliver, who were waiting with Bibles spread open in front of them. Becca slipped into the chair next to Oliver, and John sat down beside her. Reaching into her tote, Becca pulled out her white Bible case and, after a moment's hesitation, a small floral notebook. After opening her Bible to the book of Matthew, Becca found a clean page in her notebook and started writing in her careful script.

Alex made his way over to their group. "What are your thoughts, John? Are you looking forward to the big snowstorm that's in the forecast?"

John, who had been opening his own worn leather-covered Bible, glanced over at Lyle and then back at Alex. "As long as it's not too much to shovel," he said, stroking his bushy white mustache, "I would love a nice blanket of snow for Christmas."

Alex grinned at Lyle.

Violet, her hands folded carefully in front of her, looked up at the Bible teacher. "Are you working on any new paintings, Mr. Gerhartz?"

The man's brown eyes sparkled. "I'm actually just finishing up a painting of *The Widow's Mite*," he said.

Oliver cocked his head. "Mite? Like strength or like the bug?"

Violet rolled her eyes, and Alex laughed.

"Well," he said, "it's spelled like the bug but means a coin of very small value. The widow made a small contribution in the eyes of the world, but she showed great faith because it was all she could afford."

"Could we see it, please?" Violet asked.

Reaching into his side pocket, Alex pulled out his phone and scrolled until he found the photo he was looking for. He held it out for the children to see. Oliver jostled his sister in an attempt at a better view, and Violet narrowed her eyes at him and then returned her attention to the photo. They took in the beautifully depicted image of a woman wrapped in a shawl and illuminated by candlelight as she presents her meager offering.

"It's beautiful!" Violet breathed.

Unable to resist, Becca glanced up from her notebook and leaned in to view the painting as well. "Oh, Alex!" she gasped. "It's gorgeous!" She looked at Uncle John. "Did you see?"

John nodded and shifted his gaze back and forth between the phone and the Bible teacher. "You are very talented."

With a humble tilt of the head, Alex thanked the chief, and Becca returned her attention to the list she was making.

Alex glanced at the clock and stepped toward the center of the room. He clasped his hands and said, "Let's begin with prayer."

Flipping her notebook upside-down, Becca closed her eyes and folded her hands. When Alex concluded the prayer, he asked if anyone had anything on their hearts or minds. Becca turned over the notebook again. With the tip of her pen, she ran down the list of names.

Peering over at Becca's work, John read the heading at the top of the page: *Suspects*. He raised his eyebrows and looked at Becca, who smiled sheepishly at him. With a sigh, John reached over and flipped the notebook to a fresh page. Tapping the clean sheets, he said, "It will be easier to take notes from class on these."

# Chapter 11

# Puzzles

"You solved it already?" Uncle John's eyes widened. "I don't think I've ever solved this thing *once*, let alone as quickly as you just did." Oliver handed the completed Rubik's cube to the police chief. Turning the cube over, John observed the solid planes of color on each side. He placed the cube on his desk and leaned back in his leather office chair. "You must be a genius, Oliver."

The young man hooked his thumbs in the pockets of his jeans, stood a little taller, and grinned.

At the word "genius," Hazel skipped over to John's sizeable desk and stood beside her brother. "Or," she said, "he just watched a YouTube video on how to solve it a hundred times."

Oliver frowned and narrowed his eyes at Hazel.

John rocked back and guffawed. "The credit still goes to you, Oliver," he said, "for using the resources available to you."

Just then, Becca appeared in the doorway. She smiled at John, who was dressed in his police uniform and seated at the desk positioned in the middle of his spacious office. Standing near him, Hazel watched as Oliver mixed up the Rubik's cube. In a chair against the wall, Violet was engrossed in a copy of C. S. Lewis's *Mere Christianity*.

Becca took a few steps into his office. "I was just catching up with Lieutenant Harville. You didn't tell me that he was a grandpa!"

"It must have slipped my mind," John chuckled. "Now, come over here, and let's go over what to expect." He looked at Oliver and Hazel, who took the hint. Bringing the Rubik's cube with them, the children crossed the room and plopped down on the floor by a tall filing cabinet.

As Becca slid into the seat across from Uncle John, she set her comically large tumbler of water on his desk and her tote and purse on the floor beside her.

John glanced at the ornate clock on the corner of his desk. "Detective Post will be taking statements from all of you since you were all present the night of Phyllis Grant's death. A tech will also be collecting fingerprints. We still have yours on file from when you worked in the office, but we will need the kids'."

Becca glanced at Oliver and Hazel and smiled. "They'll get a kick out of that."

John nodded. "I'm sure they will." At the sound of two sharp raps, his gaze moved to the doorway. "Come in," he said loudly.

Becca looked over her shoulder to see a man in his mid-thirties enter the room. He was stocky, dressed in a suit and tie, and had blond hair and a close-cropped mustache and goatee. The man strode over to the desk, looked at John, and said, "Captain Olson, I'm ready to take statements." He then glanced at Becca and smiled.

John leaned forward in his chair. "Becca, this is Detective Christopher Post. He is investigating the Grant case and will be taking your statement this morning." His gaze shifted to the detective. "Detective, this is my niece, Rebecca Gables."

With a smile, Becca stood and held out her hand. "It's nice to meet you, Detective Post."

"Ms. Gables," he returned, shaking her hand. "I thought I would start with your statement."

Becca glanced around the room at the children and then looked at Uncle John. "Are you okay with having the kids in here?"

Oliver and Hazel looked expectantly at John.

The chief smiled. "Oh, I was counting on it," he said with a wink. "I have all kinds of work for them to do."

Becca looked over at Violet, who was still bent over her book, her nut-brown eyes transfixed on the page. "Vi, I'll be back in a little."

"Mm-hmm," Violet murmured, not looking up from her book.

John laughed. "They'll be fine."

With that, Becca picked up her tote, purse, and tumbler.

Detective Post eyed her load. "Would you like help with any of that?"

Becca laughed. "No, I'm fine. I just have to bring half my house with me wherever I go."

The detective led Becca to his office, which was small and stark except for a few framed pictures on a shelf and a faux plant. He gestured toward a chair opposite his and seated himself behind his desk, a legal pad and pen in front of him.

Reaching into her bag, Becca removed a sheet of paper and handed it to the detective. "I have a list of suspects for you... everyone who was at the party, including the staff. It's color-coded. Anyone who was near the red goblet, at least according to my observations, is listed in red. I also placed asterisks near the people whom I consider top suspects."

Detective Post scanned the paper and raised an eyebrow. "You included yourself on the list?"

"I was at the party," Becca replied.

Stifling a smile, the detective said, "Thank you, I'm sure this will be helpful." He looked up at her and laid the paper on his desk. "It's great that you all were able to come in on such short notice. The case was only classified as homicide yesterday."

Becca nodded. "It actually worked out really well. The bookshop is closed on Mondays, so this is my day off."

The detective smiled. "I'm going to ask you some questions now. Are you okay with our interview being recorded?"

"Of course," Becca said.

"How did you know Phyllis Grant?" the detective began.

Becca took a sip of water. "Everyone in Crystal Run knew Phyllis Grant," she said. "She was the relative of one of *the* Grants who founded the town. I only really knew her as an acquaintance, though, until she started coming into the bookshop weekly for her CRIS meetings."

Detective Post tilted his head. "CRIS?"

"Crystal Run Improvement Society," Becca said.

"And when did she start coming in weekly?"

Becca considered for a moment. "I'd say it was about six months ago."

The detective continued, asking Becca a series of questions covering her relationship with Mrs. Grant and when she was hired to cater for the cocktail party.

"Let's talk about the night of Phyllis Grant's death, November six-teenth," Detective Post said. "What time did you arrive at the Paper Palace?"

"The children and I arrived at 5:05," she said.

The detective's lips curled into a small smile. "That's precise."

"I know because I *meant* to arrive at 5:00 sharp, and Violet scolded me for being late again." Becca could feel warmth blooming into her cheeks.

Detective Post's light-blue eyes twinkled. Directed by his questions, Becca relayed her movements throughout the evening, giving the times to the best of her ability.

"The red wine glass..." the detective said. "From what you observed, who had access to it that evening?"

Moving chronologically through the night, Becca counted off on her fingers. "Donna Sloane removed the wine glass from the cabinet. Harvey, of course, was the bartender and poured the non-alcoholic wine for Mrs. Grant. Lexi was near it. I saw Patricia Koller pick it up, and Dr. Davis was at the bar. Violet and I were also near the goblet." She gestured toward her suspect list. "I know Donna and a few others got up during Mrs. Grant's speech and went over to the bar." Tucking a strand of blonde hair behind her ear, she added, "I was busy making preparations for the evening, so I wasn't around the wine glass the entire time."

Detective Post smiled. "That's all right, I'm only asking for your obser-vations." He tapped the desk. "Are you aware of anyone who might have had an issue with Phyllis Grant?"

Becca smiled sadly. "It might be easier to ask who *didn't* have an issue with Mrs. Grant."

"Well, do the best you can," the detective encouraged.

"Donna Sloane and Mrs. Grant had recently had a public fight... some-thing about Donna not receiving an invitation to the cocktail party, but I think they already had some bad blood between them." Becca paused for a moment. "Hazel overheard Donna say something to her husband about how Phyllis Grant wouldn't be around much longer."

Detective Post looked up from his notepad and raised his eyebrows. "I will be sure to ask Hazel about it. How did she overhear?"

A blush dusted Becca's cheeks. "She was hiding under the hors d'oeuvres table."

Stifling a smile, the detective asked, "And how did she know it was Donna Sloane speaking?"

"Donna's sparkly shoes."

"Of course," Detective Post said, a note of amusement in his voice as he scrawled on his pad and then looked up. "Now, moving on. Who else?"

"That night," Becca said, "Donna Sloane told me that Mrs. Grant had tried to get Patricia Koller fired from her position at the library."

"Do you know why?" the detective asked.

Becca pressed her lips into a line. "According to Donna, Mrs. Grant didn't like the plans for how the family portrait was going to be displayed. And then there is Harvey Veleno, Lexi's boyfriend."

"Tell me about him," Detective Post said.

"Mrs. Grant didn't approve of him and was pressuring Lexi to break up with him."

The detective nodded. "Anyone else?"

"Dr. Davis," Becca said. "Mrs. Grant wanted to give her speech, and she noticed several of the guests were missing. They were in the library, playing poker, and Mrs. Grant seemed to think that Dr. Davis was the instigator." Becca shuddered. "She said the most awful things to him. She accused him of enticing her late husband into gambling, and she called him a 'degenerate' and 'pathetic.' It felt like there was history there." Becca shook her head, and then a light laugh escaped. "Oh, and she was not very nice to me either. She always called my bookstore a '*little* shop.'"

With a half-smile, Detective Post looked up from his notepad. "Did *you* murder Phyllis Grant?"

"No," Becca laughed. "But it wasn't nice of her to say that about my bookstore."

The detective resumed his serious expression. "Are you aware of anyone else who might have had an issue with Phyllis Grant?"

Becca considered for a moment. "That's everyone I'm aware of." Furrowing her eyebrows, she slowly added, "I should also probably mention Lexi. From what I can tell, she and her grandmother had a good relationship, but she was present and had access to the wine glass."

Detective Post nodded. "Do you have anything else to add?"

Becca shook her head. "No."

"Then that concludes our interview," the detective said, shutting off the recording device and placing it in his desk drawer. "You have my cell number. If you think of anything else, please let me know, Ms. Gables."

"Yes, of course," Becca said with a smile. "I'm always happy to help. And you can call me Becca." As she rose, her eyes fell on a pair of tickets in Detective Post's letter tray. "*Hello, Dolly!*," she said. "I've heard that's a great production. I'm sure you'll be glad you bought the tickets."

Detective Post grimaced. "Ha! I actually won the tickets in a charity raffle. I don't mind theater, but I'm not really a musical kind of guy. And now I have to find a date."

Suddenly, Becca drew in a sharp breath, and she clapped her hands together. "I know *just* the person to go with you. You would love my sister-in-law, Audrey."

The detective smiled. After a moment he said, "Forgive me, Ms. Gables—er—Becca, but we just met. I think that might be a bit of an overstatement."

Becca shook her head. "I don't think so, and I can prove it."

Detective Post crossed his arms and perched on the corner of his desk. "Okay, I'll bite. Let's hear it."

"First of all," Becca said, "you play the guitar—"

"How do you know that?"

"I felt the calluses on your fingers when we shook hands," Becca said. "Audrey was in a band in college!"

Detective Post raised his eyebrows.

Pointing to the trash bin beside his desk, Becca said, "I noticed the takeout bag from Victoria's. Italian food is Audrey's favorite."

"Okay," the detective said slowly, stroking his blond beard. "Anything else?"

"And I see you have a bit of windburn on your face," she said.

Detective Post moved his fingers from his beard to his cheek.

"That, in conjunction with the keychain in your desk drawer that says Harley-Davidson on it, tells me that the motorcycle in the parking lot is yours." She bounced on her toes. "Audrey *loves* riding on the back of a motorcycle."

The detective let out a low whistle. "Okay, that was impressive."

"You should stop by the bookshop and meet her," Becca continued.

"Hmm," Detective Post murmured.

Stooping to pull her phone out of her purse, Becca quickly located a photo of her auburn-haired sister-in-law. She held it out for the detective to see, and he raised his eyebrows and smiled.

"Isn't she cute?" Becca said. "She's sweet and spunky, and I just know that she'd love to accompany you to the musical. You should stop by the bookshop and meet her."

After staring at the photo for a few more moments, Detective Post looked up with a half-smile. "I just might," he said. "But right now, I need to continue with interviews." As Becca gathered her belongings, the detective added, a note of amusement in his voice, "Unless you want to conduct them for me?"

Becca glanced at him sideways, her eyes sparkling. "Funny," she said. Slinging her tote strap over her shoulder, she followed Detective Post down the hall toward John's office.

Upon arrival, Becca and the detective were greeted by a high-pitched grinding sound. Becca cast her eyes around the room and found Oliver and Hazel seated near a paper shredder, a stack of papers at their feet. Taking turns, the children fed sheets into the machine.

John looked up from his laptop, removed his reading glasses, and grinned at his niece and the detective. "Entertainment, courtesy of the accounting department's old invoices," he said, gesturing toward the children.

Detective Post smiled and turned to the sixteen-year-old, who was still engrossed in her book. "Violet, are you ready to give your statement?"

"Yes, sir," Violet said, carefully tucking a bookmark into her book and closing it with a snap. As she rose, she looked over at her mother.

Becca smiled reassuringly at her. "It's easy. Just answer his questions honestly."

As Violet followed Detective Post down the hallway, Becca stepped toward John's desk. Plunking her tumbler on the desktop and shedding her totes, she slid into the chair opposite her uncle.

"How did the interview go?" he asked, closing his laptop.

"It went just fine," Becca said. "I like Detective Post."

"He'll do a good job," the chief agreed with a nod.

Reaching into one of her bags, Becca extracted a piece of paper and handed it to John. "This is the same suspect list I gave to the detective," she said. "It's everyone who was at the party, including the staff. Those listed in red are the ones who I know had access to the red wine glass, and I starred the top suspects."

John put on his reading glasses, and a small smile played on his lips. He nodded slowly as he scanned the list. Suddenly, he pinched the bridge of his nose between his thumb and forefinger. "Ugh," he groaned. "Andrew Curtis!"

Becca leaned forward. "Mrs. Grant's lawyer? What about him?"

With a huff, the chief laid the paper on his desk. "For starters, he was present the night of the murder, and he left for Hawaii the very next day."

"What?" Becca said, blinking. "Do I need to add another star to my list?"

A half-smile softened Uncle John's expression. "Now, before you get too excited, we've already looked into it. This is an annual vacation that Curtis takes, and there doesn't appear to be anything suspicious about it. *However*," he added, a tinge of irritation in his voice, "we still need to interview him as soon as possible. Detective Post has been trying to coordinate with the authorities in Hawaii, and it's been a bureaucratic nightmare."

"That sounds awful," Becca sympathized.

"Not to mention," John added, taking off his reading glasses again, "we have been unable to locate Phyllis Grant's will. We contacted Curtis's office, but that bumbling lawyer has seemed to misplace it. I don't even know how that's *possible* in this day and age."

"Oh!" Becca said, gripping the edge of the desktop with her fingertips. "I think I know where it is!"

John raised an eyebrow. "You do?"

"Do you remember when we were at the Paper Palace the morning after Mrs. Grant passed?" Becca's eyes were wide with excitement.

"Yes," John said slowly.

"I was looking around her room—"

Uncle John cleared his throat.

Becca blushed, and she resumed, "And I saw it on her desk buried among a stack of papers. It was a black binder labeled *Estate Planning Documents – Prepared by Attorney Andrew P. Curtis.*"

"You even remembered his middle initial? Nice detail," John said, a hint of pride in his voice. He laid the suspect list in his letter tray. "I appreciate the tip, Becca. We will look into it."

Folding her hands in her lap, Becca smiled.

John glanced at his desk clock and then at his niece. "I've got a meeting now, but I'll be back in a little while. Just keep on with the interviews and fingerprints." He grabbed a legal pad and pen and rose from his leather office chair. Smiling as he passed Oliver and Hazel, he said, "Keep up the good work."

When the children had completed their stack of shredding, they rifled through Becca's tote in search of snacks. Not only were the children rewarded with bags of sliced apples, but they also whooped in delight to find a deck of cards. Immediately, they started a game of gin rummy. Swapping out players as Detective Post called Oliver and then Hazel, the Gables passed the time. Becca *tried* to focus on the card game, but she found her gaze continuing to wander toward the suspect list at the top of Uncle John's letter tray. Finally deciding that the effort to avoid it was futile, she removed the paper from the tray, added notes to the margins, and then returned it. After the interviews were complete, a technician called the entire group back for fingerprinting.

It wasn't long before Becca and the children headed back toward Uncle John's office. John, who had returned from his meeting, was on the phone, absentmindedly fidgeting with Oliver's Rubik's cube in his free hand.

With a mischievous grin, Oliver, who hadn't wiped off the pigment yet, bent and wiggled his inky fingers at his sisters. Violet and Hazel hopped away and squealed.

John turned sharply toward them and pointed to the phone. Noticing who the culprit was, he narrowed his eyes at Oliver and then pointed at the young man. "Behave," he mouthed.

As John turned toward the window, Becca noticed that the corner of his mouth was slightly raised. "Oliver," she said, "you know better."

Violet shook her head. "The technician scolded him for that too." She looked at her brother. "Forget about art museum jail. You almost ended up in *real* jail this time."

Oliver cracked a lopsided grin.

When John completed his phone call, Becca stepped toward his desk. "Will you join us for lunch, Uncle John? I've got chicken soup in the slow cooker at home."

The chief shook his head and rose from his chair. "I'd love to, but I've got a press conference this afternoon to discuss the Grant homicide."

Becca nodded. She pointed to the marked-up suspect list that rested at the top of John's letter tray. "I added some notes to that," she said. "What do you think about—"

"Listen, Bec," John said, smiling warmly. "I know you love puzzles." His gaze fell to the Rubik's cube still in his hand, and he placed it in his niece's palm. "But you need to leave the investigating to us." He glanced over at his great-nieces and nephew, who were waiting by the door. "You have more important things to do."

Becca pressed her lips into a smile and slowly set the puzzle cube on his desk. Lovingly, she turned her gaze toward the children. "You're right," she said. "I know you'll handle it."

"Attagirl," John said, wrapping an arm around her shoulders. "You ready?"

Grabbing her tumbler and bags, Becca followed her uncle toward the office door. John took both totes from her and switched off the light on his way out. The group headed down the hall.

As they passed Detective Post's office, Becca poked her head in the doorway. The detective was arranging papers.

"Seriously!" she said with a broad smile. "You should stop by the book-shop to meet Audrey."

Detective Post looked up, and a grin spread across his face as he shook his head. "Good afternoon, Ms. Gables. I'm sure I'll see you soon... at the bookshop."

"Remember, it's Becca!" she called, already disappearing down the hall.

With quick steps, she hurried to catch up with Uncle John and the children. She glanced down at Oliver. "Do you have your Rubik's cube?"

Oliver froze, pivoted, and sprinted back to Uncle John's office.

# Chapter 12

# Law and Justice

"Becca Gables, just *what* are you doing?" Audrey plunked her hands on her waist and stared up at her sister-in-law, who stood at the top of a stepladder.

A shaft of late-afternoon gold fell upon Becca. She was dressed in a Christmas plaid button-up top and black jeans under her Tales & Tails signature teal apron. Her arms were deeply buried in the bristly pine needles of the shop's tallest Christmas tree under which both cats, Licorice and Toffee, were curled up like furry little presents. The tree sparkled magnificently by the fireplace.

"I just thought it could use a few more lights," Becca said, weaving a strand of white twinkle lights through a line of branches.

Audrey scoffed. "You know, at a certain point, more is just more."

Becca glanced over her shoulder and caught her sister-in-law's half-smile. "That's right! And with Christmas lights, more is always better!"

Shaking her head, Audrey laughed and then tilted her heart-shaped face up toward Becca. "It's slow right now, so I thought I'd do a little accounting. Do you have the receipt for this morning's bakery?"

"Hmm," Becca murmured. She held a coil of lights in one hand and rose onto her tiptoes as she continued to artfully weave the lights between the branches. "I think it's in my apron pocket. You can just grab it."

With a plump freckled hand, Audrey removed a folded piece of paper. She opened it, scanned it, and raised an eyebrow. "Funny looking receipt," Audrey said, holding up the paper, which was titled *Suspects* in her sister-in-law's neat script. "I thought your uncle John didn't want you investigating the Grant case."

"Hey!" Becca said, and the loop of lights dropped from her hand. Butterscotch, who had been dozing by the fire, raised her head in alarm. Becca hesitated for a moment and then quickly descended the stepladder. "It—it's just something interesting to think about," she sputtered, smoothing her apron. "A puzzle."

"Sure, it is," Audrey replied, her brown eyes sparkling.

With a huff, Becca snatched the paper from her sister-in-law's grasp. "I'll take *that,* thank you very much." After safely tucking away the list, she removed the receipt from her other pocket and handed it over.

"Thank *you* very much," Audrey returned.

As Butterscotch resumed her state of repose, the bell at the front door tinkled, and the two women turned their eyes to the entrance. Donna Sloane, dressed in a camel-colored wool coat with a fluffy fur collar, stepped into the shop.

"And here comes someone on your suspect list," Audrey noted quietly, her lips cracking into a half-smile. "Oh, didn't she have a *star* by her name?"

Becca shot her sister-in-law a warning look. "Be nice!" she whispered.

Head held high, Donna strode across the shop and laid her briefcase on the long gleaming table that was favored by the ladies of the CRIS. After tucking her gloves into her pockets, she shrugged out of her coat and arranged it across the back of the chair at the head of the table—Phyllis's former seat.

"Hello, Donna!" Becca said brightly. "What brings you here this afternoon?"

Donna laid her hands on top of the chair's back and gave a lipstick-lined grin. "I'm leading the meeting for the Crystal Run Improvement Society," she said, drawing out the group's full name.

Audrey tipped her head. "Oh! Are you not meeting Tuesday mornings anymore?"

"Now that I am president," Donna said, raising her eyebrows slightly, "the officers and I have found that it's more convenient to meet on Wednesday afternoons."

"It's nice that you could find a time that works for all of you," Becca said. She looked at Audrey, who gestured toward the bakery receipt. At Becca's slight nod, her sister-in-law retreated toward the kitchen, her auburn braid swinging behind her.

Becca looked at Donna and smiled. "May I get you anything?"

"Coffee, please," the woman said and then glanced at her wristwatch. "Decaf."

When Becca returned with the steaming mug, she found that the other two members of the CRIS had arrived, mousy Evelyn Hansen and apple-shaped Marjorie.

Evelyn, whose eyes were ringed red from crying, slapped a copy of *The Crystal Run Reporter* onto the table. "Murder!"

At the small woman's cry, Becca flinched, and a bit of coffee sloshed onto the saucer. She glanced at the familiar headline of the newspaper splayed out on the table: "Peril at the Paper Palace: Phyllis Grant's Death Deemed Homicide."

"Who would *murder* our Phyllis?" Evelyn choked. With a sob, she slumped in her chair.

Marjorie's already ruddy cheeks reddened even more deeply. She spun the newspaper around to face her and then pushed it away again. "*I* refuse to be a part of any scandal. I can't believe that that detective insisted on interviewing *us*—"

"Phyllis's closest friends!" Evelyn cried.

Marjorie tapped the newspaper with a short stout forefinger. "It's just shocking that something like this would happen in our little town." A fiery expression in her eyes, Marjorie looked toward the head of the table. Donna's jaw was clenched, and she was staring fixedly at the tiny puddle of coffee on her saucer.

"Evelyn, Marjorie," Becca said, taking advantage of the lull in the conversation, "may I bring you anything?"

Evelyn heaved a deep sigh. "I'll have black tea with lemon. It was Phyllis's favorite."

"Green tea for me," Marjorie said.

Becca nodded. "I'll get that right away." Then she looked at Donna, who was still uncharacteristically quiet and gazing at the spilled coffee. "I'm sorry about that. May I get you a new one?"

The woman unclenched her jaw and forced her lips into a smile. "No, darling, it's fine." Donna then turned to the other ladies at her table and said firmly, "Now, let's put all of this away." She gestured toward the newspaper and waited.

Wide-eyed, Evelyn gave a little gasp and stared at Donna for a few moments before sulkily tucking the paper into her bag.

"We have important work to do," Donna continued. "Our first order of business: Should the citizens of Crystal Run be allowed to toss coins into the fountain at Riverside Park?"

By the time the meeting concluded, the winter sun had almost set. Easing into her coat and fluffing her fur collar, Donna eyed the vacant chairs where Evelyn and Marjorie had been, picked up her briefcase, and turned toward Becca, who was waiting to wipe the table. "Becca, darling," she said, "we are still waiting on your response concerning our invitation to interview for the open position with the Crystal Run Improvement Society."

Passing the damp cloth from one hand to the other, Becca smiled and said, "Oh, yes, thank you so much for asking, Donna. I will let you know soon."

"Please do!" the woman said curtly and turned on her heel.

As Becca wiped the table, she heard a low rumble coming from outside the bookshop. Her eyes widened, and she grinned at Audrey, who was oblivious to her as she frowned at her laptop screen, a pile of receipts next to her. Expectantly, Becca turned her gaze to the bookshop entrance, and she was soon rewarded by the sight of Detective Post's stocky silhouette in the doorway. Abandoning her cloth on the table, Becca clapped and beamed and hurried toward the entrance.

Already on her way out, Donna glided past him. "Good afternoon, Detective," she said coolly.

"Good afternoon, Mrs. Sloane," he returned with a nod.

After a few steps, Donna whirled around. "Oh! Detective Post!"

He turned to face her.

Donna flashed the detective her lipstick-lined smile. "I am just wondering if you have any leads in the case... If you have any idea of who—" She flicked her eyes toward the stained-glass windows and shifted her briefcase from one hand to the other. "If you're finding evidence that points to anyone in particular?"

Detective Post pressed his lips into a straight line. "I can assure you that the investigation is continuing," he said, "and we will get to the bottom of who killed Phyllis Grant."

Donna blinked and stared at the detective for a long moment before her saccharine smile spread across her face again. "I'm so glad to hear that, Detective," she said. "Please let me know if there's any way I can help." With that, she strode toward the exit.

The detective's bushy blond eyebrows furrowed as he stared after the departing woman.

"Detective Post, you *came*!"

Becca's bubbly voice shook the man from his thoughts, and he turned to her and smiled warmly. "I'm off duty. You can call me Chris."

"All right, Chris..." Becca said, trying it out. Then she grinned. "I'm so glad you're here!" She lowered her voice. "I am *sure* that you and Audrey are going to hit it off."

Detective Post's light-blue eyes sparkled. "Well, let's just start with coffee."

Becca led the detective to the confectionery counter beyond which Audrey continued to squint at her laptop screen.

"Hey, Audrey!" Becca called. "Would you please take this customer's order?"

Audrey drummed her fingers on the table. "Could you do it? I can't get this to balance—"

Becca winked at Detective Post. "No, I really think *you* should."

Finally, Audrey glanced up toward Becca, and then her eyes moved to the detective, who, wearing a lined black leather jacket, was an image of solidity and strength. "Actually..." Audrey said, "I think that it would be good for me to take a break." She rose and stepped toward the counter. Noticing the sparkle in the man's eyes, her very round cheeks bloomed pink.

"Audrey, this is Detective Christopher Post," Becca said. "He is investigating the Grant case. Detective Post—" She tucked a strand of blonde hair behind her ear. "Um, *Chris*, this is my sister-in-law, Audrey Gables."

"It's very nice to meet you, Audrey," Detective Post said, extending his meaty hand.

"Likewise," she said, beaming as she accepted the handshake.

"Audrey," Becca continued, "you and Chris actually have a lot in common."

The detective chuckled and looked at Audrey. "Oh, yes, your sister-in-law is quite the sleuth. After spending a few minutes in my office, I felt like *she* was the one investigating *me.*"

"That sounds about right," Audrey said. "What did she find out?"

Detective Post gestured toward Becca. "Well?" he said.

"He plays the guitar..." Becca began.

Audrey looked at Detective Post and raised an eyebrow.

"He likes Italian food, which is your favorite," Becca continued. "*And* he drives a motorcycle."

Audrey nodded. "Very cool," she said to the detective. She then glanced sideways at Becca, who pretended not to notice. The rosy hue returning to her cheeks, Audrey cleared her throat and smiled at Detective Post. "What can I get for you today?"

After ordering an espresso, the detective settled into a squashy leather chair by the fire and began to scroll on his phone.

In the kitchen, Becca hopped up onto the counter near Audrey. "*Well*, what do you think?" she whispered, her emerald eyes sparkling.

Audrey positioned a shot glass under the espresso machine. "I think you're meddlesome." A smile played on her lips.

"I'll heat the milk," Becca said, sliding down from the counter. With a glance at her wristwatch, she added, "We're getting close to closing time. Violet and Hazel have already come down."

When the espresso was finished, Audrey picked up the teal-colored mug on its saucer and stepped carefully toward the fireplace to deliver it. She smiled at Violet, who was seated at one of the tables, braiding Hazel's hair, and maneuvered around the now roaming golden cat, Toffee.

"Here, kitty-kitty!" Hazel called.

Violet gently tugged her sister's braid. "Hold still, Hazel, I'm almost done."

Sitting ramrod straight as Violet secured the hair tie, Hazel watched as Toffee slunk toward the detective. Tilting his head, the cat proceeded to rub against Detective Post's ankles.

"Whoa!" The burly detective jumped out of the chair and quickly stepped to the side as several customers looked up to see what the commotion was about.

Audrey erupted in laughter, and she steadied the mug with her free hand.

"What?" Detective Post demanded, staring at the cat, who stood blinking at him.

"I'm sorry," Audrey said, still chuckling heartily. "It's just so funny! A big tough detective being afraid of an itty-bitty kitty."

The detective straightened. "I'm not afraid," he said. "I just don't like them. And what happened to its tail?"

Hopping out of her chair, Hazel scooped up the cat in her arms. "He's a Manx," the girl explained sweetly. "Daddy always liked them because they're really friendly, kind of like dogs."

"But they have no tails at all or only stubs for tails," Violet added.

Audrey was still snickering as she handed Detective Post his coffee. She removed her eyeglasses and swiped at her eyes, and the detective lifted the mug to his lips.

Hazel looked at her. "It's kind of like how you're afraid of baby bunnies, Aunt Audrey," she said brightly.

"*Bunnies?*" Detective Post spluttered into his coffee.

Audrey's jaw dropped, and she shot Hazel a look of betrayal.

The detective's eyes sparkled. "What's this about being afraid of bunnies?"

"They're actually terrifying," Audrey said, blushing deeply. "Last spring, I was watering the herbs in my herb pot, and all of a sudden, I heard squeaking. So, I lifted the leaves of my basil plant, and there at the base was a litter of tiny bunnies jumping around. I just about *died*." Although her tone was serious, she could not suppress her smile.

Detective Post threw back his head and guffawed. "Oh, yes, there's nothing more terrifying than tiny adorable bunnies."

"They had no business being there!" Audrey said defensively, her honey-colored eyes sparkling.

Still chuckling, the detective smiled at Audrey as he removed his leather jacket and tossed it on the arm of the chair. He rolled up a sleeve of his dress shirt, revealing a tattoo with the words "lex et iustitia" running down his forearm.

Violet tilted her head as she read the words. "Is the word "veritas" on your other arm?" she asked quietly.

Detective Post's eyes widened. "Do you know what this means?" he asked, pointing to the tattoo.

With a crisp nod, Violet said, "It's Latin. It means 'law and justice.'" She watched as the detective rolled up the other sleeve, revealing a bare arm. "That's why I was wondering about 'veritas'—truth. I think it would go well."

The detective raised his eyebrows. "I agree. If I ever feel the need to get another one, that will definitely be in the running."

"Violet! Hazel!"

The girls turned to see their mother waving them over from behind the confectionery counter. They smiled politely at the detective and hurried toward her, Hazel still cradling the golden-brown cat in her arms.

"It looks like you're safe from the kitty for now," Audrey quipped.

"Just so long as there aren't any *bunnies* around," Detective Post returned with a gleam in his eye.

While Violet and Hazel occupied themselves in the kitchen, Becca approached the seating area with a damp rag. She stooped to scratch Butterscotch behind the ears and then moved to wipe a table behind Detective Post.

The detective sipped his espresso. "This is good," he said, tilting the mug slightly toward Audrey. "Hey," he said, "so I want to ask you... I won two tickets to see *Hello, Dolly!* on Friday night, and I'm wondering if you might be interested in going with me."

Becca instantly straightened and grinned at Audrey. She nodded excitedly and gave a double thumbs-up.

Audrey stifled a smile and pretended not to notice. "Oh, I've been wanting to see that!" she said. "I'd love to go with you. What time?"

Becca silently hopped up and down and pretended to clap. A laugh escaped Audrey's lips, and Detective Post glanced over his shoulder. With a blush, Becca quickly bent to resume wiping the table.

The detective shook his head and grinned. "The show starts at 7:00," he resumed, "so we could grab an early dinner at Victoria's first if that works for you. Could I pick you up at 5:00?"

Audrey's lips curved into a half-smile. "As long as you pick me up in an enclosed vehicle. I do love a motorcycle, but it is *winter*, you know." She raised an eyebrow.

Detective Post grinned. "Deal," he said. "Friday, then."

After exchanging phone numbers, the detective drained his espresso, and Audrey escorted him out, standing at the doorway, chatting with him for several minutes. Glancing at her wristwatch, she scanned the bookshop to make sure it was empty, flipped the sign to *Closed,* and bolted the front door. She turned around to find Becca waiting for her with a giant smile plastered across her face. Becca linked arms with her sister-in-law, and the two walked back toward the seating area.

"I'm going to add matchmaker to my resumé," Becca said gleefully.

Audrey laughed. "As long as you don't say 'subtle matchmaker,' I think that's fair."

As the two women approached the tables, they were met by Hazel and Violet, who each cradled a mug in their hands.

"I created a new recipe!" Hazel said, eyes sparkling. "It's a Butterscotch Coffee. Will you test it out for me?"

Becca loosened her arm from Audrey's and carefully accepted the mug from her daughter. "We would love to!" She gazed down at the creamy light-gold liquid and then held it to her nose. "It smells wonderful, Hazel."

Violet handed the second mug to Audrey.

As the warmth of the mug radiated into her hands, Becca said, "You have Midweek and youth group at church tonight, girls. Make sure you have something to eat. We have leftovers, but you probably want to hurry up and claim some before Oliver clears out the fridge."

With wide eyes, the girls exchanged looks and scurried to the stairs that led to the Gables' apartment.

Settling into chairs at a small table by the fire, Becca and Audrey sipped their coffee. Butterscotch ambled over from her place by the fire and, after a few turns, curled up again at Becca's feet.

Audrey lowered the mug slightly. "Okay, this is *really* good. We need to add this to our menu."

Becca licked the cream from her lips. "I agree," she said. "Plus, I love the name." She glanced down at the dog, who was gazing up at her warmly, and then back at her sister-in-law. "Isn't Chris great?"

"You do know my type. I'll give you that," Audrey conceded with a smile.

"I know," Becca said. "You're going to have the *best* time on Friday. The two of you have a lot of chemistry. I think that baby bunny story was the clincher."

Audrey blushed. "Yes, yes. Can we talk about something else now?" She sipped the coffee and stared thoughtfully into the snapping fire. "What did Donna say to you right before she left?"

Becca smiled at her sister-in-law over the rim of her mug. "You're going to love this. I was invited to interview for the open position in the CRIS."

"Really? You totally should!" Audrey said, her eyes wide with excitement.

Wrinkling her nose, Becca said, "You're joking, right? This is coming from the woman who calls them the Crystal Run *Insufferable Snobs*."

"Well, yes," Audrey began, "that was back when they didn't want us—I mean, *you*." She plunked down her mug and gripped the edge of the table. "Look, they *are* horrible, but they know *everyone*. Just think about the networking you could do! This could be what we need to get help with the bottom line and get our name out there and more business."

Tipping her chair back, Becca slowly shook her head. "I don't know..."

"This could be a real opportunity for us," Audrey insisted. "It's the smart thing to do."

Becca narrowed her eyes. "You really think so?"

"I do. And maybe if you join their group, they might become a little less insufferable," Audrey said, offering her most persuasive smile.

With a sigh, Becca conceded. "I'll call Donna tomorrow to schedule the interview."

"Awesome!" Audrey said brightly. "Oh, and a happy little bonus for you." Her eyes flicked to Becca's apron pocket. "That puzzle you're working on. When you are being interviewed by the CRIS, you will get to talk to Donna... probably several times."

Becca straightened in her chair, a smile spreading across her face and her eyes sparkling.

Audrey grinned. "Okay, so, I have to ask... Why the star by Donna's name on your suspect list?"

Becca took another sip of coffee and searched her sister-in-law's countenance for signs of teasing. Deciding that she was being serious, Becca said, "Well, Donna and Phyllis clearly had animosity between them—"

"Case in point, the epic granny showdown when you were at the art institute," Audrey added. "And that was public. Who knows what went on just between the two of them?"

"Right," Becca said. "Donna had plenty of access to the wine glass the night of Phyllis's death, and—" She paused and glanced around to make sure no one was within earshot. "When Hazel was under the table at the party, she heard Donna say that Phyllis wouldn't be around much longer."

Audrey blinked. "What? Does Chris know that?"

"Oh, yes," Becca said. "Hazel told him when she gave her statement the other day."

"Wow," Audrey said, nodding slowly. "Donna did seem pretty comfortable sitting in Phyllis's old place at the head of the table."

"Mm-hmm," Becca agreed, swirling the last of her coffee. "I also thought it was curious how she had no interest in the newspaper article about Mrs. Grant, but she made a point of asking Detective Post"—she paused and cleared her throat—"*Chris* if he had any leads."

With a glance at the mantel clock, Audrey finished her coffee and began to rise. "Well, that certainly explains the star by Donna's name." She pushed in her chair. "Maybe you'd better give her another one for good measure."

Becca's lips curved into a small smile, and deep in thought, she stared at the dazzling Christmas tree. Slowly, she tilted her head to the side and narrowed her eyes. "Hmmm..." she murmured. "I think that branch needs more lights."

# Chapter 13

# Not-So-Secret Santa

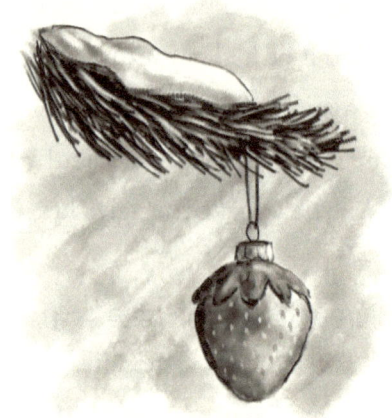

"Mom, aren't we too old for this?" Oliver complained, rubbing the sleep from his eyes.

Becca, who was seated at the kitchen table with a day planner in front of her, glanced up at her son. He was wearing a tattered royal-blue Crystal Run Homeschoolers t-shirt and athletic shorts, and his hair was fanned up on one side. In his hand was a folded pair of Christmas pajamas and a shiny gold ticket.

"Good morning!" his mother said brightly. "And no, you're never too old for the Minivan Express!"

At that moment, Hazel flew out of her bedroom, clutching a pair of pajamas that matched her brother's and her own golden ticket.

"Watch it!" Oliver warned as she nearly bowled him over.

Hazel threw her arms around Becca's neck. "Tonight? Tonight!" she exclaimed.

Becca laughed as she squeezed Hazel in return and unwound her arms from her neck. "Yes, tonight," she confirmed. "Aunt Audrey is going to cover the shop for us, and we're heading out at 5:00 sharp."

"Woo-hoo!" Hazel whooped. Her vanilla-blonde hair hung down her back in a braid, but some wisps had escaped around her face, giving her a wild look. With another squeal, she ran back to the bedroom she shared with Violet.

Swiping a hand across his eyes, Oliver said sleepily, "I'm going back to bed."

Becca stepped over Butterscotch, who had been resting by her feet, and followed Oliver toward the bedrooms. As the young man closed his door with a firm thud, Becca wrapped her fingers around the doorframe of the girls' room and peeked inside. Hazel was jumping on her sister's bed, the mattress squeaking in protest with each bounce. Violet groaned, curled up into a protective ball, and threw the covers over her head.

"Tonight, Violet!" Hazel exclaimed. "The Minivan Express rides tonight!"

That evening, Becca stood just inside the door of the Gables' apartment where the smell of buttered popcorn and warm cocoa permeated the air. Dressed in a pair of plaid flannel pajamas that matched the children's, she glanced at her wristwatch and shrugged. She cupped her hands around her mouth and called, "All aboard the Minivan Express!"

Aquamarine eyes sparkling, Hazel was the first to appear. Enthusiastically, she handed her mother her ticket.

"Welcome!" Becca greeted. "This ticket entitles you to one bag of popcorn, one cup of hot chocolate—"

"Peppermint hot chocolate!" Hazel interjected.

Her mother smiled. "*Peppermint* hot chocolate made by one of the finest baristas in town—"

The girl blushed at this.

"—and a ride on the Minivan Express to see the light displays," Becca finished. She pocketed Hazel's ticket and gestured toward the paper bags of popcorn and disposable cups of cocoa lined up on the kitchen counter.

As Hazel grabbed her snacks, Violet appeared to turn in her own ticket. Glancing at her phone, Violet smiled and said, "I see that the Minivan Express is running a little late tonight."

"The magic of the Minivan Express cannot be bound by the limits of time!" Becca replied.

Violet chuckled. "I already loaded the food pantry items into the van," she said. "And I also put all of our winter coats in the trunk."

"Thank you, Vi," Becca said warmly. "You are such a blessing to me."

Oliver was the last to arrive. He shuffled toward his mother, who held out her hand to collect his ticket.

"*Mom,*" Oliver whined.

Becca shook her head. "No ticket, no snacks," she said firmly.

Heaving an exasperated sigh, Oliver turned to retrieve the ticket from his bedroom.

When all the tickets had been exchanged for treats, Becca smiled at the children. "Shall we be off?"

"What about Butterscotch?" Hazel asked, glancing around the entranceway. "Can she come too?"

"Oh, of course!" Becca replied. "Butterscotch!"

Within a few moments, the golden retriever came loping toward them. She was wearing a bandana that matched the Gables' flannel pajamas, and even Oliver couldn't help but grin.

Becca studied the dog for a moment. "I know what's missing," she said. Turning around and reaching into a high cupboard, she pulled out an antler headband, which she gently placed on Butterscotch's head. "There," she said, stepping back to admire her work.

As the Gables' light-blue minivan pulled into the entrance of Riverside Park, Becca eased on the brakes and waited in the line of vehicles. Violet spied a sign posted to the side of the driveway instructing passengers to tune their radios to 91.9 FM. She adjusted the dial on the minivan's stereo, and in no time, Burl Ive's smooth, merry voice was inviting the Gables to "have a holly jolly Christmas." After a few minutes, it was Becca's turn to pull up to the small white shack, which was lavishly decorated in red, green, and gold. She rolled down the window, paid their admission, and handed over their food pantry donation.

Becca swiveled around to face Oliver and Hazel. "Ready?"

"Let's go!" Hazel bounced in her seat, knocking Butterscotch's antlers askew.

Switching off the minivan's headlights, Becca slowly drove forward, and they passed under an arch with the words "Crystal Run Celebration of Lights" spelled out in giant lit letters. Becca held her breath as she took in the view. On either side of the driveway, deciduous trees, whose leaves had dropped long ago, glittered with spirals of lights. Beyond, she saw a row of spotlit signs displaying gifts of "The Twelve Days of Christmas." Becca turned down the radio and issued a challenge to see if the children could remember which gifts were given on each day. (It was looking a little uncertain until Violet rescued them by recalling "eleven pipers piping.")

"Butterscotch, look!" Hazel said, pointing out the window.

Obediently, the golden retriever pressed her nose against the window as the Gables' minivan approached another arch. On one side, the outline of a reindeer flashed, its front legs tucked under, and its back legs extended. The outline disappeared, and another one appeared right in front of it along the line of the curve. The progressional flashes continued all along the arch, giving the effect that the reindeer was leaping over their vehicle.

"Do you remember?" Violet began, her eyes following the bounding deer. "This is where Dad would always do his reindeer impression. It was awful." She smiled.

Becca laughed. "*So* bad."

"What are you talking about?" Oliver chimed in from the back. "Dad's reindeer impression was the best!" Sitting up tall and drawing his shoulders back, the young man briskly shook his head back and forth as he made a noise that sounded very much like a cross between a pig snorting and a dog scarfing its dinner. His mother and sisters erupted in laughter.

"It was so funny when Daddy did it!" Hazel exclaimed. "He'd laugh so hard that his face got all red, just like Rudolph's nose!"

The Gables burst into a second round of laughter. Eyes still sparkling, Becca gazed out the window at the image of the reindeer that was there for a moment and then gone the next. She glanced over at Violet. Noticing the glistening of her daughter's eyes, she reached over and squeezed her hand. As their eyes met, Becca's lips curved into a small smile, which Violet returned as she wiped away a tear from the corner of her eye.

"Hey!" Oliver called from the backseat. "Is there any more popcorn up there?"

About three-quarters of the way through the Celebration of Lights, the light-blue minivan approached "The North Pole," which was a cluster of festively decorated shops and stands. At its center was "Santa's Workshop" where they could visit Santa and get their photo taken. Becca pulled into a parking spot.

"Oh no, absolutely not," Oliver protested.

Becca smiled and shook her head. "Sorry, this is part of it. You don't have to talk to Santa, other than being polite to him. One good photo is all I need."

With a frown, Oliver unbuckled his seatbelt and exited the vehicle along with his mother and siblings.

"Sorry, Butterscotch," Hazel said as she patted the dog's back. "You have to wait here for a little while." She held out a piece of popcorn, which the dog happily snatched with her soft pink tongue.

"We should get in line for Santa right away," Violet said. "It's always long."

Becca nodded, and the group made a beeline for Santa's Workshop. As they passed by a food stand, the warm vanilla smell of candied almonds filled their nostrils. The Gables took their place at the end of the line, which was thankfully just inside the door of the building. With glittering white snowflakes dangling from the ceiling and a myriad of dazzling evergreens, the workshop was an explosion of Christmas.

Hazel rested a hand on one of the three-foot-high candy canes that marked out the boundaries of the line and rose onto her tiptoes. "I see him!" she exclaimed. "I see Santa!"

Becca squinted across the room and saw a man dressed as Santa Claus seated in a large wooden chair. "We've got a while to wait," she said. She looked at Oliver and braced herself for an objection, but instead, the young man grinned and held up a fantasy book.

"I came prepared," he said.

"Oh no, where's Santa going?" Hazel asked.

Returning her gaze to where Santa had been, Becca observed that the throne-like wooden chair was now empty. A woman dressed as an elf was working her way along the line, and Becca strained her ears to hear what she was saying.

"Santa is taking a fifteen-minute break to feed the reindeer!" the woman said cheerfully. "He'll be back soon!"

Violet glanced at Oliver, who was already buried in his book, and frowned. "I wish *I* had thought to bring something for the wait," she said. She looked at her mother. "Would it be all right if I looked at the shops?"

Glancing at her watch and then at the line stretching in front of them, Becca said, "Oh, yes, you have plenty of time."

"Would you like to come too?" Violet asked, placing her hand on Hazel's shoulder.

Resolutely, Hazel shook her head. "Oh, no," she said. "What if we'd take too long and miss Santa? I'm not taking any chances."

Violet smiled and shrugged as her mother handed her a few dollars.

"Would you bring us back some candied almonds?" Becca asked.

"Yes, ma'am," Violet said, pocketing the bills.

She slipped through the heavy door and out into the bright, cheerful cold. As Violet made her way to the first shop, the snow-crusted ground squeaked beneath her feet. Looking up as she entered, Violet noticed that the entire ceiling was lined with gold tinsel garland. Carefully maneuvering through the store and trying not to elbow the other shoppers, she admired the tastefully arranged Christmas decor and purchased an ornament for Hazel that looked like a real strawberry.

With a glance at her watch, Violet approached the candied almond stand and took her place in line. Hugging herself as she waited, she looked longingly across the parking lot at their minivan, where her winter coat was locked safely away inside the trunk. When her turn finally arrived, she smiled up at the cashier. "One cone of candied almonds, please," she said to the man. As she fumbled for the bills her mother had given her, a strong gust snatched one of them from her frigid fingers and deposited it on the snow a few feet away. Apologetically, she smiled at the cashier. "One second," she said. Violet stooped to pick up the bill, and another breeze carried it farther away. "Goodness," she muttered. "I'll be right there!" she called to the cashier, who was drumming his fingers on the countertop. She chased the wayward bill around the back corner of the stand and finally stomped on it with her white sneaker. "Gotcha!" she said triumphantly, crouching to pick it up. As she straightened, the sound of angry voices filled her ears. She looked up to see a man she did not recognize along with Dr. Davis, who was dressed as Santa Claus. Normally a svelte man, the doctor's stomach area of his costume had obviously been stuffed. A white beard, which was significantly fluffier and longer than his own, was pulled down under Dr. Davis's chin.

"Let me remind you that the contract *you* signed said that you would not be paid until *after* Christmas." It was the man she didn't recognize.

"But I need the money *now*," Dr. Davis boomed, stamping a booted foot. "I can't wait until after Christmas. And let *me* remind *you* how many unhappy children there will be tonight if Santa Claus has to close his workshop early."

Trying to back away quietly, Violet was betrayed by the snow, which crunched noisily under her feet. At the sound, Dr. Davis turned and looked at her. The two of them locked eyes, and the doctor quickly pulled the beard back over his face. Violet spun around and made a hasty retreat to the candied almond stand where the cashier had given up on her and moved on to the next customer. She sighed and headed to the back of the line. Her eyes moved to the corner of the stand, and she fidgeted with the buckle of her purse.

A cone of warm almonds in her hand, Violet joined her family in the Santa line, which was significantly shorter than when she left.

"How was your walk?" Becca asked, plucking a sugared almond from the top of the cone and popping it into her mouth.

"It was okay," Violet said, watching as Dr. Davis resumed his place in the large wooden chair. "I'll tell you more later."

Becca raised an eyebrow. "Sure," she said. "Is everything all right?"

Violet nodded, and her mother pressed her lips into a straight line.

Tugging at Violet's sleeve, Hazel pulled her sister down and placed her lips next to Violet's ear. "That's actually Dr. Davis," she whispered, pointing.

"Yes, I know," Violet said quietly.

Before long, the woman dressed as an elf ushered the family forward. Hazel, the only one who wanted to talk to "Santa," hurried forward and perched on Dr. Davis's knee.

"Hello, Hazel Gables!" Dr. Davis said merrily. "Have you been a good girl this year?"

"Well, I haven't been *perfectly* good," Hazel said sweetly. "You know, 'for all have sinned and fall short of the glory of God' and all."

Dr. Davis glanced up at Becca, who was pressing her fingers against her mouth to cover her smile, and then he turned back to the girl with a twinkle in his eye.

"I'm sure that you did your very best," Dr. Davis assured her. "What is it that you'd like to find under your Christmas tree this year?"

Cupping her hand around the doctor's ear, Hazel whispered, "I know that you're actually Dr. Davis, but don't worry! I won't say anything. I don't want to spoil it for the rest of the kids." The doctor flicked his eyes toward Violet, who looked down at her sneakered feet. Then he resumed his gaze at Hazel and smiled warmly at her. "Thank you," he said. "Now, what is on your Christmas list?"

"I would like a pink strawberry Squishmallow, please," she said, flashing her prettiest smile. "The big kind."

After receiving a wink from Becca, Dr. Davis assured Hazel that there was a very good chance that she would find a big pink strawberry Squishmallow under her Christmas tree.

"All right, Vi, Oliver," Becca said, taking the book out of Oliver's hands. "Gather around Santa so I can get your picture!"

As Becca snapped away, the woman dressed as an elf approached her. "Oh, you're in your Christmas jammies too! Would you like a photo with you in it?"

With a grin, Becca handed the woman her phone and hurried over to stand next to Oliver.

Photos taken and candy canes in hand, the Gables trooped back to the light-blue minivan where Butterscotch greeted them, her pink tongue lolling out of her mouth. Becca turned on the ignition, and they slowly made their way down the rest of the long winding drive. The final display was a life-sized nativity. Becca pulled into a parking space near it and turned off the engine. As the family gazed upon the holy scene, Becca began to sing, "Silent night, holy night..." First Hazel, then Oliver, and finally Violet joined until the minivan was filled with the lovely sound of their acapella hymn.

As Becca drove home, she glanced over at Violet. "You're awfully quiet," she said.

"Yeah," Oliver piped up. "You didn't even tell us how that nativity scene was inaccurate because the wisemen didn't actually visit Jesus until he was about two years old."

Violet cracked a smile. "It *was* inaccurate," she confirmed. Then her expression grew sober, and she looked at her mother. "When I went for my walk, I saw Dr. Davis—"

"I *told you* that it was actually Dr. Davis, not Santa Claus," Hazel interrupted sleepily from the backseat. Butterscotch had curled up on the seat between Oliver and Hazel, and the girl was resting on the dog like a pillow. "Isn't that nice of him to play Santa Claus? You know... for the kids who don't know any better?"

Violet raised an eyebrow and said in a low voice to her mother, "Dr. Davis isn't doing it for charity. While I was out on my walk, I accidentally overheard an argument between him and what must be his boss."

"I bet that was uncomfortable," Becca said.

Running her finger along the lid of her disposable cocoa cup, Violet nodded. "It was. He said that he couldn't wait until after Christmas to get paid."

"Really?" Becca's eyebrows furrowed, and she was quiet for a few moments. "I can't imagine that he would get paid that much to play Santa Claus. He must really need the money."

Violet shrugged and gazed out the window. "I know. I thought the same thing."

For the rest of the way home, Becca drove in thoughtful silence.

It was getting late by the time the Gables filed into the apartment. Becca and Violet entered first, and Oliver, who was giving a sleepy Hazel a piggyback ride, came next, followed by Butterscotch ambling along behind. Oliver deposited his sister on her frilly pink bed and headed back to the kitchen.

"Well," Becca said, ruffling his chestnut hair. "You survived another ride on the Minivan Express. Thanks for being a good sport about it. I know you're too old for this tradition, but it's nice for Hazel."

Oliver gave her a lopsided grin. "I *am* way too old for it," he said. "But it wouldn't feel like Christmas without it." He paused, undoing a button on his flannel pajamas and then buttoning it again. "We'll ride the Minivan Express again next year, right?"

# Chapter 14

## Clubs of Crystal Run

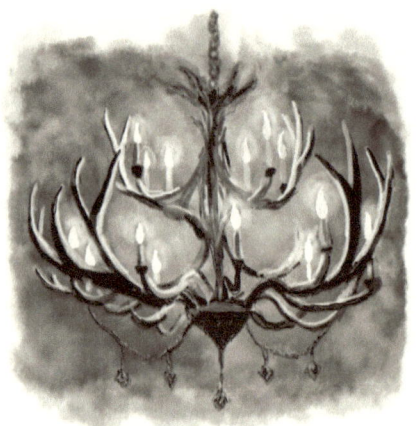

"Come along, darling," Donna said, glancing over her shoulder. The woman's black pumps click-clacked along the wooden floor.

Becca had stopped to admire the cavernous open dining space. A massive stone fireplace anchored one side of the room and stretched to the ceiling, which was supported with hefty rustic wooden beams. Embellished with white twinkle lights, windows dominated the walls and offered views of the snow-dusted golf course. An elegant Christmas tree, studded with cranberry, gold, and white ornaments, sparkled regally by the curved wooden bar. Tearing her gaze from one of the antlered chandeliers that hung in an impressive hoop overhead, Becca followed.

Donna led her to a rectangular table where Marjorie and Evelyn were waiting and gestured toward a chair. As the women greeted her, Becca unwound her scarf and shrugged out of her raspberry-colored wool coat, which she then arranged on the back of her chair. She slipped into the seat, drew her shoulders back, and smiled at the women.

"Would you like something to drink?" Donna asked, sliding a menu toward Becca.

Becca glanced down at the brown leather cover embossed with the words *Crystal Links Country Club*. She opened the menu and skimmed the beverage list. Before she had had much time to examine it, a server in her early twenties appeared. Wearing a cranberry button-down shirt with a striped apron tied at her waist, she was tall and slim and had a sprinkling of freckles across her nose.

"Good afternoon," the young woman greeted. "Would you like to hear our drink specials?"

With a quick glance at the other women's drinks—a vodka cranberry, a glass of white wine, and Donna's signature brandy old-fashioned—Becca said, "I'll have a hot chocolate, please." She handed the menu to the server.

"Becca," Donna began, the ice clinking in her glass as she set it down. "Thank you for agreeing to meet with us this afternoon. As I'm sure you're aware, we're meeting with the most respected women of Crystal Run to fill the open position in the improvement society."

Becca felt a warmth rise into her cheeks. "It's really an honor," she said.

Donna nodded. "Now, I believe we have a pretty good understanding of your family and background, but we'd like to hear it from you."

"Certainly," Becca said. "My family has lived in Crystal Run for generations—"

"Not as long as the Grants," Evelyn interjected. She missed Donna's eye-roll because she was taking a large swig of wine.

Becca suppressed a smile. "No, no one can compete with the Grants there," she said. "My family has found its place in the community by maintaining justice. My father was chief of police for more than ten years and was highly respected, and now the position is held by my uncle John, who is also an elder at Grace Lutheran."

Donna flashed her lipstick-lined grin. "And you are an entrepreneur." It was a statement.

"Yes," Becca said, tucking a strand of hair behind her ear. "After Matt and I earned our bachelor's degrees, we opened Tales & Tails."

"And your major was business, I suppose?"

Becca leaned back as the server placed a mug of hot chocolate in front of her and smiled up at the young woman. "Thank you," she said, wrapping her fingers around the mug. She looked at Donna. "Matt's major was business. I double-majored in criminal justice and English."

Marjorie raised an eyebrow. "That's quite a combination."

With a chuckle, Becca said, "I wanted to be a detective like my dad... and I have a long history of being able to get lost in a good story." She reached into her purse and pulled out a copy of *Hannah Coulter*, which she held up as evidence. "You'll never catch me without a book in hand."

Donna smiled. "Your love of reading is evident. Does that have anything to do with your decision to homeschool? Tell us about that as well as your feelings about our local schools."

"Violet has always been..." Becca gazed out the window at the snow, which had begun to take on a purple cast as the afternoon sun sank in the sky. "...different," she decided. "She's incredibly bright. We knew that we would be able to challenge her best at home. More than that, I felt God calling me to homeschool."

"It's very admirable," Donna said. "I am particularly impressed by how you were able to continue homeschooling after your husband passed."

"Oh!" Becca said. "Homeschooling was such a blessing during that time. It gave our family a unique closeness and flexibility that really helped us through." She brought the mug of hot chocolate to her lips and sipped. As she savored the hot liquid, she felt an extra warmth, a pleasant spice. *Cayenne?* She made a mental note to talk to Hazel about recreating it.

"And your thoughts on our local schools?" Donna gently prodded.

Shaking herself from her reverie, Becca continued, "As for the local schools, I think there is certainly a place for them, and they can fulfill their role well. Grace School, in particular, is amazing, and I like to support it whenever I can."

Donna frowned. "So, you don't have any"—she paused as she searched for the word—"*critiques* of our local schools? Or the families who send their children there?" The woman's eyes widened slightly, and she smiled encouragingly.

Taking a slow sip of her hot chocolate, Becca shook her head. "God trusts parents with their children, and so should we. Homeschooling is a wonderful fit for us, but families need to make the choices that are best for them."

Donna's smile flickered and faded like a faulty string of Christmas lights, but it quickly returned at the appearance of the younger server.

"Excuse me, I'm sorry to interrupt," she said, smiling brightly, one hand tucked into her striped apron pocket. "I'm just checking in. May I get anyone another drink? How about an appetizer?"

Evelyn lifted her empty glass of wine. "I'll have another glass of Riesling, please."

The server nodded and took the glass from Evelyn. "Right away," she said with a smile.

Donna lifted the olive-loaded cocktail pick from her glass and dropped it in again. She looked at Becca. "That's wonderful about the schools," she said. "Now, as you know, the Crystal Run Improvement Society is a women-led organization that works to identify, evaluate, and support opportunities to improve the town's beauty and points of interest. Your charming bookshop already brightens our little community, so we believe you might be a good fit for our group's mission."

Marjorie nodded in agreement.

"Now that the Grant portrait is no longer being donated to the library, there is a large empty wall that needs to be filled. How might you suggest that space be used?"

Becca's eyes widened. "Wait." Her gaze bounced between the three women's faces. "The Grant portrait is no longer being donated?"

"The granddaughter decided to hold onto the portrait as a family heirloom. One can hardly blame her," Donna said with a dismissive wave of her hand.

Becca frowned. "I hope that didn't cause more trouble for Patricia. You had said that she already almost lost her job over that portrait."

A chuckle escaped from Marjorie's lips. "Donna, is that what you said?" The woman sipped her drink, the cranberry color complementing her ruddy cheeks. "You are such a provocateur," she chided. She looked at Becca. "No, Patricia was never going to lose her job. Everyone knows that Phyllis complained about everyone and everything."

"Phyllis had valid concerns," Evelyn countered as she accepted the second glass of wine from the server and immediately took a swig.

Donna caught Marjorie's eye, raised a brow, and her mauve lips cracked into a half-smile. "I was just passing along what was told to me," she said with a shrug. She looked at Becca and folded her hands on the table. "But the empty wall?"

For a few moments, Becca gazed down into her mug at the almost completely melted dollop of whipped cream. Then she looked up. "Well, off the top of my head..."

Donna smiled and nodded encouragingly.

"The Grant portrait was going to highlight Crystal Run's history," Becca said, "so we could create a mural that highlights that. Perhaps a timeline that stretches across the space with vignettes branching off it depicting important moments in Crystal Run's history. We'd begin with the building of the first papermill in 1853, and we could even have three-dimensional elements added to the timeline—important documents and artifacts."

Donna leaned back in her upholstered chair and flashed her lipstick-lined grin. "I love it," she said. "The library could use more ideas like that. Honestly, the décor in there is hideous." Just then, the opening notes of "Fur Elise" along with a buzz sounded loudly from the woman's purse. Pulling out her phone and glancing at the screen, Donna said, "Excuse me, it's David. I need to take this." She stood up. "Hello, darling," she said as she slowly headed toward the Christmas tree.

With a cruel sparkle in her eye, Marjorie jerked her thumb at Donna's retreating figure and said, "She's talking with the drug dealer."

Becca furrowed her brows. "What?"

"That's what Phyllis always called David Sloane," Marjorie explained, running her finger around the rim of her glass, "because he is a pharmacist."

Becca's jaw dropped. "What an awful thing to say! Does Donna know that she did that?"

Smiling and nodding, Marjorie said, "Oh, yes, Phyllis would say it right to her face."

Evelyn pressed her lips into a line as she gazed into the remnants of her second glass of wine. "Phyllis didn't *always* call him that," she said defensively. "And even if she did, she had good reason."

Becca shook her head. "I can't imagine there's *ever* a good reason for speaking that way about someone."

Gulping the last of her wine, Evelyn glanced at Donna across the room. She then looked at Becca. "You don't understand. Donna has been after Phyllis's position as president of the CRIS for the longest time. She was talking to us behind Phyllis's back, trying to get us to support a motion for her to be our new leader."

Becca glanced at Marjorie, who nodded in agreement.

Evelyn picked up her empty wine glass and set it back down. "Of course, *I* refused to be a part of it." Lowering her voice to a whisper, she leaned forward. "And now Phyllis is *murdered...*" She glanced at Donna, who seemed to be concluding her phone call, raised an eyebrow, and shot Marjorie a meaningful look.

"My apologies," Donna said as she returned to the table and resumed her seat. "David received a dinner invitation, and he wanted to know what I had planned so he could pick the better meal. Men and their stomachs!" The woman's grin quickly melted as she took in the frosty silence. Evelyn stared out the window at the golf course, and Marjorie became very interested in rolling the corner of her cocktail napkin.

Donna pressed her lips together and looked at Becca. "I think we've heard everything we need to, darling," she said. She glanced at Marjorie and Evelyn, who were still carefully avoiding eye contact, and then back at Becca. "We will be making our decision in the new year."

Becca smiled and looked at each woman in turn. "I appreciate your consideration and look forward to hearing from you." She glanced up at the server who had appeared at her elbow.

"May I get you something else?" the young woman asked her, the tail of her dark-blonde ponytail hanging over her shoulder. "Dinner? Another hot chocolate?"

"I have to get home to my children," Becca said. "Just the check will be fine."

The girl shifted her weight from one foot to the other. "The check?"

Donna coughed daintily into her fist.

"Oh!" Becca said, feeling a warmth rush into her cheeks. "Do you not do that here?" Hastily, she pulled her credit card from her wallet and held it up.

The motionless server stared at the credit card and furrowed her brows. Marjorie and Evelyn exchanged glances, and Evelyn giggled behind her hand.

"Cash?" Becca tried again, fishing for some bills from her wallet. She held out the money toward the young woman, who stared at it repulsively. The freckles on the server's nose seemed to glow as she shot Donna a desperate look.

Donna raised an eyebrow and said to Becca, "There is no bill or payment immediately exchanged at establishments like these." She smiled as she spoke, but Becca noted a hint of condescension in the woman's tone. Donna then turned toward the server. "Please put her drink on my account."

The young woman heaved a sigh of relief. She wished Becca a good evening and beat a hasty retreat.

As Becca stood up and draped her scarf around her neck, she looked at Donna and grimaced. "I'm sorry about that."

With a dismissive wave, Donna said, "It was thoroughly amusing." She looked over at the other two women, who made insincere attempts to conceal their smiles.

"Well, thank you again for everything," Becca said and smiled at all three women. "I'm sure I'll see you soon." As she made her way across the room and passed under the antlered chandeliers, she couldn't help but think that the color of her cheeks must certainly match the raspberry color of her coat.

As Becca pushed open the door of the Gables' apartment, she smiled and inhaled the aroma of freshly baked chocolate chip cookies. Closing the door behind her and turning the deadbolt, she then eased out of her coat and hung it on the wall hook. "Vi?" she called, looping her scarf over the hook. "Oliver! Hazel! I'm home!" After a few moments of silence, she heard giggling coming from across the apartment.

Grabbing a cookie off the cooling rack as she passed through the kitchen, Becca made her way to the living room and smiled at the scene. Violet, wearing a solid black paper top hat, was sitting cross-legged on the floor in front of the coffee table. A large piece of paper was spread out in front of her, anchored by a roll of Scotch tape on one side and a pair of scissors on the other. She was fitting smaller pieces of paper onto the large one. Hazel knelt next to her sister. She was wearing her own top hat, which was patterned with pink argyle and embellished with a matching bow. The girl's eyebrows furrowed as she worked to fit a drawing onto the large sheet of paper. Oliver was draped over a tufted charcoal-gray easy chair, and he wrote on a clipboard. He, too, wore a top hat, but his was patterned with sports equipment. In his teeth was what looked like a pipe. Becca blinked hard.

"Oliver Matthew, *what* is in your mouth?"

All three children quickly glanced up at their mother.

Casually, Oliver pulled the object from his mouth and held it up. "Don't worry, Mom," he said. "It's just a chopstick stuck into a cork."

Hazel rose and skipped over to her mother, holding her hat in place with one hand. "Hi, Mommy," she said sweetly. "We're playing Pickwick Club, like in *Little Women*."

"Ah, I see," Becca said, her shoulders easing. "And where did you get these fabulous hats?"

"I made them," Hazel proudly replied. "I found a YouTube video showing how to make them out of scrapbook paper."

Becca raised her eyebrows. "Very impressive, Hazel. You checked with Violet first?"

"Of course," Violet said, continuing to arrange the slips of paper in front of her. She glanced up at her mother. "How was the CRIS interview?"

Smoothing her skirt, Becca said, "It went well overall. I think they like me and my ideas, and involvement in that society could be really good for the bookshop." She blushed. "And I also received a lesson in country club etiquette."

Violet cocked her head. "Uh-oh."

"So, apparently," Becca said, "if you are at a country club—or this one, at least—everything is paid for through a member's account."

Chuckling, Violet said, "Was it embarrassing enough to make the news?" She pointed to the large sheet of paper spread out in front of her.

"Oh, don't you dare!" Becca said, her eyes sparkling. Grabbing Hazel's hand, she stepped toward Violet at the coffee table. "Let's see this newspaper."

Violet waved a hand over the large sheet. "Here it is," she said. "I wrote the news—mostly about Mrs. Grant's murder, of course."

Nodding solemnly, Becca said, "That *is* the big news around here."

"And I drew the comic strip!" Hazel said, hopping up and down.

Becca inspected the drawing and threw her head back in laughter. "Oh! That couple is being chased by Toffee *and* a baby bunny? You have to show this to Aunt Audrey!"

Hazel giggled and slid the comic to the center of the newspaper. "Wouldn't it be better here?"

"No, here," Violet said, shifting it to a corner. "We have to leave room for the sports report."

"I'm almost done with it!" Oliver called, his legs still hanging over the arm of the easy chair.

Becca pressed her fingers over her heart. "Well, Pickwick Club members," she said, "how about we all get into our pajamas, and I'll read you some more *Little Women* before bedtime." Only a short time passed before Oliver, dressed in a tattered t-shirt and athletic shorts, switched on the gas fireplace. The flames danced and threw a soft glow across the room. Taking his usual place on the loveseat, the young man was careful to avoid crossing over onto his older sister's side. Violet, in her plaid flannel pajamas, waited quietly with her feet tucked up under her. In pajamas that matched her sister's, Hazel lay on her belly on the floor, a round cream-colored crochet pillow tucked under her chin.

Becca entered the room, and she could not help but smile as her eyes fell upon the paper top hats resting on the mantel. Settling into the charcoal-gray easy chair by the fire, Becca threw a snow-colored blanket over her lap and switched on the lamp. Her hair shining gold in the pool of lamplight, she reached into the basket that sat at the base of the lamp and pulled out a much-loved dark-green edition of *Little Women*. She found her place in the book and gazed up at the children. "Ready?"

A while later, when she had finished reading, Becca gingerly closed the book.

"Another chapter?" Hazel asked automatically, her eyelids half-closed.

With a glance at the oversized pocket watch clock on the mantel, Becca shook her head and smiled. "Not tonight."

"You know, I was thinking…" Violet said thoughtfully, "about the beginning of the book when the March girls decide to give their Christmas dinner to that poor immigrant family."

"The Hummels?" Becca offered.

"Yes," Violet said. "Christmas is only fourteen days away. Is there anyone we could bless like that?"

Becca sat up straight and laid her hands flat on the book's cover. "I *love* that idea, Violet." "What do you think, Oliver? Hazel?"

"Yeah, that would be nice," Oliver said with a shrug.

Hazel jumped to her feet. "I know just who we should bless!"

"Whom," Becca gently corrected.

"Whom," Hazel parroted. Clasping her hands together, she continued, "Mrs. Grant's granddaughter, Lexi! She doesn't have any family left, and she's all alone in that big scary run-down house."

Violet pitched forward on the loveseat, and her eyes were wide. "Yes! We could cheer her up with paper snowflakes, and Christmas cookies, and drawings!"

Hazel bounced up and down on her toes.

Frowning, Oliver said, "Drawings? Why would she want any of our drawings?"

"She *loves* art!" Hazel replied. "She's always looking at those art books we have in the bookshop."

Becca smiled and tucked the copy of *Little Women* into the basket. "It's a lovely idea, and Lexi Grant is the perfect recipient. But let's talk about this more tomorrow because it's getting late."

"Aww, Mom, five more minutes?" Hazel begged.

With a firm shake of her head, Becca pointed to the girls' room.

Sticking out her lower lip, Hazel trudged toward her bedroom. Then she doubled back, threw her arms around Becca's neck, and kissed her mother's cheek.

Becca planted a kiss on her daughter's forehead. "Remember to say your prayers," she said. "Sweet dreams."

When Hazel had disappeared down the hallway, Becca peeled the blanket from her lap and tossed it onto the chair. Reaching toward the mantel, she picked up the pink argyle top hat and pulled it onto her head. She struck a pose. "What do you think?"

"Sorry, Mom," Oliver replied. "Marmee isn't a member of the Pickwick Club."

Becca's lips rose into a half-smile as she replaced the top hat on the mantel and plopped down on the loveseat next to her son. She stared at the dancing flames in the gas fireplace for a few moments and then tousled Oliver's hair. "Just be sure that that pipe doesn't make its way downstairs. From a distance, it looks a bit too real!"

# Chapter 15

# Gifting

"Miss Violet?"

Violet sat cross-legged on the floor in a puddle of board books that had been pulled from the shelf by a tornado of a toddler. The flecks of gold in her eyes shone as she looked up into the face of a ten-year-old boy.

He pushed his glasses up on the bridge of his nose. "Is Licorice League meeting today?"

Carefully returning *Gingerbread Baby* to its place on the low shelf, Violet stood, frowned at the remaining carnage, and brushed her hands on her apron. "Hi, Paul," she said. "Actually, the book club is taking a break for December, but we'll meet again in January. We'll be reading and discussing the *Wingfeather Saga* for the next several months. Do you have the first book?"

The boy hooked his fingers in the pockets of his jeans and shook his head. "I don't think so."

Violet smiled. "Let's go find your mom." She glanced down at the pile of board books at her feet. "In just a second," she added. As she stooped to quickly file the books back onto the shelf—in alphabetical order by author, of course—the boy peeked inside the glowing windows of a stoneware gingerbread house, which sat on top of the shelf. When she had finished, Violet popped back up and smiled at Paul. "After you," she said, gesturing.

As she followed the boy through the bookshop, which was bustling with more than its usual crowd, Violet glanced out the window at the deepening shades of pink and purple in the afternoon sky. The pair wound their way through the maze of bookshelves toward Paul's mother, who was standing at a table stacked with board games. She was tall and pear-shaped and had sandy-colored hair that matched her son's. Toffee, the golden-brown Manx, rubbed against the woman's ankles. Scooping him up and stroking his head, the woman smiled as Paul and Violet approached.

"No book club today?" she asked.

Violet shook her head. "No, but Paul will want to have our January book so he's ready for when we meet again. Does your family own *On the Edge of the Dark Sea of Darkness?*" Her gaze shifted between the mother and son. "Remember, Licorice League members get twenty percent off the price of our book club books." She glanced across the room where her mother was setting up a long table with wrapping paper supplies. "*And* we're offering free gift wrapping today as community service."

The woman chuckled as she stroked Toffee's head. "Well, I don't need any more convincing." She raised an eyebrow and looked at her son. "What do you think, Paul? I could use another gift under the tree for you."

The boy nodded enthusiastically.

"I'll grab you a copy," Violet said, smiling. "We ordered several extra."

She breezed to the book club display, plucked a volume from the top of the stack, and glanced over at the nearby gift-wrapping station. The long table had been adorned with a red-and-green plaid tablecloth and evergreen branches. On top of it sat two wrapping paper dispensers, which had been loaded with coordinating rolls of paper. Carefully, Hazel set a pair of scissors and a tape dispenser by each roll. As Oliver rifled through a basket of candy canes, a peppermint hook already hanging out of his mouth, Becca affixed a hand-lettered sign that said *Free Gift Wrapping* to the front of the table.

"One second, Vi!" Becca called.

Violet stopped and turned.

"We start wrapping at 4:30," Becca said. "We'll wrap until we close, so make sure you eat something. Aunt Audrey set up a snack board for us with cheese, crackers, sausage, and fruit in the kitchen."

"Yes, ma'am," Violet said and strode toward the waiting mother and son.

Becca stepped back and smiled as she admired the festive-looking table. Her eyes locked onto a jar tied with a red-and-green ribbon and labeled *Tips appreciated – All proceeds donated to Grace Lutheran Church*. Reaching into her jeans pocket, Becca extracted a couple of bills and popped them into the jar.

Quizzically, Hazel turned her aqua eyes toward her mother.

"To get you started," Becca explained with a wink.

At 4:30 sharp, Violet and Oliver were each stationed behind a roll of gift wrap, and Hazel was ready with spools of gauzy gold ribbon and a basket of bows. Nearby stood Becca, perfecting a display of Christmas-themed books on a table.

Violet glanced at her watch and then at her mother. "Hey, we're actually ready on time."

Becca smiled. "Christmas miracles *do* happen, you know."

"Well, is this ever nice!"

Becca turned to see a woman with a cloud of frizzy red hair and black-rimmed cat-eye eyeglasses plop a heavy paper bag onto the long table.

"Not only did I get *all* of my shopping done this afternoon, but I'll also have my wrapping finished!" the woman said, beaming.

Oliver eyed the very full bag and looked at his sister, who immediately began dividing the books between the two of them.

Becca stepped toward the table. "Hi, Patricia!" she said. "I'm so glad we can make your Christmas shopping a little easier this year."

The president of the library board glanced at the stacks of books forming between Violet and Oliver and laughed. "Everyone knows what gift to expect from me. I guess that goes with the territory when you work for the library."

"We certainly appreciate the business," Becca said. Her gaze paused over the mounds of books. "And keep in mind that, if you ever decide to purchase something other than a book, even if it's from another store, we're happy to wrap that too. Do you think you'd like something from the café while you wait?"

Violet handed Hazel a package wrapped in white paper patterned with red Christmas trees. As Hazel dug into the bow basket, she said brightly, "I recommend the Red-Hot Chocolate, Mrs. Koller. It's not *really* spicy... It's got a nice cinnamon flavor."

Patricia smiled warmly at the girl. "That sounds like just the thing!" With another glance at the stacks of books waiting to be wrapped, she took a few steps toward the café. Patricia paused, and her gaze settled on the artwork on top of the mantel. Looking at Becca, she pointed to the maps of Narnia, Avonlea, and Neverland and said, "I've always admired those."

"Thank you," Becca said, casting her eyes on the trio of framed pieces. "I enjoy picking out decor for the bookshop."

Patricia sighed. "I've got a large wall to fill at the library now that we're no longer receiving the Grant family portrait."

"So, it's true?" Becca said. "Lexi rescinded the donation to the library?"

The woman nodded. "Yes, she submitted a letter to the board saying that she never agreed with her grandmother's decision to donate the portrait. She believes that it should be kept in the family."

"That must have been very disappointing," Becca said.

Patricia chuckled. "Not really. Working with Phyllis Grant was a headache. She had a complaint for *every* way we proposed to display the portrait." Lowering her voice, she added, "By the end, it was rather a joke among the board members."

Becca smiled. "If you're looking for ideas, I think the Crystal Run Improvement Society is already working on it."

"Oh, I'm sure they are," Patricia said, rolling her eyes. She laughed and headed toward the café. "I do love those maps!" she called over her shoulder.

Time passed quickly as Violet and Oliver turned Patrica Koller's mound of books into a merry-looking stack of red and green. In front of the gift-wrapping station, various residents of Crystal Run lined up. The children not only wrapped books but also board games, basketballs, pajama sets, and science kits. The only difficulty came when Becca noticed a bottleneck in the assembly line. Hazel, who had dubbed herself "embellishment expert," lingered over each gift and dressed it up to perfection. With a gentle reminder, Becca convinced her daughter that perhaps *one* bow per present was enough, and she didn't have to tuck sprigs of evergreen into *every* ribbon.

"Oh, *thank you,*" said a woman's voice, thick with gratitude.

Becca turned and looked into the face of a mother in her late twenties. The woman was pale, and her eyes had dark circles beneath them. She wore a light-gray sweatsuit, and her hair was thrown into a messy ponytail. From her arm hung an infant car seat laden with a pink-cheeked baby, who was gnawing on the leg of a rubber giraffe.

"You have no idea how much this helps me to have the gifts wrapped," the woman continued. "Sophie is teething, and I am up with her all night long. I feel like I'm behind on *everything*." She shifted the car seat to her other arm.

Becca smiled warmly at the woman. "That's exactly why we do this," she said. "And, trust me, these days will be gone before you know it." For a moment, tears pricked her eyes as she gazed at Violet, Oliver, and Hazel, who were continuing to wrap gifts. Glancing at the woman's multitude of bags filled with presents, Becca said, "I will help you carry these to your car."

The woman shook her head. "Oh, no, that's okay—"

"I insist," Becca said, smiling as she stooped to pick up the bags. "I'm Becca, by the way."

"Abigail," the woman said. With words of thanks tumbling from her lips, the exhausted mother tucked several bills into the tip jar and led Becca toward her vehicle.

The bell at the front door tinkled as Becca let herself back inside the bookshop. Recognizing Donna Sloane's camel-colored coat with its fur collar, she found herself following Donna and Marjorie Marston as they made their way toward the gift-wrapping station. Becca watched as Donna took her place in line, a light-blue shopping bag dangling from the crook of her elbow.

"Hi, ladies!" Becca said, smiling at Donna and Marjorie in turn. "I'm so glad that you stopped in."

The women exchanged quick glances, and Donna pressed her lips into a small smile. "Hello, Becca."

Marjorie raised her eyebrows, and Donna gave a slight wave as her friend headed toward the café area to secure a table.

Becca gestured toward the shopping bag. "Is that a Christmas gift for your daughter?"

"Actually," Donna said, "this is a cashmere sweater that David purchased for me. He just doesn't know it yet." She folded her arms across her chest and cast her gaze around the bookshop.

"We've had quite a few people stop in," Becca tried again. "Patricia Koller was here, and she mentioned the empty wall at the library."

Donna picked an imaginary piece of lint from her sleeve. "Oh? That's nice."

A small sigh escaped from Becca's lips. "Listen, Donna," she said, "I want to apologize again for how things ended at the country club—"

"There's no need to apologize," Donna said coolly, placing a hand on Becca's arm. "It's not your fault. That environment requires a certain background. But you can be at ease because you won't be in that awkward position again. We've found a suitable replacement for the position." At that, the woman handed the light-blue bag to Violet, placed a twenty-dollar bill into the tip jar, and then turned on her heel to join Marjorie at the café.

Violet glanced up at her mother and raised her eyebrows.

Becca sighed and bit her lip. "Well," she said, "I guess the interview didn't go as well as I'd thought." Pushing her shoulders back and smiling, she looked at her children and said, "I think we need some bolstering in the form of Christmasy drinks. Hot chocolate, everyone?"

At the children's eager nods, Becca headed to the kitchen. After helping Audrey with a few drink orders, she poured the thick chocolatey liquid into four teal mugs and crowned them with swirls of whipped cream. A mug in each hand, she delivered the first two to Oliver and Hazel. As she was about to embark on her second delivery, she glanced up and beamed in delight at the sight of Detective Post, dressed in a navy-blue suit, standing in line at the confectionery counter. Sidling up to him, she said, "You just had to have an evening espresso?" Her eyes flicked to her sister-in-law, and she grinned.

Letting his gaze fall on Audrey, the detective smiled and cleared his throat. "I like a warm drink on these chilly evenings."

Becca's eyes sparkled as she headed back to the gift-wrapping station with the final two mugs. Finding several people in line, she quickly set down the hot chocolates, stepped behind the table between Violet and Oliver, and began tearing small pieces of tape for them. As the family wrapped furiously, Becca snuck an occasional peek over at the confectionery counter where she saw Detective Post and Audrey, heads bent toward each other and laughing. By the time the Gables had the gift wrapping under control again, the whipped cream had melted into a frothy layer at the top of their mugs. Becca glanced up to see that Detective Post had made his way over to the wrapping station and was now hovering by it. His suit coat was slung over his arm.

Becca smiled at him. "How's the espresso?"

"Best in town," the detective said, raising his cup. He cleared his throat. "Hey, Becca," he said, "I'm wondering if you have a minute."

Smoothing her apron, Becca stepped out from behind the table. "Sure thing. How can I help?"

Chris glanced across the room at the auburn-haired woman, who was punching an order into a tablet. "I want to get your sister-in-law... Audrey... something small for Christmas. We've been out a couple of times, and I want to get her something, but, well..." He shifted his weight from one foot to the other. "Well, I'm not the best at stuff like this, and I'm wondering if you have any ideas. I have been studying her and the things she likes, but I want to know if you could give me any... you know... leads."

Becca's eyes widened as she suppressed a giggle at the detective's word choice. Then she grinned. "Oh my goodness, I would *love* to help." Her brows furrowed as she considered for a few moments. She cast her gaze to Hazel, who was carefully trimming the tails of a bow into perfect peaks. Suddenly, Becca clasped her hands and rose to her tiptoes. "I have a great idea!" Leaning toward Chris, she spoke in a low voice, and the detective responded with a chuckle and a nod.

"Hey, Vi," Becca called, "do you think I could borrow Hazel for a couple of minutes?"

Violet scowled at the pileup of gifts that had begun to form by Hazel again as the young girl fussed over an arrangement of three bows. "Feel free to take her for a while."

Becca smiled sympathetically at Violet but said, "Hazel, you are doing a beautiful job." She waved the girl over and whispered in her ear.

Hazel bounced on her toes and looked up at the stocky detective. "This way!" she called. Skipping in the direction of the hollow tree, Hazel glanced over her shoulder to make sure that Detective Post was following.

When the pair returned to the gift-wrapping station, Chris was clutching a miniature coffee-colored stuffed rabbit. He held it close to his body on the side opposite Audrey at the confectionery counter. The detective handed the stuffed animal to Oliver. Grinning mischievously at Becca, he said, "A baby bunny. She is going to freak out."

"In a good way or in a terrified way?" Becca asked.

"Both, I hope," the detective said with a twinkle in his eyes.

Within a few minutes, Violet had helped him make the purchase, and Hazel handed him the elaborately decorated gift. The detective suppressed a smile as he examined the assortment of ribbons and bows, which almost completely hid the wrapping paper underneath. Stuffing some bills into the tip jar, he thanked Becca and the children for their help, waved to Audrey across the bookshop, and headed out into the frosty night.

Becca smiled as the door closed behind Detective Post. She turned toward the children. "Are you okay here for a few minutes? I'd like to chat with Aunt Audrey."

"We're fine," Oliver said. His words were muffled by the candy cane sticking out of his mouth.

Violet nodded. "Yes, we've got it under control."

With quick steps, Becca made her way toward the confectionery counter. As she passed the shining wooden tables near the fireplace, she heard Donna's syrupy voice.

"Becca, darling, please come over here."

Stopping and forcing her lips into a pleasant smile, Becca addressed the woman. "May I help you with something?" She glanced at Donna's empty mug with a cinnamon stick resting on its side. "Another mug of apple cider?" She smiled in acknowledgment at Marjorie, still wrapped in her crimson velvet coat.

Donna laughed. "I'm fine," she said. "I just noticed you were talking to the detective over there." She gestured vaguely toward the gift-wrapping station and paused.

"Yes," Becca said. "He stopped by to talk with my sister-in-law and to have a gift wrapped."

"Oh, how nice." She flashed her lipstick-lined smile and picked up her cinnamon stick. "There is so much going on in this little town of ours. Did he happen to mention anything about the Grant case? I know they are so very busy down at the station. I would love to help in any way that I can."

Becca glanced at Marjorie, who was poised in her chair, eager for a morsel of gossip. Pressing her lips into a line, she said, "No, he didn't mention it. Sorry."

Donna dropped the cinnamon stick into her mug. "Well, if he does, I'm sure you will be a dear and let me know. We're all working on this together." The saccharine smile spread across her face again.

Tucking a strand of blonde hair behind her ear, Becca gestured toward the two empty mugs. "May I take these?"

As she headed toward the kitchen with the dishes, she glanced back over her shoulder at the women whose heads were bent together in quiet conversation. Her frown quickly shifted into a smile, though, as she passed Audrey on her way to the sink. Softly, her sister-in-law hummed as she used a pair of tongs to load two gingerbread cookies onto a plate, which she handed to a waiting customer.

Audrey surveyed the café area and then turned to Becca. "Phew! The rush is finally over."

"Do you want to sit down for a couple of minutes?" Becca inclined her head toward the tiled table, which was laden with a wooden board half-filled with cheese, crackers, and fruit.

"Do I ever!" Audrey replied, sinking into a chair. She slipped off a clog, crossed an ankle over her knee, and rubbed her toes.

Becca seated herself opposite her sister-in-law and selected a strawberry from the board. "Things seem to be going well with Chris." She bit off the end of the strawberry, and her lips curved into a smile.

"They really are," Audrey said. "We just went out the other night, actually."

Becca pitched forward in her chair. "You did? You didn't tell me that!"

Audrey nodded. "We had such a great time at *Hello, Dolly!* that we decided to go out again. He took me bowling."

Leaning back, Becca laughed. "Well, now I see why you didn't say anything. " She took another bite of the strawberry. "*Bowling?* I thought you hated bowling!"

"Oh, I do—did," Audrey said, her eyes sparkling. "But Chris made it fun! He showed me how to throw a hook."

Becca's eyebrows rose. "Really?"

Audrey hopped out of her chair and slipped her foot back into her clog. "I'll show you!" Supporting an imaginary bowling ball in her hands, she took several steps forward. Just before releasing the "ball," she paused and said, "As you let go, you turn your hand like you're extending it for a handshake." She mimicked the motion and watched as her "ball" sailed down a make-believe lane.

"Wow!" Becca said. "Were you actually able to throw a hook?"

"No, not at all!" With a goofy smile, Audrey collapsed back into her chair. She jerked her thumb behind her. "Didn't you just see that land in the gutter?"

A laugh burst from Becca's lips.

"But it was so cute how he was trying to teach me," Audrey continued, a blush blooming on her cheeks. "Today he said he was thinking of me and wanted to stop in and say hi." Lowering her voice, she leaned toward her sister-in-law. "And he actually asked me to come over to his apartment on Monday because he wants to make dinner for me."

Becca arched a brow. "He cooks? That's amazing! What is he making?"

"I have no idea," Audrey said cheerfully. "He would only tell me it was something Italian. Apparently, he loves to cook."

"Perfect." Becca nodded. "I cannot *wait* to hear all about it. You'd better not hold out on me this time." She glanced at her wristwatch. "We're getting into the final twenty-minute stretch. I am going to check on the children." As she rose from her chair, she imitated the bowling motion Audrey had used. "Like this?"

Audrey shrugged. "That looks good to me!" she said, laughing and reaching for a slice of black pepper cheese.

As Becca made her way across the bookshop, she noted that the table previously occupied by Donna and Marjorie was now empty. Flicking her gaze to the gift-wrapping station, her eyes lit up to find Maggie Sharpe standing in front of the table. The Grace School librarian wore a dark-green wool peacoat with a plaid scarf wound around her neck, and she twisted a class ring around her thumb as she eagerly cast her gaze around the shop.

"This is the *cutest* bookshop!" the young woman bubbled.

"I'm glad you made it in!" Becca said, smiling. "I had a feeling it would be right up your alley."

"Well, you know I've been meaning to, and I couldn't pass up an opportunity for help with gift wrapping. I'm hopeless at it and usually just stuff everything into gift bags." She grinned as she handed a few gift-filled bags over the table to Oliver, who immediately began to unroll a length of Christmas tree wrapping paper. "Thank you," she said. "And I'd love for one of you to help me pick out a book or two for the library at Grace School."

Hazel's aqua eyes sparkled. "I can, Miss Sharpe!" The girl ducked out from behind the table, grabbed Maggie's hand, and pulled her toward a display of Christmas books. In a matter of minutes, the volumes—*Mr. Willowby's Christmas Tree* and *Red & Lulu*—had been selected and paid for, and Maggie was back at the gift-wrapping table, watching as the pile of wrapped packages grew.

Becca felt a rub against her ankles and glanced down to find Licorice. Scooping up the cat, she looked at Maggie. "Would you like Licorice and me to give you a tour of the bookshop while you're waiting?"

Maggie grinned. "I would love that!"

With Licorice curled in her arms like a baby, Becca led the young librarian around the shop. Maggie nodded appreciatively at the story time area and remarked on the clever names of the two book clubs, Licorice League and Butterscotch Brigade. Breathing in deeply as she passed the café area, her eyes lingered on the single remaining lemon-lavender cupcake. She exclaimed over the hollow reading tree and stared up in wonder at the twinkle lights winking from the ceiling as she followed Becca toward a mysterious section near the front of the shop.

"This is a fun little spot," Becca said, lowering Licorice to the floor. She straightened and paused as Maggie read the sign on what looked like an ordinary oak door with an old-fashioned handle.

"Grandmother's Attic," Maggie read softly. She looked at Becca and raised a brow.

Becca's lips curved into a smile as she reached out and slid the door to the side, revealing bookshelves set back behind the wall that had previously been concealed. The shelves were loaded with faded and worn volumes organized by the decade they were published. Nestled among the books was the occasional vintage toy, including a Raggedy Ann doll and a Lionel train engine. "This is where we keep our antique and vintage books," Becca explained.

As the two women returned to the gift-wrapping station, Maggie could hardly contain her excitement as she thanked Becca for the tour. Lacing her fingers together, she took a deep breath, settled herself, and smiled at the children. "Violet, Hazel," she said, "my boyfriend, Barton, and I are really looking forward to the performance of *A Christmas Carol* on Saturday. Look for us in the third row."

Hazel grinned. "I'll sign your programs afterward too, if you want!"

Violet scowled at her sister. "Hazel!" she scolded softly.

"We would love that," the young librarian said, taking the bags, which were now loaded with wrapped packages, from Oliver. Placing a few bills into the tip jar, she said, "I'd better be getting home. The snow is starting to fall." She glanced at Becca. "Thanks again for the tour!"

As Maggie headed out of the bookshop, Oliver reached into the basket of candy canes. He grabbed one, snapped it in half, and peeled off the wrapper. "Do you think Miss Sharpe was our last customer?"

Before Becca could reply, the bell at the front of the shop tinkled, and Uncle John appeared, wearing a tan sheepskin coat and brown cabbie cap. As he approached the gift-wrapping station, the Gables could see that he was carrying a large lumpy bag.

"Hello!" he greeted, his voice as rich as hot chocolate.

"Hi, Uncle John!" the children chorused.

Becca hurried over to peck her uncle's cheek, and Violet reached for the bag, but John held it protectively to his chest.

"Oh, no!" the police chief said with a grin. "Your service hours are finished for the day." He reached into his bag and pulled out a plastic container of frosted cookies. Handing them to Oliver, he said, "Go put your feet up by the fire, and see if you and your siblings can find something to do with these."

The children looked at their mother.

"You're dismissed," she said, smiling and waving them toward the café area.

When Violet, Oliver, and Hazel were a safe distance from the gift-wrapping table, John held out the lumpy bag to Becca and raised his eyebrows. "Please? You do such a good job."

Becca smiled. "Of course," she said, taking the bag from him. As she stepped behind the table, John pulled up a folding chair and set it across from his niece. From the bag, Becca pulled a crochet kit of sea animals. Glancing over her shoulder at the café area, she saw a bundled-up Audrey pull a pom-pom stocking cap onto her head and waved goodbye. Turning back to John, Becca said, "Hazel is going to like this."

John smoothed his mustache with his thumb and forefinger. "I thought so."

"So," Becca said, guiding her scissors through the wrapping paper, "are there any updates on the Grant case?"

John chuckled and shook his head.

"Donna Sloane was in earlier," Becca said. "She was very interested in my conversation with Detective Post, who stopped by to see Audrey. Is Donna pretty high on your suspect list?"

John's lips raised into a half-smile. "We're continuing to investigate all relevant leads," he said cautiously.

Becca glanced up at her uncle and then back down at the crochet kit as she centered it on the gift wrap. Undeterred, she said, "Did you find Mrs. Grant's will? Was it on the secretary desk?"

"Yes, thank you for that," John said with a smile. "I sent an officer to the Paper Palace to collect it, and it was right where you said it would be."

"Good," Becca said, carefully creasing the wrapping paper.

After a beat, John held up his phone. "Do you like my new lockscreen?"

Becca glanced up to see a photo of herself and the children in their matching pajamas gathered around Santa Claus.

"I love that picture," the chief said. "Very sweet."

Tearing a strip of tape from the roll, Becca frowned. "About that... Did you see who was playing Santa?"

"It looks like Dr. Stephen Davis," John said, squinting at the screen.

"Mm-hmm," Becca murmured. She paused and then continued, "I know this isn't my business, but I feel like I should let you know..."

John leaned forward. "What's that?"

"Well," Becca said slowly, "when we were at the Celebration of Lights the other day, Violet saw Dr. Davis arguing with his supervisor. Apparently, he is really in need of money."

Furrowing his eyebrows, the chief clasped his hands and sat quietly for a few moments. Finally, he said, "Now, I share this with you because I know that you will keep this to yourself and also because we wouldn't have found Phyllis Grant's will nearly as quickly without your help."

Becca paused in her wrapping, her green eyes twinkling as she stared at her uncle.

With a soft chuckle, he went on. "According to that will we found, Dr. Davis was set to inherit a legacy of twenty-thousand dollars."

"Really?" Becca's eyes were huge, and she bounced on her toes.

John nodded and gestured toward the bag. Obediently, Becca reached into it and pulled out a pocketknife. She held it up and arched a brow.

"Every young man needs a good pocketknife," he said.

Becca smiled and gave a low whistle as she measured the paper. "Twenty-thousand dollars..."

John removed his cap and shifted it from one hand to the other. "Before you get too excited, it seems that this is not the most current version of the will. Now that the lawyer, Andrew Curtis, is back in town from his Hawaiian vacation, he's searching for it."

"Searching for it?" Becca frowned.

Raising his eyebrows, John said, "Oh, yes. It would seem the good Mr. Curtis doesn't believe in computers. He says that a handshake is a contract, and computers are not to be trusted. So, for the past week, he has been searching for the latest version of Phyllis Grant's will. He put it in a safe place, and safe it most certainly is—even he can't find it."

Becca laughed, and she clapped a hand over her mouth. "I'm sorry," she said. "That's got to be so frustrating."

John dropped his cap into his lap and rubbed his temples. "You have no idea."

When Becca placed the bow on the final gift, she tucked it into the lumpy bag along with the others and handed the bag to John. She grabbed the overflowing tip jar from the table and tilted it toward her uncle as they made their way to the café area. "As an elder of our church, would you be able to handle this donation for us?"

"Happy to," John said, placing the jar in his bag. "And just know that I'll be adding my own sizeable tip for a job very well done."

The fire popped in greeting as the pair found Violet and Oliver on the floor, embattled in a game of chess. Violet was sitting cross-legged, and Oliver was on his stomach, his chin resting on his palm. Hazel, eyes half-closed, was lying on top of Butterscotch and stroking her ears. On the floor beside them was a plastic cookie container, empty except for a few crumbs.

"You know," John said, "I received a picture recently that made me smile." With a grin, he held up his phone and displayed the lockscreen of the pajama-clad Gables gathered around Santa Claus.

Oliver's jaw dropped. "*Mom,*" he complained, "you said that you wouldn't post that photo on social media."

Becca opened her mouth to defend herself, but John beat her to it. "Leave your mother alone," he said to Oliver. "Privately texting a photo is not the same thing as posting it to social media." With one hand, he pulled his cabbie cap onto his head and turned to his niece. "I do have a question for you, though, Bec." He paused dramatically. "Where do I get a pair of those pajamas?"

# Chapter 16

# Winter Storm Warning

"It's really coming down out there," Becca said, dropping her hand from the heavy door that led into the alley behind Tales & Tails. As the door shut with a thud, a surge of frigid air washed over her, and she shivered.

Oliver grinned. "I know. Isn't it great?" He picked up his sled, an old-fashioned wooden one with metal runners, and tucked it under his arm.

"Just promise me you'll be careful," Becca said, hugging herself for warmth. "Do you have your watch on?"

Pushing back the cuff of his glove, Oliver held up his arm and showed his mother the black timepiece looped around his wrist.

Becca nodded. "You need to be back no later than 4:00 so you have time to get ready for your sisters' performance of *A Christmas Carol*," she said. "They're already at Steeple Hall." She smiled and tousled his chestnut hair. "You have your hat?"

Oliver patted the chest of his coat. "It's in my pocket. Can I go now? My friends are waiting for me."

"Yes," Becca said, "I need to get going for story time too." She smiled as Oliver adjusted the sled under his arm and heaved open the heavy door. "Love you," she said.

Through the whipping wind, Becca could hear a faint, "Love you too!" as the young man disappeared behind a curtain of slanting snow.

Smoothing her teal apron, which was pinned with a sprig of holly, Becca crossed the bookshop and picked her way through the children who were already settled on the carpet. She plucked the mallet from the basket and struck the wall-mounted chime. As she waited for the dawdlers to make their way over, she took a survey of the children's favorite Christmas cookies—frosted cut-outs being the easy favorite. Butterscotch was the last to join the story time area, and she signaled her readiness by making three slow turns and curling up at Becca's feet.

"Hello, boys and girls, and welcome to a very special Christmas story time!" Becca greeted. "Let's begin with our good morning song."

From *Christmas Trolls* to *The Legend of the Candy Cane*, time passed quickly as Becca made her way through the basket of picture books. Ending with a finger play, she stood as she led the children through the final verse. "One little Christmas tree stood all alone," she said, holding up one finger. "His heart was very sad for he hadn't found a home. *Chop*! went the ax. Down fell the tree." She and the children tumbled to the ground.

Amidst a round of high-pitched giggles, they all rose and marched in place. "And off it went with a happy family!"

Laughing, Becca collapsed into the rocker and clapped her hands for attention. "Our time together is over for today, children. Parents, if you want to take home any of the books that we read today, they are all available for purchase at the display table." She reached behind her, pulled out a white basket filled with miniature candy canes, and held it up. "And since this is our last story time before Christmas, I have a little gift for you! But..." Becca paused, and her eyes twinkled mischievously. "You need to earn them!" She held up *The Legend of the Candy Cane*. "Who can tell me the three ways candy canes remind us of Jesus?"

Almost all the children's hands shot into the air.

"Yes, Lily?" Becca smiled at a six-year-old girl. Her long red-gold hair hung prettily over her thick sweater-jacket, which was patterned in broad brightly colored stripes.

"It's shaped like a 'J' for Jesus!" the girl said.

"Very good! That's one. What else?"

Becca pointed to a hazel-eyed boy whose head was topped with thick golden curls. "Yes, Theo?"

"The stripes," the boy said, taking a large bite of the chocolate chip cookie his mother had just handed him.

Raising her eyebrows, Becca said, "I'm impressed! That was the hardest one. Isaiah said that by His stripes we would be healed. Does anyone know the last one?"

"Yes?" Becca said, pointing to a pair of blonde twin girls.

"It's shaped like a shepherd's hook—" the first girl said.

"And the shepherds were the first ones to find out about Jesus's birth," her sister finished, ignoring the glare from the sibling she had just interrupted.

Becca laughed. "Excellent, children! As you enjoy these candy canes, it is my prayer that you will always remember Whom Christmas is all about." She waved them forward. "Come on, you earned them!"

When the sea of candy-grabbing children had subsided, red-haired Lily stepped forward and tentatively chose a candy cane from the basket. "Thank you, Ms. Gables," she said sweetly.

"You're very welcome," Becca said, smiling.

As the girl continued to stand there, Becca glanced around the story time area and furrowed her eyebrows. "Is your mom here, Lily? Maybe in the café or looking at books?"

Lily shook her head. "Mom dropped me off. Grandpa was supposed to pick me up."

Becca cast her gaze around the bookshop and frowned. Seeing Lily's worried expression, she quickly gave the girl a reassuring smile. "Well, I'm sure he's here or on his way. Let's take a look around."

Becca took Lily's small hand in her own, and the two of them wandered the bookshop. When neither Lily's mother nor grandfather could be found, Becca crouched by the girl. "Do you know your mom's phone number? Or your grandpa's?"

Lily's bottom lip trembled. "I know my mom's."

"Good girl!" Becca said, pulling her phone from her back pocket. She dialed the number that Lily gave her. The phone went to voicemail, and she forced her lips into a smile as she left a message.

Crouching again, Becca said brightly, "This actually works out really well. My daughters, Violet and Hazel, are at play rehearsal right now, so I could use some help. Would you like to be my helper until your mom or grandpa arrives?"

Lily's face broke into a smile, revealing a gap where a front tooth had been. "Yes, I would!"

Grabbing Lily's hand, Becca led her to the café area and behind the confectionery counter. After showing the girl how to wash her hands, Becca popped Hazel's apron over Lily's head. "It fits great!" Becca said. "Maybe a tad big."

Lily smiled and slid her hands into the apron pockets.

"Shall we make the rounds and check on the customers?" Becca asked.

At Lily's enthusiastic nod, Becca led the girl around to the front of the confectionery counter. As they passed, Audrey caught Becca's eye and arched a brow.

"I have a helper," Becca explained, "until her mom or grandpa comes to pick her up."

"Ah!" Audrey said with a nod. "She looks like she's a good worker." The auburn-haired woman returned to her task of waiting with measured patience as a customer chose between chocolate chip and orange-vanilla scones.

Becca's eyes fell on Alex Gerhartz, the Bible teacher, seated at a table, typing on a laptop. He wore a white cable-knit sweater, and his leather jacket and a brown patchwork scarf were slung across the back of his chair.

Crouching, Becca looked into Lily's honey-colored eyes. "Are you ready?"

The girl nodded shyly, and the pair made their way to the man's table.

"Hey, Alex!" Becca said. "Are you loving the snow outside?"

Alex looked up from the laptop screen and beamed. "You bet I am."

"Lily and I are just checking to see how you're doing," Becca said, placing a hand on the girl's shoulder.

Lily's eyes widened hopefully. "Can we get you anything?"

Alex picked up his mug and inspected the contents. "I have a good amount of cider left," he said. Seeing the girl's disappointment, he added, "But I could really use a napkin."

Lily glanced up at Becca, who smiled and nodded, and the girl hurried away.

"You're taking a break from painting to work on the Matthew study," Becca said. It wasn't a question.

Alex raised his eyebrows and leaned back in his chair. "Now, how do you know that I was painting?"

"By the dark-green paint on the side of your neck," Becca said, pointing.

Drawing his fingers to the spot where Becca indicated, Alex shook his head and chuckled as he felt the dried paint beneath his fingertips.

"And based on the color, I'd say you were working on *The Widow's Mite*, specifically the robe of the man on the far right."

The Bible teacher looked up at Becca, and his lips curved into a half-smile. "Well, now you're just being a show-off."

Becca laughed and shrugged as Lily returned and plunked about fifty napkins onto the table beside Alex's mug. "We'll let you get back to it," Becca said, reaching for Lily's hand. "I know you've got to get that done for tomorrow."

Alex eyed the thick stack of napkins and smiled at Lily. "Thank you," he said, brown eyes twinkling. "You are quite the overachiever." He caught Becca's eye and chuckled as the two made their way to the next table.

Becca blinked in surprise as she took in the sight of Harvey, his sandy-colored head bent over a sketchbook. Even with the additional bulk of the young man's green-and-gray coat, his frame looked delicate. On the tabletop sat a half-consumed peppermint mocha, a dark-gray winter beanie complete with visor and earflaps, and a copy of the *Crystal Run Reporter* with a formal portrait of Phyllis Grant centered on the front page.

"Good morning, Harvey," Becca said.

He glanced up from his sketchbook. "Oh, hello."

"Lily and I are just wondering if we can get you anything," Becca said, smiling down at her helper.

Harvey tilted his head as he considered the girl for a moment and then shrugged. "No, I'm fine."

Lily watched as Butterscotch made her way over to the fireplace and laid down, settling her muzzle between her paws. "Ms. Gables?" the girl asked. "Would it be okay if I pet Butterscotch for a while?"

Becca crouched down. "Oh, yes," she said, her eyes crinkling in amusement. "Petting Butterscotch is an important part of the job description."

As Lily skipped away toward the golden retriever, Becca smiled at Harvey and stepped toward the next table. "Just let me know if you need anything."

"Actually..." Harvey's voice was high for a man's and a bit nasaled.

Becca stopped and turned to face him.

"Well," Harvey said, shading in a corner of his drawing, "I'm just wondering if you've seen Lexi lately."

With a quizzical tilt of her head, Becca said, "She stops by the bookstore every now and then." She hesitated for a few moments and then added, "But we are going to see her on Monday when we bring her a meal."

Harvey sat up. "Really? Can you ask her to call me?"

Becca furrowed her brows. "Why would you need me to do that? Did something happen?"

Harvey's face flushed, highlighting the sprinkling of freckles across his nose. "She broke up with me about a week ago, and she's not responding to any of my phone calls or texts."

"Oh," Becca said softly, "I'm sorry to hear that."

Setting down his charcoal pencil a little too roughly on the sketchpad, he continued, "I just don't get it. We've been having such a good time."

Becca cleared her throat.

"I mean, yeah, I know I wasn't there the day her grandma passed. But I explained to her how my phone died, and I thought she had gotten over that." He shook his head, and his voice grew louder as he continued. "And we even went down to Chicago to see this art auction, and she was talking to all these people down there. She seemed to have fun. I don't know." He paused, picking up the pencil and shading another corner. "It's like one day everything was great, and now she doesn't want anything to do with me."

"That's really tough," Becca said, tucking a strand of hair behind her ear. "Now, of course, I don't know all of the circumstances between the two of you, but Lexi is going through a lot right now."

Harvey looked up at her, his eyes shining with tears. "That's the thing. I know she's going through a lot with having to stay at her grandma's to put herself through law school. Now she has to sell the estate, and she was really upset about her grandma being gone and all. The young man picked up his peppermint mocha and set it back down. "So, I tried to point out to her that now we are free to be together without anyone standing in our way. And a few days later, she just breaks up with me!"

At his words, Becca stiffened.

Heaving an exasperated sigh, Harvey continued, "Could you *please* just have her call me? Whatever is going on, we can work through it." He looked up at Becca, his eyes like a wounded puppy.

Becca shifted her weight from one foot to the other. "I'll see what I can do." She bit her lip as she considered what else to say, but before she could continue, a loud bang came from the front of the bookshop. Becca turned to see the teal door ricochet off the wall as a woman stormed inside.

"Lily!" The woman's voice pierced the otherwise pleasant sounds of Christmas music and cheerful chatter, and her straight red hair streamed behind her as she strode to the back of the shop. "Lily!"

"Mommy!" the girl cried. She popped up from where she had been kneeling by Butterscotch and ran to her mother.

"Manicure!" Jumping back in alarm, the woman raised her hands as Lily flung her arms around her mother's waist.

Becca smoothed her apron and stepped toward the pair. Smiling at the girl, she said, "See, Lily? It wasn't long at all before someone came to pick you up. I will be sad to be losing my helper, though." Becca turned her eyes to the mother. Her red hair was striking against her elegant white coat with its wide lapel collar. Beneath the coat, which was cinched at the waist, the woman wore a gray pantsuit, and a puddle was beginning to form beneath her short boots as the snow melted from them.

An embarrassed smile spread across the woman's face. "I am so sorry," she said. "I don't know what happened. Lily's grandpa was supposed to pick her up."

Becca's lips curved into a slight frown. "Is he all right? Did you try calling him?"

"I did," the woman said. "He didn't answer his phone, but I'm sure he's fine."

At the woman's careless certainty, Becca raised her brows.

Unnoticing, the woman continued with a smile, "I'm not sure that we've ever been formally introduced. She glanced down at her daughter. "Lily, would you reach in Mommy's bag and hand Ms.—"

"Gables!" Lily supplied cheerfully, flashing her gap-toothed grin.

"Gables... one of my business cards?" She blew on her nails, which were painted a deep purple, and waved them in the air.

"You can call me Becca."

Obediently, Lily reached into the front pocket of her mother's designer purse, pulled out a card, and handed it to Becca.

Becca glanced down at the dark-gray card, which featured a headshot of the red-haired woman standing in front of an impressive waterfront property. Running along the bottom of the card was a beige band with the words: *Harper Davis – Realtor.*

"Harper Davis," the woman confirmed. "I would shake your hand, but..." She held up her hand and wiggled her fingers in explanation. The woman glanced down at her boots and then back up at Becca. "Thank you for watching Lily. I really appreciate it."

"It ended up all right," Becca said, smiling as she tucked the card into her apron pocket. She placed her hand on Lily's shoulder. "And Lily was an excellent helper. However," she continued in a serious tone, "I do need to tell you that a guardian must be present during story time. This isn't a drop-off program."

The muscles in Harper's jaw tightened, and she narrowed her eyes. "Well, I'm sorry, but someone was *supposed* to be here." The woman's eyes flicked to the doorway. "And here comes Mr. Unreliable now."

Becca followed the woman's line of sight and watched as Dr. Stephen Davis stamped the snow from his boots just inside the teal door. He wore a long chocolate double-breasted peacoat and a brown leather fedora with a floppy brim. Spying Harper, he made his way to the back of the bookshop.

"Sorry I'm late," Dr. Davis said, slightly out of breath. "It's nasty out there!" He removed his hat, revealing eyebrows and a beard crusted with snow.

Lily gazed up at her grandfather and giggled. "You look so funny, Grandpa!"

"What's the excuse this time?" Harper asked flatly, crossing her arms over her chest. The doctor gaped at his daughter.

Becca cleared her throat. "Is everything all right? Are you okay, Dr. Davis?"

"Everything's fine now, thank you," he replied. "My car got stuck in the driveway, but some nice young gentlemen came along and pushed me out."

"Oh no!" Becca said. "But what a blessing that those young men came along."

The doctor chuckled. "Indeed! I'd probably still be there if it weren't for them."

Tenderly, Lily reached up and wrapped her hand around two of Dr. Davis's gloved fingers. "Is it still a Lily-Grandpa Day?"

"I'm here, so I might as well take you now," Harper replied, looking at her daughter. "Take off that apron, and let's go."

The doctor's eyes widened. "What? Why? Can't she even stay for a hot chocolate?"

"Please, Mommy?" Lily begged, ducking behind her grandfather and clutching his arm.

A look of pain shot across Harper's face. "No," she snapped. "Absolutely not." Turning toward her father, she said, "You are completely unreliable, just like you've always been. I can't even count on you to pick up Lily from story time so that I can get my nails done—"

"It was the snow!" the doctor interjected, stamping his foot.

Harper narrowed her eyes. "Snow," she said coldly. "There's always an excuse. You were never there for me growing up, and you are not even here for your granddaughter now." Her gaze fell on the copy of *The Crystal Run Reporter* that Harvey had left at his table. Clenching her jaw at the sight of Phyllis Grant smirking out at her, she picked up the newspaper and brandished it at Dr. Davis. "You spent all your time with your precious Grants. Always the Grants!" She flung the paper back onto the table. "I heard you tell Mom that you were investing all that time with that family *for us*. That it would pay off someday. And what did Mrs. Grant eventually do? She dumped you because she saw you for the pathetic gambling bum you've always been!"

"Harper!" The doctor's eyes flashed. "Don't you dare take that old bag's side! After all I did for that woman—that *family*!"

"You did more for that family than you ever did for your own," Harper replied icily. "And now look at what you have to show for it." Reaching behind her father and snatching Lily's hand, the woman said, "Come on, Lily, there's no Lily-Grandpa Day today." Tossing her fiery hair over her shoulder, she stalked away, dragging her daughter behind her. Halfway to the exit, she remembered the teal apron, hastily removed it, and pitched it on top of the nearest bookshelf.

With jaw and fists clenched, Dr. Davis watched as the pair exited.

"Oh, dear," Becca breathed. "I'm so sorry, Dr. Davis. I know that you were looking forward to your day with Lily."

Face still flushed with anger, the doctor heaved a sigh.

Pressing her lips together, Becca hesitated and then said softly, "What did she mean by Mrs. Grant 'dumping you'? I thought she was your patient right up until the end?"

"Oh, she was still my patient all right," the doctor replied sharply. "But she completely wrote me out of her will... about six months ago." A vein bulged in his forehead, and he continued, "After the *decades* I've served that family. After I sat with her dying father and read him the sports section day after day." His eyes fell on the newspaper with Phyllis Grant staring up judgmentally at him. "Whoever killed that woman did the world a favor. That old goat had it coming."

Wide-eyed, Becca held her breath as the red-faced doctor furiously pulled his hat onto his head, turned on his heel, and strode out of the bookshop into the howling wind and snow. She stared after him for a few moments, blinked, and then retrieved the teal apron from the top of the bookshelf where Harper had discarded it. As Becca headed back to the kitchen area to hang up the apron, Audrey caught her eye.

"Is everything okay?" her sister-in-law asked, plating a cinnamon roll. "I heard shouting."

Raising her eyebrows and drawing in a breath, Becca said, "I feel bad for that little girl... for the whole family." She glanced at her watch. "Is it okay if I head upstairs to start getting ready for the show?"

"Go ahead. I've got it," Audrey said, the shop's twinkle lights reflecting in her glasses. "With the weather, the customers are starting to dwindle anyway. I'll see you there."

Becca gave her sister-in-law a quick hug, hung up her apron, and headed toward the steps that led to the Gables' apartment. She was so deep in thought she almost tripped over Toffee, who trotted up to her with a toy mouse in his mouth. "Goodness!" she gasped as she regained her balance. Stooping, she stroked the cat's back, gently removed the toy from its mouth, and tossed the mouse several yards away. As the cat scampered after it, the door to the alley burst open, and Oliver bustled inside, sled tucked under his arm. He had his hood pulled up over his head, and his entire body was covered in a layer of snow.

"Hey, buddy!" Becca said brightly. "How was sledding?"

Oliver leaned the sled against the wall and pushed back his hood. His hair was damp and matted, and his cheeks were flushed pink.

Becca arched a brow. "I can see you didn't wear your hat."

"Nah, I had my hood," the young man said with a grin. "It was lots of fun. I tried going down the hill backward, and I ended up doing a double-backward somersault."

Cringing, Becca said, "There are some things that may be better for me not to know."

Pulling his gloves from his hands, Oliver continued, "My friends and I helped push Dr. Davis's car out of his driveway. He had gotten it stuck in the snow."

"Oh, that was you!" Becca said, smiling. "That was wonderful of you all to do that. Dr. Davis stopped by here, and he was very grateful."

Oliver blushed and shrugged. "It wasn't a big deal." He kicked off his boot in the general direction of the alley door.

Becca smiled warmly at her son. "You'd better head up and shower. We're going to have to leave for the play soon."

"Will they have concessions?" he asked, shrugging out of his snow-crusted coat.

"Of course," Becca said. "I believe I heard that there will be Marley's Popcorn Chain, Fezziwig's Fudge, and Cratchit's Cookies."

With a grin, Oliver mounted the steps two at a time. He stopped suddenly, turned, and descended again. "Oh, hey, Mom... As I was coming home, I passed Harvey—you know, Lexi Grant's boyfriend?"

"You did?" Becca's eyes widened.

Oliver frowned. "Yeah. I waved to him, but he didn't respond. I dunno, he just seemed really..." The young man paused as he searched for the word. "...weird." He kicked at the step with his socked foot. "It didn't feel right."

Becca smiled at her son. "Thank you for sharing this with me. Is there anything else?"

Oliver shook his head.

Pointing up the stairs, Becca commanded, "To the shower with you!"

Obediently, her son leaped up the stairs, and Becca bent to turn his boots upright. As she lined them against the wall, she felt a draft slip around the doorframe like a whisper. Echoing in her head were Harvey's words: "without anyone standing in our way." She shivered, wondering whether the impulse was triggered by the icy air or the icy words.

# Chapter 17

# Blessing Backfired

"Uh-oh." With a lid in one hand, Hazel peered into the stockpot. Her vanilla-blonde hair was wound into an elegant twist, and she wore a ruffled apron patterned with gingerbread men and candy canes.

"What's the matter, Hazel?" Becca, wearing an apron that matched her daughter's, had barely caught the utterance over the cheerful piano notes of "I Saw Three Ships."

"I don't remember if I put salt in the soup," Hazel said, wringing her hands. "I'd better add more, just in case." She picked up the wooden salt cellar and measuring spoons.

Becca spun around. "Freeze!" She looked at her daughter, whose face was flushed and dewy from leaning over the soup. "Did you taste it?"

"No, not yet."

Removing two spoons from a light-oak drawer, Becca handed one to Hazel. "A good chef tastes as she goes." She ladled out a small amount of soup, and the mother and daughter tasted it. Becca arched a brow. "Well, chef?"

Hazel smacked her lips. "I think I did add the salt already."

"I think you did too," Becca said, smiling.

"Oliver!" Violet scolded. She wore a plum-colored sweater and jeans, and her hair was pulled back into her signature messy bun. "If you eat any more peppermint bark, there won't be any left for Miss Grant."

Defiantly, the young man popped another piece of bark into his mouth. "A good chef tastes as he goes," he said.

Becca laughed as she seized the tray, rose onto her tiptoes, and placed it safely on top of the refrigerator. "That's not what I meant."

Just then, a knock to the rhythm of "Shave and a Haircut" sounded from the apartment door. "Come on in, Audrey!" Becca called.

Within moments, the auburn-haired woman appeared and cast her gaze around the kitchen. Her eyes lingered on the evergreen swag hung over the range hood and the sparkling white bottlebrush trees that adorned the floating shelves. "Well, isn't this a merry scene?"

"Aunt Audrey!" Abandoning her ladle, Hazel raced across the room and wrapped her arms around the woman's waist. Taking a step back, she surveyed her aunt. "You look fancy!"

"Do you think so?" Audrey asked, popping her leg forward and pointing a booted toe. She wore a cropped leather jacket over a long flowy evergreen dress that was cinched at the waist with a broad leather belt. In her hand was a floppy wide-brimmed Panama hat, and a brown leather tote bag hung from her shoulder.

"You look adorable!" Becca said, eyes twinkling. "Almost like you're ready to enjoy a romantic Italian dinner."

Audrey waved the comment away, but a blush rose into her round cheeks as she hung her tote on the back of a chair.

Oliver, who had been leaning against the counter, straightened. "Aunt Audrey, would you like to see the latest issue of the *Pickwick Portfolio*?" His eyes twinkled mischievously.

"Your newspaper?" Audrey asked. "I would say yes, but I'm not sure I like that look on your face."

Hazel glanced at her brother, clapped her hands, and bounced on her toes. "I'll go get it!"

As the girl bolted in the direction of the living room, Audrey looked at Becca. "Do you know what this is about?"

"I might," Becca said, smiling and tossing a handful of chopped dates onto a bed of greens.

Soon Hazel returned with a long cream-colored scroll, which she unrolled, revealing a patchwork of pasted articles and drawings. Holding it up to her aunt, she asked in her high, sweet voice, "Do you see anything interesting, Aunt Audrey?"

Audrey's eyebrows furrowed as she studied the newspaper. Suddenly, she gasped and clapped a hand over her mouth. "The comic!"

Hazel exploded into a fit of giggles, and Oliver grinned. Even Violet set down the plastic knife she was using to cut brownies and smiled as she joined the little group around the *Pickwick Portfolio*.

Placing her hands on her hips and doing her best to keep a straight face, Audrey said, "That looks an awful lot like me and Detective Post."

"Being chased by Toffee and a *baby* bunny!" Hazel added helpfully.

Becca raised her hands, palms out. "I plead innocence."

"Well," Audrey said to the children, trying to sound stern, "I can't wait until the next edition of the *Aunt Audrey Post*." She wagged a finger at them. "You should all be afraid!" As the very unafraid children erupted into laughter, her eyes returned to the comic. She shook her head, but she was unable to hide the smile that played on her lips. "Oh!" she suddenly exclaimed, her face brightening. "This reminds me! I want to show you what I'm making Chris for Christmas." Handing the paper back to Hazel, she hurried to her tote bag, plunged her hand inside, and pulled out a tailless golden-brown crocheted cat about the size of a coffee mug.

"It's Toffee!" Hazel said, her eyes crinkling in delight.

Audrey stroked the top of the cat's head with two fingers. "He's not quite finished yet. I need to sew on his eyes and embroider his little pink nose and mouth." She glanced at Becca and the children and gave a shaky smile. "I don't know. What do you think? Is he going to like it?"

Becca grinned as her thoughts flashed to the baby bunny Chris had purchased for Audrey. The children, who had burst into a fresh round of giggles, were clearly thinking the same thing.

"What?" Audrey asked, her eyes widening in dismay. "Is he going to hate it?"

"Actually," Becca said, raising her voice over the children's laughter, "I couldn't think of a more perfect gift."

Violet shot Hazel a *don't-you-dare-say-anything* look, and Oliver coughed into his fist.

With a raised brow, Audrey searched their faces. Then she looked at Becca and smiled. "All right, I trust you."

"May I hold him?" Hazel asked, reaching for the cat.

As the woman handed over the crocheted cat, Audrey looked at Becca. "Could we head down and grab that dessert now?"

Becca scanned the kitchen. Finding that the preparations for Lexi's blessing basket were nearly complete, she said, "Are you okay with being in charge for a bit, Vi?"

"Yes, go ahead," Violet said. She glanced up from the brownies to find her brother furtively reaching toward the top of the refrigerator. "The only challenge I expect is keeping Oliver away from the peppermint bark."

With a jerk, Oliver lowered his arm and hid it behind his back.

As Becca stepped lightly down the steps toward the bookshop, she glanced up at Audrey. "Yesterday I moved a turtle cheesecake from the freezer to the refrigerator. Does cheesecake sound okay?"

"That will be perfect," Audrey said, adjusting her tote strap on her shoulder.

Becca's green eyes sparkled. "I'm envisioning one slice, two forks..."

"Knock it off," Audrey said, swatting at her sister-in-law with her Panama hat as a wide smile spread across her face.

The women neared the door that led out to the alley. When her gaze fell upon Oliver's boots lined up against the wall, Becca's thoughts shifted to her conversation with Harvey, and the playful smile faded from her lips.

In silence, Becca led Audrey into the bookshop, which felt strange and eerily dark except for the Christmas tree that glimmered in the corner. The two made their way to the kitchen. Becca's face glowed in the refrigerator light as she carefully removed a cheesecake drizzled with caramel and chocolate and sprinkled with chopped pecans.

Clasping her hands in delight, Audrey exclaimed, "It's beautiful!"

"Mm-hmm," Becca said absently, setting the cheesecake on the counter.

Audrey studied her sister-in-law's face. "Hey, is everything okay?"

"Oh, sorry," Becca said, pulling her lips into a smile. "What do you think about putting it on that pretty red crystal platter we keep up there?" She pointed to an upper cabinet. After a few moments' hesitation, she added, "I was just thinking about a conversation I had with Harvey the other day."

Audrey moved to the cabinet Becca had indicated. "Oh, what about?" she asked, standing on her tiptoes as she reached for the red platter. "Does it involve the Grant case?"

Tucking a strand of blonde hair behind her ear, Becca slid into a chair at the tiled table. "Harvey Veleno was always high on my suspect list, but now he's even higher. He told me that Lexi broke up with him soon after he shared the silver lining that now they could be together without her grandmother 'standing in their way.' The conversation just gave me the creepiest feeling. And then Oliver had an encounter with him afterward too, and he said it just felt 'off.'"

Setting the platter on the counter, Audrey raised a brow. "And for *Oliver* to say that..."

"Exactly," Becca said. She paused, drumming her fingertips on the tiled table. "But how would Harvey have known about Mrs. Grant's medication? Obviously, Lexi would know about it, but I can't imagine that it was exactly a conversation point between the two of them."

Audrey spun around to face her sister-in-law. "Oh, that's easy!" She grinned and continued. "Do you remember when Hazel was working on her veggie-chopping skills?"

Becca laughed. "How could I forget? I had enough chopped onions, carrots, and celery to make chicken soup for the entire town."

"Well," Audrey continued, "I was at Sloane's Apothecary, stocking up on Band-Aids, and I saw Harvey in there with Lexi, picking up Phyllis's prescription. He definitely knew about the sleeping pills."

Lost in thought, Becca gazed at the glistening cheesecake for several long moments. "After that," she said slowly, "all Harvey would have to do is sneak into her bedroom and take a few pills when she wasn't around."

Audrey nodded as she gingerly placed the cheesecake onto the platter and licked the caramel from her fingers. "Who else is high on your suspect list?"

Shaking herself from her thoughts, Becca looked up. "Donna Sloane," she said. "It's not a secret that she had a grudge against Mrs. Grant. And there are few who have more access to her prescription than the pharmacist's wife."

Becca rose and extracted a box of toothpicks from a drawer. With a glance at her sister-in-law, she said, "So we don't smudge the top when we wrap it." She inserted the first toothpick and continued thoughtfully. "Well, I had a couple of people drop down on the suspect list. The story about Patricia Koller nearly being fired because of Phyllis Grant was exaggerated. And Dr. Davis's motive recently got a whole lot weaker."

Audrey, who was bending to pull a roll of plastic wrap from a drawer, glanced up at Becca and raised her eyebrows.

"Do you remember that big blow-up between Dr. Davis and his daughter?" Becca asked as she inserted the final toothpick.

Audrey gave a low whistle. "Do I ever!"

"Dr. Davis said that Phyllis Grant had at one time left him a legacy in her will, but she had written him out completely about six months ago. I can't eliminate him completely because he clearly did not like Mrs. Grant, but the motive for money is gone now."

Audrey pulled a long piece of plastic wrap from the roll. "Okay," she said slowly, "So that leaves Donna and Harvey as our top suspects?"

Becca nodded. "And I'd put a double star next to Harvey's name."

"Okay, so Harvey and Donna," Audrey said slowly, tucking the edges of the plastic wrap under the platter.

Hopping up onto the counter, Becca beamed. "Why the sudden interest in the Grant case? Does it have anything to do with a certain detective heading it up?" She waggled her eyebrows.

"No..." Audrey said defensively, her cheeks flushing a bright pink. "I have *always* found this kind of stuff fascinating."

"Liar!" Becca laughed heartily as she slid down from the counter.

Audrey made a face and glanced at her watch. "Yikes! We should both be going."

Becca nodded. "I want a full report when you get home tonight. I'm dying to know what he's cooking for you."

"That makes two of us," Audrey said with a smile as she picked up the wrapped cheesecake. "And I want to hear all about your meal drop-off at the Paper Palace."

"Oh," Becca said, "I'm sure that will be far less exciting."

It wasn't long before the Gables' light-blue minivan was pulling into the winding snow-covered cobblestone driveway of the Paper Palace. Although the two lamps on the stone pillars pierced the darkness, Becca's eyebrows furrowed as she realized this was the only residence on Grant Boulevard completely devoid of Christmas lights. She pulled into the circular driveway and switched off the engine. From the trunk, Oliver hefted an insulated tote with ham-and-potato soup, soft golden dinner rolls, and a thermos of piping-hot chocolate. Violet carried a small cooler with a salad and bottle of dressing, and Becca grabbed a paper bag filled with her trademark Symphony brownies, a loaf of banana bread, and peppermint bark. Hazel clutched a stack of *Nutcracker*-themed drawings. She had been careful to make sure that her sketch of the Sugar Plum Fairy was on the top.

As the family headed toward the massive arched front door, Hazel skipped ahead. Glancing over her shoulder, she beamed at her mother and siblings. "Do you think the March girls in *Little Women* were this excited when they were delivering their meal?"

Becca smiled warmly at her daughter. "You have a beautiful servant's heart." Transferring the paper bag to her left hand, she extended a finger and rang the doorbell.

Hazel frowned at the huge unadorned front doors. "Maybe I should have made Miss Grant some paper wreaths."

"Your drawings are going to bring her lots of Christmas cheer," Becca said, placing a hand on Hazel's back.

Oliver's husky voice broke in. "Someone else is here."

Becca turned and watched as a black Mercedes Benz pulled in behind their minivan.

Just then, the house door opened, and Lexi appeared. Her blue-black hair was pulled back into a ponytail, and she wore a gray sweater tunic over leggings. With one hand on the door, she surveyed the group.

"Merry Christmas!" the children called in unison.

Pushing her way to the front, Hazel grinned at the woman. "We brought you dinner for tonight, breakfast for tomorrow, *and* peppermint bark!" She glanced at her brother and scowled. "Well, what's left of it anyway."

Oliver jabbed an elbow into Hazel's side, and Becca gave them both a stern look.

"And I drew these for you!" Hazel continued brightly, thrusting the stack of drawings toward Lexi. "I know you love art. You can hang them up or set them around the house. Whatever brings you the most Christmas cheer."

"Well, thanks, all of you," Lexi said, smiling as she accepted the drawings. "That's so generous." She stood on her tiptoes and peered over their heads at the woman approaching the front door. "The realtor is here early for our meeting, but it shouldn't be very long." Looking at Becca, Lexi said, "You're familiar with the kitchen. Would you mind putting the food in the fridge for me? You can wait in the library when you're done."

Becca smiled. "I don't mind at all."

Lexi opened the door wider, and the Gables entered the foyer. As they set down the packages and hung up their coats, the realtor entered. She was a tall, heavyset woman with muddy-blonde hair and choppy sideswept bangs. Her eyes were framed by rectangular eyeglasses, and she wore a brown skirt suit under a trench coat, which was knotted in the back.

While Lexi greeted the woman and led her to the office, Becca and the children resumed their blessing basket offerings and trooped toward the kitchen. As they entered the spacious room, Becca's gaze was drawn to the collection of shining pots and pans that hung from a rectangular rack over the granite countertop. The family set to work unloading the insulated tote, cooler, and paper bag. Placing her hands on either side of the disposable container that held the soup, Becca said, "It's still nice and hot. I think I'll leave this out for now so Lexi can have it for dinner."

Violet glanced at the salad. "This should go in the fridge, though." She picked up the plastic container and opened the refrigerator door. As she tucked the salad inside, she turned toward the others. "Come here," she said softly.

Becca, Oliver, and Hazel stepped toward the refrigerator and looked inside as Violet stepped back. Apart from an expired carton of milk and a couple of small takeout boxes, the refrigerator was empty.

"She really needed this," Hazel whispered.

Becca gave a small smile as she closed the refrigerator door. "God is blessing Lexi with something she needs. Isn't it wonderful how He is allowing us to be a part of it?"

Job complete, the Gables made their way to the library, dropping off the tote, cooler, and bag by the door. Becca flipped on the light as they entered the library, which, like the rest of the Paper Palace, was a picture of elegance. A chandelier hung from the molded ceiling and cast light on the wood-paneled walls. A stately writing desk stood in front of a set of three tall, narrow curtained windows, forming a corner of the room. Towering bookshelves flanked the carved stone fireplace, and an octagonal side table stood nearby topped with a chess set.

Standing in front of the bookshelves, Oliver scanned the spines of the gold-embossed hardbacks. "The Grants must not be fans of the fantasy genre," he observed. He glanced at Violet. "Do you feel like getting beaten in a game of chess?"

Violet cocked a brow. "I'd like to see you try!"

As the brother and sister slid into the upholstered chairs at the octagonal table, Hazel gleefully pulled a book from the shelf. "*A Christmas Carol!*" she exclaimed, holding up the volume to show her mother. Clutching her treasure, she skipped over to a powder-blue loveseat opposite the fireplace and plopped down. Carefully, she opened the antique book and turned the pages. "Oh! And it's illustrated. I'm going to see if they have a picture of the Ghost of Christmas Past."

With the children entertained, Becca slowly walked the perimeter of the room. As she ran her fingers along the edge of the writing desk, she eyed a large book on its surface titled *The Grant Paper Company: A History*. Moving along, she paused to study a landscape hung over a side table. Then she stepped toward a globe mounted on a stand. Becca gave it a spin, and her fingertips ended up in the Mediterranean Sea. With a smile, she recalled what Oliver had always said about that body of water—that it looked like a duck with the Adriatic Sea as its wing.

She strolled away from the globe and noticed that the door leading to the living room was ajar. She gazed into the space. Even though the room was still nothing short of grand with its colossal stone fireplace and gleaming tiled floors, Becca marveled at how different it looked from the night of Phyllis Grant's cocktail party. That evening, the room had been alive with food, flowers, and a delightful mixture of music and the buzz of conversation. Now it stood bare, cavernous, and almost tomblike. Most jarring was the naked stretch of wall above the carved fireplace. Becca's eyebrows furrowed as she noted that the Grant family portrait now sat on the floor, leaning up against a wall.

With a glance over her shoulder at the happily occupied children, Becca stepped into the sepulchral space and allowed herself to be drawn to the painting. The closer she got, the more she felt dwarfed by it. At one point, she paused and let out a low whistle. "That must be about nine feet tall," she said softly to herself.

Finally stopping a few feet in front of the portrait, Becca's gaze swept over the surface, and her eyes widened in dismay as she took in the condition of the painting. At the cocktail party, she had noticed that it had been covered with a web of hairline cracks, but now that the portrait was directly in front of her, Becca could see that it was incredibly dusty, and the damage was significantly worse than she initially thought. The entire surface was bubbled and wrinkled. Betsy Grant's elegant gold evening gown had the texture of a rumpled bed sheet. Becca's eyes moved to teenage Phyllis's baby-blue mini dress, which was shot through with dark lines. William Grant III's black suit was covered with what looked like silver spiderwebs. Tragically, the worst damage of all was located at the center of the painting. On William Grant's otherwise dignified brow, a large chip of paint was beginning to peel away from the canvas. Just below the forehead, the man's expertly painted brown eyes stared out at her, and Becca was captivated by them. She leaned in and studied the lashes, the upper lid, the gold-flecked iris... Alberti had captured a gleam in Grant's eye. What was it? Pride? Confidence? Perhaps a touch of fear? Becca frowned. *If only this weren't so dusty!* Without thinking, she blew a short sharp puff at the eye. Her breath was all that was needed to dislodge that loose paint chip entirely. Gasping in horror, Becca watched as the four-inch fragment floated to the floor like an oak leaf. "Oh *no!*" she breathed. She crouched down, gently picked up the flesh-colored paint chip by its edges and examined it. Her eyebrows raised in surprise as she noticed a piece of double-sided tape on the back. Becca rose and flicked her gaze back and forth between the fragment and its original place until her eyes locked on the portrait. Drawing in a sharp breath, she whispered, "What is this?" She squinted at what she had thought was a void but, upon closer inspection, was actually an image, smudged and dim. She leaned in. It appeared to be a banner with the letters "D-E-C" printed across it. Carefully, Becca transferred the paint chip to her left hand, pulled her phone from the back pocket of her blue jeans, and took a photo of the image. As she tucked the phone back into her pocket, she continued to stare at the hazy illustration. She was so engrossed that she only vaguely became aware of Lexi's approaching footsteps.

"WHAT. DID. YOU. DO?" With each staccato word, Lexi's voice grew louder until it was echoing throughout the cavernous room.

Becca jumped backward, and her hand flew to her heart as she turned toward the young woman, who was red-faced and trembling with rage.

"What did you do?! What are you doing?!" Lexi repeated, her fists balled at her sides.

Cheeks blooming with shame and embarrassment, Becca stammered, "I-I-I'm sorry. I'm so sorry. There was so much dust! I was just trying to clear some away so I could see better, and this piece fell off." She paused and bit her lip. "But—but, Lexi," she continued, "I think there's a painting under here."

Lexi's red face turned white and then red again. For several moments, the young woman stared at Becca, her mouth gaping. "I *know*!" she finally snapped. "I know that there's a painting underneath. Alberti reused canvases." Lexi glared at Becca and turned her gaze to the paint chip in Becca's hand. "Set that on the mantel and leave. *Now!*"

Having nearly forgotten the painting fragment in her hand, Becca glanced down at it. "Of course," she said. She stepped toward the mantel and carefully placed it on the surface. "Lexi, again, I am so, so sorry—"

Lexi stamped her foot. "Take your bratty children and go!"

Looking toward the door leading to the library, Becca saw that Violet and Hazel were cautiously entering the room. Oliver, on the other hand, crossed the space with bold strides and stood beside his mother.

Narrowing her stormy eyes at Becca, Lexi spat, "I hope you teach these kids to have more respect for people's personal property than you do. You ruined my family's portrait!"

Oliver clenched his jaw and gestured toward the painting. "It doesn't exactly look like it was in the best shape to begin with," he said coolly.

Becca shot Oliver a warning glance as Violet and Hazel finally joined the group.

Lexi's face contorted with rage. "Out!" she screamed, pointing in the direction of the doorway.

Grabbing Hazel's hand, Becca and the children hastened out of the room and toward the front door of the Paper Palace, Lexi following closely on their heels. The Gables quickly pulled on their coats.

Oliver snatched up the thermal tote. "You're welcome for the meal," he said icily.

"Merry Christmas?" Hazel squeaked.

"OUT!" Lexi bellowed.

Becca scanned the young woman's face, and a wave of regret and pity washed over her. "Merry Christmas, Lexi," she said softly.

In reply, Lexi clenched her jaw, narrowed her eyes, and pulled open the colossal door. She glared after the family as they stepped out into the frigid night. The door banged shut behind them, and Violet jumped, rattling the ice pack in the cooler she carried. For several long moments, the Gables stood stunned on the doorstep.

Hazel looked up at her mother, her eyes filled with tears. "I want to go home!" she said in a warbled voice.

Steeling herself, Becca sucked in a breath and squeezed her daughter's hand. "Let's get in the van and talk about it at home."

As the family headed toward their vehicle, which now sat alone in the circular driveway, Becca couldn't help but cast one last look back at the Paper Palace. The curtains were being furiously thrust closed, and Becca imagined a red-faced Lexi behind them. She shuddered.

The drive home was silent until Oliver finally said, "Mom, she went ballistic."

Becca sighed. "I know, but I did damage her painting."

Violet's eyebrows furrowed. "What did you do?"

"It was dusty," Becca said, gripping the steering wheel tightly. "I was just trying to get a better look at it. I blew on it, and a piece of paint fell off."

Violet's jaw dropped. "Mom, you blew on a damaged painting?"

"I know! I'm sorry. I didn't even realize what I was doing." Becca's face flushed in embarrassment, and she fidgeted with the tiny cross that dangled from her necklace.

For a few moments, Violet stared at her mother. Then she shook her head and looked out the window.

Becca shrugged as she slowed to a stop. Their faces were cast in yellow then red light, and silence filled the vehicle again as they waited.

"Mom?" Hazel whispered. "I don't think this is how the March girls felt after they delivered the Christmas meal to the Hummels."

# Chapter 18

---

# Christmas Eve Consultation

"Careful now," John said. The sleeve of his charcoal suit brushed against Becca's arm as he tipped the flame of his candle toward hers.

The wick of Becca's candle sparked to life, casting a soft glow on her face and the bodice of her red satin dress. Slowly, she pivoted toward Hazel. "Are you ready?" she whispered.

With wide eyes, Hazel looked up at her mother. She wore a green satin dress with a thin black belt at her waist. Her cascade of ringlets was half-up and embellished with a black satin bow. The girl lifted her ivory candle toward her mother's. When it was lit, Hazel started to turn toward Oliver.

"One second," Becca whispered to Hazel. Catching her son's eye, she gave a small shake of her head and mouthed, "No funny business."

Oliver sighed. "That was years ago," he muttered.

Becca had to admit that, with his hair neatly combed and dressed in a navy-blue suit and red checkered tie, he looked like quite the young man. Becca smiled and then nodded her permission for Hazel to light her brother's candle.

When Oliver's candle was lit, he guarded the flame with one hand and swiveled toward Violet. Her candle flickered to life.

Becca's breath caught as she watched the light and shadow play across Violet's face. Since it was Christmas Eve, Violet had actually allowed Becca to style her hair, which hung in shining chestnut waves down her back. She looked beautiful and grown-up in a cream-colored sweater and forest-green pleated skirt.

The usher continued to make his way down the pews, lighting candles, and Becca gazed up at the sanctuary, which was anchored by the Glory Cross and studded with jewel tones. Immediately her eyes were drawn to the altar with its gleaming gold communion ware, the special antique set used only for Christmas and Easter. A pair of sparkling emerald Christmas trees framed the altar, and voluminous ruby poinsettias were placed on the altar and steps. The choir, dressed in their sapphire-colored robes, assembled on the steps in front of the altar.

Eventually, the congregation's candles were lit, and the sanctuary lights dimmed. The first acapella notes of "Silent Night" floated through the air, and Becca glanced back at the assemblage and the multitude of tiny lights. Closing her eyes, she imagined that very first Christmas night, the velvet black sky pinned back by stars as the heavenly host appeared in praise of God. Tears filled her eyes.

On their way out of the sanctuary, Pastor James shook John's hand. "Merry Christmas, friend. I assume you're heading out?"

"After Bible study," John replied.

Pastor James nodded. "That actually works really well. Could I grab you for a few minutes afterward? I've got an elder matter to run by you."

John smiled. "As long as it doesn't mean that I'm late for Becca's shepherd's meal."

The pastor looked at Becca and raised his eyebrows.

Adjusting the faux fur wrap on her shoulders, Becca blushed. "Oh, it's a simple meal—something I imagine the shepherds might have eaten on that first Christmas night: potato soup, freshly baked herb bread, dried fruit, and nuts."

"What time should I be over?" Pastor James said, eyes twinkling.

Becca laughed. "You're always welcome!"

The pastor chuckled and turned toward Violet, Oliver, and Hazel to wish them a merry Christmas. Filled with holiday spirit, Hazel bobbed a curtsy, and Becca covered her mouth with her fingers to hide her smile.

As the congregation streamed out of the church, the Gables and John filed into the classroom for Alex's special Christmas Eve Bible study. John took Becca's wrap from her, and while the others found seats, she stepped toward a small table near the classroom entrance where she had previously stashed a cranberry almond bundt cake and a tote bag of supplies. Embellished with sprigs of rosemary and a few plump cranberries, the golden-brown cake looked festive on its glass cake stand. Removing a sifter from her tote, she dusted the cake with powdered sugar, which fell on the surface like snow.

"She's at it again!" Maggie Sharpe exclaimed as she entered the room, clutching the handle of her lavender Bible cover.

Becca grinned. "People who come to Bible study on Christmas Eve are devoted. I say that we should reward them with cake!"

"That's right!" Alex said cheerfully, striding toward his place in the center of the U-shaped tables. "We don't take a break from studying the Bible because it's Christmas Eve. That would be like not setting off fireworks because it's the Fourth of July!" Alex set his Bible on the podium and flipped it open. He was dressed in a burgundy button-down shirt topped with a tweed sport coat.

Becca tucked the sifter back into her tote and exchanged it for a knife. She sliced the cake and carefully deposited a piece on a shiny gold plate. Glancing around the room, she noticed that the class was much more sparsely attended than usual. Besides her family, it was Maggie, Lyle Gregory, and a few other devoted Bible scholars. She looked at her younger daughter. "Hazel, will you help distribute?"

Popping up from her chair, Hazel skipped to her mother's side, her curls bouncing on her shoulders.

"Remember to grab a fork for each one," Becca said, smiling.

With a little too much enthusiasm, Hazel stabbed a fork into the first piece and split it in half. She frowned.

"I'll take that one," John said, a note of amusement in his warm bass.

When she had delivered a slice of cranberry-studded cake to everyone seated at the tables, Hazel held out a plate to Alex.

He smiled warmly. "I'll have mine at the end."

Hazel set the plate down on the table, and, cake delivered, she and Becca slid into their seats.

Alex clapped. "Welcome, everybody," he said, smiling. "I'd like to thank Becca for the wonderful Christmas treat."

Hazel loudly cleared her throat.

"And Hazel for delivering it, of course," Alex added, his eyes twinkling. "Let's begin with prayer."

The class bowed their heads and folded their hands, and Alex led them in prayer, asking that the Lord open their hearts and minds.

Over the next hour, the class proceeded in lively discussion over the story of the paralytic man healed by Jesus in Matthew 9. When Alex said, "All right, final point!" Becca's eyes widened in surprise. She shifted her gaze from the Bible teacher, who was perched on the edge of his high stool, to the clock and could hardly believe that class was almost over.

"It's such a blessing that we can get together and share openly with each other about our struggles," Alex said. "God can certainly remove any one of them because everything is possible with him." He rose and began slowly walking around the inner edge of the tables. "But it's absolutely crucial to recognize what God, who sees all things clearly, knew was the *real* challenge of this man who was paralyzed." He paused and looked around the room. "It's the same challenge each one of us has today—sin." Hooking his thumbs in his pockets, Alex resumed his slow trek around the tables. "God can remove any burden we carry. We call out to him, and we trust that he will hear us. We know that, as our heavenly Father, he will do what is best for us." He stopped again, his voice rising as he looked earnestly into the students' faces. "But while we wait expectantly for his answer to those prayers, let us *rejoice* in the fact that he says those most important words to us, the same words he said to that man: 'Son, daughter, your sins are forgiven!'"

Tentatively, Violet raised her hand.

"Yes, Violet?" Alex said, smiling warmly at the young woman.

Her voice was quiet, and she fidgeted with one of the long chestnut curls that hung over her shoulder. "Doesn't that forgiveness tie in really well with Christmas?"

"How so?" Alex asked encouragingly.

"Well," Violet said, looking down at her hands and then back up at the Bible teacher, "it's nice to think of how Jesus could fix all of our problems in this world and the things that make us sad." She glanced over at her mother, who met her gaze and returned a small smile. "But today—Christmas," Violet continued, "is the day he came for the purpose of doing something so much more important: forgiving our sins. And that is why Christmas is so special."

Alex beamed. "You are absolutely right! This text speaks so clearly to why we celebrate Jesus's birth today. It's not because he can make our backs hurt less, or restore our sight, or even help us walk again," he said, counting off on his fingers. "The reason his birth is the defining moment in history is because through his life and death, our sin has been removed and our relationship with God restored. He is why we know we will live forever in Heaven, and it all started with his birth!" Alex stepped back to the podium and smiled at the people seated before him. "Merry Christmas to all! We really can't top that, so let's close there with prayer."

The Bible students followed his lead as he folded his hands and closed his eyes.

"Lord," Alex prayed, "we thank you for the gift of your son. Be with us as we celebrate your coming into this world and the restored relationship we find with our heavenly Father. All this we pray in Jesus's name, Amen." He looked up and into the faces of the people seated in front of him. "Merry Christmas, everyone."

As those in attendance expressed their thanks and mutual good wishes to Alex, Pastor James appeared in the doorway. He nodded in acknowledgment of the Bible teacher and smiled. "How was class?"

Alex raised his arm in a half-wave. "Hello, Pastor. We had a great discussion today. I think it was beneficial."

"Wonderful," the pastor said. After thanking Alex and wishing him a merry Christmas, he caught John's eye and inclined his head toward the door.

John turned to Becca. "It should just be a few minutes."

"No problem," Becca replied, smiling as she zipped up her Bible case. "I need to clean up anyway."

John followed Pastor James out of the room, and Maggie crooked her finger at Becca, who made her way toward the petite young woman. Clutching an envelope, Becca stood by Maggie's side as the young woman placed a medium-sized poinsettia in Alex's hands.

Maggie beamed. "Merry Christmas from your Bible students!"

"Thank you," Alex said. He glanced down at the plant, and his eyebrows furrowed as he studied the petals, which were mostly pink with white edges. He paused a few moments and asked hesitantly, "Is it sick?"

Throwing back her head in laughter, Maggie said, "No! It's a *marbled* poinsettia."

"Oh, okay," Alex said. "I'll do my best, but I have to tell you that I've never been great with plants." He smiled apologetically.

Becca grinned and handed an envelope to Alex. "We also pitched in for a gift card to The Thai Bistro. I *know* that you'll know what to do with this."

With a smile, Alex accepted the envelope and tucked it into his pocket. "Oh, yes, I see red curry in my future." He waved and wished the librarian a merry Christmas. Then he stepped toward Becca. "Oh, hey," he said, "just a reminder that I'm not teaching painting classes this week. We'll resume in the new year."

"Thank you," Becca said. "I need all the reminders I can get!"

Violet nodded vigorously at this.

Shooting her daughter a sideways glance, Becca said to Alex, "I'll have the children work on drawing exercises over the break."

As she made her way out of the classroom, a rail-thin woman with straight gray hair cut into a bob smiled at Alex. "It's so nice that you offer classes to our community. I'll make it to one of them yet!"

"I'm happy to do it," Alex said. "It helps keep my mind on positive things."

Even though his tone was cheerful, Becca noticed a look of sadness in the man's eyes. She met his gaze in understanding and offered a sympathetic smile.

"Would you like a piece of cake *now*, Mr. Gerhartz?" Hazel asked brightly as the gray-haired woman exited the room.

Alex shook himself from his thoughts and smiled. "Sure, I'd love a piece of cake now!"

Hazel ducked under the table and crossed the room to retrieve the plate.

"May I have another one?" Oliver asked.

Becca turned to her son and sighed. "Will you have room for dinner?"

"Aren't you always saying that I'm a bottomless pit?" Oliver replied with a grin.

"Touché," Becca laughed. As Hazel handed Alex a piece of cake, Becca stepped around the table to slice an extra-large piece for Oliver.

"Are we going to go now?" Hazel asked.

Becca glanced at her watch. "We need to wait for Uncle John. He should just be a few minutes."

"Tic-tac-toe?" Hazel asked, turning to her sister. In reply, Violet pulled a small notepad from her Bible case and flipped it open to a clean page.

Becca stooped to pull out a roll of plastic wrap from her tote. Straightening, she looked at Alex. "What are your plans for the evening?"

"I'm having dinner with my parents and my brothers."

Pulling a long sheet of plastic from the roll, Becca hesitated. Then she asked, "Do you have a few minutes? I'm hoping to pick your artist's brain."

Alex lifted a forkful of cake in response.

Becca smiled. "We were at the Paper Palace on Monday, delivering a Christmas meal to Lexi Grant."

"That was nice of you," Alex said.

Becca raised an eyebrow. "Well... While we were there, I was able to get a close look at the Grant family portrait. You know, the one that was going to be donated to the library."

"Mm-hmm, I've heard of it," Alex replied.

Carefully, Becca tucked the plastic around the remaining bundt cake. "And while I was looking at it, a piece fell off."

"Fell off?" the man repeated skeptically.

"Mom blew on it!" Hazel called happily from her tic-tac-toe game.

Alex's jaw dropped. "You blew on a *cracked* painting?" He stared at Becca in disbelief.

Becca bit her lip and tucked a strand of hair behind her ear. "Thank you for that, Hazel." Turning to Alex, she said, "I don't know what I was thinking. Up close, it was just so dusty."

"And a leaf blower wasn't available?" he asked, suppressing a smile.

Becca blushed deeply. "Very funny," she said, her eyes narrowed. "But here's the thing. I wasn't the first person to cause that piece to fall off. There was double-sided tape on the back. It can't be normal for a painting to be repaired like that, can it?"

Alex paused, his fork suspended in midair. "With tape? Certainly not. Only someone who knew nothing about painting restoration would do something like that."

Becca nodded and carefully tucked the remnant of the cake into her tote. "And there's something else... There was another painting underneath the Grant family portrait."

"Really?" Alex said, raising his eyebrows. He took another bite of cake and chewed thoughtfully for several moments. Then he said, "Well, some artists do reuse canvases. They can be quite expensive, especially big ones like that."

Retrieving her phone from the table, Becca swiped the screen and opened her photo album. "Look at this," she said, selecting an image. "I took a picture."

Alex shook his head. "So, you blow on a painting 'til it's in pieces and take pictures of the carnage. You sound like a wonderful house guest." He chuckled.

With a grin, Becca handed him her phone. Violet and Hazel abandoned their game of tic-tac-toe and hurried over. Oliver popped a giant piece of cake into his mouth, joined the group, and leaned in to get a view of the screen.

"What do you think of this?" Becca asked. "It's smudged and faded, but it looks like a banner with the letters D-E-C on it."

Alex zoomed in on the photo and examined it closely. "The painting's really well done," he observed. He paused and studied it further. "But artists don't paint over masterpieces, so this is likely some copy or master study the artist gave up on." He looked at Becca. "However, if you want to research it further and see what he might have been copying, it looks like the style is Renaissance... maybe Baroque." Shifting his gaze back to the phone, he zoomed in a little more and squinted at the screen. "And I don't think those letters are D-E-C. They're probably D-E-O."

Violet lit up. "*Deo* is *God* in Latin!"

Alex nodded. "I'm betting you have art history books at your bookshop. If you want to look more into it, you could flip through those and see what you come up with." He handed the phone back to Becca.

"This is great!" Becca said, her green eyes sparkling. "We'll turn our research into a school assignment!"

Oliver groaned.

Becca gave her son's shoulder a playful shake. "It will be fun! Like a puzzle!"

Raising a brow, Oliver said, "I think you and I have different ideas of fun, Mom."

At that moment, John poked his head into the doorway. He looked at Becca. "You ready?"

"Yes," Becca told her uncle. Turning to Alex, she said, "Thank you for your insight. You have been incredibly helpful."

The Bible teacher flung his empty plate into the trash. "It's really an interesting situation," he said. "Let me know if you discover anything, and I'll keep thinking too." Alex put away his Bible and, with a swing of his arm, picked up his leather satchel. He waited while John and the Gables gathered their belongings, gestured for them to exit first, and then switched off the classroom light.

As the group headed toward the coat room, Becca glanced back. "Alex! You forgot your poinsettia."

"Oh!" Alex doubled back and soon reappeared with the pink-and-white plant in one hand. Looking at the poinsettia, he slowly shook his head.

"Sorry, buddy. I don't know what you did that these people would send you off to be executed."

A laugh burst from Becca's mouth. "Maybe you'll be able to keep this one alive!"

Alex cocked a brow. "There's a first time for everything, I suppose," he said, clearly unconvinced.

In the coat room, Alex slipped on his black double-breasted wool pea-coat and waited patiently for the family. Hazel took an exceptionally long time as she fussed with her beret, scarf, and mittens.

John smiled apologetically at the Bible teacher. "It's okay," he said. "I can lock up."

Becca looked at Alex earnestly. "Thank you for a wonderful Bible lesson," she said. "And for your help with the painting."

With a humble nod, Alex said, "You're very welcome. I'm looking forward to hearing what you find out."

"I can't *wait* to dig into this," Becca said. Suddenly, her eyebrows furrowed, and she stood in thoughtful silence for a moment. "Do you think," she said slowly, "that there would be any value in having a background check done on Alberti, the artist?"

Alex considered. "I can't say that I've ever had the ability to ask for one of those. But sure, it couldn't hurt. It might help you narrow down where he lived and then studied."

Eyes twinkling, Becca spun toward John. "If I give you the name of a painter, would you run a report on him?"

"A painter?" John repeated, pulling on a leather glove.

"Yes," Becca said, "from fifty years ago."

John's thick white eyebrows shot up. "Fifty years?" He shook his head. "We are very busy at the station."

"*Please*," Becca cajoled. "There's no rush." She smiled charmingly and batted her eyelashes at her uncle.

John chuckled. "Send me the name, and I'll see what I can do."

"Yay!" Becca said. "Thank you so much!" She rose onto her tiptoes and pressed her lips against her uncle's rough cheek.

Gazing into the mirror, Hazel gave her cream-colored beret a jaunty slant. "There!" She grinned approvingly at her reflection. Violet rolled her eyes, and Oliver pretended to swat at the beret.

Alex raised his eyebrows at Becca and smiled. "I'll leave you to it. I'd better head out. It's a decent drive to my parents'." Glancing at the family, he lifted his arm in a wave and said, "Merry Christmas, all!"

"Merry Christmas!" the Gables returned as the Bible teacher headed out into the chill.

Becca pulled her wrap tightly around her shoulders. "Are you still up for the shepherd's meal, Uncle John?"

The man's bushy white mustache spread as he grinned. "I wouldn't miss it!" Holding the door for Becca and the children as they exited, John closed it behind him. After ensuring the lock was engaged, he gazed into the building momentarily and watched as the lights went out.

# Chapter 19

# Yuletide Hunt

The gentle tinkling of windchimes sounded from the direction of Becca's nightstand. Reaching toward her alarm clock, she switched it off and turned it to face her. 4:30. With a delicate moan, she snuggled back under the covers and savored the warmth of her buttery-soft sheets for a few more minutes. Finally, Becca stretched her limbs, wiggled her toes, and swung her legs over the side of the bed. She smiled down at the golden retriever who had kept guard by her side all night. "Merry Christmas, Butterscotch," she whispered.

Pulling her plush ivory robe over her plaid Christmas pajamas and stepping into her slippers, Becca padded into the hall. As she approached the living room, her breath caught at the beauty of the Christmas tree that glowed in the corner by the fireplace. Ornamented in red, white, and gold, the tree emanated warmth and light.

Becca crossed the room and gently touched a glittering ornament, a thin white salt-dough cross with a heart cut out of its center. Her attention was drawn to a glimmering gold snowflake frame ornament, and a smile spread across her face as she admired the circular photo of her parents inside it. Her father, Joseph Olson, was in his police chief uniform, looking remarkably like Uncle John except for his distinctive square jawline. Her mother, Nancy, smiled from the frame, wearing a cream-colored tie-neck blouse. Her light-brown hair skimmed her shoulders in soft waves, and her green eyes, the same color as Becca's, sparkled with cheerful crinkles at the corners. "Merry Christmas, Mom and Dad," Becca said softly. "Someday, we'll all be together again." She turned her gaze out the window into the darkness and saw the world covered in a soft white blanket. The snow fell steadily as big flakes slanted across the auras of light radiating from the streetlights. She closed her eyes and thanked God for the gift of His Son.

Tearing herself away from the peaceful scene, Becca headed toward the kitchen, where she found her cookbook open, her stand-mixer loaded with a dough hook, and all the ingredients for her homemade cinnamon rolls laid out on the counter. She switched on the oven. Grabbing her nutcracker mug from the drying rack, she poured herself a cup of coffee and added two big splashes of cream. Then she turned on her favorite Christmas album, *Behold the Lamb of God* by Andrew Peterson, and slow piano notes rose and fell as a man's voice, rich with childlike wonder, filled the room.

Becca placed the glass measuring cup of water in the microwave. Slowly, she stirred the yeast into the warm water, and her thoughts turned to her conversation with Alex. While she waited for the yeast to activate, she grabbed her phone and looked at the picture of the underpainting again. Tracing her finger along the line of the banner, she murmured, "Deo." Becca bit her lip. Alex had suggested looking through the art history books stocked at the bookshop, and she resolved to do just that during the dough's first rise.

The kitchen timer sounded, and Becca prepared the dough and turned it out into a bowl. With a damp cloth, she covered the bowl and set it by the warm oven to rise. Grabbing her phone, Becca set a one-hour timer. She dropped the phone into the pocket of her robe, tied the belt tightly around her waist, and rose on her tiptoes as she thought of the art history books just waiting for her on the shelf. She stepped toward the foyer but was stopped by the sound of a sweet, high-pitched voice.

"Merry Christmas, Mommy!"

Spinning around, Becca found Hazel dressed in her plaid Christmas pajamas and rubbing the sleep out of her eyes. Becca held out her arms, and Hazel ran into them as her mother enfolded her in a hug. She kissed the top of Hazel's head and murmured, "Merry Christmas, sweetheart."

"May I check my stocking?" Hazel asked, aqua eyes sparkling.

Becca smiled. "Did you look at the clock?"

"Yes," Hazel replied slowly, suddenly very interested in her bare feet.

"What did it say?"

The girl made a face. "5:15."

"And what is the rule?" Becca asked, raising her eyebrows slightly.

Hazel stuck out her lower lip then said glumly, "We have to stay in our rooms until 7:00."

"That's right," Becca said. "So, back to bed with you! 7:00 will be here before you know it!"

With a sigh, Hazel trudged back to her bedroom. When her daughter was out of sight, Becca turned to Butterscotch. "Do you want to join the hunt, girl? I know this isn't exactly a duck or a rabbit." The dog panted in reply and clipped along at Becca's heels as she made her way out of the apartment and down the stairs toward the bookshop.

The lights were off, but the lofty, ever-illuminated Christmas tree cast a glow over Tales & Tails. As she strode to the art section, two sets of yellow-green eyes gleamed in the dark, and Becca smiled. "Merry Christmas, kitties!" she called. Crouching in front of the art history books, she ran her finger along their spines. "Alex said to look for the Renaissance period," she said to herself. "Or Baroque." Grabbing as many relevant books as she could carry, she headed over to the Christmas tree and plopped down. From the top of the stack, she selected a book, *The Oxford Illustrated History of the Renaissance*. Flipping through it, page by page, she searched carefully for a painting with a white banner inscribed "Deo."

It seemed as though almost no time had passed before the timer on Becca's phone sounded. With a frustrated huff, she abandoned the two books she had searched through, tucked the rest under her arm, and headed upstairs.

Back in the apartment, she set down the stack of books on the bench in the foyer and held the door for Butterscotch, who followed her inside. "Don't worry. We'll keep at it," Becca promised the dog. Making her way to the kitchen, she peeked into the cloth-covered bowl to check the dough's progress. She grinned as she saw that the dough had risen to an impressive height. It wasn't long before Becca had smothered the dough in butter, brown sugar, and cinnamon. After rolling it up and slicing it, she carefully nestled the rolls in a glass baking dish and returned them to the warm spot by the oven. Setting her timer for another forty-five minutes, she gleefully stepped toward the foyer to retrieve the stack of art history books and headed to the living room.

Becca switched on the gas fireplace, set the stack on the side table, and lowered herself into the pillowy gray easy chair. As she spread a blanket over her legs, she looked out the window and noticed that the darkness was beginning to fade into weak tones of blue and gray across the Wisconsin sky. Hefting a book onto her lap, *Art in Renaissance Italy: 1350-1500*, she slowly turned the pages. Before long, she heard squeals and grunts of complaint coming from the children's rooms. Glancing up at the oversized pocket watch clock on the mantel, Becca smiled as she saw it was exactly 7:00. In anticipation, she set the book on the side table and watched the living room entrance.

Within moments, Violet, Oliver, and Hazel appeared in the doorway, dressed in matching Christmas pajamas, and Becca was sure that her heart would burst at the sight. Violet, whose brown hair hung in a braid down her back, yawned and stretched. Hazel, bright-eyed and bouncing on her toes, tugged Oliver's arm as he shuffled forward, eyes half-closed.

"Merry Christmas!" Violet and Hazel greeted in unison.

Hazel gave her brother's arm another jerk. "Merry Christmas," he mumbled sleepily. "Are the cinnamon rolls ready?"

Becca rose from her chair, hurried toward her children, and folded them in an embrace. "Merry Christmas, loves," she said. She ruffled Oliver's fanned-up hair. "The cinnamon rolls will be going into the oven soon, but you may check your stockings."

The morning flew by like a whirl of snowflakes as the Gables pulled chocolate oranges and ornaments from their stockings, gorged themselves on cinnamon rolls, scrambled eggs, and fruit salad, and dashed out the door for Christmas morning worship.

Time finally seemed to slow as the family arrived back at their apartment. Becca and the children stomped the snow from their boots, lined them up on the boot tray against the wall, and headed upstairs to change out of their church clothes. Violet and Hazel helped their mother tidy up the kitchen and set the dining room table for dinner. Armed with a sturdy shovel, Oliver cleared the snow away from the door in the alley and made a path.

Before long, the young man joined his mother and sisters in the kitchen. His cheeks were pink, and his hair was damp from the snow and exertion. "I don't think the storm is over," he said, leaning against the kitchen counter as he gnawed a Christmas cookie. "But at least Uncle John should have an easier time getting in."

With Oliver back inside, Becca gathered the children and dialed Matt's parents for a video call. The conversation started with Hazel excitedly recounting how Violet had nearly lowered the curtain on the cast of *A Christmas Carol* during the curtain call. Blushing deeply, Violet cleared her throat and asked Hazel if she wanted to show Grandpa and Grandma the cookie she had decorated to look just like Butterscotch. The chatter then shifted to Oliver, who shared his adventure of helping to rescue Dr. Davis's car from a snowdrift. Audrey's goofy faces in the background reassured the children that their aunt had arrived safely in Minnesota. After many laughs, blown kisses, and festive greetings, the Gables told Audrey they would see her soon, and Becca ended the call.

As soon as the screen was dark, Hazel, dressed in a cream Fair Isle sweater and jeans, looked at her mother. "Is it time to open gifts now?" she asked excitedly.

"Let's wait for Uncle John," Becca said. Seeing the look of disappointment on her daughter's face, she offered a small smile and added, "But I think it would be all right if you opened one gift."

Grabbing Hazel's hand, Becca led her into the living room and pointed to a large wrapped gift tucked near the base of the tree.

Hazel retrieved the package and, after glancing at her mother to confirm that she had selected the right one, quickly unwrapped it. "My big pink strawberry Squishmallow!" Hazel exclaimed, squeezing the plush toy and throwing her arms around her mother. She raced to her room to fetch the smaller one she already owned. "Now I have a big one *and* a baby one!"

Becca grinned. She wore a crimson button-up silk blouse tucked into black slacks. Her soft blonde curls were loosely pulled back, and a few tendrils framed her face. "Do you know the perfect way to break in that Squishmallow?" she asked.

Violet's eyes lit up. "Oh, yes! Let's finish *It's a Wonderful Life!*"

"Exactly!" Becca said, smiling at her oldest daughter. "Do you mind cueing it up?"

After finding their place in the movie, Violet settled next to Oliver, careful to stay on her side. Hazel laid on her stomach on the floor. Setting the leftover cinnamon rolls and fruit salad on the coffee table for the children to munch on, Becca sank into the gray easy chair. She watched for a few moments as a panicked George Bailey fruitlessly retraced Uncle Billy's steps in search of the missing $8,000. She then picked up a book from the side table titled *Michelangelo.* Carefully, she flipped the pages and searched the paintings for a white banner with the word "Deo."


Becca flinched in surprise as the timer on her phone buzzed. She had made it a good way through the book but sighed as she realized that her search thus far had been as futile as George Bailey's. Reaching into the basket at the lamp's base, she extracted a bookmark, tucked it into place, and replaced the book on the stack. As she passed the coffee table on her way to the kitchen, she snatched a piece of cantaloupe from the fruit salad and popped it into her mouth.

Once in the kitchen, she turned on the oven and pulled a large cream-colored roasting pan from a lower cabinet. She then grabbed a smoked ham from the refrigerator and freed it from its wrapping with kitchen scissors.

"Mom, do you need help?" Violet called from the living room.

Becca placed the ham into the roasting pan. "No, thanks, Vi!" she called back. "You just enjoy your movie!" She added water to the pan, covered it tightly with foil, and transferred it to the oven. Becca had just finished setting the timer when she heard the apartment door thump open and heavy footsteps.

"Hello!" a man's warm bass called from down the hallway.

Becca beamed as, within moments, John appeared in the kitchen. In his hand was the large lumpy bag Becca recognized from the gift-wrapping event at the bookshop. "Hi there!" She hurried to peck his cheek, which felt cool and rough against her own.

"I'm sorry I'm late," John said. "I was caught up at the station."

Becca's green eyes twinkled. "With the Grant case?"

"Yes," John replied, raking his fingers through his thick white hair.

"Can I get you something to drink?" Becca asked. Trying to sound nonchalant, she added, "Are you close to making any arrests?"

"Yes, I'd love a beer," John said. He cleared his throat. "And as for an arrest, we are getting closer..."

Becca peeked into the refrigerator to check on the prepared dishes of scalloped potatoes and Brussels sprouts. Before closing the door, she grabbed a bottle of Spotted Cow and then handed it to her uncle. "Are Donna Sloane and Dr. Davis still your top suspects?" she asked.

Prying off the bottle cap, John responded with a crisp nod.

"Uncle John! Uncle John!" Hazel bounded into the kitchen. She flung her arms around the man, who laughed as she nearly knocked the lumpy bag of gifts from his hand.

At a more dignified pace, Violet and Oliver entered the room and greeted their uncle.

Clasping her hands and rising on her tiptoes, Hazel gazed up at her mother. "*Now* may we open gifts?"

Becca laughed and looked into the faces of her other children. "What do you say? Did you finish the movie?"

Oliver grinned. In his best imitation of a little girl's voice, he said, "Every time a bell rings, an angel gets its wings."

Gesturing to her uncle, Becca smiled and said, "Lead the way, Uncle John!"

"You know," Violet said as the group made their way to the living room, "some angels likely do not have wings. Cherubim have four wings, and Seraphim have six wings, though."

While Oliver rolled his eyes, John raised his eyebrows. "Is that so?" he said.

Helping himself to a cinnamon roll, John sank into a soft leather chair. He looked at Becca. "Why don't you hand out your gifts first?"

The fire burned merrily as Becca and the children exchanged gifts. Violet admired her eight-volume box set of C. S. Lewis classics, and Oliver whooped with joy when he unwrapped his new basketball.

Cracking open the dove-colored velvet jewelry box in her hands, Hazel looked down at the pair of sparkling earrings. "Ooh!" she cried. "They're pretty!"

Becca nodded. "Look at the back," she encouraged.

Hazel removed the earrings from the box and turned them over. Furrowing her eyebrows, she said quietly, "They're pierced..." Suddenly, she jumped up and shrieked. "They're *pierced*! I can finally get my ears pierced?"

"You've gotten so grown-up," Becca said, smiling.

Hazel squealed in delight, and Oliver clapped his hands over his ears.

After reminding Becca and the children that the main part of his gift was the children's painting lessons with Mr. Gerhartz, Uncle John reached into his bag and called Violet and Hazel forward to collect their gifts. Although Violet declared that she couldn't wait to get started on her Agatha Christie-themed jigsaw puzzle, and Hazel "oohed" and "ahhed" over the crochet kit of sea animals, John's eyes had a particular gleam when he handed Oliver his present. Knowing what was coming, Becca perched on the arm of the loveseat so she could get a better view.

As Oliver returned to his spot, he turned the small box over in his hands. He looked up curiously at John as he tore the wrapping. "YES!" the young man exclaimed, pulling a pocketknife from the box. "Thank you, Uncle John! I've always wanted one!" Immediately, Oliver unfolded the blade and waved it at Hazel, who was sitting pretzel-legged on the floor a few feet away from him. "Hey! Do you want me to pierce your ears right now?" he asked with his lopsided grin.

Grabbing her earlobes, Hazel whimpered.

"And I'll take that!" Becca said, holding out her hand palm-side up. "You can have it back when you learn to be responsible with it."

Violet glanced at her watch and then at her brother. "Wow... Forty-five seconds. You held onto it longer than I would have expected."

"What?" Oliver protested. "Mom, no! I was just kidding!"

John pressed his lips into a straight line. "Your mother is right," he said soberly. "You have to respect things like knives. They are tools, not toys."

With a sigh, Oliver reluctantly folded the knife and placed it in his mother's hand. Becca reassured him that they would try again in a little while. Between the consolation, Uncle John's joy at receiving his highly anticipated tin of homemade peanut brittle, and the aroma of ham beginning to permeate, Oliver's mood lightened quickly. He and John sat down to a game of chess while Becca and the girls headed to the kitchen to prepare dinner.

Before summoning everyone, Becca surveyed the candlelit table one last time. On either side of the Advent wreath, a miniature holly wreath hugged an ivory pillar candle. Each place at the table was set with a gold charger, one of Becca's white china plates, and topped with a red plaid napkin cinched in the center by a gold napkin ring that looked like a jingle bell. With its maple-orange glaze, the baked ham gleamed in the candlelight. Casting her eyes over the steaming scalloped potatoes, balsamic roasted Brussels sprouts, and golden-brown dinner rolls, Becca decided that the meal was ready and asked Hazel to gather everyone.

The Gables joined hands and bowed their heads as John said grace. Rising, the man began to carve the ham and lavished his praise generously on Becca and the girls for the delicious meal.

As the dishes made their way around the table, Hazel wrinkled her nose at the bowl of Brussels sprouts and passed them to Violet without taking any.

Spooning a single sprout onto Hazel's plate, Violet said, "You have to try at least one."

Hazel narrowed her eyes and sniffed the little green vegetable. "Ew, that smells!"

"Indeed, it smells great!" John said cheerfully, looking up from the thick slices of ham piling up in front of him.

Becca stifled a smile and then looked at Hazel. "Your sister is right. You do need to try one. Besides," she said, spearing a Brussels sprout on her own fork, "these were your father's favorite."

Closing her eyes, Hazel pierced the vegetable, popped it in her mouth, and chewed. With much effort, she swallowed.

"Well?" Becca asked.

"It's not my favorite," Hazel said, a look of disgust on her face.

Becca smiled. "Thank you for trying it. Maybe you'll like it next year!"

Hazel shot her mother an alarmed glance, which Becca ignored as she scooped scalloped potatoes onto her plate.

The meal was capped off with a dessert of chocolate cheesecake topped with crushed peppermint. Becca and the children quickly tidied up while John, rubbing his stomach in appreciation, retrieved his Bible case from the lumpy bag he had brought and slowly turned the pages. When everything was in order, the Gables joined John in the living room. The only light in the room came from the flames dancing in the fireplace and the warm lights from the Christmas tree. Becca settled into the gray easy chair by the fire, and Violet and Oliver took their places on the loveseat. Hazel plopped down between her siblings. Oliver opened his mouth to protest then changed his mind and closed it again.

Reaching into his pocket, John put on his reading glasses and opened his worn leatherbound Bible to Luke chapter two. "In those days," he read, "Caesar Augustus issued a decree that a census should be taken of the entire Roman world."

Gazing at her children, Becca held her breath as John read one of her favorite parts: "But Mary treasured up all these things and pondered them in her heart."

As he reached the end of the reading, John glanced up and couldn't help but smile as he watched Hazel rest her head on Violet's shoulder and close her eyes. "The shepherds returned, glorifying and praising God for all the things they had heard and seen, which were just as they had been told," John's warm voice finished, and he carefully closed his Bible. Lifting a hand to remove his reading glasses, he looked at Oliver. "Someday, this will be *you* reading the Christmas story to your own family."

Oliver sat up a little taller, and Hazel lifted her head from Violet's shoulder to smile at her brother. The family sat in stillness for several minutes, listening to the snowstorm howling outside the window.

Finally, Becca sat up and said brightly, "Well, who is up for a game of charades?"

The family enthusiastically agreed and quickly divided themselves into teams of boys versus girls. Between Hazel taking the acting far too seriously and Violet overanalyzing every syllable, John and Oliver easily won the game.

"Well," John said, rising from the leather chair with a grin, "I had better leave on that note of victory."

Becca glanced out the window at the snow as it slanted determinedly across the light of the streetlamps. "Be careful out there, Uncle John," she said. "It's really coming down. I heard we're supposed to get up to ten inches overnight." Becca bit her lip. "Are you sure you don't want to stay? Oliver could sleep on the couch."

John chuckled and assured his niece that he would be fine since he had decades of experience driving in Wisconsin winters. After promising to text when he arrived home, John hugged the children while Becca loaded leftovers into his lumpy bag. With a kiss on the cheek goodbye and many wishes of "Merry Christmas!" John headed out into the storm.

Becca gazed at the closed door for a few moments. Noticing the children's worried expressions, she said, "Let's pray for Uncle John." The children followed their mother's lead as she bowed her head and folded her hands. "Heavenly Father, we thank you for Uncle John and the blessing that he is to our family. Please watch over him and bring him home safely through this storm. In Jesus's precious name, we pray, Amen." She smiled at the children. "How about you get into your pajamas? I'll make cocoa, and we'll finish reading *A Christmas Carol* before bed."

"Woo-hoo!" Hazel cried, scurrying down the hall.

As Violet and Oliver followed, Becca grabbed the *Michaelangelo* book and took it to the kitchen. She added sugar, cocoa, a dash of salt, and hot water to a medium saucepan and heated it. With one hand, she whisked the mixture until it boiled, and with the other, she flipped the pages of the Renaissance art book. She added the milk and vanilla and stirred again as she studied the pages.

Soon, the pajama-clad children appeared, and Becca ladled the cocoa into their mugs. They all headed to the living room, snuggled into their places, and Hazel rested her chin on her big pink strawberry Squishmallow. Plucking the novella from the basket at the base of the lamp, Becca smiled as her phone lit up with a text from Uncle John:

> *Made it home. Thanks for a wonderful evening, Bec. Merry Christmas. Love you.*

Becca smiled at the children. "God kept Uncle John safe!" she said. She gazed out the window at the snow building up against the glass, and Butterscotch lay down at her feet with a sigh.

The minutes flew by, and soon, Becca read, "And so, as Tiny Tim observed, God bless us, every one!" She carefully closed the book and clapped a hand over her mouth as she saw that Hazel had fallen asleep and was snoring softly on her Squishmallow. With a warning glance at Violet and Oliver, she put a finger to her lips and rose from her chair. Bending, she kissed

Hazel's porcelain cheek and carefully picked up the untouched mug of hot chocolate. She made her way over to the other children, kissed the top of Violet's head, and ruffled Oliver's hair while she looked lovingly into his eyes. "Merry Christmas," she whispered to them.

Becca watched as Oliver scooped up Hazel and carried her toward her bedroom. Violet followed and glanced back at her mother with a wave.

"Good night!" Becca mouthed.

Returning to the kitchen, Becca hopped up on the quartz countertop and pulled the *Michaelangelo* book into her lap. As she turned the final page, she blew a tendril out of her face with a frustrated puff. Glancing down, she saw that Butterscotch was waiting patiently by her feet. Sliding down from the counter, she scratched the dog behind her ears. "Do you want to hunt with me downstairs for a bit?" After poking her head into the children's rooms to ensure that they were sleeping peacefully, Becca collected the art history books she had brought upstairs.

With Butterscotch at her heels, she headed down to the bookshop. On her way to return the books to the shelf, she paused at a window. Big flakes of snow battered the glass, and the wind howled and moaned. Filing away the books she had already searched through, Becca grabbed the remaining two volumes and pulled up a chair by the lofty Christmas tree. Faithfully, Butterscotch followed, and Licorice and Toffee offered their support by rubbing against Becca's ankles. Becca paused and bent to scratch the cats under their chins. As she straightened, she rubbed the back of her neck and wondered just how long she had been searching through these books. She yawned and continued her quest.

Finally, Becca closed the last book with a disheartened snap. She looked at Butterscotch, who lay at her feet, her head resting between her paws. "Well, girl, that was the last of them. I guess we're not getting our duck or rabbit after all."

With a sigh, Becca stepped toward the art history section to reshelve the books. Job complete, she straightened and found Butterscotch watching her, head tilted slightly. Becca shook her head. "I'm sorry, Butterscotch. I've looked through them all. If it's a book about art, this is the only place where it would..." She paused and then finished softly, "...be." Suddenly, Becca gasped and rose on her tiptoes. "Unless!"

She quickly strode to the opposite side of the bookshop toward the collection of antique books for sale. Her gaze settled on the sign attached to the door labeled "Grandmother's Attic," and she slid the door to the side, revealing the hidden nook. Systematically working across the shelves, Becca ran her phone's flashlight over the spines. Her eyes brightened as they fell on the title *Caravaggio: His Life and Work*, and she plucked the book from the 1950s shelf. Becca felt a thrill run down her spine as she gazed at the cover, which displayed an astonished-looking Saint Thomas poking a finger into Jesus's side while two other disciples looked on. Triumphantly, Becca held out the book to Butterscotch. "This is the one that Lexi was reading!"

Energy renewed, Becca had a skip in her step as she returned to her chair at the Christmas tree. Butterscotch followed closely. The dog wagged her tail hopefully as her mistress flipped through the pages for several minutes. Becca turned to a page that featured a colored picture of a nativity scene. "Woo-hoo!" she exclaimed, jumping out of her chair. "Gotcha!" The dog startled, and Becca laughed and stroked its head consolingly. "I'm sorry, Butterscotch. I'm sorry. But look!"

Lowering herself back into the chair, Becca laid the book on her lap again as the golden retriever rested her chin on Becca's leg. The painting was a nativity scene centering around Mary, dressed in Renaissance-style clothes and kneeling in adoration before a supine baby Jesus. Shepherds and others, including an ox and a donkey, worshiped the baby, and a winged angel in the upper-left corner of the painting carried a banner inscribed with the words *GLORIA IN EXCELSIS DEO*. With her finger, Becca traced the banner on the page. "Deo," she breathed. Bringing up the picture on her phone, she compared the two images. She nodded excitedly. "That's it, Butterscotch," she said. "Alberti must have been copying this painting, which is called..." Setting down her phone, she ran her finger along the page to the caption. "*Nativity with Saints Lawrence and Francis*," she continued. "1609." Silently, she read the rest of the caption: *Oil on canvas, 105 1/2 x 77 5/8 in. (268 x 197 cm). Oratory of the Compagnia di San Lorenzo, Palermo*. "So, the original is in Italy," she mused, tapping the painting with a finger.

With a contented sigh, Becca closed the book, tucked it under her arm, and stroked Butterscotch's head. "A nativity scene found on Christmas night," Becca said, slowly shaking her head in wonder. "God gave us an unexpected gift today." Rising from the chair, she smiled and yawned, suddenly feeling the weight of her fatigue. "Come on, girl. We can rest knowing we had a successful hunt after all." By the light of the Christmas tree, Becca headed back toward the apartment, warmed by thoughts of snuggling into her downy sheets with Butterscotch keeping guard at her side.

# Chapter 20

# Memory Montage

Becca shielded her eyes from the bright sunshine streaming through the side window as she flipped the Tales & Tails sign to *Open*. Striding back to the café area, she heard the bell at the front door tinkle with the entry of the day's first customers. Behind the confectionery counter stood Audrey. Her auburn hair was piled on top of her head, and the tiny stud in her nose glinted in the light. She was a picture of readiness.

Becca smiled at her. "Do you need anything before we head out?"

Audrey shook her head and gestured to Violet, who was standing next to her, wearing a turquoise apron that matched her aunt's. "We've got everything under control," Audrey said. "Just promise that you'll send score updates."

"You got it," Becca said, zipping up her gray puffer jacket over her "Hawks" t-shirt. She paused and glanced at Violet. "Vi, did you happen to notice if I turned on the slow cooker this morning? I know I put a chicken in there, but I don't remember if I switched it on."

Violet gave a small smile and half-wave to an approaching customer and quickly glanced at her mother. "You did. I could smell the chicken as I was heading down."

"Good!" Becca said, nodding. She turned to her sister-in-law. "Oh, hey, did you get that garlic pasta recipe from Chris? The way you were talking about it after your date, I'm dying to try it."

Audrey stepped to the side as Violet took the customer's order for a vanilla latte. "No, sorry, I keep forgetting to ask him." She glanced at her watch. "But he's off duty today and will be stopping by any minute. If you're still here, you can ask him yourself." She laughed. "But then you might have a difficult time getting out the door because once you get him talking about cooking, it's hard to get him to stop." Still smiling, she glanced at the tablet Violet was holding and turned to prepare the drink.

Becca shifted her gaze toward her other two children by the fireplace. Hazel lay on the floor, running Butterscotch's tail through her fingers. The girl's vanilla-blonde hair was parted down the middle and plaited in two braids interlaced with blue and white ribbon. Oliver, suited up in his blue CRH Hawks basketball uniform, was sprawled in a squashy leather chair with a burgundy duffel bag by his feet.

"Oliver!" Becca called.

Grabbing his duffel, Oliver hoisted himself out of the chair and stepped toward his mother. Even though she hadn't been summoned, Hazel popped up and joined them too.

Becca looked over her son. "Do you have your basketball shoes?"

"Yes," Oliver said, his voice husky.

"Your water bottle?"

The young man toed the side of his duffel. "Yes."

"Mom?" Hazel said, tugging on the sleeve of her mother's coat.

Lifting a finger in Hazel's direction but keeping her eyes on Oliver, Becca touched her son's bare elbow. "How about your winter coat?"

"I don't need one," Oliver said matter-of-factly.

Arching a brow, Becca said, "It's fourteen degrees outside. This is not negotiable." She jerked a thumb toward the steps that led to their apartment.

With a heavy sigh, Oliver plodded away to retrieve his coat.

Becca turned to her younger daughter. "Yes, Hazel? Now it's your turn."

Hazel pointed to the hand-lettered chalkboard listing the daily specials. "It's December thirtieth."

"Yes, it is," Becca agreed. The bell at the front door tinkled, and she turned to see Detective Post materialize out of the sunshine. He stomped his boots on the mat and headed toward the café area. Turning toward Audrey, Becca smiled.

Hazel's aqua eyes widened in urgency. "So, do you have our video done?"

Becca felt a knot twist in her stomach. Drawing a breath, she crouched down and met Hazel at eye level. "You know that takes me a lot of time," she said softly.

"How far are you?" Hazel asked.

"Well," Becca said, straightening, "I think I've made it through October."

Hazel clasped her hands together and grinned. "You're almost done, then! You can do it, Mommy! That video is *tradition*."

"Morning," Chris's gruff voice cut in as he approached the pair. He wore a hooded flannel coat over a white t-shirt and jeans. "What video is this?" He glanced over at Audrey, who was frothing coffee, and waved.

Smiling at the detective, Becca said, "Oh, every day, I try to take a short video of daily life." She tucked a strand of hair behind her ear. "I have an app on my phone that grabs a few seconds of each day's video, and it compiles them all into a montage. On New Year's Eve, we watch the complete video and review our year."

Chris raised his eyebrows slightly. "Add some popcorn and cocoa, and that sounds like a great tradition."

"But it takes me a while," Becca continued, "and I just don't think I'm going to have the time—"

Her braids bouncing on her shoulders as she hopped up and down, Hazel exclaimed, "You can work on it at the basketball game!"

Becca raised a brow. "Shouldn't I be *watching* the game?"

Hazel stilled and shook her head. "I'll tell you when Oliver's in, and then you can watch. And when he's on the bench, you can work on the video. I bet you can get it done!"

Chris chuckled. "It sounds like she's got it all planned out."

Becca shot the detective an *aren't-you-supposed-to-be-on-my-side* look as Oliver returned with his lumpy winter coat tucked under his arm.

"Are you talking about our video?" the young man asked. "Yeah, Mom, you need to get that done."

Becca sighed. "I can try..." she said feebly.

"Plus," Oliver added, "that means you'll be doing less cheering from the stands."

Green eyes twinkling, Becca brightened. "Oh! That reminds me! I need to bring in my pom-poms when we get to the game."

Oliver rolled his eyes, but the corner of his lips rose in a half-smile.

Glancing at her watch, Becca said, "We'd better head out now." Audrey was helping a customer, but Becca managed to catch her eye and waved goodbye.

Audrey pointed at Chris and mouthed something.

Becca tilted her head and mouthed back, "What?"

"Re-ci-pe!" Audrey tried again.

"Oh!" Becca said, turning to the detective. "Chris, could I please get that garlic pasta recipe from you? Audrey can't stop talking about it, and I think it would go really well with our chicken tonight."

Chris paused for a moment and then beamed. "The Pasta Aglio e Olio?"

Becca nodded. "I think so." She smiled sweetly at him. "It's the one that you made for Audrey."

"Oh, it's delicious! I'd be happy to give it to you," the detective said. "The key to that one is the preparation. There are so few ingredients involved that you have to treat them properly." He rubbed his hands together in excitement, and Becca stifled a smile. "One of the Italian chefs that I like shared that the real secret to this dish—"

Oliver elbowed his mother and murmured, "Mom, I'm going to be late for warm-ups."

Smiling apologetically at Chris, Becca said, "I would love to know the secret, but we have to go now. Would you email the recipe to me?"

The detective sped up his words. "Sure, I can email it to you, but the secret is you have to add the *sliced* garlic to the oil in a *cold* pan and slowly heat it up—"

"Hey, babe!" Audrey said, appearing at Chris's side and pecking his cheek.

As the detective lifted his girlfriend's hand to his lips, Audrey mouthed to Becca, "Go!"

Becca turned to find that Oliver and Hazel were already heading toward the exit. She followed them for a few steps, waved goodbye to Violet, and then called over her shoulder, "I really appreciate the recipe, Chris! And thanks for the tip!"

The detective raised his arm in a half-wave. "I want to hear how it turns out!"

"Sure thing!" Becca said, hurrying after the children.


It wasn't long before Becca pulled up to the main entrance of Crystal Valley Christian School. Before she had even come to a complete stop, Oliver flung open the minivan door.

"Hang on!" she said then smiled. "Have a good game and no injuries, please."

The young man mumbled a "yeah" and bolted, duffel in hand, to join his team.

After paying admission for Hazel and herself, Becca stepped into the modestly sized gymnasium and was greeted by the familiar sound of squeaking shoes combined with the thunder of dribbled basketballs. The scoreboard counted down the time until the start of the game while the CRH Hawks, in their blue-and-white uniforms, practiced shots on one side of the court. The CVCS Lancers, clad in silver and red, ran plays on the opposite side of the court. With her pom-poms clutched in one hand, Becca scanned the gym in search of her son and found him standing on the edge of the three-point line. She cringed as she watched Oliver lick the fingers of one hand and then wipe them on the bottom of his shoe. "Ew!" she said, exchanging a disgusted look with Hazel. With a quick shake of her head, she dismissed the image and asked, "Shall we go find a seat?"

As the mother and daughter made their way to the Hawks' side of the gym, Hazel spotted her friend Logan, a tall blond boy about her age, seated with some other kids near the court. Hazel waved hello to him and looked up at Becca. "No sitting by your mom friends today," she said, her aqua eyes serious. "All you moms do is talk, and you've got a video to make!"

Becca laughed. "All right, we can sit by ourselves."

Hazel pointed to the topmost bleacher, and she and Becca began to climb. As Becca passed the other Hawks' moms, she crouched by them and explained the situation.

"She's got important work today," Hazel confirmed, tugging at her mother's sleeve.

When Becca and Hazel had made their way to the top of the bleachers, they shrugged out of their coats, and Hazel relieved her mother of the pom-poms.

Becca glanced down at the court and watched as Will Sloane, muscular and towering, easily sank a free throw. The teen had sandy-blond hair cropped short on the back and sides and topped with messy curls. "I wonder if Donna is here," Becca said softly, squinting across the court to the other set of bleachers. She was soon rewarded by the sight of the teen's grandmother, Donna Sloane, who was seated beside her husband a few rows up from the court. Her camel-colored coat was draped over her shoulders, and she wore a stylish black-and-white striped t-shirt. Knotted jauntily at her neck was a silver-and-red silk scarf.

"Mom, focus," Hazel said, pulling her mother's phone from her purse and placing it in her hand.

Becca unlocked the phone and opened the video montage app. "Right!" she said. "Focusing." The screen of her phone displayed a calendar on which most of the dates showed a thumbnail photo, but beginning partway through October, the squares were completely blank. She tapped on the first empty date and selected a video.

Leaning over her mother's arm, Hazel watched a clip of herself blowing out the candles on a very pink cake. "Oh! It's my birthday!" she exclaimed.

Becca laughed and covered the screen with her hand. "Hey, no peeking until it's done!"

Time passed quickly as she engrossed herself in selecting videos and choosing the most interesting five-to-ten-second clips. Suddenly, an impossibly loud buzzer blared, signaling the start of the game. Becca jumped several inches and let out a squeak. Placing a hand over her heart, she looked out at the court and saw that the players were positioned for the tip-off, including Oliver, who was lined up by the Hawks' free-throw line as point guard. She tucked her phone into her purse and grabbed her pom-poms. Shaking them, she called, "Go, Hawks!"

Becca held her breath as yet another of the Hawks' shots refused to sink. Will Sloane snagged the rebound, crossed the court with easy strides, and made a layup. Becca frowned at Hazel. "You'd think at least *one* of our shots would go in."

The Hawks finally went on the board after Oliver was fouled and sank two free throws.

"Yay, Oliver!" Becca and Hazel cheered in unison. Hazel tossed a pom-pom in the air and caught it again.

The referee's whistle blew, and several players on both teams exchanged places, including a red-faced Oliver whose gaze flicked up to his mother and sister.

"Now! Go!" Hazel said excitedly, tapping her mother's knee with the flat of her hand.

Fishing her phone from her purse, Becca reopened the app and added more clips. After a while, she came to November 16. She clicked the cell and was directed to a video of Oliver playing his violin at the Paper Palace. "Oh!" she said. "I forgot that I had this!" She grimaced as she watched the images move across the screen. "I wonder if it's appropriate to add a clip of Mrs. Grant's cocktail party..." she mused aloud.

Hazel nodded. "It is if you only add the part with Oliver playing the violin." Her aqua eyes sparkled with mischief. "He will *love* that."

Becca nodded and added the clip. When she had initially recorded the video, she had been a distance across the room, but she could still see her son's bow rise and fall and hear the soaring notes of his violin.

"Ouch!" Becca cried as Hazel's bony elbow jabbed her side.

"Sorry," Hazel said, smiling sweetly. "But he's back in!"

Becca dropped her phone into her purse and watched as the Hawks lined up on their side of the court. Oliver dribbled the ball a few times and looked out at his teammates. "Motion!" he barked and took a few steps forward.

Before long, the buzzer blared again, this time announcing halftime. Becca flinched and shook her head. "Does it *have* to be so loud?" She glanced at the scoreboard. The Hawks were down twenty-seven to twelve. As both teams huddled around their coaches, the players' younger siblings raced onto the court. In a melee of laughter and squeals of delight, the children began throwing basketballs up at the hoop.

"Could I get a couple of dollars for popcorn?" Hazel asked.

Becca frowned. "You know, we can save money by making our own popcorn at home."

"May *I* buy this young lady a bag of popcorn?" a warm bass asked.

Glancing up, Becca smiled at Uncle John, who was breathing heavily and had one hand on Hazel's shoulder. He was wearing his sheepskin coat, and his bushy white mustache stretched as he grinned. "You're very welcome to," Becca said.

John held out his hand to Hazel. "Shall we?"

Hazel looked at her mother. "This is a great time to keep working on the video!" she said, pointing a commanding finger.

John arched a bristly brow at Becca. "Video?"

Becca, who had retrieved her phone from her purse, held up the calendar grid to show her uncle.

"Oh yes," he said, "your annual montage. How are you not finished with that? What else have you been doing?" John chuckled at his own joke.

Becca made a face. "Very funny," she said, smiling.

As John and Hazel began to descend the bleachers, the police chief glanced over his shoulder at Becca. "I just winded myself climbing up this mountain of bleachers only to head right back down... I'm not sure I thought this through."

Hazel grinned and tugged John's hand, and the pair continued their journey toward the concessions.

After tapping the next video clip into its place, Becca glanced up to see Uncle John and Hazel near the court. She winced as she watched a particularly bad shot from a third grader ricochet off the rim and sail directly toward Hazel's head. Before Uncle John could block the ball, Hazel's friend Logan grabbed it out of the air. Smiling, the boy handed the ball to Hazel and glanced up at the hoop. Becca stifled a laugh as she watched her daughter try with all her might to shoot the ball, which drifted through the air in an arc that didn't even come close to the basket. As Hazel shrugged and flashed a smile at Logan, Becca laughed softly and reminded herself that her daughter always had acting to fall back on.

With only seconds left on the clock before the end of halftime, Hazel returned with a bag of popcorn in one hand and a package of Skittles in the other. Carefully, John followed, balancing a plastic tray of nachos. As John settled himself beside Becca, the buzzer blared.

"Want some?" John asked, tipping the tray toward his niece.

Becca shook her head. "No, thanks." Noticing that Oliver was out on the court, she put away her phone.

As the young men took their places, John gazed across the gym at the opposite set of bleachers. "Donna Sloane," he said quietly, narrowing his eyes. "It's only a matter of time before we have everything we need on her."

"What about Dr. Davis?" Becca asked with a sideways glance at her uncle.

Pulling his wallet from his jeans pocket, John gave Hazel a few bills and asked her to buy bottles of water for the three of them. As the girl bounded down the bleachers, the chief cleared his throat and looked at Becca. "Confidentially..." he began.

Becca leaned in toward her uncle.

"Andrew Curtis, Phyllis Grant's lawyer, *finally* found the current version of her will." John's blue eyes sparkled as he picked up a nacho and set it back down. "You'll never guess where it was."

Becca shook her head. "I have no idea."

"It was in a mayonnaise jar in the back of his freezer for safe keeping."

Becca's eyebrows raised. "A *mayonnaise* jar?" She threw back her head and laughed.

John nodded. "Yeah, he's not a very good lawyer."

An amused smile still playing on her lips, Becca glanced over at the concession stand where Hazel was paying for the water.

"But the point is," the chief continued, "that the will confirms that Davis was written out, and he was not going to benefit financially from Phyllis Grant's death. Davis knew about it as well. According to Curtis, about six months ago, Mrs. Grant took some pleasure in informing Davis of his being disinherited. So, he is no longer considered a main suspect."

Becca nodded. She opened her mouth to ask a question and then closed it again.

John's gaze flicked to Hazel, who was mounting the bleachers, carrying three bottles of water. He placed a hand on Becca's knee and smiled. "No more work talk. Let's enjoy the game."

While Becca intermittently worked on the video montage and watched Oliver play, the game continued. In the fourth quarter, the Hawks made a bit of a comeback, and Becca finally found occasion to use her pom-poms again. The entire side of the Hawks' bleachers exploded into cheers as Oliver intercepted a pass and drove down the court in a breakaway. Only Will Sloane was fast enough to come close to Oliver, and even then, there was no chance he could position himself between Oliver and the basket. Becca whooped in delight at what would surely be an easy two points, but her expression of joy quickly shifted into dismay as Will desperately thrust his foot between Oliver's and tripped her son before he could lay the ball up. Oliver tumbled to the floor, a tangle of lanky arms and legs, and the ball sailed out of bounds and bounced off the concrete wall.

"Foul!" Uncle John shouted.

Becca jumped to her feet. "Oh no! Is he okay?" she gasped.

John gently touched his niece's arm. "He's fine. He's tough. And now he'll get two free throws."

Keeping her eyes locked on her son, who was picking himself up from the floor and brushing off his shorts, Becca slowly sank back down.

The referee gave a short blast of his whistle and tossed the ball to Will, who was positioned outside the court where the ball had flown out of bounds. Both teams lined up for the throw-in, and Oliver, jaw hanging open, looked back and forth between the referee and his coach.

"What! No foul? Come on, ref!" John shouted as Becca sat wide-eyed.

Hazel shot upward. "That's not fair!" she cried, shaking her package of Skittles in protest.

"Shhhh," Becca hushed her daughter. "It's going to be all right." She patted the bench beside her, and Hazel plopped down in a huff.

The referee blew his whistle. Smacking the ball with an open hand, Will scanned the blur of silver and blue and looked for an open teammate. Finding one, he threw in the ball with a bounce pass to the Lancers' point guard, and both teams raced to the other side of the court.

Becca watched her son as he positioned himself on defense. He had both hands on his knees, and his eyes were narrowed. "Shake it off, buddy," Becca said softly.

"Strike!" the Lancers' point guard called, and his teammates leaped into motion. As Will jogged toward Oliver, he slowed his pace and, leaning in, said something into the young man's ear. Oliver straightened. Looking up into the skyscraper of a teen's eyes, Oliver pushed him in the chest with both hands, knocking him flat on his back. From the ground, Will blinked up in disbelief as Oliver stood over him.

With a whistle blast, the referee stopped the game and called a technical foul for unsportsmanlike conduct. A hush fell over the gymnasium.

Becca buried her face in her hands. "Ugh, he did *not* just do that."

"Now, now," Uncle John said soothingly as the assistant coach ushered in another player to take Oliver's place.

Working up the courage to peek between her fingers, Becca saw Oliver standing next to the Hawks' bench, hands on his hips and looking down as he accepted his coach's rebuke.

"I cannot *believe* that he pushed that boy," Becca said, her fingertips turning white as she gripped the pom-poms. "How often do we talk about being peacemakers? And how we don't retaliate?"

With a beautiful arc, Will sank the first of his free throws.

John chuckled at his niece. "Breathe, Becca, breathe. Talking about those things is good, but this is how boys are when they play sports. It's okay."

The second of Will's free throws swished through the net.

"Who knows," John added with a smile, "they'll probably end up being friends."

Becca tilted her face toward her uncle and arched a brow. "Friends?" she said incredulously. "After *that?*"

"Sure," John said, popping a nacho into his mouth and casting his gaze over the court. "You've heard me talk about Robert, my best friend growing up?"

Becca nodded. "Oh, yes, I've heard stories about the two of you."

John's blue eyes sparkled. "Well, the first time I met him, I punched him in the nose."

"You didn't!" Becca said. Her grip on the pom-poms relaxed, and she grinned.

Dipping another chip into his sour cream, John said seriously, "You bet I did. He tipped over my bike." He bit off the corner of the nacho and glanced at his niece. "Three weeks later, we were inseparable. This is how boys grow and bond."

Becca laughed and shook her head. She glanced down at Oliver, who was now intently watching the game from the bench.

"Well," Hazel said happily, "now that Oliver's out of the game, you have plenty of time to work on the video!" Seeing her mother's bewildered expression, her grin melted into a shy smile.

With a playful tug on one of Hazel's braids, Becca said. "Let's just watch the rest of the game, okay?"

Before long, the final buzzer bellowed, and Becca clenched her teeth. She glanced up at the scoreboard: 64-31. She sighed.

"Well," John said, raising his eyebrows, "another character-building game."

Becca made a face. "A couple of opportunities to be gracious victors would also be okay." She gestured to Hazel to pick up the wrappers and empty bags from their snacks.

As the Hawks and Lancers lined up on the court to exchange low fives and mostly sincere compliments of "Good game," Becca, John, and Hazel made their way down the bleachers. Several of the Hawks' moms expressed their sympathy over the uncalled foul and Oliver's being benched from the game. Becca felt warmth rise into her cheeks as she thanked them and said that it would certainly provide her and the children with substance for conversation at home.

Feeling a touch on her elbow, Becca turned to find Donna Sloane, her lips stretched into a lipstick-lined grin. Becca's eyes widened in surprise. "Hi, Donna!" she said. "There was quite a bit of—err..." She paused and tucked a strand of blonde hair behind her ear. "...*excitement* in today's game, wasn't there?"

The woman touched the knot of her silver-and-red scarf and tilted her head. "Well, I suppose the important thing is that the Hawks tried. Better luck next time!" She raised her hand, wiggled her fingers goodbye, and then hurried off to join the family members congratulating her towering grandson.

John narrowed his eyes as he watched the elegant woman stride away. "Just a matter of time..."

Becca glanced around in search of her son and found that he was now the sole player packing up at the Hawks' bench. Glumly, Oliver tucked his basketball shoes into his duffel and slid his socked feet into a pair of black slide sandals.

John spotted him too and gave Becca a reassuring smile. "How about I drive Oliver back to the apartment?" he said. "It will give us a chance to talk man-to-man."

"Would you?" Becca breathed. "That would be *wonderful*." She took a deep breath and gazed at her son. Keeping her eyes on him, she asked, "What will you say to him?"

Buttoning his sheepskin coat, John said, "I'm going to tell him that I'm proud of him for standing up for himself, especially against a boy who is so much bigger than him." Becca turned to John, her eyes wide. He held up a finger. "But I'm also going to tell him that he has to play by the rules with honor because that is *also* the mark of a man. You can't just have courage *or* honor—a man has to have both."

Tears pricked Becca's eyes, and she wrapped her arms around John's neck. "I don't know what I would do without you," she said, her voice muffled against his coat. After a long moment, she stepped back and looked affectionately into his eyes.

"I'm always here for you," John said warmly. He then glanced at Oliver, who was trudging toward them, eyes cast down toward the gleaming floor of the court. "And for this guy," he added, wrapping a muscular arm around Oliver's back.

Becca placed her hand on Oliver's cheek and brushed his cheekbone with her thumb. "Hey, buddy."

The young man leaned into his mother's caress and closed his eyes. Finally, he said, "Did you get the video done?"

Becca laughed and lowered her hand. "I'm close. I'll have it ready for New Year's Eve." "I'm sorry about your game, Oliver," Hazel said. She reached out and, uncurling her brother's fingers, thrust the remnants of a package of Skittles into his hand. "These are for you."

Oliver looked down at the candy, and a chuckle escaped. "Thanks."

"Come on," John said, lightly cuffing the young man's shoulder. "I get to drive you home."

As John led Oliver toward the exit, Becca glanced down at Hazel. "Let's give them a head start," she said softly. She pulled her phone from her purse and opened her email. "Oh! Chris sent the garlic pasta recipe." She scrolled a bit. "I only need a couple of things from the store. We can stop there on the way home, and that will give Uncle John and Oliver more time together, just the two of them."

She glanced up and gazed lovingly at the two men in her life as they opened the set of double doors and disappeared into the sunshine.

# Chapter 21

# Old Acquaintance Not Forgot

"Violet Whitman…" Hazel said the words slowly, trying them out. "I think it sounds nice!" She grinned at her sister.

Sliding into the passenger seat of the Gables' light-blue minivan, Violet slammed the door shut. "Knock it off, Hazel."

Hazel's eyes sparkled as she clicked her seatbelt into place. She was wearing a hot-pink-and-silver *Happy New Year* tiara headband. Spilling out from beneath her winter coat was a pink sequined tulle skirt. "All I'm saying," she said sweetly, "is that it seems like more than a coincidence that Trevor Whitman would pick you *three times* during the broom dance."

A blush rose into Violet's cheeks, and she gazed out the window.

"Ugh, I hate the broom dance," Oliver said, sliding the minivan door closed.

Becca frowned. Her gaze locked onto the rearview mirror as she backed out of their parking space at Steeple Hall. "Broom dance? What is that, and how did I miss it?"

"You were in the kitchen, getting the pizzas ready with the other moms," Oliver said. "Next time, I'm going to see if you need help."

Becca's silver-and-gold tiara headband sparkled in the afternoon sunlight. "So, you each danced with a broom?"

Hazel giggled. "No…"

"The broom dance," Violet said crisply, arms folded across her chest, "is a silly dance in which there is a line of boys and a line of girls. Someone holds a broom, and they are the 'selector.' So, if it's a girl holding the broom, the two boys at the front of the line will address her. The girl will pick one of the boys, and the two of them will dance off toward the back of the lines. The boy who was not chosen is now the 'selector,' and he gets to choose his partner from the next two girls in line."

"And if you're Trevor Whitman," Hazel added, "you'll switch up your place in line so that you can choose Violet every time."

Narrowing her eyes, Violet shot her sister an icy look. Hazel began examining the contents of her prize bag with a small smile.

"All right," Becca said brightly. "Now that we've seen the ball drop at our *Noon* Year's Eve party, let's go over our plan for the rest of the day."

"I know my plan," Hazel said. "I am staying up until midnight to see the *real* ball drop!"

Oliver scoffed. "There's no way! You barely made it past ten o'clock last year."

Hazel glared at her brother. "I'm a whole year older now! And I have a plan."

Violet rolled her eyes and turned to her mother. "What time is Aunt Audrey coming over?"

"Actually," Becca said, easing on the brakes as she approached a stop sign. "Aunt Audrey called to say that she has different plans this year. She and Detective Post are spending New Year's Eve together."

Hazel stuck out her lower lip. "Aww! It won't be the same."

"We'll still have lots of fun," Becca soothed. "Besides, we should all be happy for Aunt Audrey. She was saying how nice it will be to finally have someone to kiss at midnight."

Oliver wrinkled his nose at the thought, and Hazel's face lit up as she pitched forward in her seat, excitedly tapping Violet on the shoulder. "Someday that's going to be you and Tr—"

"Don't you *dare* finish that sentence!" Violet snapped.

Hazel's eyes twinkled with mischief as she flopped back into her seat, and Becca covered her mouth with her fingers to hide her smile.


Just inside the apartment door, Butterscotch was waiting for them. "Hey, sweet girl," Becca said, scratching the dog behind her ears. Becca pulled off her raspberry-colored wool coat, revealing a silver turtleneck tucked into a black midi-length skirt. Glancing sideways, she saw the backs of Violet, Oliver, and Hazel as they headed down the hallway. "Wait a minute!" Becca called after them, kicking off her black pumps. "We need to finish going over the plan for the rest of the day."

Oliver turned and heaved an exasperated sigh.

"Give me five minutes at the kitchen table," Becca said, smiling.

As she lowered herself into a chair, Becca set a platter of chocolate chip cookies in the center of the table. "Since you can all sleep-in tomorrow morning, you are allowed to stay up until midnight to watch the ball drop."

"Woo-hoo!" Hazel whooped.

Violet raised a brow at her sister, and her lips curved into a half-smile as she slowly shook her head.

"So," Becca continued, carefully removing her tiara headband and placing it on the table, "I encourage all of you to take naps. I know *I'll* be taking one."

Reaching for a cookie, Oliver frowned. "I can't sleep during the day."

Becca smiled patiently at her son. "Then you can read or do something else quiet and restful in your room. We have New Year's Eve worship at 6:30, and we'll have dinner as soon as we get—"

"And then we'll watch our yearly video?" Hazel interjected, her eyes wide with excitement. "You finished it, right?"

With a laugh, Becca said, "Yes, I finished it." Picking up her tiara, she tilted it and watched it twinkle and flash in the sunlight. "So then, we'll watch the video, play Clue, maybe I'll read aloud—"

"And Hazel will fall asleep..." Oliver added.

Hazel's jaw clenched. "I will not! I have a plan this year!" She pounded her little fist on the table. "Just wait a second." With that, Hazel rose from her seat and dashed toward her bedroom. She soon returned and triumphantly held up a piece of paper titled in sparkly purple gel pen: *Operation: Midnight.* "Phase one," Hazel read in her high, sweet voice, "take a nap. Phase two. And"—she raised a pointer finger as she explained—"this will be once I start feeling sleepy."

"So, you should probably start phase two right now," Oliver said and then popped the rest of his cookie into his mouth.

Hazel ignored him. "Phase two: caffeine." Her eyebrows furrowed, and she quickly turned to her mother. "Is that okay, Mommy?"

"For New Year's Eve, it's all right," Becca said with a smile. "You may have one Coke."

Satisfied, the girl nodded and continued. "Phase three: jumping jacks. Phase four: dance party!"

"Oh no," Violet groaned, bringing her fingertips to her forehead. "Not in *our* room?"

"Where else?" Hazel asked innocently. "And finally, phase five..." She paused dramatically. "A cold shower." She grinned and slowly looked into the faces of her mother and siblings.

Oliver brushed the crumbs off his hands and straightened in his chair. "Wow, Hazel, I take it back. I really think that's going to work!"

"You do?" she asked, raising a thin eyebrow.

"Yeah," Oliver said. "That will keep you up until at least 9:30!"

As Hazel glared at her brother, Becca stifled a laugh and then smiled at her younger daughter. "It's a very well-thought-out plan, Hazel," she said. "And now it's time for all of us to enact phase one: take a nap."

The children headed to their bedrooms, and Becca, followed by Butterscotch, stepped into her own room. She flipped on the ceiling fan, lowered the blinds, and plumped her pillow. Tossing a cream-colored throw blanket over herself, she lay down on top of the covers. With a final glance at the golden retriever, who had curled up on her rug with her head resting on her paws, Becca smiled and closed her eyes.

She had just drifted off to sleep when she felt a strange sensation pulling her from her slumber. Although the room was silent, Becca felt a definite presence. Rolling to her side, she opened her eyes to find a pair of aqua-colored ones only inches from her own. She let out a squeak, and her hand flew to her heart. "Hazel!" she scolded.

The girl blinked. "I couldn't sleep."

With a frown, Becca reached over to her nightstand and turned her clock to face her: 2:15. "It's only been twenty minutes."

"It feels like it's been much longer than that," Hazel said, sticking out her lower lip. "There's no way I'm going to fall asleep."

Becca sighed. "Then just rest. Read your book or work on your crochet."

"Oh!" Hazel said, clasping her hands together. "I do need to add the beak to my penguin!"

"Perfect." Becca pulled the blanket up to her chin and rolled onto her back. As her daughter retreated from the room, she stared at the ceiling. Her heart was still thumping, and she knew that another attempt at a nap was hopeless.

She sighed and made her way to the living room where the Christmas tree sparkled, and the flames in the gas fireplace flickered and danced. Throwing a blanket over her legs, Becca settled into her chair and reached into the basket at the foot of the lamp. The light-green copy of *Pride and Prejudice* felt warm and familiar in her hand, and the volume opened easily to the inside of the front cover. The corners of Becca's lips curled upward as she gently ran a fingertip over the uneven peaks of Matt's "M" in his inscription to her. With a sigh, she found her place in the book and continued to read it for what was likely the hundredth time. She glanced up to see Hazel plunk down on the loveseat with her crochet kit, and then her eyes returned to the page. Becca read for some time, eventually smiling sleepily at Mr. Darcy's snobbish behavior at the Netherfield ball. She allowed the book to fall into her lap as she closed her eyes.

She woke to the sound of clinking and clattering in the kitchen. With a sleepy glance at the oversized pocket watch clock on the mantel, Becca closed her book and returned it to the basket. Making her way to the kitchen, she leaned against the doorway and watched as Violet pulled a rectangular cake from the oven, and Hazel whisked the contents of a bowl.

"What are you girls up to?" Becca asked, rubbing the sleep from her eyes.

Violet and Hazel turned toward their mother.

"We're making parfaits!" Hazel said brightly.

"Well," Becca said, "since you girls have everything under control for dessert, I'll put together our seafood platter."

As Becca and the girls moved about the kitchen, the food preparation went smoothly, except for Oliver's occasional appearances to "taste test." Soon, a cheerful-looking feast filled their kitchen table. In the center was a platter ringed with imitation crab and shrimp with a bowl of cocktail sauce nestled in the center. Beside it stood several tall glasses layered with vanilla pudding, cake, and strawberries.

By the time the Gables had put the treats away for later, cleaned up the kitchen, and then plied themselves with a light dinner of sandwiches and fruit, it was time to leave for the 6:30 New Year's Eve service. The sun had set hours ago, and it was dark when the family stepped into the frosty night to head toward their minivan. The worship service at Grace Lutheran Church was lightly attended but beautiful.

Later, as Becca and the children trooped back into their cozy apartment, she let out a contented sigh. "Isn't worshiping in God's house a wonderful way to end the year?"

"I can't think of anything better," Violet said quietly, hanging up her coat on its hook.

Oliver and Hazel, who were tossing their hats and gloves into their baskets, nodded in thoughtful agreement.

Suddenly, Hazel bounced on her toes and looked up at her mother with wide eyes. "It's time! It's finally time for our video!"

Becca laughed. "Yes, it's that time. Let's all get changed and meet in the living room. Whoever finishes first, would you please grab the seafood platter and parfaits?"

In almost no time, the family was assembled in the living room. Violet and Hazel wore their matching Christmas pajamas, and Oliver was in an old Hawks t-shirt and athletic shorts. Becca had exchanged her elegant outfit for a gold t-shirt printed with the word "Cheers," black joggers, and sparkly slippers. Slipping the silver-and-gold headband tiara onto her head, she surveyed the coffee table, which was loaded with their special New Year's Eve seafood platter, plates, and diminutive forks for the crab legs and shrimp. Beside all this stood a colorful cluster of parfaits with spoons tucked into them.

Spying her mother's headband, Hazel raced to her bedroom to retrieve her own. When the girl returned, she had a can of Coca-Cola clutched in one hand. She held it up to show her mother and siblings. "Phase two!" she announced proudly.

Pinching off a tail, Oliver dunked a shrimp in cocktail sauce. "Wouldn't you rather have some nice warm milk, Hazel?"

The girl narrowed her eyes at her brother, and Oliver chuckled.

Primly, Violet pierced a piece of crab with her fork. "Mmm," she said. "I wait for this all year long."

Plates and parfaits in hand, the family settled into their places, Violet and Oliver on their respective cushions on the loveseat, Hazel sitting pretzel-legged on the floor, and Becca in the tufted charcoal-gray easy chair. Balancing his plate on the arm of the loveseat, Oliver leaned back and pulled out the pocketknife from Uncle John. Carefully, he unfolded the knife, looked over at his mother, and mimed eating the crab with the blade.

"May I?" he asked, flashing her a lopsided grin. Becca shook her head, but her green eyes twinkled, and she smiled her approval. The young man quickly speared a piece of crab and dipped it in the cocktail sauce. Despite her amusement, Becca couldn't help but cringe as Oliver pulled the piece of crab from the knife with his teeth.

Becca picked up the television remote. As she pointed it at the screen, she said, "I would just like everyone to take a moment to appreciate that I finished the montage in time." She laughed as the children burst into a round of applause, and Oliver even whooped. "All right," she said, still grinning. "Without further ado... the Gables' year in review!"

The video began with a clip of Hazel taking a running leap onto a sled and zipping down the top of a hill. Every three to ten seconds, the video changed, showing a different scene from the family's life. An image of the children waving palm branches at the Palm Sunday worship service filled the screen. "Aww!" Becca said, smiling. "I just love that tradition!"

The family watched as Oliver stepped onto a coach bus headed to Camp Wartburg with his friends. "The zipline there is the *best*," he commented. "I get to go back again this summer, right?"

Becca nodded. "You bet!" She turned to Violet. "Vi, do you think you'd be interested in being a junior counselor?"

"Maybe," Violet said, shrugging and keeping her eyes on the screen.

"Oh, the Art Institute!" Hazel exclaimed, pointing at the screen where Violet sketched *Allegory of Peace and War*.

Violet made a face. "That was such a beautiful painting, but my sketch looked nothing like it."

"The art there was fine," Oliver said, his voice a bit muffled as he took a bite of crab. "But the best part was the stolen painting exhibit."

Crumpling her napkin, Hazel pivoted and hurled it at her brother. "Oh nooooooo! Don't start with that again!"

Oliver dodged the napkin. "What?" he said. "It was cool! I actually liked writing that report."

The smile quickly disappeared from the young man's face as a clip of him playing the violin at the Paper Palace filled the screen, and Hazel giggled gleefully.

"Ugh," Oliver groaned. "I look like such a dork all dressed up like that!"

With a nod, Violet smiled at her brother. "Yes, you do, but at least it's far enough away that you kind of fade away into the background."

Becca dunked her spoon into her parfait and frowned. "Yeah, this is not the best video of Oliver's performance, but it was my only opportunity. Otherwise, Mrs. Grant was always in the room." She turned to her son. "And you do *not* look like a dork. You look very handsome."

As Oliver arched a brow at his mother, the family burst into laughter as a close-up of Uncle John filled the screen. He had been taste-testing one of Hazel's drink creations, and as he lowered the mug from his lips, a large dollop of whipped cream clung to the tip of his nose.

The image shifted to a basketball court where Oliver, suited up in his blue-and-white Hawks uniform, called a play into motion.

"Against the Crusaders?" Oliver complained. "Mom, couldn't you have used a video from a game we won?"

"Well," Hazel said sweetly, "there weren't many of those to choose from."

Oliver narrowed his eyes at his sister, who smiled back at him.

Not knowing whether to grimace or laugh, Becca spluttered her bite of pudding.

The video shifted to the CRH actors onstage in their *A Christmas Carol* costumes, bowing and then pointing upward as the audience roared in applause.

Becca cleared her throat. "That's my favorite part... How you all give the glory and honor to God."

Toward the end of the applause, Violet, dressed in all black and wearing a headset, peeked out from behind the curtain and waved.

On the screen, the scene changed to the bookshop, where Audrey and Chris leaned across the confectionery counter, making googly eyes at each other. The couple was so engrossed in their playful chatter that they were completely oblivious to the camera.

"Oh, Aunt Audrey is going to get her kiss tonight!" Hazel said dreamily, clasping her hands by her heart.

Violet smiled, Oliver shuddered, and Becca laughed.

The final clip showed a mirror ball slowly descending as voices called out, "Three, two, one... Happy *Noon* Year!"

"And that's from today!" Hazel said. She glanced over her shoulder at Violet. "It's too bad Mommy didn't get a video of you and Trevor dancing."

Violet rolled her eyes, picked up the crumpled napkin, and flung it back at her sister's head.

As the montage faded from the screen, the family sat in silence for a moment, looked at each other, and then finally burst into applause.

"Again! Again!" Hazel cried.

Becca laughed. "You can watch it again another time. How about we keep the traditions rolling with a game of Clue?"

Oliver groaned. "Okay, we can play. But we already know that you're going to win, Mom."

Smiling innocently, Becca said, "You never know..."

Violet shook her head as she rose to retrieve the game from the closet.

After a quick clean-up in the living room, the Gables took their places around the dining room table. Hazel, as usual, insisted on being Miss

Scarlet. As she moved her pawn into its starting place, her mouth stretched open in a loud yawn.

Oliver grinned. "What was that, Hazel? Are you starting to feel a little sleepy?"

The girl froze, her aqua eyes wide. "Phase three!" She took a couple of steps back from the table and flung her limbs outward like a star. Pulling them in again, she shouted, "One!" As she continued her jumping jacks, she called out, "Two! Three!"

After a while, Violet glanced up from her Clue notepad on which she was recording an intricate series of codes. "How many of those are you going to do?"

"A hundred!" Hazel gasped. Then she stopped. "You made me lose my place! Now I have to start over."

Becca laughed and shook her head. "You were at eighty-two."

"Eighty-three!" Hazel resumed.

Before long, the girl slid into her seat, breathing hard and pushing her damp vanilla-blonde hair off her forehead.

"Make sure you look *carefully* at your cards this time," Violet warned her sister.

Oliver began humming, and Hazel looked at him curiously as she arranged her cards in her hand. After a moment, she recognized the tune as "Brahm's Lullaby" and kicked at her brother under the table. "Knock it off, Oliver!"

The young man grinned mischievously. Violet and Becca exchanged glances and burst into giggles while Hazel shot them a look of betrayal.

The Gables proceeded to play the game, and Oliver's prediction proved correct as Becca called out, "Mrs. Peacock with the rope in the library!" After she opened the envelope confirming that she was right, the children flung their cards on the table.

"I was one turn away!" Violet bemoaned.

Becca smiled sympathetically at her daughter and glanced at her watch: 10:28. "How about you children clean up," she said, "and I will go record the ball dropping in New York, so we can play it back in Central Time at midnight?"

Oliver turned to Hazel whose eyelids were beginning to droop. "That's a whole hour-and-a-half away. How are you feeling, Hazel?"

The girl straightened in her chair. "I'm feeling wide awake…" she said, her voice wavering at the end. She turned toward her mother. "Is it okay if I start phase four—dance party now?"

Becca laughed. "Sure. How about we all do our own things for a while, and we'll meet in the living room at 11:00 for read-aloud?"

Hazel popped up from her chair, twirled, and struck a pose. Looking at Violet, she asked, "Are you coming to the dance party?"

Violet made a face. "No, sorry, I can't find my ticket." She looked at her mother. "I'll make popcorn and cocoa for the read-aloud."

"Your loss!" Hazel said brightly, skipping off to her bedroom. Within moments, the twangy opening notes of Anne Wilson's "Hey Girl" began to blare throughout the apartment.

Pulling his knife from his pocket, Oliver said, "I'm going to my room to do some more soap carving."

Becca smiled. "What are you making?"

"Not sure," Oliver said with a shrug. "The design hasn't worked its way out yet."

With the children entertaining themselves, Becca found herself alone and made her way to the living room. She curled up on the gray tufted chair and resumed her copy of *Pride and Prejudice* to see if, this time, Lizzie would be more immediately forgiving of Darcy's indifference to her. The smell of melted butter caught her attention, and she glanced up and smiled as Violet set a large bowl of popcorn on the coffee table.

"The cocoa is on the stovetop to keep warm," Violet said. "I've successfully avoided the dance party." The young woman grabbed her own book, *Hercule Poirot's Christmas*, and settled on the loveseat.

At exactly 11:00, an alarm on Violet's phone sounded. She laid the book in her lap and looked at her mother. "Should I get Oliver and Hazel?"

Becca nodded, and Violet left to collect her siblings. After ladling out mugs of cocoa and filling up bowls of popcorn for themselves, the older children took their usual places on the loveseat. On the floor, Hazel curled up with her Squishmallow. Violet handed her mother her nutcracker mug, and Becca allowed the warmth of the cocoa to radiate into her fingers. She took a long slow sip, and then, swapping her copy of *Pride and Prejudice* for *Little Women*, Becca began to read.

After several pages, she glanced up to find Hazel's eyes mostly closed. "Hazel, are you still with us?"

The girl perked up at the sound of her name. "I—I—I'm totally awake!" she stammered.

"You're never going to make it," Oliver said in a singsong voice, and a laugh burst from Violet.

"Phase five!" Hazel cried desperately. "I'm going to go take a cold shower now."

Becca smiled reassuringly at her daughter. "You know, Hazel, it's okay if you want to go to bed. You already stayed up later than last year."

"No!" Hazel said determinedly. "No, I can do this! I *want* to do this."

Picking herself up from the floor, she headed to the bathroom as Oliver and Violet exchanged knowing glances. With a smile, Becca shook her head and resumed reading.

After a couple of minutes, a piercing shriek came from the bathroom, followed by a high-pitched exclamation of, "COOOOOOOOLD!"

Becca, Violet, and Oliver exploded into laughter.

Before long, Becca glanced up from the page as Hazel stepped into the living room. Her hair was wrapped in a white towel turban, and her mother noticed flashes of ankles and wrists under last year's too-small pajamas.

"Welcome back," Becca greeted.

Settling on the floor, the girl frowned at her Squishmallow and pushed it away from her. She sat up ramrod straight.

"What are you doing, Hazel?" Violet asked. Her nut-brown eyes were focused on her phone as she set another timer.

"I'm making myself as uncomfortable as possible," Hazel said. "I am *not* falling asleep."

Sliding down from his place on the loveseat, Oliver reached behind his neck and pulled a pendant necklace over his head. He plunked down next to his sister and, pinching the clasp between two fingers, swung the pendant back and forth in front of her eyes. "You are getting sleepy..." he said in a low, monotone voice. "Very sleepy..."

"Stop it!" Hazel said, batting the necklace and sending it flying.

As Oliver crossed the room to retrieve his pendant, Becca stifled a laugh. "Oliver," she said, "you may want to be careful. You remember what happened when Jo teased Amy too much, don't you?" She held up the copy of *Little Women*.

Hazel grinned at her brother. "Do you still have your pocketknife? I wonder if it would melt..." she said sweetly. With a mischievous glint in her eyes, she looked over at the flames dancing in the gas fireplace.

Looping the necklace over his head again, Oliver chuckled and flopped back down on the loveseat beside Violet.

Becca smiled. "Shall we continue?"

Time passed quickly as the Gables entered the world of *Little Women,* and at 11:50, the timer on Violet's phone sounded. Becca snapped the book shut with a soft thud. She bent to tuck it into the basket at the base of the lamp, and as she straightened, she heard Violet and Oliver snickering. Following her older children's line of sight, she saw Hazel, sound asleep on her Squishmallow. One of Hazel's arms was curled around the plush toy, and her lips were slightly parted as she snored softly.

Becca laughed and clapped a hand over her mouth. "Oh no!" she said in a loud whisper, her eyes twinkling in amusement. "She almost made it."

Pressing a finger to her lips, she padded over to Violet and Oliver. "Vi, would you please pour the sparkling juice? And, Oliver, would you go into the dining room and grab the bowl of noisemakers?"

Oliver glanced at Hazel and cocked an eyebrow.

"I have a plan," Becca said.

As she cued up the recording of the ball drop in Times Square, Becca smiled as she saw Oliver, wearing his Pickwick Club top hat, return with the bowl of noisemakers and set them on the table. In another minute, Violet joined them, carrying three plastic champagne flutes, which she then filled with sparkling apple juice.

Becca glanced down at the basket of noisemakers and fished out a tiara. Looking at Violet, she asked, "Would you like one?"

Violet wrinkled her nose and shook her head. Pulling out her phone and swiping to the world clock, she then picked up the television remote in the other hand and assumed the duty of playing the recording at the exact time.

On the television screen, clouds of confetti drifted through Times Square as the digital numbers counted down. At "ten," the crowd began shouting the countdown, and the Gables joined them in a loud whisper. "Nine, eight, seven..." Becca's eyes twinkled as she pressed a noisemaker into Oliver's hand, dropped one into Violet's pocket, and then pointed to the fire escape.

"Ah!" Oliver said, nodding at his mother.

The glistening ball continued to descend. "Three, two, one! Happy New Year!" Becca, Violet, and Oliver said as loudly as they dared.

Becca led them in picking up her glass of sparkling juice. "Cheers!" she whispered. The children echoed her, and the three of them clinked their glasses together. As Becca sipped, the delicate fizz tickled her nose. Setting down her glass, she dropped a kiss on Hazel's forehead, grabbed the thick cream-colored blanket from her tufted chair, and motioned for the older children to follow her.

As the Gables stepped onto the fire escape, Becca threw the blanket around her shoulders like a cloak. She offered one corner to Oliver and the other to Violet, and the three of them huddled together in the chill. Glancing sideways at each of the children, Becca grinned. "Happy New Year!" she shouted into the frosty night and raised the noisemaker to her lips. The children joined her, and a merry cacophony filled the evening air. Oliver gave blasts of varying lengths, Violet blew three sharp staccato notes and quit, and Becca tried to play "Auld Lang Syne."

Tipping her face upward, Becca gazed at the stars, which blinked back at her like diamonds. "The heavens declare the glory of God," she began.

"The skies proclaim the work of his hands," Violet and Oliver finished in unison.

Under the blanket, Becca wrapped her arms around her children's shoulders. The nearly full moon cast a soft silvery glow over the family as the mother prayed. "Heavenly Father," she said, "we thank you for the blessings of this past year. May you fill our hearts with your wisdom and grant us your blessing and protection in the year to come. In Jesus's precious name, Amen." The three of them gazed up at the night sky for several long moments, their breath hanging in the icy air like clouds. Finally, Violet shivered, and the three of them headed back inside.

Tossing the blanket back onto her chair, Becca picked up the remote and switched off the television. She and the children drained their glasses of sparkling apple juice, and Violet collected the glasses and took them to the kitchen.

With a slow shake of his head, Oliver smiled down at his sleeping sister. "Maybe next year," he said. Gently, he picked her up and turned to exit the living room.

"Wait!" Becca hurried after him and ruffled his hair. "Love you," she said warmly. Unwinding the towel from Hazel's head, Becca kissed her daughter's forehead. As she looked up, she saw Violet wave goodnight as she headed toward the bedroom. Butterscotch followed at her heels as Becca put the apartment to sleep for the evening—closing the curtains, clicking off the lights, turning off the Christmas tree and the fireplace, and making sure that the doors were locked.

Finally, she headed to her bedroom. With a yawn, she peeled back the covers and slipped between the sheets. She rolled to her side and smiled sleepily at the golden retriever, who had finished her three slow circles and settled down on her rug. Reaching down, she scratched the top of the dog's head. "Happy New Year, Butterscotch," she murmured.

Becca rolled onto her back and waited expectantly for sleep to come. Despite her fatigue, her brain buzzed as it played the video montage over and over again in her mind. Hazel jumping on the sled. The children waving their palm branches. Oliver stepping onto the bus. After what felt like a long time, Becca blinked up at the ceiling. Reaching over to her nightstand, she turned her clock to face her. "Ugh," she groaned as she looked at the time. Flopping back onto her pillow, she sighed as the images from the montage continued to flash across her mind. Violet sketching. Oliver playing the violin. Becca's entire body tensed, and she sucked in a breath at the realization that *that* was the image that was bothering her. Violet's words echoed in her consciousness. "At least it's far enough away that you kind of fade away into the background," she had said.

Becca sat up so suddenly that Butterscotch raised her head and looked at her mistress in alarm. Reaching down, Becca soothed the startled dog. "Sorry, girl, but I just had an idea." She picked up the phone and excitedly held it up to Butterscotch. "Oliver was in the *background* of the video. I have the full clip on my phone, and we can see a lot of what is happening at Mrs. Grant's cocktail party." A shiver ran up and down her spine. "I wonder if I caught Harvey poisoning the goblet!"

Flinging off the covers, Becca jumped out of bed and smiled apologetically at the dog, who had now risen. She stepped into her slippers. "There's something I need to check out." As she pulled on her robe, Butterscotch looked at her and tilted her head. Becca patted her thigh. "Come on, girl! We'll be able to get a better view on the television screen."

Becca entered the living room, snatched the remote from the coffee table, and turned on the television. She settled into the charcoal-gray chair, tucking her feet beneath her, and Butterscotch sat attentively by her side. As Becca scrolled on her phone in search of the full three-minute video clip, the cold blue light emanating from the screen shone on her fair complexion. She cast the video onto the television and narrowed her eyes in concentration as it played, this time focusing on everyone in the video *except* her son. Suddenly, her eyes widened, and she held her breath. She paused the video, rewound the clip, and played it again. A cold wave washed over her body, and she shivered. Pausing it and watching it one more time, she realized that her hand had moved to her mouth in horror.

Glancing up at the oversized pocket watch clock on the mantel, Becca noted the time: 2:15 AM. After a moment's hesitation, with trembling fingers, she selected a contact on her phone.

"Hello? Becca? Is everything okay?" It was a warm bass, thick with sleep.

"I'm fine. The kids are fine," Becca said, her voice wavering slightly. "But I've just discovered something, and I had to tell you about it right away."

"What?" the deep voice asked. "What did you find?"

Becca drew in a breath. "I know who killed Phyllis Grant."

# Chapter 22

# What Becca Found

Framed by the jagged frost that had crept along the edges of the glass panes, the steely gray early morning light filtered through the living room windows of the Gables' apartment. With a shiver, Becca pulled her green knit cardigan more tightly over her white t-shirt and glanced at the two men who were standing next to her, staring intently at the television screen. She was wearing jeans, and her hair was plaited in a French braid with a few loose strands framing her face. Detective Post, dressed in a navy-blue suit, folded his arms across his chest and looked at the chief.

"Please play it again, from the beginning," John said, his bass voice grave. He was wearing his police uniform, and his eyes were locked on the screen.

Looking down at her phone, Becca restarted the video. She studied the men's faces as the scene from Phyllis Grant's cocktail party played out in front of them for the fourth time. Detective Post squinted at the screen, occasionally running his thumb and forefinger across his light-colored beard and glancing over at the chief. John stared unwaveringly ahead of him. His keen gaze took in every second of the clip, not drifting from the screen for even a moment.

As the video ended, Becca's eyes twinkled with excitement, and she looked back and forth between the detective and her uncle. However, instead of looking pleased, John's mouth was set in a straight line, and his eyebrows were furrowed. The detective hooked his fingers in his pockets, and his expression clouded over as he glanced at the chief. Confused, Becca opened her mouth, but before she could form her question, the creaking of a door coming from the hallway broke the silence.

Within moments, Oliver appeared in the doorway. He was wearing a Hawks t-shirt and athletic shorts, and his hair was fanned up on one side. His eyelids, which were heavy with sleep, widened as he took in the sight of the two men standing in the living room.

"Oh, hey, Uncle John," he said, rubbing the sleep from his eyes. "What are you doing here?"

Quickly, Becca crossed the room to her son. "Oliver," she said, "please go back to bed."

Glancing at the television and seeing the clip of himself with his violin poised on his shoulder, the young man's face brightened. "You're watching the montage? I looked really—"

"Oliver, go," Uncle John said sternly.

Oliver's mouth snapped shut. After a moment's pause, he slowly turned to head back to his bedroom.

Becca placed a hand on her son's shoulder and said softly, "Everything is okay. I will come and get you in a little bit." Once she ensured that Oliver was in his room with the door shut behind him, Becca rejoined the two men.

Uncle John looked at her. "Again, from the beginning."

With a touch of her phone screen, Becca restarted the video, and the grand living room of the Paper Palace filled the screen. Off-center and slightly to the right was a distant Oliver, whose eyes occasionally closed as he eased his bow back and forth across the strings of his violin. On the far-left side of the frame, the dark cherrywood bar gleamed. Carefully lifting trays loaded with filled champagne glasses, Harvey moved away from the bar, leaving Lexi standing there alone. The young woman wore a black sheath dress, and her ebony hair was pulled back in an elegant twist. Her back was to the camera, and she was barely in the frame.

Becca held her breath, and her gaze flicked to Uncle John, whose eyes were narrowed slightly as he studied the screen.

After a quick glance around, Lexi picked up the ruby-colored goblet and tossed its contents down the sink behind the bar. Her pale hand shot out, grabbed the distinctive green bottle of champagne, and refilled her grandmother's glass.

"I know for a *fact* that Mrs. Grant's non-alcoholic wine was in a blue bottle," Becca said.

John nodded, his gaze still locked onto the figure on the screen. "Yes, you've said that."

The goblet disappeared from their view as Lexi, her back still to the camera, pulled it in close to her. She threw another glance over her shoulder, and Chief John, Detective Post, and Becca watched as the young woman grabbed her clutch and apparently rifled through it. Her exact actions were blocked from their view, but it was clear that she was doing *something*.

"That must be when she put in the eszopiclone," Becca whispered.

When Lexi was finished, she returned the goblet to its original place and set the clutch back down on the countertop of the bar. Within moments, a loud bang could be heard in the video, and Becca bit her lip.

"That's the library doors crashing open," she explained. "This is when Mrs. Grant came back in with the three men who were playing poker, and I had to stop taping."

"Yes, yes," John murmured, continuing to frown at the screen.

Detective Post folded his arms across his chest again and shook his head. "It's always the family members," he said in a low voice.

Becca glanced back and forth between the two men's faces, rising hopefully on her tiptoes. "This is what you needed, right?"

Uncle John turned toward his niece. "Becca," he said, the warmth returning to his voice, "could the detective and I have a moment?"

"Oh! Oh, certainly." The woman tucked a strand of hair behind her ear. "How about I make a pot of coffee?"

Detective Post gave a curt nod, and Becca headed to the kitchen. As she scooped the fragrant grounds into the coffee maker, she couldn't help but strain her ears. Although the men's voices were low, she picked up the words "judge" and "warrant."

When the coffee was brewed, she poured it into three mugs. After adding cream to her own, she grabbed one of the mugs of black coffee and headed toward the entrance of the living room. She caught John's eye, raised her eyebrows, and lifted the mug. "Ready?"

The chief smiled at her. "Yes, thank you."

Becca stepped into the room and handed her uncle the mug. She returned to the kitchen to grab the other two. Handing the second black coffee to the detective, she kept the creamy one for herself.

Detective Post sipped the hot liquid and then looked at Becca. "We are going to need a copy of this video."

With a nod, Becca set down her mug on the coffee table. "Certainly. I'll put it on a thumb drive for you right now." After rifling through a drawer, she found a fresh data storage device and plugged it into her laptop. The two men watched as she loaded the video onto the drive, ejected it, and placed it in the detective's palm.

Detective Post looked at John. "I'm going to work on authenticating this, Chief."

"Very good," John replied.

The detective turned to Becca. "Thank you for your time and for bringing this to our attention," he said, holding up the thumb drive. "I will let myself out."

Becca picked up her coffee, and she and John stood, listening to the clacking of Detective Post's wingtips as he made his way down the hallway.

At the thud of the apartment door, Uncle John turned to his niece, his blue eyes twinkling with their usual geniality. "I trust you understand that you should not mention this to anyone."

"Of course, I will be discreet," Becca said. She frowned, looked down at her slippered feet, and then back at her uncle. "But I don't understand. Isn't this a good thing? Isn't this the evidence you needed?" Her eyes widened. "I mean, the video shows that Lexi did it. It's right there!"

With a sigh, John gazed down into Becca's confused countenance. "Yes, it's exactly as you said. The video shows that Alexandra Grant killed her grandmother. You know it, and I know it." Becca tilted her head, and John continued, "But any mediocre lawyer will view this tape and say that all it shows is her pouring out one drink and pouring in another. They will frame it as an innocent mistake. Maybe she saw a hair or a bug in there, so she dumped it out and accidentally refilled it with the wrong beverage.

The point is that we don't see her adding the eszopiclone, so they will say it was an accident, and we can't prove that it wasn't." He paused and took a long sip of his coffee. "Even that oaf Curtis could get her off that charge."

Becca's shoulders drooped as she considered her uncle's words. After a few moments, she brightened and said, "Yes, but this will at least give you enough to open an investigation on her to find something else to convict her."

The corners of John's bushy mustache rose slightly in a small sad smile. "We *have* been investigating her," he said, and an even deeper sigh escaped his lips. "She was our very first suspect. Just as Detective Post said, it's always the family members..." He gazed down into the contents of his coffee mug and then looked at Becca again. "But following every angle we could, we found nothing. No motive. The Grants have no money. There is no inheritance, no company, no position, no other family left. And according to every witness we interviewed, the two had a good relationship. In fact, it seems to be one of the only decent relationships Phyllis Grant *did* have..." Slowly, the chief shook his head. "When she gets arrested and goes to court, this is not going to be nearly the conviction it should be."

"So, she's just going to get away with it?" Becca said weakly, her spirit sinking like a stone.

John smiled, and his blue eyes twinkled. "Not if we can help it." He reached out and lightly stroked Becca's shoulder with his thumb.

With a wink, John thanked his niece for giving him work to do on New Year's Day, pecked her on the cheek, and headed out to join Detective Post at the police station.

# Chapter 23

# Reports and Revelations

As the bookshop's fireplace popped and crackled nearby, Licorice effort-lessly leaped onto the wide windowsill, settled himself with a regal air, and looked out at the softly falling snow. With a slight frown, Becca gazed at her cat silhouetted against the dove-gray sky. She tried to ignore the knot that had formed in her stomach two days ago when she had shared the incriminating video with Uncle John and Detective Post. An exasperated sigh escaped from Violet's lips, and Becca was shaken from her thoughts. Quickly, she shifted her attention to her oldest daughter.

"I know a bank where the wild thyme blows," Violet read, her cheeks a bright fuchsia. "Where oxlips and the nodding violet grows."

"Violet!" Hazel echoed excitedly.

Flicking her gaze up from the page, Violet shot her sister an annoyed look. "Quite over-canopied with luscious woodbine," she continued, "With sweet musk-roses and eglantine." The young woman thumped both hands on top of her book and looked up at her mother. "Can it be someone else's turn now?"

Oliver raised the mug of hot chocolate to his lips to hide his grin.

"It's good to have challenges," Becca said encouragingly. "They help us grow. You can do this, Vi."

With a puff of air from the side of her mouth, Violet blew at a wayward strand of chestnut hair. She glared down at the page, ready to engage it in battle. "There sleeps—" She paused and looked up at her mother again.

"Ti-TEY-nee-*uh*," Becca said softly.

Violet wrinkled her nose. "Titania," she repeated, "sometime of the night. Lull'd in these flowers with dances and delight. And there the snake throws her enamell'd skin, Weed wide enough to wrap a fairy in." She heaved another sigh and turned to her mother. "*Now* can it be someone else's turn?"

Becca gave a small shake of her head, and with much effort, Violet finished Oberon's part.

"Fear not, my lord, your servant shall do so," Hazel said, raising her already high voice into an even higher pitch.

Oliver cocked a brow at his little sister.

"What?" Hazel asked innocently. "Puck is a fairy."

"End scene!" Becca declared, closing her copy of *A Midsummer Night's Dream* and reaching down to scratch Butterscotch behind her ears.

Violet snapped her book shut and shoved it across the table. "Good riddance!" She paused and looked at her mother. "I don't mind Shakespeare in general, but reading his plays aloud is a nightmare. My tongue gets all twisted up."

"You know, she's right," Oliver said. "This would be way better if he had just written it in English, but I'm getting more out of it now than before."

Becca stifled a smile. "It *is* in English, Oliver. But I am happy it's making sense to you." She reached over to tousle her son's hair, but he ducked out of the way. "There are so many good reasons to study Shakespeare," Becca continued, "one being to develop your cultural literacy." She glanced at Violet. "We'll just keep plugging away, and it will get easier with time. You'll see."

Plucking a small stack of 8x10 art prints from her morning time basket, Becca distributed them face-down around the table. "Now, as you are studying the image, remember what Mr. Gerhartz told you about how to read a painting." She paused. "And flip!"

Becca and the children turned over the art prints to reveal Leonardo da Vinci's *The Last Supper.* They were so engrossed in their examination of the painting that no one noticed when the shop's twinkle lights suddenly reflected on the prints' surfaces or when light swing jazz music began to drift through the bookshop. Suddenly, Becca felt a hand on her shoulder. She jumped and let out a squeak.

"Morning!" Audrey said, laughing at her sister-in-law's reaction. The front pieces of her auburn hair were damp with melted snow. "You are all in your own little world this morning." She leaned over and scanned the art print. "Still Rembrandt?"

Violet shook her head. "No, da Vinci."

"Oh." Audrey shrugged and then turned to Becca. "We're all set. I'm going to look at our accounts until we open."

Becca shuddered. "Be my guest," she said and then flashed a smile at her sister-in-law. As Audrey made her way behind the confectionery counter, Becca scanned her children's faces. "Close your eyes," she instructed. "Can you see all of the painting in your mind's eye?"

Obediently, all three children shut their eyes. Oliver and Violet nodded, but Hazel screwed up her mouth. "The objects on the table are a little fuzzy," the girl said.

"That's okay," Becca encouraged. "Open your eyes and study the painting a little more."

The children bent their heads over the art prints, and Becca glanced over to the window where Licorice had now settled into a sphinxlike pose.

"Hey, Becca!" Audrey called from her seat at the tiled table behind the confectionery counter. "Have you heard anything about that shipment of books for Licorice League? The payment posted, but we haven't received the books yet. We're going to need those soon."

Becca frowned and looked at Violet. "Vi, would you—"

"I've got it," Violet said.

With a grateful smile at her daughter, Becca rose from her chair, stepped over the golden retriever, and headed toward her sister-in-law. Finding that Audrey had already set Becca's laptop opposite her own on the table, Becca slid into a chair and flipped it open. She propped her chin on her fist and scanned her inbox. "There might be something here," she murmured. "I haven't checked my email since yesterday." Suddenly, she narrowed her eyes. "Mallory Smith? Why is Uncle John's secretary emailing me?" She clicked on the email, and her eyebrows furrowed as she began to read. "Oh!" Becca cried. "Oh, oh!"

Eyes wide, Audrey looked at her sister-in-law. "What is it?"

"This is the background check that I asked Uncle John for... on that painter!" Becca said excitedly.

Audrey raised her eyebrows. "What does it say?"

Silent for a moment as she read the email, Becca shook her head and sighed. "Not much, actually. It just confirms what Mrs. Grant said during her speech. Apparently, Alberti was deported from the U.S. He was then arrested in Italy, but there aren't any details on that. He never made it back to the States again." Becca slumped back in her chair. "Her father really did a number on that guy."

"I'm sorry it's not much help," Audrey said sympathetically.

Becca shrugged. "It's okay. I actually already found out what I wanted to know... the name of the painting that Alberti had copied." She returned her attention to the laptop screen. "Aha!" she said triumphantly. After a few clicks, she glanced across the top of her screen at Audrey. "According to the tracking information, the books should be here in three days."

Audrey gazed up at the vaulted ceiling as she calculated. "Okay, that should give us enough time. I'll mark it down."

Becca nodded, closed her laptop, and rose from her seat.

When she returned to the long table where her children were seated with the art prints, she found that Toffee had claimed her chair, his toy mouse in his teeth. He blinked up at Becca, who held out her hand and allowed the cat to drop the toy into her palm. Tossing the mouse as far as she could, Becca laughed as the Manx happily bounded after it. She scanned the table as she resumed her seat. "How is it going over here?" she asked.

"We noticed something," Hazel said, twirling a strand of vanilla-blonde hair around her finger. "If this is the Last Supper, where is the cup?"

Becca grinned. "Excellent observation!" Green eyes twinkling, she looked at each of her children in turn. "I have a fun fact for you. The chalice *was* originally in the painting. After da Vinci painted it, he asked someone what they thought of it. That person said that it was so well done, he felt like he could just reach out and touch it. At that, da Vinci immediately went up to the painting and scratched it out."

Violet gasped. "Why would he do that?"

"He didn't want anything overshadowing Jesus," Becca explained. The children slowly nodded, and Becca smiled at them as she collected the art prints. "Now, does everyone have their assignments for the day?"

In reply, Hazel held up her checklist, and Violet and Oliver pointed to their planners.

"Very good," Becca said. "I'm here if you need me, but I have to warn you that I'll be a little more preoccupied than usual." She hefted the morning time basket onto the table and indicated the thick, haphazard stack of papers at the back of the basket. "I have to organize all of the work you turned in for the first semester." She glanced down at the stack and ran her thumb along the top edge. "I need to make room for all of the new assignments and reports you'll be turning in for the second semester."

Oliver grimaced. "You know, Mom," he said, "you would have a lot less filing to do if we didn't write reports at all."

"Ha!" Becca said. "Nice try." As she ruffled Oliver's hair, a lopsided grin spread across the young man's face.

Hazel jumped from her chair to clip one of the art prints to the strand of twinkle lights by the mantel, and Violet stacked the volumes of *A Midsummer Night's Dream*. As she handed the pile of books to her mother, she asked, "Will you need my help this morning?"

Becca shook her head. "I don't think so, but thank you. I'm expecting a pretty slow day today with just the regulars." She paused to glance out the window at the softly falling snow. "In fact," she said, smiling, "you and Hazel could do your work by the fireplace today if you'd like."

Hazel, who had returned to her mother and sister's side, looked up hopefully at her sister. "Please, Violet? *Please?*"

Violet made a face. "All of our books are upstairs."

"I'll get them!" Hazel insisted, tugging on her sister's sleeve. "I'll bring them all down."

From the fireplace came a cheerful pop, and the gold flecks in Violet's eyes twinkled as she gazed down at her sister. "*Fine,*" she relented. "But I'm bringing down my own books." The faint chime of a timer sounded, and Violet glanced down at her sweatshirt pocket.

"Ten o'clock!" Becca said, smiling at her daughter. "I'd better open for the day!" As Violet and Hazel headed toward the apartment to retrieve their books, Oliver hefted his backpack on his shoulders and made his way to his hollow tree. Becca stepped toward the confectionery counter, where Audrey was waiting with her sister-in-law's apron in hand. She tossed it, and Becca snatched it out of the air. After looping it over her head and tying it around her waist, she headed to the entrance, flipped the storefront sign to *Open,* and unlocked the glossy teal door.

Becca's prediction of a slow morning proved correct as only a few customers trickled into the bookshop with coffee orders. Drumming her fingers on the countertop, she glanced at her daughters, who had settled themselves by the fire. With her legs tucked under her in one of the soft chairs, Violet held up multiplication flashcards for her sister, who sat by her feet and stroked the back of the toffee-colored Manx. Becca turned to Audrey. The auburn-haired woman was keeping herself busy by rearranging a stand loaded with carrot cake muffins drizzled with cream cheese frosting. "I'm going to start organizing the kids' schoolwork now," Becca said.

Audrey nodded, replacing the glass dome over the stand. "You've certainly got the opportunity. If things don't pick up, I'm going to start a load of laundry." She pointed to the linen closet. "We're getting dangerously low on kitchen towels."

Becca crouched and pulled out the thick stack of papers from the morning time basket. She laid it on the tiled table and, with Butterscotch's companionable supervision, began sorting the assignments by child.

As the morning eased into afternoon, Becca made substantial progress, turning the disheveled stack of papers into three neat piles of her children's best work. Shortly after Audrey headed upstairs with a laundry basket tucked under her arm for the third time, the bell at the entrance tinkled. Glancing up, Becca smiled as she saw Uncle John closing the door behind him and brushing the snow off the shoulders of his police uniform. She laid Oliver's report from their field trip at the Art Institute on the top of his stack and hurried to greet her uncle.

"Good afternoon, dear," John said in his warm bass as Becca unwound her arms from around his neck. His mustache rose as he smiled. He waved at Violet and Hazel, who looked up absentmindedly from their schoolwork to greet him. As the girls quickly returned to their studies, John raised his eyebrows at Becca. "Studying?"

"Studying," Becca confirmed. "It looks like they're working on first declension noun endings."

With a chuckle, John shook his head in wonder. "Black coffee, please."

"Sure thing! For here?" Becca said hopefully, stepping behind the counter again.

John pulled his wallet from his pocket. "Yes, I've got time." He eyed the glass dome. "And I'll take one of those delicious carrot cake muffins too." His blue eyes twinkled. "I want to eat healthy today."

The corner of Becca's lips rose in a half-smile as she poured coffee into a teal stoneware mug.

"What? No laugh?" John said, sliding a fifty-dollar bill across the counter. "I thought that was pretty good." The smile faded from the chief's face as he looked at Becca, whose eyes were wide and serious as she carefully set the mug in front of him.

"Have there been any... *changes* in the Grant case?" she asked, her voice low. Becca noticed the fifty-dollar bill and, with a frown, pushed it back toward the chief.

Glancing around him, John found that the girls were far enough away to be out of earshot, and the only other customer around was a middle-aged man in a business suit speaking into his cell phone by the fireside. The chief settled onto a stool and leaned toward Becca. "After verifying the authenticity of your video," he said, "we were able to go to a judge on Tuesday and obtain a warrant to search the Paper Palace."

"Oh? And?" Becca's fingertips turned white as she gripped the edge of the countertop.

John's bushy eyebrows raised slightly. "There, they were able to find Lexi's bag from the cocktail party," he continued. "After running some tests on it, they discovered trace amounts of eszopiclone inside."

"I knew it!" Becca breathed. She straightened and started bouncing on her toes.

John nodded patiently. "Yes," he said, "you were right." He crooked a finger at her, and she leaned close to him again. "Now, I remind you that this is confidential because we have to arrange action on this." He paused, his eyes solemn. "But it's enough to arrest her."

Becca's eyes widened, and she grinned. Clasping her hands at her heart, she resumed her hopping.

A small smile played on John's lips as he gestured with the flat of his hand for his niece to settle down. "Becca," he said, "we're going to continue to work this case, but again, this is all circumstantial evidence. We can arrest her, but it's a long road ahead making this stick."

Becca froze, and her mouth fell open as she looked at her uncle in dismay.

"Hey," he said cheerfully. "Don't give up hope. This is what we do! We're going to make sure that justice is served." He smiled and pointed to the mound of carrot cake muffins. "Are you forgetting something?"

With a sigh, Becca lifted the glass dome and used a pair of tongs to plate a muffin, which she set in front of her uncle. "With all of those vegetables," she said, glancing at the treat, "it's basically a salad." Becca forced her lips into a smile.

"That's the spirit!" John said. Giving the plate a slight turn, he smiled down at the muffin and then glanced up at his niece. "Oh, did Mallory email you the results on that background check? It's not too easy running a report from fifty years ago, you know."

Becca replaced the glass dome over the stand. "She did! It was helpful." She looked at her uncle, and her eyes twinkled. "I appreciate it. It's nice knowing I've got someone at the top I can count on."

Color rose into John's cheeks, and he cleared his throat. As Audrey returned to the kitchen, he greeted her with a nod and held up the fifty-dollar bill. "Audrey, will *you* accept this please?"

Audrey beamed, crossed the room to John, and plucked the money from his fingers. "Thank you!" she said appreciatively as Becca, placing her hands on her hips, smiled and shook her head.

Ambling over to John, Butterscotch nudged the man's hand and looked up at him with soft brown eyes. The dog panted in delight as John scratched under her chin, and then the chief glanced up at the piles of schoolwork. He looked at Becca. "And what have you been up to?"

"Oh!" Becca said. "I need to put those away. I was organizing the kids' assignments." She turned to place a clip on each of the piles and then stacked them all together. As she bent to tuck the papers into the basket, she heard the bell jingle at the front door. Straightening, she saw Donna Sloane and Marjorie Marston stepping into the bookshop with Evelyn Hansen trailing after them. Becca looked at Uncle John. "CRIS meeting," she said quietly and bit her lip.

Hearing the tinge of rejection in his niece's voice, Uncle John said wryly, "Oh, good. Hopefully, they will take care of that house on Lilac Lane that had a tree out front without Christmas lights. I was afraid I'd have to send my officers."

Becca giggled and looked affectionately at Uncle John. Violet and Hazel glanced up as the women settled into their usual seats at the long wooden table. After allowing the CRIS members a few moments to settle in, Becca smoothed her apron and picked up her notepad and pen. Still perched on the windowsill, his long tail curved slightly at the bottom, Licorice blinked serenely at Becca as she approached the table to take the women's orders.

Task complete, Becca resumed her place behind the counter and handed the notepad to Audrey, who had just finished restocking the linen closet with neatly folded towels.

Audrey flicked her eyes to the empty seat at the long wooden table, and a mischievous smile played on her lips. She leaned toward Becca. "Now we finally get to see who the new insufferable snob is!" she whispered.

Becca stifled a smile and set to work plating a frosted chocolate brownie as Audrey reached for the vanilla and marshmallow syrups to begin making a crème brûlée latte. With a tilt of her head, Becca surveyed the plated brownie for a moment and decided that it could use a pop of color. Remembering she had some fresh mint to use up, she opened the refrigerator door. As her fingers found the package of mint, she heard the tinkle of the front door followed by Donna's sing-song exclamation, "There she is!" Becca closed the refrigerator door, and the little package of mint slipped from her fingers as she took in the sight of Lexi Grant. Wide-eyed, she stared as Lexi, dressed in her olive-green puffer coat, strode toward the café. Remembering herself, Becca quickly stooped to pick up the herb, sprung up again, and cast Uncle John a sideways glance.

Hands stuffed into her pockets, Lexi approached the long wooden table and then draped her coat over the back of the empty chair.

"Oh!" Donna said, flashing a wide lipstick-lined smile. "We have already ordered, darling."

Lexi nodded. "Okay."

Becca held her breath as the young woman made her way to the café and stepped up to Audrey to place her order.

John snuck Becca a surreptitious look of warning, and then, turning his head, casually looked over at Lexi, who returned his gaze with a crisp nod and a hint of a smirk.

"The usual?" Audrey said with a smile.

"Yes," Lexi said, hooking her thumbs in the pockets of her jeans. "I'll take a black tea with lemon and a scone with jam and clotted cream."

As Audrey tapped the order into her tablet and Lexi paid, Becca tried to keep her breathing even.

She watched as the young woman took her place among the society ladies.

Pushing the untouched muffin away from him, John looked at Becca. "Excuse me," he said softly. "I need to make a phone call."

The chief got up from the stool and, pulling his cell phone from his pocket, slowly disappeared among the tall distant shelves of books.

Becca set her mouth in a line and turned to assist Audrey with the tea.

"Is everything okay?" Audrey asked, glancing sideways at her sister-in-law.

"Oh, yes!" Becca said as she set the teacup and saucer on the counter. "Everything's totally fine." She flashed a smile.

Unconvinced, Audrey raised an eyebrow and shook her head as she scanned the collection of refreshments on the counter to ensure everything was accounted for. Looking at Becca, she said, "Shall we?" and the two headed toward the CRIS ladies.

Becca's hand trembled as she placed the tea tray beside Lexi, causing the cup to rattle on its saucer. Lexi glanced at Becca with a mixture of disdain and annoyance before turning her attention to Audrey, who was setting the crème brûlée latte and brownie in front of Marjorie. The CRIS secretary paused her reading of the previous meeting's minutes and licked her lips in anticipation. Noticing this, Donna rolled her eyes while sipping her vanilla latte and then flicked her gaze to Evelyn, who was daintily blowing across the surface of her coffee.

In a couple of minutes, Uncle John coolly resumed his place on the stool. Although he was facing the kitchen, his eyes were fixed on Lexi's reflection in the glass-fronted cabinets.

Becca drew in close toward her uncle. "What do we do?" she whispered, a note of desperation in her voice.

John's gaze shifted from Lexi's reflection to his niece's wide eyes. "*We* will do nothing," he said evenly and quietly. "You will continue to take care of your bookstore and serve your customers. My officers and I will take care of the rest." He glanced at the young woman's reflection again and then gave a small reassuring smile.

Becca drew in a deep breath and nodded. "Okay," she said. She stood frozen for a moment and then nodded again, this time with determination. "Okay!" Spinning slowly, she cast her gaze over the kitchen, desperately looking for something to do. Finally, she snatched a dishcloth from its hook by the sink, opened the drawer of teaspoons, and dumped the contents onto the counter. One by one, she picked up the spoons, polished them with her cloth, and returned them to the drawer.

Glancing sideways at Becca, John mouthed, "What are you doing?"

"I don't know!" Becca mouthed back, stifling a nervous laugh.

John's eyes twinkled as he returned his gaze to the glass-fronted cabinet.

Only three teaspoons remained when the bell at the front door tinkled, and Detective Post appeared, followed by two uniformed police officers. Becca recognized the first as Officer Spencer with his tall lean build and tidy crew cut. The second policeman was young, and his dark-blond hair was gelled firmly into place. His pale eyes gleamed with eagerness as his gaze darted back and forth between the detective and Officer Spencer.

Detective Post strode toward the back of the shop, and John rose from his place at the counter and turned to face him. Audrey's face lit up, and she raised her hand in greeting, but she slowly lowered it again as the detective stared fixedly at the chief. John directed his gaze to Lexi, who was sipping her tea as she listened to Marjorie continue to read the CRIS meeting minutes. Following John's line of sight, the detective and officers stepped toward Lexi, and John followed them. As the officers approached, Marjorie fell silent, and the four women looked up.

Donna picked up the stack of papers in front of her and whacked it down again. "Detective Post," she said in an exasperated tone. "I have told you and *told* you. I had nothing to do with the murder of Phyllis Grant. When I said that Phyllis wasn't going to be around much longer, I was purely referring to her *position* as president of the Crystal Run Improvement Society."

Hazel's eyes snapped up from the page she was reading, and she jerked on Violet's sleeve. "Did you hear that?" she whispered.

Expressionless, Detective Post looked at Donna and then turned to Lexi. "Alexandra Grant," he said in a loud commanding voice. "Please stand up. You are being placed under arrest for the murder of Phyllis Grant."

At the words, Hazel rose and squeezed in beside Violet on the soft leather chair. Oliver poked his head out of the hollow tree on the other side of the bookshop to see what was happening.

With the CRIS women's gazes locked on her, Lexi didn't move. "Under arrest?" she asked skeptically, narrowing her eyes. "On what grounds?"

"We have video evidence of you pouring alcohol into Phyllis Grant's glass," the young officer blurted. His gelled hair gleamed as he fumbled for the handcuffs clipped at the back of his belt. "And when we searched your premises, we found that the purse you had the night of her death contained residue of the sleeping drug found in her system."

Shooting the young officer a sideways glance, Detective Post narrowed his eyes and gave a slight shake of his head.

Lexi laughed as she set the teacup onto its saucer. "Is that all?" she said. "That's nothing. You can arrest me now, but I'll be out by this evening." With a toss of her blue-black hair, Lexi stood and straightened her arms in front of her.

From behind the confectionery counter, Becca stared as the young officer began to fasten the handcuffs over Lexi's wrists. The woman's chin was tilted upward, and her ocean-blue eyes flashed haughtily. Becca shook her head at the irony that, finally, in this moment, Lexi had the bearing of a Grant. Becca's breath caught as Lexi's lips curled into a smirk—the exact smirk that a young Phyllis Grant had expressed in the Grant family painting. *The painting*, she mused, a chill running up and down her spine.

"You have the right to remain silent," the young officer droned. "Anything you say can and will be used against you in a court of law..."

The officer's voice faded into a buzz as Becca's thoughts swirled. *The painting, the painting, the painting...* Suddenly, she gasped, and her eyes widened. Ducking behind the counter, Becca fished Oliver's Art Institute report from the basket and slapped it down in front of her. She flipped to the second page and ran her finger down the words. She paused, and as she read the surrounding passages, her eyes gleamed. Rising, she gave one big hop of excitement.

Uncle John glanced over his shoulder at his niece and then turned back to the scene in front of him.

Looking directly at Detective Post, Lexi arched a brow. "You are wasting your time. At *best* what you have is circumstantial. There is no *motive* behind your theory." The woman's lips curled into a triumphant smirk. "Why would I have killed my own grandmother?"

The question hung in the air for a long moment. Finally, the silence was broken by the sound of Becca's voice.

"Because of the painting," she said evenly.

Every head in the room swiveled to look at Becca, and an incredulous laugh escaped Lexi's lips. "My family's portrait?" she scoffed.

Stepping out from behind the counter, Becca said, "No, the one underneath it. *Nativity with Saints Lawrence and Francis* by Caravaggio. It's the original, isn't it?"

With Oliver's report in her hand, Becca stepped in front of the fireplace. Every eye was on her. She took a breath and slowly exhaled. "About two and a half weeks ago," she said, "the children and I delivered a blessing basket to Lexi at the Paper Palace. While we were there, I was looking at the Grant family portrait. I accidentally knocked off a chip of paint, and I saw a painting underneath." She flicked her gaze to Hazel and felt a warmth rise into her cheeks. Then she continued, "But what I also saw was a piece of double-sided tape on the back of the paint chip. No art restorer would ever use tape. That was you." She looked at Lexi, whose complexion had taken on an ashen hue.

Lexi opened her mouth as if to speak, but no words came out.

"A few months ago," Becca resumed, "Phyllis Grant had decided to donate the painting to the library. She couldn't afford to have it professionally cleaned, so, of course, she asked Lexi to do it." She glanced over at Lexi and arched a brow.

Lexi's expression remained unchanged.

With a slight shrug, Becca continued. "As you were cleaning, you chipped off some paint and saw the painting underneath. And you did the same thing I did... You researched the painting. You found out what painting it is and that the original is from Palermo, Italy." She winked at Oliver, who had made his way over to the group, and held up her son's report about famous art thefts. Then she returned her attention to Lexi. "You learned that the original painting was stolen—cut out of its frame right above the altar—at the Oratory of Saint Lawrence in 1969." Becca paused. "1969," she repeated slowly. "Shortly before Alberti, who was also from Palermo, came to the United States and approached Elizabeth Grant with a proposal to paint a large family portrait for her living room. You noticed that the Grant portrait was just slightly smaller than the original Caravaggio painting." Becca gave a small smile. "Things began to line up."

Lexi shot Becca a deadly glare.

"Now," Becca continued, crossing to one side of the fireplace, "you realized that Alberti, who was a talented artist in his own right, was on the run with this large painting. He had to hide it where it was safe, and he could find it again." She gazed out at the faces of the people who were hanging on her every word, and John nodded at her encouragingly. "What better place to hide it than underneath a painting that wasn't going to go anywhere? A portrait of a wealthy family. He knew it would be safe there."

Clasping her hands behind her, Becca slowly paced back and forth in front of the fireplace. "After a while, Alberti tried to recover the painting. Again and again, he tried to enter the Paper Palace." She let out a small laugh and raised an index finger. "*That's* why he kept trying to sneak into the house. It wasn't to see Phyllis Grant. He wanted to get the painting back!"

"Oh!" Evelyn blurted and then immediately clapped her hand over her mouth.

"But Phyllis thought that Alberti wanted *her*," Becca continued, "so she had her father get rid of him. William Grant had Alberti shipped back to Italy. He was arrested as soon as he got off the boat, and he never made it back to the United States to retrieve the painting."

Resuming her original stance in front of the fireplace, Becca looked at John, her eyes twinkling. "If you check the painting underneath that portrait, I'll bet you anything you'll find that it is an original Caravaggio." Her gaze flicked to Lexi and then back to her uncle. "Mrs. Grant had already decided to give the portrait to the library. And if she did that, Lexi would never be able to get her hands on it again. But Lexi also couldn't tell Mrs. Grant about it because she—and the rest of Crystal Run—knew that Phyllis Grant had squandered the family fortune. She reasoned her grandmother would likely do the same with any money from the painting. And that's why Lexi killed Phyllis Grant." A flush rose into Becca's cheeks. "She killed her because, if that painting is real, which I'm sure you're going to find it is, it's worth millions. Tens of millions!"

"That painting is mine!" Lexi roared, her face contorting with rage. "It belongs to me! That old hag was going to give it away! Even if I told her about it, she'd just blow through that money, like she did with the family fortune!" Desperately thrusting, she twisted out of the officer's grasp and lunged toward Becca.

"Whoa, now," John said. With an effortless swing of his arm, he restrained the woman, who was wild with fury.

"That money belongs to me!" Lexi spat as John led her back to the officers.

Detective Post raised his light-colored brows. "Not anymore."

Officer Spencer gathered Lexi's belongings, and the detective glanced over at a beaming Audrey.

"Dinner tonight?" the auburn-haired woman mouthed.

In reply, Chris flashed her a smile and winked.

Audrey's round cheeks flushed pink as she stepped out from behind the counter to join Becca and the others, and Detective Post returned his attention to the arrest. As the wide-eyed CRIS ladies looked on, the detective and the young officer led an irate Lexi, fussing and fuming the whole way, out of the bookshop. The woman's ranting faded and finally dissolved into silence as the glossy teal door shut behind them. After giving Becca a small smile, Officer Spencer hurried after the others with Lexi's property.

"Well, I *never!*" Donna exclaimed, her expression a mixture of shock and glee. "In our town, such a thing... People are never, *never* going to believe this!" She glanced at the meeting minutes. "Ladies, I don't see how we could possibly continue. The meeting is adjourned!"

Rising from her chair, Evelyn dabbed at the corners of her eyes. "Poor, poor Phyllis."

In stunned silence, Marjorie stared at the remaining brownie in her hand, shook her head, and placed it on her plate. Standing up, she pulled on her coat and, after a moment's hesitation, mumbled, "Well, maybe later." She wrapped the treat in a napkin and tucked it in her purse.

Within moments, the three women had left the shop, a flurry of gossip, grief, and gasps.

Sliding her hands into her apron pockets, Becca smiled at John. The corners of the man's mustache were raised with his wide grin, and then he turned at the sound of a young woman's voice.

"What is going to happen to Lexi now?" Violet asked.

John smiled. "We are going to check out that painting and confirm everything. But if it's true—and based on the confession she just gave, it sounds like it is—Alexandra Grant is going to go away for a long time. This is now going to be an open-and-shut case."

Becca felt herself lift onto her toes, and her lips curved into a smile. "Oof!" she said as Hazel, who had dashed to their side, flung her arms around her mother's waist.

Oliver bounded over. "Uncle John!" he exclaimed. "You just solved an art theft!"

The chief chuckled. "No," he said, "I can't take credit for it. Your mom solved this one." He looked at Becca warmly.

Green eyes wide with admiration, Oliver gazed up at his mother.

"Oh no, he's never going to stop talking about this!" Hazel's voice was muffled as she moaned into her mother's apron.

The young man flashed his lopsided grin, and then his gaze drifted over to Lexi's unfinished scone.

Watching him, Audrey laughed. "Don't even think about it. I'll get you a fresh one." As she made her way to the counter, Audrey suddenly stopped in her tracks. She spun and looked at the chief. "What about Harvey, her boyfriend?"

John nodded. "We looked carefully into him and found no reason to think that he was involved."

"Yes, those two never made sense to me," Becca said. "I have a feeling Lexi was just using Harvey for his access to the art world." Feeling a nudge at her knee, the woman looked down to find Butterscotch's chocolate eyes looking up at her. She knelt and scratched the dog behind her silky ears.

Smiling, John watched his niece. "You did well, Becca," he said in his warm bass. "Really well. Your father would be proud."

Becca rose, her eyes glistening with tears. "God had us all play our parts," she said. Lovingly, she gazed at each of her children's faces in turn, smiled, and then arched a brow. "Shouldn't the three of you be working on your schoolwork?"

# Epilogue

"The brushstrokes are much more precise and finished-looking than in many of Caravaggio's later works. However, the artist's newfound depth of humble feeling was not entirely lost." The docent drew her eyes up the massive painting of the nativity scene, which glowed impressively from its thick gilded frame against the charcoal-colored wall. She gestured to a man wearing a broad-brimmed hat on the right side of the canvas. "Observe the peasant-like Joseph figure with his workworn hands." The woman smiled as she turned again to admire the painting. She was tall with a medium build, and her reddish-brown hair was pulled back into a severe bun. The docent wore a black suit over a white button-down shirt, and an Art Institute of Chicago badge dangled at the end of a lanyard around her neck.

Rising onto her tiptoes to see beyond the tour group, Hazel squinted at the colossal painting and then looked up at her mother. "*That's* Joseph?" she whispered.

"Mm-hmm," Becca murmured softly, smiling down at her daughter. She took Hazel's hand and gently led her several feet to the side. They now had a better view of *The Nativity with Saints Lawrence and Francis*. Becca caught Violet's eye and motioned for her older children to join them. With a tug of her brother's sleeve, Violet beckoned Oliver, and the two joined their mother and sister.

"In 1608, Caravaggio was commissioned to create this painting for the Oratory of Saint Lawrence in Palermo, Italy," the docent continued, "where it remained for over 360 years. On the night of October 17, 1969, the painting's path took an unusual turn." With a gleam in her eye, the woman scanned the faces in the crowd.

Oliver's eyes widened. "Stolen," he breathed.

Becca stifled a smile.

"Two thieves broke into the church," the docent resumed, "cut the painting from its frame, rolled it up in a carpet, and carried it out. A week later, one of them was found dead. The remaining thief, Francesco Alberti, smuggled the painting to America. Alberti was a talented painter himself, and he hid this masterpiece underneath a family portrait he painted for a paper magnate in Wisconsin. He planned to retrieve it when it was safe."

Violet's gaze flicked to her mother, but Becca kept her eyes on the docent.

"Before he could recover the painting," the woman said, "he was deported back to Italy where he was immediately arrested for murder and died shortly thereafter in prison. For more than fifty years, the painting remained hidden in the wealthy family's living room."

"So, how was it recovered?" an elderly man near the front of the tour group asked in a thin voice.

The docent's eyebrows raised. "One of the last remaining family members eventually discovered the painting's identity... along with the fact that it is valued at twenty million dollars. To ensure the painting would be hers alone, she poisoned her grandmother, killing the only other heir. The plan would have succeeded, and this masterpiece would have been lost to the world in illicit channels if it had not been discovered by the police. And what's more, the police credit the discovery of all of this to none other than a mother who owns the town's local bookshop."

Someone from the front of the crowd let out a long, low whistle.

"Because of their efforts, this beautiful painting has been recovered and restored. The public can enjoy it here where it's on temporary loan until it finally, and at long last, returns to its rightful home—above the altar in the Oratory of Saint Lawrence in Italy." The woman stepped back and, with a flourish of her hand, said, "Please, enjoy."

The wide-eyed and slack-jawed tour group buzzed as they stared at the painting with newfound appreciation.

After several minutes, the docent smiled and said, "And if you'll join me over here, we have another one of Caravaggio's works, *The Cardsharps*." The woman's black pumps clicked as she crossed the shining parquet floor.

One of the last to follow was a dark-haired man dressed in a pale-blue Oxford and jeans, who was staring at the painting with his arms folded across his chest. He leaned toward the woman next to him and arched a brow. "Do you think they make this stuff up to make the paintings more interesting? I mean, that story seems pretty far-fetched."

At the man's words, Oliver turned to his mother and sisters. "That was us," he mouthed. Hazel bounced on her toes, Violet frowned deeply, and Oliver opened his mouth to speak. "Actually—" the young man began.

Gently, Becca laid her hand on her son's arm and shook her head at her children. With wide eyes, they stared at her. Smiling, she took Hazel's hand. "Let's move on to the next wing," she said. "There is so much more out there, just waiting for us."

# Afterword

Goodness, truth, and beauty. One of the main goals of the Gables' home-school is to search for and cultivate these virtues; therefore, it is important that you, dear reader, know what is truth and what is fiction. *The Nativity with Saints Lawrence and Francis* is a real masterpiece painted in 1608 by Michelangelo Merisi da Caravaggio, more commonly known as Caravaggio. It is true that, for 360 years, the painting was displayed in the Oratory of Saint Lawrence in Palermo, Italy. It is also true that the painting was stolen on the night of October 17, 1969. Tragically, what is fiction is that the painting has been recovered. While several theories abound regarding this masterpiece's whereabouts, its fate is a mystery that exists to this day. Perhaps someone, maybe even you, will be inspired by the Gables' adventure and be the one to bring this painting to light.

*Soli Deo Gloria*

# Acknowledgements

First and foremost, we give glory to God, who created us in His image and instilled within us the desire to create, along with a deep longing for goodness, truth, and beauty. Like the lamp in Psalm 119, He has illuminated our path step by step on this literary journey. His presence has been constant, His grace unmistakable. *Soli Deo Gloria.*

To our families—thank you for your patience, encouragement, and love. Kristin especially thanks Dan and their children—Shane, Conner, Logan, and Theodore—who graciously gave her the space to write and cheered on every draft. She also thanks her mom, who signed her up for her first writer's workshop in fifth grade and passed down her love of a good mystery. Ben especially thanks his family, and in particular his mom, who became one of our biggest supporters.

To Leah Dobrinska, a fellow cozy mystery author and true inspiration—thank you for your generous guidance and encouragement. Your wisdom and warmth shaped this project more than you know.

To our beta readers—Elizabeth, Amber, Paula, Nancy, David, Susan, and especially Sarah—thank you for diving into the earliest drafts, offering thoughtful feedback, and cheering us on.

To our "gamma readers" (a title we invented for the faithful friends who read the nearly-final version)—Carolyn, Melissa, Angela, and Julie—your insight, care, and encouragement strengthened this story in its final steps.

To Ally, Conner, and Estelle—thank you for so beautifully bringing Violet, Oliver, and Hazel to life on our cover.

To our church family at Faith Lutheran Church—thank you for walking alongside us as brothers and sisters in Christ and for encouraging us as we seek to shine His light into the world.

And finally, to you, dear reader—thank you for stepping into Crystal Run, for meeting Becca and her family, and for joining us on this mystery. Stories only truly come alive when they are read, and we are deeply grateful to share this one with you.

# About the Authors

**Kristin Brellen** is the author and writer of the Tales & Tails Mysteries, a cozy mystery series featuring a homeschool mom, her three children, and their whimsical bookshop. She earned her degree in Elementary Education with a specialization in Language Arts from UW-Eau Claire. For as long as she can remember, Kristin has dreamed of creating her own Nancy Drew or Hercule Poirot. Thanks to the encouragement and support of her co-author and by the goodness of God, that dream is now being realized through the character Becca Gables.

Kristin lives in a small Wisconsin town with her husband, four sons, and her faithful feline writing companion, Minnie. Fueled by cups of creamy coffee, she has the joy of homeschooling her children, teaching English grammar and writing to their homeschool community, leading women's Bible study at church, and of course, writing. When her fingertips aren't on a keyboard, Kristin enjoys reading, exercising, cooking, baking, and watching Hallmark movies.

**Ben Alexander** is the co-author and artist of the Tales & Tails Mysteries. He holds a Bachelor of Arts and a Master of Divinity. Although he has always been a natural storyteller, he is actually new to the mystery genre and had never read a murder mystery before helping to craft *Death at the Paper Palace*.

Ben has lived in several states but currently resides in Wisconsin's heartland with his adorably quirky green parakeet, Rembrandt (Remy, for short). He works a 9-to-5 job, but his greatest passions include teaching weekly adult Bible studies, writing devotions, and occasionally preaching at his church when requested. Additionally, he is a self-taught professional artist, contributing the cover art and chapter illustrations for *Death at the Paper Palace*. An accomplished home chef, Ben's kitchen is often filled with the aromas of garlic, onions, and wine. In his spare time, he practices martial arts, researches swords, sculpts, and watches Hallmark and Great American Family movies.

# Coming Soon

*Fall from Grace*—the second installment in the Tales & Tails Mysteries, continuing the adventures of Becca Gables.

Stay connected at www.talesandtailspublishing.com.

www.ingramcontent.com/pod-product-compliance
Lightning Source LLC
Chambersburg PA
CBHW021958130726
47903CB00014B/1703